Phantasmagoria

Phantasmagoria

Robert Spina

To order additional copies of this book, contact:
Xlibris
1-888-795-4274
www.Xlibris.com
Orders@Xlibris.com
797115

CONTENTS

Chapter 1

What the Hell, Smoke?

Rain looks into Marlene's eyes. He runs his fingers through her hair and kisses her.

"I can't believe we are going to do this."

"I know," she replies with a smile.

Marlene wraps her arms around Rain's back and squeezes him as he kisses her and moves his hips until they are joined. They kiss and move for the first time making love with each other. The bedroom is dark with a little light shining in from the kitchen. The ambiance is perfect; a single scented candle is burning on the dresser, and after an hour of Rain flirting, touching, kissing, and playfully trying to get Marlene out of her clothes, she gives in to his charm. She has been exhausting every excuse she can think of to not get naked with him, and now their bodies are one. The couple is happily feeling each other, and Rain runs his lips down Marlene's neck as they make love. Marlene hears a creek in the floor and opens her eyes to see a man standing over the two of them with his arms raised over his head, and she screams. She sees the man swing at her and instinctively raises her arms to block the attack. The man swings a bat just as Rain is raising his head, and the bat hits Marlene's arm and Rain's head. Fortunately, Marlene's arm broke the brunt of the attack, which would have knocked Rain out cold. This leaves a very painful welt on Marlene's left forearm and on the back of Rain's head. Rain rolls to the right, taking the covers and, with a very painful headache, tumbling to the floor. He slams into the wall and stands holding his head. He sees a man covered in black clothing and mask, striking Marlene with a bat.

"What the fuck!" yells Rain.

He dives headfirst at the assailant. Rain hits the man in the stomach with his shoulder, and the man falls back into the wall. Rain falls on the bed, on Marlene, who is now crying with painful welts growing on her forehead and forearms. The assailant never falls to the ground; he bounces back from the wall, raising the bat to swing at Rain, who gets up very fast on the bed and jumps, raising his right knee, striking the man on his left jaw. Rain comes around with his right fist, striking the man in his neck under his left jaw. The assailant drops the bat. Rain comes up with his left fist, snapping the man's head up, and he falls to the ground.

"Marlene, baby."

Rain lowers to Marlene, who is crying, and tries to comfort her.

"What the hell is going on, Rain? Who is that? Why is he hitting us?"

"I don't know, baby. I don't know."

Rain can see Marlene has been hit very hard on the head, and it looks like a big egg is growing from her forehead and both her arms.

"Rain, why did he do that? It hurts so bad."

She barely touches the still growing welt on her head. She is crying, and the two of them can hear tumbling and thrashing around in the living room.

"I'm scared, Rain. What is going on?"

Rain gets up and grabs some shorts from the dresser. He grabs a large sweatshirt for Marlene and hands it to her.

"Here, put this on."

Just then, another man dressed in black is thrown into the bedroom and lands on the man Rain had knocked out. Still, Marlene and Rain can hear thrashing around in the living room. Marlene gets off the bed and squats down into the corner of the room. Rain walks toward the door when the man thrown into the bedroom gets up, grabbing the bat. Rain faces him at the end of the bed, and the man swings the bat. He swings from his left to his right, which is awkward for the assailant since he is right-handed. Rain catches the bat with both hands and kicks straight into the man's sternum, sending him back tripping over the other man, who is now standing up. The man standing is groggy and dazed, which does not last too long because Rain swings very hard, striking the man dead center of his head with a loud crack. The man falls like a sack of potatoes out cold. The other man gets up quickly facing Rain. Rain gets ready to swing again when he is attacked by a third assailant running into the bedroom. Rain is hit from behind as the third assailant is actually thrown into the bedroom and lands on Rain, sending both of them to the floor next to the bed, landing on the assailant already knocked out.

"Get off me!" yells Rain.

The man on Rain raises to his knees. A fourth man runs into the bedroom. This man is not covered in black; he is dressed in jeans and a T-shirt. He stabs the assailant on Rain in the back with a knife three times. Rain hears the stabbing and the man groaning with each insertion of the knife into his lower back. The attacker stands throwing the knife at the second assailant that entered the bedroom. This is an accurate throw with the knife as it enters the man's throat, slicing his windpipe and jugular vein. The man is heard gasping out of his neck as blood and oxygen gargle from the wound. Rain stands looking at the man, who slowly falls to his knees and leans against the wall, trying to hold on to life. Rain turns and grabs the man behind him, running him across the bedroom, slamming him into the wall.

"Rain, Rain, Rain!" yells the man.

Rain pulls back his right arm, tightening his fist.

"Rain! It's me, Smoke! Rain! Easy, Rain, easy."

Smoke gently raises his hands, opening his palms, facing Rain.

"Easy, Rain, calm down. It's me, Smoke. It's me."

"Smoke! What the hell, Smoke! I thought I was through with you. You just won't be happy until you are the death of me, will you?"

"Rain, behind you!"

Rain turns to see the last living assailant standing. Smoke bends to his left shin, pulls a knife from a sheath strapped to his leg, and throws it. The knife enters the man's throat much like the knife in the other assailant's throat, and he falls dying. Rain turns to Smoke.

"What the hell, Smoke? What the fucking hell? There are dead men in my bedroom. What the fucking hell?"

Rain hears Marlene crying on the floor in the corner of the room. He walks over and bends down, hugging her.

"Rain, I don't like this. I don't like this, Rain. I just wanted to be with you, just you and me. I don't know what this is, but I'm scared, and I don't like it."

Marlene cries louder. Rain hugs her.

"Come on, Marlene. Come on."

Rain helps her onto the bed. Marlene starts to feel the pain intensify in both her arms and her head, and she starts to cry louder.

"Rain, why? Why, Rain?"

She looks at her arms, and both have huge welts on them from being struck with the bat. The welt on her forehead is terrible, and she touches it gently with tears streaming from her eyes.

"Why would someone do this to me, Rain? Why?"

"I don't know, Marlene. I don't know what is going on yet."

Rain turns to Smoke, who pulls the knives from the assailants. He wipes the blood from the knives on the assailants and puts the knives back in the sheaths on his shins. Smoke starts to drag the bodies out of the bedroom into the living room.

"What the hell is going on, Smoke? Why did these guys attack us? Who are they?"

Rain pulls the masks from the three men, looking them over. They are lying in the living room, and Rain has no idea who they are.

"You don't remember them? You don't remember who they are?"

"No, Smoke. Who are they?"

"That there is Randy Smilderkent. That's Kevin Tresblense, and that there is Melveroykel."

"Are you serious, Smoke? The three guys from Willsdus that always had it in for us in high school? Why the hell would they come into my home now? Are you trying to tell me they are holding a grudge? Whatever that grudge would be for, what, twenty-five years now? You can't be serious? That does not make any sense even for these idiots who are now dead. Smoke, there are three dead men in my house. Are you fucking kidding me?"

Marlene walks into the living room like she is in a daze. She has rinsed off with cold water in the bathroom off the side of the bedroom. She has dressed herself and walks to the door.

"Rain, I want to go home now. Rain, please take me home."

"I would not go home if I were you. They know who you are. You may have been targeted like Rain has been targeted," says Smoke.

"Targeted? Why would someone target me? Rain, why have I been targeted?"

Marlene starts to cry.

"Marlene, don't cry. Don't listen to this guy. Like always, he is being overdramatic."

Rain hugs Marlene and escorts her to the bedroom so he can dress himself. They can hear Smoke dragging the bodies out the front door of the house. Rain gets dressed, and by the time he and Marlene leave the bedroom, Smoke has dragged the bodies into a van and is waiting for them in the living room.

"Do you still go to the planning zone? You remember where we used to meet, right?" says Smoke.

"I left that behind me with you, Smoke. I have not been there in over five years. I don't even know if it is still there."

"Well, it is still there. You remember where it is, right?"

"Yeah, I remember."

"Meet me there in an hour and bring Marlene with you. I have to get rid of the bodies, and then I will be right there. One hour, Rain, be there."

Smoke leaves the house and closes the door behind him. Rain walks to the door and watches the van pull away. He closes the door, and Marlene is there to hug him. She is shaking and in a lot of pain.

"Rain, what was he talking about? Do you know what is going on? Who was he anyway?"

"That is someone I thought was left in my past. I don't know what is going on, but surely, he has a lot to do with it." Rain walks to the couch, holding Marlene, and sits by her.

"His name is Smoke, and your name is Rain. Are you two brothers or something? You look like you could be brothers," she says.

"No. Smoke is not his real name. It's just what I call him. We met in first grade. We were best friends all our lives. We were very competitive, and those three guys that attacked us were from Willsdus, the town right next to Farmsvern, where Smoke and I are from. They were always out to get us because we beat them at all the sporting events like basketball games and track events. What really made them mad was that Smoke and I dated two girls from Willsdus. This made them really jealous of us, and they used to fight us all the time."

"That was high school. Why are they coming after you now? Why are they after me? Do they want to kill us?"

"I don't know. None of this is making any sense."

"This guy, Smoke, why have you never told me about him?"

"I have not seen Smoke in a long time. Let me think for a second. It has been five years now since I have seen Smoke."

"I thought you were best friends all your life."

"We were, but Smoke is a daredevil. He is crazy. He was always like that. I am ambitious and adventurous, but Smoke is crazy. I had to pull his ass out of the fire one too many times, and I finally said enough is enough. I broke ties with him because he was going to get me killed. He still is. I mean, look at this. Here we are all beaten up. There were three dead guys right here in this living room, and neither of us know what is going on. That is why I broke ties with Smoke. He will never grow up, and things are getting more serious. I don't want to go to the planning zone, which is just a restaurant/coffee shop where we used to meet. I know better than to go there, but it's the only way we will find out what is going on."

"I don't want to go, Rain. I want to go home. I don't know what this is all about, but it has nothing to do with me, and I want no part of it. Me being targeted is a bunch of crap. Look at me, Rain. My head looks like a bird's egg is growing from it. Look at my arms. I am scared, and I want to go home."

"OK, Marlene, I will take you home."

Rain gets his car keys, and Marlene gathers her things. They leave the house and lock up behind them. Rain drives Marlene home. It is a very quiet drive to her house. When in her driveway, she starts to get out of the car. Rain gets out and walks over to the passenger door, opening it for her. He hugs her as she gets out.

"Marlene, I am so sorry about tonight. I still have no idea what is going on, but I will get to the bottom of it."

"Rain, I was really liking you a lot. I do like you a lot, but I think I need some time away from you for a while. Please give me some space, and when I am ready, I will call you."

"I hope you don't need much time. All right, you take care. You don't want me to call you? I mean, I will find out what is going on from Smoke, and if it is something serious that involves you, I will let you know."

"OK, Rain, but I need some time to be alone right now."

Rain walks her to her front door, and she goes in without a hug or a kiss good night. He goes back to his car and stands by the driver side door, looking at Marlene's house. He can see the light go on in her bedroom, and he gets in his car and starts it up. Rubbing his forehead, he gets very mad with Smoke at how things have gone this evening. He is starting a serious relationship with Marlene. They have been dating for a month now, and this was their first intimate evening. Rain has not been serious in a physical way with any woman for over ten years. Now at forty-three years old, his physical ambitions just are not the way they were when he was younger. He is very much in love with Marlene, and now he feels this evening may be his last with her. This makes him very angry at Smoke. Rain has saved Smoke's ass and covered for Smoke so many times throughout their lives. He remembers when he exploded on Smoke and told him he never wanted to see him again. Here he is again in a very awkward situation, and he has no idea what is going on. Just like old times with Smoke. Rain hears the dancing footsteps of rain start to fall on the hood and roof of his car. He starts up his car and heads toward Sandy's restaurant/coffee shop on Route 34, where he and Smoke always used to meet after they got out of the service. The rain starts to fall harder and harder. By the time he gets to Sandy's, it is pouring rain. He sits in his car for almost fifteen minutes, and still it is raining hard and not letting up. Rain runs into the coffee shop and gets drenched. He sits in a booth where he and Smoke always used to sit.

"Stormy, Stormy Clouds, is that you? I haven't seen you in, what, five years?"

"Hi, Renee. I can't believe you still work here."

"I know. I guess I'm a lifer. Can I get you some coffee like always?"

"Yeah, that would be great."

"So where is Kenneth, or do you still call him Smoke? Everyone still calls you Rain, right?"

"Yeah, I call him Smoke still. Of course, I still go by Rain. You can get two cups. He is supposed to be joining me."

"All right, I'll be right back with two coffees. You know I still love your name the best of all the names I have ever heard. Stormy Rain Clouds. I love that name. I always have."

"Yeah, my parents are probably the most eccentric ever."

"One second, honey, I'll be right back with the coffee."

Renee brings Rain some coffee and a cup for Smoke. She talks with rain for thirty minutes in between serving customers. It is not like Smoke to leave Rain waiting. Smoke is very punctual and has been his whole life. Rain is quite sure he is not coming after waiting for nearly an hour. He leaves money on the table and waves good-bye to Renee, who is busy serving customers. It is still raining outside, but now it's just a light but steady rain. He drives home still pissed at Smoke for the intimate evening with Marlene that was violently ruined by Smoke.

Chapter 2

Ajaunta

Rain gets back home, and the rain is still falling. He loves the rain probably because that is his name. His first name is actually Stormy, but everyone has always called him Rain, and he likes it, so he always tells everyone Rain is his name. He notices how much damage has been done inside his house. He picks up the knocked-over lights and vacuums the broken glass. He picks up the bedroom and sits in the kitchen, looking out the sliding glass door, eating a ham sandwich, thinking out loud. "What have you got us into this time, Smoke?" He finishes his sandwich and glass of milk, listening to the lightly falling rain through the screen door that leads from his kitchen to the porch. His phone rings, and he finds it under the couch in the living room. It must have been knocked there during the skirmish earlier. He forgot about his phone all evening until now. He picks the phone and sees an unfamiliar number on it. The way this night has gone so far, he figures he may as well see who it is.

"Hello."

"Hi, is Rain there?"

Rain's heart flutters. Butterflies form in his stomach as the voice is familiar to him. He freezes for a moment. He has not heard this voice in twenty-five years, but he recognizes it.

"Hello, hello," the voice says.

"Hi, this is Rain."

"Rain, this is Ajaunta."

Rain gulps.

"Ajaunta, Ajaunta from school Ajaunta?"

"Yes, Rain, it's me. I know this is probably way out of line for me to ask of you, but I need to see you, if I can? Can we meet? Can we talk somewhere?"

"Ajaunta, aren't you married? Don't you have kids and, you know, the whole family thing going on?"

"Well, that's what I need to talk to you about. My husband has gone with the kids, and I don't know whom to talk to. I remember you said you always loved me, so I am taking a chance that you will meet with me. I need someone to talk to, and I don't know whom I can trust. There is a lot of really crazy things going on in my life. Suddenly, my life is upside down. I need someone to talk with. I am scared, Rain, and you are the only one I can think of to help me. I don't know who else I can talk to."

"That sounds familiar. A lot of crazy things are happening in my life suddenly as well. OK, I mean, I don't know where you live these days."

"You know where Summersfield is, right?"

"Sure, that's not far from where we grew up. I live in Lilston now. Summersville is about an hour drive for me from here."

"You know where Route 265 meets with 84?"

"I know exactly where that is. That's actually in Crens."

"Yes, yes, there is an all-night diner on the corner. Can you come meet me there?"

"What, you mean right now? It's eleven o'clock."

"Yes, I really need someone to talk to, Rain."

"You know, Ajaunta, when I said crazy things were happening to me, I meant like tonight, crazy things are happening. My house was broken into, and it's still a mess. Now you are calling me wanting to meet with me. This is beyond crazy. All right, give me an hour and a half. I'll be there by 12:30 a.m. Is that OK?"

"I will be waiting for you, Rain."

"All right, Ajaunta, I will be there."

"Thank you, Rain. Thank you."

"OK, I will see you in a little while. Bye."

"Bye, Rain."

Rain hangs up the phone and leans against the wall right next to the sliding glass door in his kitchen. He inhales the warm air, which smells of lilacs and rain. He rubs his forehead, dumbfounded to the way this evening has been going. From starting to make love with Marlene to being beaten and having three men killed in his home by Smoke, whom he has not seen in five years; taking Marlene home and waiting for Smoke, who never showed up to meet with him at the coffee shop, which is very uncharacteristic of Smoke; to having the girl of his dreams call him, asking him to come meet with her. Rain's body and brain have been twisted and turned all night long, and still the roller coaster rolls on. He stares out the screen door seeing only darkness, but he can hear the steady light rain falling in the trees behind his house. He walks through his house, looking all the rooms over, making sure all the windows and doors are shut and locked, which is not something he worries about, but tonight has just been a crazy night, and everything about his life seems to be out of whack. He puts on a new shirt and locks the door behind him.

He drives for nearly an hour, and it is has been raining the whole way to Crens. Rain parks in front of the diner, which is nearly full on this Saturday night with an early twenties crowd of late-night partiers. Rain walks into the crowded and loud diner, instantly being taken back to the days when he was young and full of energy just like so many of the kids in here now. He looks around and sees Ajaunta sitting in a booth all by herself just looking at him. It's like Rain is a twelve-year-old boy again. His heart pumps fast, and he is already thinking about what he is going to say. His nerves cause his throat to dry up and, after one step toward her, he feels like he is going to be sick. *What the hell? Are you serious, Rain? Get it together.* He takes a deep breath and walks over to the booth and sits across from Ajaunta, who has a cup of coffee in front of her.

"Hi, Rain. I was afraid you would not come," she says, reaching her hands to his.

"Your call definitely caught me off guard. You wanting to meet with me is very surprising."

"Hi, sir, would you like a menu?" says the waitress walking up to their booth.

"No, thank you, coffee will be fine."

"Coming right up."

"So, Ajaunta, what has you so scared that you called me and asked to me to come meet with you?"

"Rain, I don't know what is going on. I mean, I do, but I am afraid to say exactly what it is because you will think I am crazy. You will think I am losing my mind, and maybe I am. I don't know if I can even say it without you laughing at me or walking out on me thinking I am crazy."

"Well, first of all, where are your husband and your kids? Why are you talking to me and not them?"

"That's part of it, Rain. Sully, my husband, whom you have never met, has taken our boys and girls to Texas to be with his family. Sully was scared for their safety, so he took the kids to his parents' home and left me here."

"You have identical twin boys, right? They must be all grown up by now."

"Yes, and then I had identical twin girls. Our boys are twenty years old, and our girls are seventeen years old."

"Wow, what are the chances of that?"

"The chances are about one in seventy thousand. I know because I get asked that all the time."

"Well, that is amazing. Why did Sully leave with your kids? That makes no sense to me. You must have been married over twenty years. Don't you have a house together?"

"Yes, we do have a house, and we have been married for twenty-two years now."

"So what is going on?"

"OK, Rain, I am going to tell you." Ajaunta grabs both Rain's hands with hers. "OK, Rain, here goes. Don't laugh at me. Don't walk out on me. Hear me out, OK?"

"All right, Ajaunta, don't worry, just tell me."

"About six years ago, Sully and I were having difficulties with our marriage. He cheated on me, and I thought we were going to break up. I got involved with a man who sweet talked me and charmed my pants off literally."

"Sounds like me tonight—almost," Rain says out loud.

"What?"

"Nothing, nothing. Go on."

"Anyway, this man and I started dating, and as I started to get closer to him, I realized he was not a good man. I mean, he is actually a part of a demonic cult. I had no idea the bad things this man had done. When I found out he was a part of this cult, I broke ties with him immediately. I convinced Sully to start seeing a counselor with me, and we started talking and working our problems out. Things started to get good with Sully and me. We actually worked out our problems and got back together. Counseling worked for us. Well, this man whom I had dated over the years has come back into the picture, and he started threatening my family. He said if I do not come back to him, he will have my husband and kids killed. Rain, I don't know what to do. Sully is truly scared. This cult has threatened my kids and my husband, and they left me." Ajaunta starts to cry.

"Ajaunta, I can't even believe this. I mean, OK, this cult is threatening you. I can believe that, but what do you think I can do about it? Isn't this a problem for the authorities?"

"I went to the authorities, but there is nothing they can do. I don't know where this cult is. I don't even know the real name of the man I was dating. I told the authorities, but they have no people or locations to investigate. I don't know how to find these people. They can find me anytime, though. They know where I live and where I work. They know where my husband works, where my boys go to college, and where my girls go to high school. This cult has turned my life upside down. Rain, I am afraid to go home. I need help, and I don't want to involve my parents because I know they will be threatened as well. I know it is so unfair for me to ask you for help, but there is nowhere else for me to turn. I always remember you and Kenneth were bad ass. No one messed with you two. I know you always had a crush on me, and I always wished you would have made a move on me, but you never did. I don't know what to do. I am afraid they are watching me right now. Can I please stay with you at least for a little while?" Ajaunta is wiping her eyes with a napkin, trying not to cry out loud.

"Oh my god, Ajaunta! Of course, you can stay with me. I'll tell you right now, if anyone comes to my house with the intent of hurting you, I will fucking kill them. There were already three corpses in my house tonight, and that is no lie. This night is getting stranger and stranger. I almost made love earlier for the first time in over ten years, and we were attacked by three men who were killed by Smoke. I have not seen Smoke in five years. This scared Marlene to death, and she has left me for the time being. Smoke left me high and dry. I waited for him at a coffee shop so he could explain why he killed those men whom I may have killed if he had not showed up at my house. Smoke did who knows what with the bodies, and I go home to get a call from you, and now here I am. So knowing that, do you still want to come to my house?"

"Yes, Rain, yes. I know you would never hurt me."

"No, I would not. I have loved you every day of my life since the first day of seventh grade. My only regret in life is not making you my girl. I guess I am old now, and I'm not afraid anymore."

"Rain, afraid? Afraid of what?"

"I was never afraid of anything ever in my life except for one thing."

"What was that?"

"The only thing that ever scared me, the one thing that absolutely terrified me was Ajaunta Macari."

"Why would you be afraid of me?"

"Because I got to watch this little girl in my class. She was nothing but long arms and long legs from here to the moon. She had scraggly blond hair and teeth as crooked as mine. I got to watch her grow into the most stunningly beautiful young woman I ever saw in my life. Now sitting here seeing you twenty-five years later, looking into your eyes and seeing your face, there is no question you are the most beautiful woman I have ever seen in my life."

"Rain." Ajaunta blushes.

"The most terrifying thing in my life was to hold, to try and take care of the most precious, the most beautiful girl I had ever seen in my life, and that was always Ajaunta Macari."

"Rain, I can't believe you are saying this to me. Why didn't you say that when we were kids?"

"I couldn't get close to you. My heart was in my throat. My legs felt like they were going to give way every time I walked toward you. Simply put, I was chicken shit. It's my fault we never got together."

"Rain, I love my husband and my kids. I want my life back. Right now, I just don't know what to do, where to go, or whom to turn to. I'm not looking to start a relationship."

"I understand. I am just proud of myself to finally tell you how I have felt all my life. I am glad that I am not going to go to my grave with that bottled up inside me."

Ajaunta is blown away by Rain's words, and the waitress comes by offering to fill their coffee cups, which they accept. The diner is very loud, so they can talk freely without anyone listening or hearing what they are saying. Ajaunta feels safe with such a large crowd, and it seems more and more people are streaming in all the time.

"Rain, I can't believe you just said that. That breaks my heart in a way. I would not do anything to change my life with my husband and my kids, but when we were young, I always had a crush on you. Makes me wonder, what if? I guess I was afraid to."

An awkward silence falls over them as they sip their coffee and watch the young adults laughing, smiling, and eating in the diner. It reminds them when they were in their early twenties.

"So what is your plan? You want to come to my house and, what, just stay there? I mean, what are you going to do? If you can't call the police and you don't want to tell your parents, what are you going to do? Why didn't you go with your husband and kids to Texas?"

"People from this cult went to my husband's work and threatened him and our kids. They told him if he did not leave, he and our kids would be killed, and if I were to disappear with them, we would all be killed. Sully got so scared. He left me. He even lost his job. I don't know what is going to happen. I don't know if we can survive this, but for right now, I just don't know what to do. I need you to help me, Rain. I don't want to go home. I don't want to go near there because I am afraid they are waiting for me, and who knows what they will do?"

Rain rubs his forehead and sips his coffee.

"Well, all right, come on, let's go. You can come with me to my house, but I don't know what to do. I don't know what you are going to do, but we will figure something out. You do have a car, right? You drove here, right?"

"Yeah. I have a nice SUV. I can follow you."

"Do you think you are being followed? Does this cult have you under some sort of surveillance, or are they following your car?"

"I don't think so."

"So you coming to my house should be safe. I mean, they won't know where you are, right?"

"Rain, I don't know. I don't think so. They may be watching my house waiting for me to go back there. That's why I don't want to go there."

"So do you have clothes and things in your car?"

"No, just what you see."

"Well, in that case, I will probably see you naked, so, fuck it, let them come after me."

"Rain, please, I'm old and getting fat. I'm not what I used to be."

"Well, that happens to all of us. Come on, at least you can hold my hand."

Rain stands up and drops money on the table. Ajaunta stands up and holds his hand with a smile, walking out of the diner into the lightly falling rain. Ajaunta scans the parking lot looking for anything or anyone suspicious. She notices nothing and follows Rain in her SUV back to his house.

Chapter 3

Dreams and Ajaunta

Eight-year-old Rain walks down the pavement toward the swing sets. He is all alone, but kids are walking, running, and yelling all around. Samantha runs up to Rain and kisses him on the cheek. She runs away smiling and yelling.

"If you catch me, you can kiss me."

Rain smiles and ignores her. His attention is on Kenneth, who is standing by the cement wall next to the tennis courts. Reid, Gavin, and Tim have Ken surrounded, and it seems like they are taunting him. Rain walks up behind Tim.

"What do you want, Rain? We are busy here," says Gavin.

"I came to see Ken. I have some things I want to ask him," says Rain.

"Yeah, well, Ken is busy. You can see him after school," says Reid.

"Yeah, I can see him right now," says Rain.

"Listen, Rain, get out of here right now," says Gavin.

"Or what? Huh, Gavin? What are you going to do? You don't feel quite so tough when it's three on two instead of three on one, do you, Gavin?" says Rain.

"You ain't so tough, Rain, you little faggot. Get out of here before I kick your ass just because I feel like it," says Reid.

"Take your best shot, Reid," says Rain.

Reid takes a step toward Rain and punches him dead in the face, knocking him to the ground. Ken takes a step forward, punching Reid in the jaw, knocking him down. Gavin starts to punch Ken, and Tim watches, yelling, "Fight, fight, fight!" Rain gets up, feeling the blood dripping from his torn lip. He hears Tim yelling and dives at him, tackling him to the ground. Rain straddles him and punches him repeatedly in the face. Tim covers his face with his arms, blocking most of Rain's punches. Rain gets up and kicks his right knee into the gut of Gavin, who bends over falling to the ground, curling up in a fetal position. Reid gets up and punches Rain on the back of the head, and Rain turns to get punched in the face again, being knocked down. Ken punches Reid in the face, and he falls to the ground and starts to cry. Tim gets up and runs toward the school, yelling, "I'm telling, I'm telling!" Reid and Gavin are both curled up on the ground crying, and Ken reaches his hand to Rain, helping him up. Rain's lip is swelling up very badly, and blood has dripped all down the front of his shirt. He spits blood and torn cheek from his mouth.

"Damn, Rain. You got fucked up," says Ken.

"Yeah, well, I'm not the one crying on the ground. I told you to stay away from these guys—they're thugs," says Rain.

"Yeah, I know they are liars too," says Ken.

"Goddamn it, Ken, we are only in first grade and already I know you are going to be the death of me. I don't know how I know that, but I do. You are going to get me killed someday, you know that," says Rain.

"Well, if I am going to get you killed, then I need a cool name like you have. Rain—that is such a cool name. Now I need a cool name. What can I be called? I know—Smoke. From now on, call me Smoke," says Ken.

"I will call you Smoke because wherever there is fire, there is smoke, and I am always dragging your ass out of the fire," says Rain.

"Oh, gee, here comes Mr. Thomas. I'm sure we are getting in trouble for sure," says Ken.

"Yeah, I'm sure you are right," says Rain.

Rain wakes from his dream and sits on the edge of his bed. If it were not for the excruciating pounding on the back of his head, he would think this whole night is a dream. He looks at his phone next to his bed to see it is only 3:15 a.m. He goes to the bathroom and rinses the back of his head with cold water. He walks into the living room. Ajaunta said she would sleep on the couch tonight, and Rain gave her a few blankets and pillows. He walks over to the couch and sits next to her. She rolls from her side to her back, looking at Rain, who runs his fingers through her hair.

"I can't believe you are here. The girl of my dreams is here in my lonely house with me."

"I can't believe you never got married. I find it hard to believe some beautiful girl out there didn't scoop you up."

"You ever hear that saying, 'Things happen for a reason'?"

"Of course, everyone has heard that."

"Well, I still remember seeing you the first day of seventh grade, the first day we were in high school. That was the first time I really knew how beautiful you were. Your body started catching up with your arms and legs. You were transforming. You were undergoing female metamorphosis."

Ajaunta laughs and slaps Rain on the side.

"Shut up, you jerk. You are so funny."

"No, I'm serious. You were my princess. I just never had the nerve to tell you, but I know you knew. You saw the way I looked at you, and you never let me near you. The very few times I did get close to you, I choked up badly, but you knew I was so in love with you. Girls know these things. Guys too."

"I knew, Rain. Well, you're close to me now, and you are not choking. You are spilling your guts."

"I'm not afraid anymore. I'm too old to be afraid."

Rain reaches his arms under Ajaunta's back and stands with her in his arms.

"Rain, what are you doing?"

"You're not sleeping on the couch. Come to bed with me," he says as he walks into the bedroom with her in his arms. He lays her on the bed.

"Rain, I'm not a little girl anymore. I'm not petite anymore. I'm ugly now."

Rain kisses her.

"Rain, I love the way you make me feel."

He kisses her some more.

"Rain."

He looks in her eyes.

"You can do whatever you want with me, Rain."

He makes love with her slow and powerful, and soon afterward, they both fall asleep.

Rain runs through the parking lot, yelling, "Smoke, Smoke, behind you!"

Smoke turns to see Melveroykel swinging a bat at him. Thanks to Rain, he noticed just in time to dodge the attack. Randy and Kevin are already facing off with Smoke, and Shelly is yelling at the boys to leave Smoke alone. Stacey is running behind Rain, who is now running full speed to get to Smoke. Rain gets to Smoke and pulls him from the center of the three boys who are from Willsdus, and Shelly stands next to Smoke.

"Hey, guys, calm down. We don't even know you. What seems to be the problem here?"

Melveroykel does not give Rain a chance. He swings the bat, hitting him right on the head. Rain falls like a ton of bricks. Shelly runs up screaming.

"Melveroykel, you fucking asshole!"

She leans down to protect Rain from another attack, but that matters not. This infuriates Smoke, and Smoke punches Melveroykel in the face twice, dazing him and knocking him to the ground. Randy makes a move at Smoke, and Smoke grabs the bat, which fell to the ground, and hits Randy in the head, dropping him almost unconscious to the ground. Smoke flares the bat at Kevin, and he runs away. Smoke then kneels down to Melveroykel and puts the bat on his throat and starts to crush his windpipe. Melveroykel gets very scared. He raises his hands, showing submission. Smoke lets off the pressure and backs away. Rain is getting up, and Smoke helps him to his car. Shelly and Stacey go with Rain and Smoke.

"Yeah, you better go. You better get out of here!" yells Melveroykel, sitting up, laughing, and rubbing his throat.

"This isn't over. You hear me? This isn't over!" yells Melveroykel.

Smoke and the two girls from Willsdus help Rain to his car, and he is still dazed.

"Goddamn it, Smoke. You are going to get me killed someday, you know that? I'm serious. Someday, I am going to get killed. I mean, what the fuck was that? I never even saw those guys, and he, what, hits me with a fucking bat. What the hell was that all about?"

"Those guys are jealous because I am dating Smoke," says Shelly.

"Yeah, and they know I like you, Rain," says Stacey.

"Really, you like me?" says Rain.

Stacey smiles and puts her arms around Rain's neck, hugging him tight.

"I guess you do like me," says Rain.

"Hey, Rain, you must be having some sort of wild dream. One minute, you are kicking, and the next minute, you are laughing. You woke me up," says Ajaunta.

Rain looks up to see Ajaunta leaning over him.

"Hmmm. I woke you up. Oh, I'm sorry. Yeah, I was having a dream about Smoke of all people. That's the second dream I have had about him tonight. Must be because I saw him earlier. You know Smoke was always in trouble, but tonight was the worst ever. Three people died. You know what—they were in my dream. Do you remember when I got knocked out in the parking lot in Willsdus at that soccer game?"

"I do remember that."

"Well, the three guys from Willsdus involved in that incident are the three guys that Smoke killed here in my house earlier tonight before you called me. This is freaking nuts. It still has not even sunk in yet. Three guys were killed in my house earlier tonight. This is just not normal. Here I am looking at you. I must be insane. I must be dreaming."

"Rain, calm down. It seems like you are as scared as I am. We both can't be scared. Let me lie next to you. Let me hold you."

Ajaunta snuggles up next to Rain and puts her head on his shoulder. This calms and relaxes Rain a lot, and in no time, Ajaunta is fast asleep. Rain lies there next to Ajaunta, but he cannot fall back asleep. He thinks about the first week he and Smoke were in boot camp together.

"Smoke, are you sure about this? You know we are signing our lives away here. We are literally saying we have no family. If we get in a bad situation and that is exactly where we are heading, then there is no next of kin for us. Is that what you want? If we die, that's it. We are burned, buried at sea, or shot off into space—that's it."

"Come on, Rain, you always worry about every little thing. If it were not for me, you would still be in Farmsvern. Come on, Rain, this is going to be awesome. This is the only way we are ever going to get ahead. If we don't sign, we are going to be stuck with all the other losers doing the same thing the same way all the losers do. You are not a loser—you never were, so come on shut up and sign."

Ajaunta leans up and kisses Rain on the neck. She can tell he is half asleep. She rolls to her side with her back to Rain, and he rolls to his side, falling into a dream.

"Smoke, where are you, Smoke?"

Rain is running through the thick jungle with his finger near the trigger of his M15A4. This is his preferred gun in combat. He wears light body armor and is completely camouflaged. "Smoke!" he yells, looking down, seeing Smoke's gun lying in the brush. He retrieves the gun and moves on, coming up to a clearing. He sees a tall building where Smoke is being dragged by two men into the building. Rain pulls back into the bush, staying out of sight. He bends down next to a tree when he feels a sharp pain and immediate burning on his left shin. Looking down, he realizes he was bitten by a green snake. Like he was in some sort of delayed reaction, he suddenly jumps after he sees the snake. The pain starts to intensify, and he grabs his leg as the snake slithers away from him. He grinds his teeth, trying his best not to cry out.

This wakes Rain, and he sits on the side of his bed, rubbing the back of his head, which is still throbbing. He squeezes his head with his hands and twists his head from side to side, trying to ease the pain. He looks behind him, and Ajaunta is in deep sleep. He lies back down closes his eyes and remembers that the snake that bit him was poisonous and very common to the region. He happened to have antivenom and administered it to himself. Rain starts to fade to sleep, dreaming about the second week in boot camp when Smoke and Rain were picked as a two-man team to go on special missions that are not on the books.

No records of their missions were ever kept. The two of them went on twelve missions all over the world and survived them all. On this particular mission, Smoke was captured, and Rain happened to get him out before he was tortured to death. This was their last mission in the Special Forces, and they both retired from military service. They were paid very handsomely, and Rain used his money to buy his house. Smoke— he could never settle down; he was always on the go and had to travel all the time, seeking adventure. Rain could not keep up with Smoke anymore, and Smoke continued on his way. Rain did love the service, but soldiering is a young man's game, and at forty years of age, Rain said enough is enough. Smoke agreed it was time to leave the service, but settling down was never something Smoke could do, at least not yet in his life. They both retired. Rain bought his house and opened a gun shop here in the town of Lilston. Now, Smoke is back after five years, and all hell has broken loose.

Rain dreams of the tall building in the clearing of the jungle. He can still hear Smoke screaming from within. After injecting his femoral artery with the antivenom, Rain runs toward the building, throwing a grenade into the bottom window of the building. He runs around the side of the building where there is a doorway with no door. He squats and points his rifle. Shortly after, the corner of the building explodes and the dust settles. Rain sees men running down the stairs, and he shoots them. He charges up the stairs in a fury, shooting everyone he sees. He can hear Smoke yelling the whole time, and Rain follows his voice right to him. Rain shoots six enemies and finds Smoke tied to a bed where he was being tortured. Rain cuts the ropes and realizes Smoke has been sliced with knives on his arms and legs. He is bleeding badly, and Rain puts Smoke over his shoulder, carrying him out of the building. This is the only time Smoke has ever been captured and the only time Rain ever saw Smoke with wounded pride. Rain carries Smoke for three miles through the jungle until he feels they are safe and rests, leaning Smoke against a tree.

"Rain, you got me out. You got me out."

Rain pulls a canteen of water and drinks.

"Smoke, drink. Drink some of this."

Rain puts the canteen to Smoke's mouth, and he drinks.

"Rain, you saved my life. They were going to kill me. I was not going to tell them a thing, and they were going to kill me. Look what they did to me, those bastards. They cut me up. They cut me up."

"No sweat, Smoke, we're going to fix you up. A few stitches and you will be good as new."

"Rain, I can't believe you saved me. You charged right in there and you pulled me out. You are the best friend anyone could ever have. You hear me? You are the best. I won't forget this ever. I will always be there for you. The time will come when I will be there for you. You can believe that."

"I know you will, Smoke. I know you will."

The two of them can hear the sound of a rocket, and the earth around them explodes. Dirt and debris fly all over. Rain kicks his legs, which shakes him from his sleep. He is lying on his back, and the sun is up shining in the window. He breaths deeply and rubs the back of his head. He looks over to see only he is in the bed.

Chapter 4

Log Cabin

Rain sits up on his bed. He rubs his head in disbelief thinking about what happened last night. He gets up, puts on a pot of coffee, and listens to it percolate. Starring out the window, he can see the sun already high in the sky. He looks at his phone and wants to call Marlene, but he can still hear her saying, "Don't call me. I'll call you." Then he thinks of Ajaunta, and the phone rings while he is looking at it. He can see the number showing from the caller; he already remembers it is Ajaunta.

"Hello."

"Rain, it's me, Ajaunta."

"Hi, Ajaunta. I was surprised to see you had gone before I got up this morning. I did sleep in, but, hey, it's Sunday."

"Rain, my husband came back with the kids. He called me early this morning, and I went back home. Rain, my kids have been kidnapped. They took my kids."

"What about your husband?"

"He is here. They beat him up. They left his eyes black and blue and his lip all swollen. He said they beat him up and left him here at our house to tell me they wanted me. They will let our kids go if I turn myself in to them."

"What do you mean turn yourself in to them? What the hell is that supposed to mean?"

"Rain, they want to sacrifice me for some sort of satanic ritual. They are going to kill me, and if I don't go to them, they are going to kill my kids."

"Ajaunta, I can't even believe this. I never would have thought this of you. I guess you really don't know somebody. I was in your class from elementary school to high school, and I never would have thought you would be involved with people like this."

"Rain, you are the only one I can turn to. Can you help me?"

"You can't be serious? No, I can't help you. You need to call the police. You need to call the police and tell them exactly what you are telling me."

"Rain, everyone knows you were a bad ass in the marines. You were some sort of special unit commando or something. This is what you do, isn't it?"

"No, this is not what I do. When you are in the military and you do things for your country, that is something completely different and separate from civilian life. Sure, I could go kill some people, but I'm not going to."

"What am I going to do? I can't let them kill my kids."

"Then you better call the police and let them handle it. Listen, this is crazy, this is nuts. I can't believe I am hearing this from you. I can't deal with this right now. I'm sorry, but I have to go. You are going to have to figure this out with your husband. I'm sorry, I have to go."

"Rain, please."

Rain hangs up the phone. He rubs his eyes and takes a deep breath, tossing his phone on the table, rubbing his eyes red like he has a never-ending itch.

"What the hell kind of bullshit is this? Satanic cults killing people—what the hell? I can't believe this. Why the fuck isn't she calling Smoke? He would love this shit."

Rain is interrupted while talking to himself by his phone ringing.

"Ajaunta, are you for real? Seriously, you live in Summersfield, which is pretty much a huge city, and it's not like 1800 anymore. A satanic cult is kidnapping people and sacrificing them. I just can't believe this."

Ajaunta is hysterical and crying.

"Rain, Sully is going to get our kids. He is going after them. Rain, they are going to kill Sully. I know they will. Rain, please help me, please."

Ajaunta is sobbing on the phone.

"Ah!"

Rain sighs loudly, slapping the top of his head with his right hand. "All right, all right, just what do you want me to do? What can I do?"

"Come get me, and we can go there and try to save my husband and my kids."

"I don't even know where you live?"

"Meet me at the diner where we had coffee last night."

"All right, Ajaunta, I will meet you at the diner, and you better get rid of your winey ass tears and put on your serious face because I am treating this like life and death for real, am I clear?"

"Yes, Rain, loud and clear. I am going to the diner right now."

"I will be there shortly."

Rain hangs up the phone not believing he is going on this crazy goose chase. He goes to his back yard and unlocks his shed next to the big barn, and inside is a whole lot of guns, rifles, ammunition, cleaning kits, supplies, and more. Rain does have licenses to carry concealed firearms, and he puts on a shoulder harness, which holds two handguns, one under each arm. Both .357 magnum revolvers have six shots, and that is plenty, he figures. He puts on a sports jacket, which hides his weapons, and wastes no time to go see Ajaunta.

Pulling into the driveway of the diner, Rain can see Ajaunta is standing at the back of her SUV waiting for him. She jumps into his car as he drives up.

"Well, it sure looks like you have calmed down."

"You said to put on my serious face, and this is it. No one fucks with my family. It's time to go fuck them up right, Rain?"

Rain laughs sarcastically.

"Whatever you say, Ajaunta. So where are we going?"

"You know where Fright Hill is, right?"

"Fright Hill? That's where you are supposed to park your car on the hill and your car rolls up the hill instead of down the hill, right?"

"That's it, that's where we are going. Let's go."

"I was there once or twice in high school, but I don't know how to get there. All I remember is that it's on the way to Cansdale, I think?"

"Don't worry, I'll show you the way. Just start heading down 84."

"All right."

Thirty minutes later and they are at fright hill. When they get to the top of fright hill, Ajaunta directs Rain to head west, which he does. She then directs him south down a dirt road, and it seems like civilization has been left behind as they head into deep woods. Rain stops the car and gets out. It is a beautiful day. The sun is shining. The light breeze is blowing through the trees. Ajaunta gets out.

"Rain, what are you doing? We are not there yet."

"So you have been here before?"

"Yes, John took me here once before."

"Oh, so now this mystery man has a name."

"That's the name he told me, but he told me later that the name was a fake one. It's just what I know him by. Come on, Rain, we have to get to Sully and my kids."

"Listen, Ajaunta, this is what I do, and the first rule is you do not go into a bad situation blind. That is exactly what we are doing. For all we know, there are eyes watching us right now, which makes us dead ducks. So tell me exactly where we are going. When we get there, what is there?"

"There is a big log cabin at the end of this road."

"How far is it from here?"

"It's another fifteen to twenty minutes from here."

"All right. So how many people are in this cult?"

"I'm not sure. I was only seeing John."

"You don't even know how many people are a part of this cult? So this log cabin, is it the only house there? Are there other log cabins or barns or anything?"

"It's just one big log cabin, and it is gorgeous. John took me there, and I fell in love with the place. It's so beautiful there. John told me it was his place, but now I know he was lying. It is a place where people from this cult take people and seduce them. They lure people here and sacrifice them."

"So if they had you there, why didn't they sacrifice you?"

"I don't know. I guess they wanted access to my family. Maybe John just wanted to have sex with me first. I don't know. Rain, I messed up so bad. I can't believe I ever got involved with this. Rain, you are right. This is not something I would ever knowingly be a part of."

Ajaunta breaks down sobbing and walks to Rain, hugging and hanging on him.

"Rain, I don't know what to do. You are the only one I thought could help me. I don't have a lot of friends, not friends that are like you. You were always so strong, so independent. I am so sorry to involve you, but I have to save my family. I will do anything to make sure my children are not hurt especially because of something stupid I did. Please help me."

"Calm down, pull yourself together. Listen to me and listen good. There is only one reason why I am here right now, and that is you. There is nothing I would not do for you because I have loved you every day of my life since the first day of seventh grade. Now having said that, I want for your kids and your husband to be OK. I want you to go back to your life the way it was before this cult bullshit. You are going to follow me from this point on, and you are going to keep quiet, do you understand?"

Ajaunta shakes her head up and down.

Rain starts to walk along the road and veers into the woods, which gives the two of them some cover. Ajaunta follows him quietly. Rain moves slowly, stopping periodically to scan the surroundings. He is very familiar with wooded landscapes, and he is looking for possible traps. He keeps many thoughts to himself as they move through the woods. He can tell there has been no human activity in the woods at all. He sees no traps of any sort and no sign of human activity all the way to the cabin. He stops inside the woods and scans the entire area with his eyes. There are no cars, no signs of people in or around the cabin.

"This must be it."

"Yes, this is it."

"Does not look like anyone is here at all. Are they expecting you to come here? I thought you said your husband went to get your kids? How did he know where this place is? I don't see any cars. Where would he have parked? Did he know how to get here?"

"No, Sully was never here, but they have his phone number. They called him while he was in Texas and tricked him to come back home. Sully told me this morning he came back home to save me. He told me he came back home to fight for me, and our kids came back with him. The cult members were waiting at our house and took our kids. They beat up Sully, and he called me after they left with our kids. I went home, and when I got there, Sully told me he was going after our kids. They called him just before I got there, but he didn't tell me where he was going. I just figured it was here. He told me to stay home, and I called you."

Rain and Ajaunta instinctively bend and crouch down in the brush as they hear loud chanting from behind the cabin. It sounds like a dozen people chanting the same thing but in a language neither Rain nor Ajaunta understands.

"Ajaunta, you never met any of these supposed cult members except this John? You only met this one guy?"

"I dated him on and off over the years, and when Sully and I started working things out, I tried to break things off with John. That is when he started telling me about this cult that he is a part of. At first, I thought he was just trying to scare me into staying with him. He was telling me how they kill people and he is two hundred years old. They sacrifice people to give them youth and eternal life."

"Yeah, right."

"That's what I said to his face. I broke ties with him, and now he and this cult started threatening my husband and our kids."

"You have me here now. Time to start threatening them. When you are afraid of the unknown, it's usually best to face it head-on, so let's let them know we are here."

Just as Rain pulls his revolvers, they both hear a scream above all the chanting from behind the cabin.

"Sully!" yells Ajaunta, and she runs toward the sound.

"Ajaunta, Ajaunta, wait!"

Ajaunta runs around the cabin. Rain follows behind her, wielding both his guns. What Rain sees when he rounds the cabin takes his breath away. Ajaunta is quickly captured by two very large men and taken to the front of a large rock, which has a man lying on his back, tied at the hands and feet. The ropes are held by large men holding the man in place. These men are all wearing some sort of devil mask with long vines hanging from the masks to their knees. One man is holding a large knife, and he thrusts it into the man's chest just below his throat and drags the knife along the center of the man's chest, cutting all the ribs. The man drops the knife and grabs the ribs with both hands, pulling them apart.

"Sully!" screams Ajaunta.

"Motherfucker!" yells Rain, and he points his guns and shoots the man twice in the chest. He then shoots the men holding the ropes. The men holding Ajaunta put her in between them and Rain, hoping he will not shoot at them, and it works. They back into the woods, taking Ajaunta with them. There are nearly a dozen other men and women all wearing red-and-black hooded cloaks covering their heads and bodies. These people are chanting some gibberish Rain cannot understand, and their chants get louder and louder. Ajaunta is screaming as the men drag her through the woods, and already she is out of sight. Rain instinctive goes to Sully and pushes down on his ribs, closing his chest cavity. He is still alive, and he looks at Rain, trying to talk with blood dripping out of his mouth. He is gagging and coughing blood.

"Don't talk. Don't talk. I am going to get you out of here."

Rain looks up to see the cloaked people are not moving at all. They are just chanting louder and louder when the earth below Rain starts to shake. He loses his balance and falls to the ground. The earth to the front of the rock explodes as a huge blood-red creature erupts from the ground. It slams two front hands with long talons on the ground on either side of the rock and lifts its twelve-foot body out of the ground. Rain is just missed by the left hand that slams on the ground right beside him. He rolls out of the way and stands up as the creature lifts bipedal legs from the earth and stands. Its feet has three toes and one big toe all with long thick talons.

"What the fuck!" says Rain.

The creature looks at the individuals chanting in their cloaks and reaches down, grabbing the man on the rock around his neck with its left hand. It has a humanoid body arms and legs. The head is humanoid except it has a large blood-red bill like a toucan. It raises the man in the air and bites the head three times, crunching it, tearing it from the man's neck, and swallowing it. Rain watches as the blood-red demon bites, rips, and swallows the head in a few quick bites.

"Motherfucker!" exclaims Rain.

Rain had slipped his guns back in their holsters, and he pulls them, shooting the remaining six shots into the demon. The demon screams very loudly, very deeply, facing its bill right at Rain as he shoots it. This makes Rain's chest thump. He feels like his ribs are going to crack. Rain is very accurate hitting the demon in the head and chest with all his shots, and the beast falls back into the hole it rose from, taking the unfortunate man with it. The earth falls back into place, covering the hole. Rain is out of ammunition and suddenly wishes he had brought more. The people chanting in their cloaks stop, and they start to approach Rain. Rain lost sight of Ajaunta a while ago and runs back down the road toward his car.

Chapter 5

Fright Hill Woods

Rain runs back down the road toward his car. He really is not too worried of the cloaked people who are running after him. He does have a tactical soldier knife hanging in a sheath from his belt, and he is very confident with his hand-to-hand ability. He is actually really freaked out by the creature that he saw with his own eyes. After a quarter of a mile, Rain looks back to see he is not being pursued, and he slows to a brisk walk. He hears Ajaunta screaming off in the woods, but he does not see her. He wields his knife and heads toward the screams of Ajaunta. The woods are very thick with lots of green everywhere. He can tell he is getting close to Ajaunta because her screams are getting louder and louder. He can tell she is being beaten. He can now see the two men wearing large coconut-like masks with long vines hanging down to their knees. They have Ajaunta against a tree, and they are tearing at her clothes, ripping them from her body. Ajaunta is screaming and holding her arms to her breasts now covered by only her bra, and her skin is scratched and torn from the long, sharp fingernails of the very large men.

"Aye!" yells Rain, getting the attention of the two men, who face him and walk toward him. Rain moves toward them in an offensive stance with his knife ready. The men are much larger than Rain, standing roughly six and a half feet tall each. Rain can't get a real good look at them. They wear a mask, which looks like a large coconut shell with holes cut out for the eyes and nose, but he can't see eyes or noses.

The vines hanging from the bottom of their masks cover a lot of their bodies, but Rain can see they are very scarred, and the flesh on them looks deformed.

"Come on, motherfuckers. Keep coming at me. Get what you get," says Rain.

They keep approaching until within striking range, and Rain attacks ferociously. He kicks with his right shin at the left knee of the man to his right. The man bends down to grasp his knee, and Rain kicks up with his knee, hitting the mask, sending it flying. The man stands facing Rain, and this is enough to scare even Rain. The man has his eyelids sewn shut. His nose has been sliced off, showing his nasal cavity, and Rain can see into his hollow skull.

"What the fuck! This is not even real," says Rain.

Rain immediately strikes upward with his knife, driving it hilt deep from under the devil man's chin into his hollow head. Rain pulls his hand back to see what happens. There is some sort of clear slime that drools onto his hand and knife from the brainless man, and that really freaks Rain out. He shakes his hand frantically to try and rid his hand of the slime. It looks at the other creature holding the bottom of its chin. The other creature slaps both of his hands on the creature's bare head, crunching the bones, and it falls crumbling like its bones and flesh are granite being crushed. The creature falls apart as it hits the ground, and Rain jump kicks the other creature and stabs it under the chin like he did the first one. He comes around stabbing it in the neck with his knife, and it falls crumbling like the first one did. He sheaths his knife and runs to Ajaunta, who is standing against the tree in some sort of daze. He grabs her hand and heads for his car.

"Come on, Ajaunta, we have to get out of here."

She is crying, holding her arms over her breasts. She is unresponsive, and Rain grabs her shoulders, shaking her.

"Ajaunta, Ajaunta, get a hold of yourself. Come on, we are getting out of here."

"Sully. Where is Sully?"

"That thing. That monster, whatever the fuck it was, got him. I'm sorry, he is gone. It took him into the earth. It's not taking me into the earth. I ain't fucking around anymore. If you are gonna just give up and let them have you, then that's on you. I'm fucking out of this nightmare."

Rain lets go of Ajaunta and turns to head back to his car. He sees all the cloaked cult members have surrounded him and Ajaunta, and they start chanting his name.

"Stormy Rain Clouds, Stormy Rain Clouds, Stormy Rain Clouds, Stormy Rain Clouds."

Rain sees Ajaunta's torn shirt lying on the ground, and he uses it to wipe the slime from his hand and knife, which he pulls from its sheath. He faces the people a little hesitant because he still has not seen their faces, which is kind of freaking him out.

"Come on, motherfuckers, you want some of me? Here I am. Who's first?"

Rain waves his knife from side to side, facing the cloaked crowd.

"Ajaunta, are you coming with me? I ain't wasting my time with you if you are going to be all wuss. If you're coming, let's go, otherwise I'm leaving you."

Rain faces Ajaunta and holds his hand to her. She grabs his hand and follows Rain's lead. He walks slowly away from the crowd chanting his name. One of them speaks.

"Go, Stormy Rain Clouds, go, but you cannot hide from us. We will find you. Our lord will feast on your flesh, and your soul will nourish our youth."

Rain has never backed down from a threat ever in his life, and now is no exception. He lets go of Ajaunta's hand and approaches the one he thinks is speaking.

"Who is hiding, you coward fuck? You want me, don't search for me. I am right here. You think I am afraid of you—you little ball sack piece of shit motherfucker."

Rain approaches him and flips the hood over his head. This freaks Rain out. It's just a skull, no flesh, no muscle, just a skull, and it starts to laugh. Rain kicks it in the chest, and it's just a human frame of bones.

"What the fuck! This can't be real. What the fuck is going on here?"

Rain talks to himself, flipping the hood of the man next to the one he just kicked, and it is a real human man who punches Rain in the face, sending him backward and falling to the ground. The rest of them are real, and they flip their hoods and pursue Rain. He gets up fast and runs, grabbing Ajaunta by the hand, and they run back toward his car. The cult members chase after them. Rain realizes he lost his knife. That punch really took him by surprise, and now Rain is truly freaked out.

The cult members are catching them and grabbing at their clothing. Rain has his shirt torn as he pulls Ajaunta from the grasp of cult members who are trying to pull her from Rain. One dives on Ajaunta's legs, dropping her to the ground, and she screams. Rain turns and starts to fight with them. Rain is well trained and uses simple but very effective fighting techniques, punching and flipping the overmatched cult members. He pulls the man on top of Ajaunta and punches him several times in the face. The cult members keep piling on Rain just to be punched, kicked, and flipped away from him. They grab Ajaunta over and over, and Rain is always there to bloody their face and knock them away from her. The cult members realize they are not enough to overpower Rain even though he is tiring. They circle the two of them and start to chant. Rain helps Ajaunta to her feet and holds her, realizing they are surrounded. The chant is similar to the one at the log cabin, and the earth starts to shake.

"Oh, not again. Come on, Ajaunta, we have to get out of here now."

He runs at one of the cult members and kicks him out of the way. Ajaunta follows Rain, and they run toward his car. Erupting from the earth is one of those humanoid demons, and the cult members point at Rain and Ajaunta, and the demon chases after them.

"Rain, what is that thing? What is that?"

"I don't know. I have some speed clips in my car. We have to get to my car quick. Come on, run like you have never run before."

Rain is way faster than Ajaunta, and he leaves her behind, trying to get to the ammunition clips in his car. They are actually pretty close to his car, and Rain gets there, unlocking the car door and accessing the clips in the center console. He ejects the empty casings from his guns and inserts new bullets. Ajaunta is exiting the woods, and the demon is right behind her, biting at her with its massive bill.

"Rain, Rain, it's gonna get me."

Rain is right there with both guns pointed at its beak, and just as it is getting ready to clamp down on Ajaunta, Rain blasts away. He shoots fast and accurately, cracking and breaking the beak with four shots. Another four shots crack and break its skull, and the remaining four shots blast holes in its chest. The demon screams a deafening high-pitch frequency, almost popping their eardrums, and they both have to cover their ears as the demon shrinks and floats backward through the trees into the woods from where it came.

"Come on, let's get the fuck out of here!" yells, Rain getting into the car. Ajaunta gets into the passenger side. Rain starts it up and starts to drive away. It takes about five seconds for him to realize something is very wrong. He gets out of the car, and sure enough, the tires have been cut and are flat.

"Goddamn it. Come, we are on foot, let's go. Wait a second, where is your phone?"

Ajaunta feels her pants.

"I don't know. I lost it somewhere."

"It's OK. Mine is right here."

Rain looks in the center console of the car.

"Damn, where is it? It should be right here. Damn, where is my phone? Damn it. It looks like we are on foot after all. Come on, let's go."

Rain starts to walk down the dirt road back to the main road. Ajaunta walks beside him, and she really can't believe her husband is dead.

"I have no idea what happened to my kids. I don't know where they are."

"Listen, evil people do what evil people do. They probably never had any intentions of sparing any of you."

"You think my kids are dead?"

"I have no idea. I can't believe what I have seen here in these woods today. Now I am tempted to believe what you said about this evil cult sacrificing people for longer life or special powers or whatever. This is crazy. Why did they want you and your family, I wonder? I mean, is it anyone they can sacrifice, or do they need certain people? How did you know they wanted to sacrifice you? Maybe it was your husband they wanted all the time?"

"I didn't know about the sacrifices. I mean, I did, but just like you said, it is so crazy, so hard to believe. When I got home this morning, my husband told me all this stuff they told him. John had made threats toward my family, but I thought it was just to get to me, and now they are dead."

"This John guy, did you see him at the cabin or in the woods?"

"No, I have not seen him today. I have never seen any of these people. I never even heard of that monster that came out of the ground."

"Yeah, me neither. I'm still baffled to what that was, but there is no doubt it was real."

Rain keeps watching behind and around them. Looks like the cult members have broken off the pursuit.

"Would you feel more comfortable wearing my shirt?"

"If you would not mind, I would appreciate that."

Rain gives Ajaunta his shirt to wear. They walk for nearly an hour, making it to the main road, and finally, a car passes by, which they flag down. The car stops, and the driver lets them call the police. The driver keeps going, while Rain and Ajaunta keep walking down the road. A police car will meet up with them soon. They walk and talk for nearly an hour before a police car shows up. He pulls over and exits his car.

"Mr. Clouds? Mrs. Brenner?"

"Yes, Officer, I go by the name Rain, and this is Ajaunta."

"Hi, I am Officer Stephen Brace. I got here as soon as I could. So let me see if I understand this correctly. You two were being attacked by some sort of cult?"

"Yes, Officer, that is correct. They cut the tires on my car, and it is stranded. If you can drive us there, I will show you where it is, and I can show you a log cabin where these cult members were. I know this sounds crazy, but they were committing an actual sacrifice. They murdered Ajaunta's husband behind the cabin."

"Well, that is a pretty extraordinary statement. How far from here is your car?"

"Well, we have been walking for about two hours now, Officer. I would imagine we could drive there in less than twenty minutes."

"All right, jump in the back of my cruiser, and we will take a drive."

Rain and Ajaunta get in the back of the police car. There is a metal wire mesh separating the back and front seat, but they can talk freely with the officer. Once the officer starts to drive down the dirt road, he starts conversation with his passengers.

"You know there have been a lot of disturbances recently here in the Fright Hill Woods."

"Well, we can surely attest to that, Officer," says Rain.

"Well, look at this. This must be your car."

"Yes, Officer, that is my Fusion."

The officer gets out of his car and walks up to the car. Rain and Ajaunta get out and walk up to his car.

"I thought you said the tires were slashed?"

"They were, Officer. This is odd."

All the tires look like they are brand new.

"Well, since we are here, let's take a look at this log cabin and where this sacrifice was taking place."

"Yes, it's right down the road past these trees," says Rain.

Rain and Ajaunta start to walk toward the cabin. The officer gets back in his cruiser and drives behind them into the clearing. Rain and Ajaunta walk into the clearing with their jaws hitting the ground. The officer gets out of his car and looks onto an open patch of land that has been mowed with no log cabin.

"I don't know what to say, Officer. Less than five hours ago, there was a huge log cabin right here."

Rain is standing where the log cabin was. He walks over to where the rock was that Sully was being held on, the spot where the demon erupted from the earth, but he does not tell this part to the officer. He looks around rubbing his head. The ground has no bare spots at all. It is completely filled with grass. Ajaunta is speechless.

"Officer, I can't believe this. How did they do this?" says Rain.

"Well, there seems to be no signs of disturbance here. Someone obviously likes to keep the grass freshly mowed and looking neat out here in the middle of nowhere, but that is not much of a crime," says the officer.

"Ahh. No, Officer, it is not. Again, I don't know what to say," says Rain.

"Listen, you two, it is a beautiful day. I took a ride in the country, no harm done. Why don't the two of you walk back to your car, make sure it starts up? Then I'll make sure you can drive out of here safely, and we will all go on our way. Sound like a good plan?"

"Yes, Officer, sounds like a good plan," says Rain.

Rain and Ajaunta walk back to Rain's car, and it is still locked. Rain gets in his car, and to his amazement, his phone and his knife are in the center console. He looks at Ajaunta, holding his phone and knife with a baffled look on his face. Ajaunta looks in the console, and her phone is in there as well.

"Somebody wants to get in touch with us," says Rain.

He starts his car and drives out of the woods to the main road. The officer follows behind them and follows them to the bottom of Fright Hill, where he heads on his separate way.

"What the fuck is going on here?" says Rain.

Ajaunta starts to cry.

"My husband is dead. My kids are probably dead. What am I going to do? What am I supposed to do?"

"We are going back to my house for now. We are going to figure some things out. You are with me now, and we are going to get to the bottom of this. Playtime is over. These cult motherfuckers want a war. A war we will give them. They killed your husband, and they probably ate your kids. What are you going to do about it?" says Rain.

"I am going to kill those motherfuckers with your help."

"That's right. We are going to hunt those motherfuckers down."

Chapter 6

The Fire

Rain takes Ajaunta to her car at the diner, and she follows him home. Back at his house, they are both dirty and exhausted. Ajaunta goes to the bathroom and starts to clean her cuts and scratches. She leaves the door open, and Rain watches her. She seems to be oblivious to everything around her. Rain watches as she strips down to her underwear, washing her arms, legs, and stomach with a wet washcloth. She notices Rain watching her, and she holds the washcloth out toward him. He walks into the bathroom and takes the washcloth. She turns removes her bra, and Rain gently rubs her back with the washcloth. She leans into his naked chest, and he kisses her neck, rubbing her chest with the cool, damp cloth. She turns to face him, and they kiss slowly, making their way into the bedroom, where they shower each other with affection.

"Rain?"

"Yeah?"

"Secretly, I always did love you. A lot of times, I wished you would have made me your girl when we were in school. I wish I had the nerve to tell you how I felt sometimes when we were younger. I remember when your family moved to Farmsvern. I used to make my dad drive by your house just so I could see you."

"You did?"

"I did. I guess I just thought you were never interested in me."

Ajaunta's phone rings, and she rolls over to the nightstand on her side of the bed and picks her phone.

"It's John. Hello. Yeah, this is Ajaunta. You killed my husband, and I don't know if my kids are still alive. Everything you have told me so far is all for nothing. I am with a man now, John, a real man, and he is going to hunt you down. He is going to hunt you down and kill you. Of course, I want to see my kids. Where are they? When? Rain, he said my kids are home. I'm calling right now to see if they answer."

Ajaunta dials on her phone. She sits on the side of the bed, biting her nails. Rain can see she is anxious.

"Mark, Mark, is that you?"

Her voice cracks in excitement hearing her son's voice.

"Mark, are your brother and sisters there with you? They are. Listen to me. I want you all to stay right there. I will be home shortly. Stay right there and do not let anyone in the house. You hear me? Lock the doors and wait for me to get there, OK? OK, I am on my way. I will be there soon."

Ajaunta gets up looking all confused. She looks around remembering her underwear and pants are still in the bathroom.

"Do you by any chance have anything I can wear?"

"Sure. Look in the middle dresser drawer to the right."

She does, and she finds sweatpants she can wear. She does not even worry about underwear.

"What about a shirt?"

"Middle drawer."

She finds a shirt, and she does retrieve her bra from the bathroom. She puts the shirt on. She puts her shoes on without the socks and heads out the front door.

"Hey, wait a minute. So you are going home now. I take it your kids are home? What are you going to do when you get there?"

"I don't know. First things first. I need to see them. I need to know they are all right. Then I will get them out of there. We will go somewhere."

"Well, do you want me to come with you?"

"Yes, I do. Come on, let's go."

Rain gets up and gets dressed. Ajaunta is rushing. She is standing in the doorway.

"Come on, Rain, let's go. I need to get home fast."

"OK, let's go. I'll follow you this time."

Ajaunta gets in her SUV and speeds off toward her home. Rain follows. Rain has never been to her house. He has never met her kids or her husband until he saw him being sacrificed. Rain thinks to himself how crazy the past few days have been as he follows Ajaunta. He follows her all the way to Summersfield, and he gets a very uneasy feeling as she drives down back roads to her house. She turns off onto a dirt road and pulls into a driveway. The name of the road she lives on is so odd— Doctors Way Road. He pulls in behind her, and he can already hear her screaming. Rain looks around, and there are no other houses in sight. He can see a man in front of the house, and he has a bottle with a rag hanging from it that is on fire. Ajaunta is screaming.

"Mark, Mark, it's OK, honey. I'm going to get you out of there."

Rain runs up beside Ajaunta, and he can see a young man inside the house with his mouth taped, and it looks like he is bound to a chair.

"Where are Matthew, Willow, and Wendy?" Ajaunta says to the man holding the bottle.

"They are in the house. They are safe for the time being. If you come with us, the house will be left as is, and your friend can go in and get them out. If you do not come with me, I will throw this bottle at the house, and you will not like the result of that," says the man.

The man is wearing a black-and-red cloak. The hood is down, so Rain can see the man's face.

"Ajaunta, do you recognize this man?"

"Yes, this is John, or whatever his name is."

Rain walks toward the man and pulls his .357 Magnum, pointing them at the man.

"Listen up, you fuck. Let's see how well you throw that with no fucking head."

"No, Rain. No, Rain, don't!" yells Ajaunta, and she jumps on Rain from behind. She swings her arms down on Rain's arms, dropping them to his sides and tripping him. He stumbles forward with Ajaunta on him.

"Ajaunta, what are you doing? I had him dead in my sights. What are you doing?"

"No, Rain, my kids are in the house. I am not taking any chances with my kids' lives."

Rain and Ajaunta look up, seeing the other three siblings bound to chairs with their mouths taped. They are brought to the window and set in front of it so they can be seen from outside. The kids are struggling to free themselves. They are struggling to yell and scream, but the duct tape prevents any sounds from leaving their mouths.

"Willow, Wendy, Matthew!" yells Ajaunta.

"There are no more warnings. Now you all will be sacrificed. You will all burn in hell." says John, and he throws the bottle at the house, which breaks and instantly starts a fire that races around and up the house. Before Rain and Ajaunta are even able to get up off the ground, the house is in flames, and as soon as they stand, it explodes five times, sending glass, splinters, metal, and debris flying all around. John starts to charge Rain. From out of nowhere, a sporty black BMW comes speeding around the bend into the lawn, hitting John. The car skids in the grass, and John is sent flying twenty feet through the air, landing hard. Rain dodges and dives being missed by the car. Ajaunta is crying hysterically, running toward the house, but she cannot get close to it. She can't even get within thirty feet of the house. It is an inferno, and she watches as her children burn and expire in agonizing pain. Ajaunta falls to her knees like the life has been drawn from her. Rain gets up to see Smoke exit the BMW.

"Smoke, where the hell have you been? It's not like you to leave me hanging like you did the other day. What the hell, Smoke? How, why are you here? How did you know I would be here?"

Rain looks to see Ajaunta standing, crying, and walking toward the burning house.

"Ajaunta!" he yells and runs after her. He grabs her, but she fights to enter the burning house.

Rain grabs her arm and turns her, facing him. He slaps her hard across the face.

"Listen, I still do not know what the fuck is going on here. The only thing I know is how to get even. You want to kill yourself, I won't stop you. You want revenge? You want to make sure these cult fucks cannot do this to anyone else, then you want me."

Smoke walks up behind Rain.

"Ajaunta. Ajaunta Macari, is that you? I knew Rain was always in love with you, but I thought you had married someone else. You have kids, don't you?"

Ajaunta cries and leans into Rain's chest.

"Smoke! I cannot believe how crazy these past few days have been. Absolutely nuts. First, you come to my house and kill three people, and then you leave me hanging all alone at the planning zone, which you have never ever done. Marlene breaks up with me. Ajaunta calls me, and apparently, some sort of demonic cult has been terrorizing her and her family. I saw her husband get sacrificed and eaten by some sort of demon that rose from the ground and took him into the earth, and that's no shit. I saw it with my own eyes. Her kids are in the house right now, and they were just murdered by this evil cult. This is the most fucked-up situation I have ever seen in my life, and now you show up again. How the hell are you here?"

The three of them turn toward the burning house because they hear the loud chanting of over a dozen men and women wearing black-and-red cloaks, which cover their heads and bodies completely. They are walking around the fire with their arms folded in front of their chests. They are chanting in a similar fashion that Rain remembers from the log cabin.

"Oh, shit, here we go again," says Rain.

"Yeah, well, let's give them a little surprise," says Smoke.

"I heard that," says Rain.

Smoke and Rain walk to the trunk of Smoke's car.

"What are you guys doing?" asks Ajaunta.

"We're gonna fuck them up," they say in unison.

Ajaunta walks to the back of the car where the trunk is now open, and her eyes light up to see all the guns and ammunition. Smoke's trunk is like a very large armory. Smoke gets a super big type of M16, and it looks like it has ten times the space for ammunition. Rain grabs a similar gun, and the two of them walk around the front of the car. They look at each other and ready their guns.

"Fucking kill them bastards!" yells Ajaunta from behind her classmates from long ago.

The Special Forces veterans start to unload on the cloaked individuals. Rain heads toward the right side of the burning house. Smoke heads toward the left side of the house, and the two of them pelt the cult members with a barrage of bullets, easily killing them all. They know something is not right as they shoot them. After being shot, it is not like they fall with gunshot wounds. Instead, the cloaks fall to the ground like there was never anyone in them. Rain walks up to the cloaks on the ground and lifts one with the superheated muzzle of his gun. He looks the cloak over. No skin, no flesh, no hair, no nothing.

Smoke does the same to the cloaks on the left side of the house. They go back to the front of the house, looking baffled at each other. They stand in front of the burning house, and Ajaunta walks up in between them.

"You see what I mean, Smoke? Crazy shit," says Rain.

"Yeah, well, I have some crazy shit of my own to tell you about. Hey, Ajaunta, what, it's been twenty-five years now since we have seen each other?" says Smoke.

"Yeah, Kenneth, it's been a long time. I see Rain is still calling you Smoke," says Ajaunta.

They all take a step back as the house starts to crumble. The two-story house is caving in, and the flames are thirty feet in the sky. The house starts to buckle and rumble like it is on some sort of fault. Timbers and burning beams start to fly upward.

"What the fuck? Oh, don't tell me," says Rain.

They all see something in the middle of the house. Something big bursts from the center of the house and stands. It has blood-red skin that is hard to see in the rising flames, and the fire does not bother it at all. It pounds its front paws on the burning cinders and starts to walk up from the earth. Ajaunta starts to cry as it obviously finds the burned remains of her children and chomps them down. It is a four-legged creature looking like a monitor lizard only it is blood red and stands ten feet at its shoulders on all fours. It is easily big enough to eat the three of them whole. Rain and Smoke look at each other and start to unload their weapons on the demonic beast. It rears its head back and forth and then charges at the puny humans. Rain and Smoke back away with a constant bombardment on the monster. They are backing toward the back of Smoke's BMW, and they notice Ajaunta is driving away in her SUV. They don't worry about her right now.

"Rain, keep firing at it. I have something a little more powerful," says Smoke.

"Hurry up, go get it," says Rain.

Smoke runs to the trunk and grabs what he calls a Tommy shotgun. This is an automatic shotgun that holds twenty-four custom-made eight-gauge slugs, and it is very loud when shot. Smoke walks up shooting at the demon lizard and its sensory tongue that is five feet long.

Rain runs to the trunk and grabs a machine gun loaded with hollow-tipped ammunition. He walks up beside Smoke, firing fully automatically, blasting, bursting, and exploding the flesh all around the neck of the creature. This weapon is very effective slicing and dicing the unknown creature. Smoke sees how effective this ammunition is and gets a similar machine gun. The two men are now blasting the creature to bits, and it retreats into the fire and down the hole from where it came. The house is still burning, and the smoke has been seen for miles around. Sirens can be heard, and fire rescue is on the way.

"Come on, Rain, put the weapons back. They will be on us soon. We better get out of here unless you want to be stuck filling out statements and paperwork for the next two weeks," says Smoke.

"No, I don't. We are out of here," says Rain.

"Follow me. Let's meet at the planning zone. I have a lot to tell you," says Smoke.

"You got it. Let's go," says Rain.

Rain gets into his car, and the two of them speed away, avoiding all the rescue services on the way.

Chapter 7

The Longest Sunday Ever

Rain is speeding following behind Smoke's BMW. He looks at the digital clock on his car dashboard, seeing it is already four in the afternoon. He has already been to the Fright Woods this morning. He's been to Ajaunta's house for the first time and obviously the last since it is burning to the ground. Of course, the log cabin in the Fright Woods is gone. He has shot at two different demons. He has shot at cult members, and he has been reunited with Smoke. *This is the longest Sunday ever,* Rain thinks to himself. Now he is on his way to the planning zone with Smoke. Just when he thinks the day is starting to wind down a little bit and he can go get some answers from Smoke, his phone rings, and he sees it is Marlene, so he answers.

"Hi, Marlene."

"Rain, I don't know what is going on. I am really scared. I don't know what to do."

"Whoa, whoa! Calm down, Marlene. What is going on?"

"There are these guys all wearing cloaks and hoods. I don't know who they are or where they came from. There are a lot of them, and they are standing around my house. My dad called the police, and they said they are sending a police car here. My mom is scared, and so am I. This made me think of the other night when that guy said I was a target. What do these people want? Are they here to kill me?"

"I don't know. Does your dad have any guns? If he does, tell him to get them. I don't know what is going on, but my life has been crazy ever since the other night. All kinds of crazy things are happening. These men are they dressed in red-and-black cloaks?"

"Yes."

"I have seen them too. They are some sort of demonic cult. I have no idea who or what they are, but I have been shooting them today. I know this sounds crazy, but they are dangerous. Protect yourselves, you hear me? I am about an hour from your house, and I am on my way there right now."

"Hurry, Rain."

"You and your parents protect yourselves. I am with Smoke right now. We are coming from Summersfield, where we just shot some of these cloaked people. Damn, there are a lot of them. They are everywhere. Protect yourselves until the police get there, OK? I am on my way."

"OK, Rain."

Marlene hangs up. Smoke and Rain are on Highway 990 West, and Rain pulls up beside Smoke's car. He hits the automatic widow, and the passenger window rolls down.

"Smoke, those demonic people are at Marlene's house. You said the other night she and I were targets. Well, they are at her house. Are they there to kill her?"

Smoke yells back, "That's what I need to talk to you about. This demonic cult is trying to kill you both!"

"What the fuck, Smoke? You got me and Marlene mixed up in some demonic cult? Why? Why would you do that? How did you even know about Marlene? You know this is why I stopped protecting you because you are just looking for trouble all the time. You keep dragging me into shit that is going to get me killed. Now you have done it, haven't you?"

"It's not like you think, Rain. This is not something that I initiated. I need to explain to you what is happening. You need to meet with me at the planning zone."

"I am heading to Marlene's house right now. They are there. Are they going to try and kill her?"

"Rain, it's a trap. It's a trap to get you and her together, and, yes, they are going to kill you both."

"You fucker, Smoke. You better do right and help me save her and her parents. If anything happens to her, I'll never forgive you. Whatever is going on should not involve her at all."

"Rain, you can't go there. You have to come with me. I'll explain best I can. You can't go to Marlene's house, you just can't."

"Oh, that is exactly where I am going, and you better be coming to help me blow those cloaked motherfuckers away."

Rain steps on the gas and speeds in front of Smoke's vehicle.

"Rain, don't go there, Rain!" yells Smoke, but Rain has sped in front of his car, and now Smoke is following Rain. Rain is driving about ten to twenty miles faster than the speed limit. He prays he makes it to Marlene's house without drawing attention from police for speeding. Smoke tries to pass and communicate with Rain, but Rain steps on the gas every time Smoke speeds up. It takes Rain about twenty minutes to reach his exit and another twenty minutes to make it to Marlene's house. It just so happens she lives on a dirt road and there is no other houses by her house. Rain pulls up to her driveway, which goes down a fairly steep hill for about twenty yards until you reach her old house. Rain pulls up to her house, and there are no signs that anyone is even here. No police, no cloaked cult members, no nothing. Rain runs up to the house and knocks on the door.

"Marlene, Marlene!" he yells.

Smoke pulls up behind Rain's car and gets out. He runs to the back of his car after popping open the trunk. He runs toward the front door where Rain is calling for Marlene.

"Rain, here, take this."

Smoke throws a shotgun, and Rain catches it. He also throws a shoulder harness with two of Rain's favorite handguns in it, .357 Magnums.

Rain puts on the harness.

"You remembered, Smoke. Nice. Smoke, what have you gotten me into this time?"

"Rain, it's not what you think. It's not something I did. It's something or someone trying to drag you and me into something."

"Yeah, explain it later. Right now, we need to find Marlene and her parents. Are you ready?"

Smoke shakes his head up and down. Rain knocks on the door again, holding the shotgun.

"Marlene, are you in there? Mr. Shailes, are you here? Mrs. Shailes, it's me, Rain. Is anyone here?"

Rain tries to open the door. He turns the door handle, but it is locked. He takes a step back, nodding his head to Smoke. Smoke nods his head up and down. Rain kicks the door three times, but he cannot break in. He takes a step back and hurls his body at the door. This works as he drives his body through the door, falling into the living room. He quickly pops to his knees, looking for anyone. Smoke is right behind him, aiming his machine gun. Rain looks around from his knees.

"What the fuck is going on around here?" says Rain.

The living room looks like it has not been walked in for a hundred years. There are cobwebs strewn all over. There is no furniture in the room. There is one rug that is round and covers most of the floor. The windows are letting light in but very little, so the room is mostly dark. They can see dust floating around in the air. Rain stands up.

"Hello. Is anyone here?" calls Rain.

His voice echoes through the empty house. He walks from the living room into the next living room. Again, there is no furniture in here. There is a fireplace built into the wall, and still there is dust just floating about in the dimly lit room. He walks into the kitchen and opens one of the dusty cupboards to see no dishes in there.

"Smoke, this is absurd. I was here in this house last week. It was fully furnished. I had dinner with Marlene and her parents. They are wonderful people. Where are they? Where are all the furniture?" says Rain.

Rain walks into the living room where the fireplace is and walks up the stairs.

"Marlene, Mr., Mrs. Shailes, is anyone here?" calls Rain.

Rain walks around the upstairs bedrooms and bathroom. The whole house looks like it has not been walked in for many years. The dust is so thick they leave footprints where they walk.

"Smoke, what the fuck is going on? Do you know what is happening here? How can this be like this? This house looks like it has been abandoned for years. Where could Marlene and her parents be? Smoke, do you know what is going on here?" says Rain.

Smoke looks around.

"We better get out of here. Come on, let's meet at the planning zone where we can talk," says Smoke.

Smoke turns and walks toward the stairway. Rain walks into Marlene's bedroom and looks out the window. He sees Marlene standing in the front yard, and she is looking up at him. She points at him and starts to laugh.

"Marlene, Marlene," calls Rain.

Rain tries to open the window, but it won't budge.

"Marlene, Marlene," he calls.

Marlene turns with her back facing Rain and bends down.

"Marlene, Marlene," he calls again.

Rain looks around the room, and it is empty except for an old dresser with cobwebs all over it.

"Rain, what is going on? What do you see?" asks Smoke.

"It's Marlene. She is in the front yard," says Rain.

Rain turns his shotgun and breaks the small square glass panes with the butt of his gun.

"Marlene!" he yells.

Rain looks out the window, and Smoke looks out the window too. Marlene stands and turns to the men in the window. She is crying.

"Marlene, wait right there. I am coming. I am coming down right now!" yells Rain.

"Rain, it's too late. You are too late. Why didn't you save me, Rain? Why did you let them get me? Rain!" cries Marlene.

Rain can see one of those demon lizards rise from the ground at the back of Marlene, and it touches Marlene with its massively long tongue. Marlene turns to face the much larger creature, and she screams as it swoops with its head, grabbing her and biting a few times, pulling her into its mouth. It crunches down on her body, breaking off her legs and head. Rain can see it raise its head, swallowing her, and it sniffs around, finding her legs and head, biting and swallowing them as well.

"Marlene!" cries Rain.

Rain starts firing at the beast with his shotgun. The demon hell lizard falls back into the earth, and it reforms like the earth has not been disturbed at all.

"Marlene!" cries Rain.

"Smoke, did you see that? Smoke?" says Rain.

Rain turns around, and Smoke is leaning against the wall with his back to Rain.

"Smoke, did you hear me?" says Rain.

Rain walks to Smoke. He puts his hand on Smoke's left shoulder and turns him. It is not Smoke. It is some sort of demon with red skin and blue-black eyes. It has sharp pointy teeth. It grabs Rain around the throat and lifts him in the air. Rain feels helpless. He feels so weak that he cannot even lift his arms. He drops the shotgun.

"Smoke!" cries Rain.

Rain takes a deep breath. He sits up in his bed and is breathing very heavily. His heart is pounding so hard he feels like he is having a heart attack. He is breathing like he just sprinted for a mile. He touches his chest and feels his face. He is soaked with sweat.

"Honey, honey, what is wrong?" says a voice from his bed.

Rain almost jumps out of bed being startled by the voice and touch. He turns to see Marlene. She puts her arms over his shoulders.

"Oh my god, Rain! You are soaking wet. The bed is all wet. What happened?" she asks.

"Marlene, Marlene, it's you. You are right here," says Rain.

"Yes, I'm right here. I didn't go anywhere," says Marlene.

"Oh, Marlene," he says.

Rain hugs her.

"Honey, why are you so wet?" she asks.

"I don't know. I have never had a dream like that. I mean, I have never had a nightmare in my life. Now I have. It was so real. They were coming after you and me. They got you. They were coming for me. It was so real," says Rain.

"Honey, honey, it was just a dream. I am here. I hope those is not signs of things to come because last night was fabulous," she says.

Rain does not remember last night at all.

"I would normally say come back to bed, but you sweat right through the sheets into the mattress. I mean, really, honey, this is bad," says Marlene.

Marlene gets out of bed and takes the sheets off the bed.

"Come on, baby. Let's get into to shower and rinse you off. Then we can pick up right where we left off," says Marlene.

"Where we left off?" says Rain.

"Yeah, baby, you were amazing. You sexed me so good I fell asleep right afterward. That means you were great, and it was our first time. They say the first time is the most awkward time. I have a feeling you are going to rock my world for a long time to come if you like?" says Marlene.

Marlene smiles and walks toward the bathroom.

Rain looks down to see he and she are both naked. He does not mention that he does not remember anything about last night. He remembers parts of his dream. He has visions of his dream popping into his head. He sees short segments of what was happening, and it feels so very real.

"Oh, yeah, well, you were so good last night I don't even remember what day it is," says Rain.

"Silly, it's Sunday. We have all day to do whatever we want to do. Come on in, the water is warm," says Marlene.

Rain thinks most of his dream took place on Sunday, and it is Sunday morning. *This is still Sunday,* he thinks to himself. *This is going to be the longest Sunday ever.* Marlene grabs Rain by the hand and pulls him into the bathroom. She pulls Rain to the shower and stands under the running water.

"Well, are you coming in?" she says.

"Yeah. I just can't get over why I had this nightmare last night. I mean, being with you was so wonderful, and I have wanted to be with you ever since I met you. Maybe I am scared of commitment? There, I said it, but I think I am in love with you, and I want to be with you," says Rain.

"That's one thing I love about you, Rain—you just say what is in that head of yours. I love that. It's like you are telling me who you are without me having to ask you. You are not afraid that I will judge every little thing you say. You just keep being you because I love you," says Marlene.

"I love you too," says Rain.

Marlene hugs Rain under the falling water. Rain hugs her looking at the tile wall of the shower as confused as he has ever been in his life.

Chapter 8

Breaking Free

Rain cannot remember anything of the immediate past. He is completely focused on the nightmare he had last night. It is consuming all his thoughts. He and Marlene get out of the shower and dry off.

"I will put the sheets in the wash later on. Right now, you relax and forget about that dream you had last night. I can tell it is still bothering you. I tell you what. You relax and I am going to make a nice breakfast for us both. Don't get used to it, though, because I am not a big cooker," says Marlene.

Rain smiles to Marlene as she heads downstairs, just shining with happiness.

"The kitchen is yours," he says as she walks down the stairs.

Rain sits on his bed, rubbing his head. He has never had a nightmare where he actually woke up in a sweat breathing heavily. He is still seeing visions of his friend Smoke, whom he has not seen in years. He remembers seeing Ajaunta, his high school crush, whom he has seen only one time since they graduated high school twenty-five years ago. The demons, the cloaked and hooded cult members, the log cabin, and Ajaunta's house burning are all visions he remembers from his dream. He can see them all so clearly in his head. He wonders, *Was it a dream, or was it real?* He remembers Marlene was eaten by that demon lizard, and yet she is with him right now. He cannot remember being with her at all last night. He remembers nothing about last night outside the dream. He tries to remember the last thing he can remember before the dream, and this scares him more than anything so far. He cannot remember anything from last week at all. He keeps having thoughts about that damn dream. He puts on some clothes and heads downstairs. Walking into the kitchen, Marlene is standing at the sink, looking out the window, and she is talking on the phone with someone.

"All right, I will talk to you later. I have to go," she says.

"Who was that?" asks Rain.

"Oh, that was my dad. I was just telling him I won't be home for lunch today," she says.

"You're forty-five years old and you still tell your parents what you are doing?" says Rain.

"Yeah," she says.

"Huh, so what's for breakfast?" says Rain.

"How about some bacon and eggs?" says Marlene.

"Mmmmm. Sounds good. I'm going outside for a few minutes. I'll be right back," says Rain.

"All right, honey, take your time. I haven't really started yet. I still have to get used to where all the pots and pans are," says Marlene.

Rain walks out the sliding glass door onto the porch. This morning is bothering him a lot. He still can't place anything about last night outside of the nightmare. Everything seems fine, everything seems normal, but he just can't get over how real that dream felt. He goes to the barn and looks inside. All is normal. He unlocks his shed next to the barn where he keeps all his guns and ammunition, and sure enough, all seems like it should be. He closes up his arms storage and locks it up tight. Looking around the back of his house, all seems exceptionally good. It seems too good. The birds are chirping, the sun is shining, and it is a nice, warm morning here in Lilston. It is odd how sore his lower back is. This happens to him when he sleeps too long. For some reason, his body seems much more sore if he sleeps too long, and that is how he is feeling right now. He usually ramps up his activity when he feels like this, so he runs back into the kitchen. Marlene is talking on the phone and looking out the window again. She pulls the phone to her stomach, hanging up as Rain walks up behind her and hugs her.

"Good I caught you before you started making breakfast. I have a treat for you. I am going to take you out to breakfast," says Rain.

"You're going to what?" says Marlene.

"Yup, come on, we are going to get some breakfast. Pancakes and eggs and bacon. Let someone else do the cooking. You said it yourself you are not a big cooker. Come on, let's go," says Rain.

"Rain, I'm not even dressed," says Marlene.

"Well, get dressed," says Rain.

"Rain, I want to stay here and have a nice quiet breakfast with you—just you and me," says Marlene.

"Yeah, well, if you want breakfast with me, get ready because I am not waiting. I am leaving," says Rain.

Rain is serious; he is walking out the door.

"Rain, Rain, you are not leaving without me," says Marlene.

"If you don't hurry up, I am," says Rain.

Rain is getting into his car, and he notices something very odd when he sits in his driver's chair. He looks out the rearview mirror, and there is a car at the back of his car. He gets out of his car.

"What the fuck is this?" says Rain.

Rain walks to the other car and looks it over.

"Marlene, Marlene, there is a car in my driveway. I wonder whose car this is," says Rain.

Marlene comes to the front door.

"Oh, Rain, that's my car," says Marlene.

"What do you mean that's your car? How did your car get here? I drove you here. I did not even know you had a car," says Rain.

"Yeah, that's what I was talking to my father about. He dropped my car off earlier this morning for me," says Marlene.

Rain just looks at Marlene confused.

"You know, Marlene, this whole day is just not making any sense. I think your car being here is a blessing in disguise. Listen, last night was great, and I love being with you, but I need to organize my thoughts. I need to get out and just do whatever. You are more than welcome to stay here, or you can go home. I am going to get out for a while," says Rain.

Rain gets into his car.

"No, Rain, this is our first morning together after being intimate with each other. Of course, there are going to be confusions and things out of place. We should face them and work them out together. That's what people do," says Marlene.

A silver Monte Carlo drives by Rain's driveway and comes to a stop.

"Rain, Rain, is that you?" calls a voice from the car.

The car backs up and pulls into the driveway. A man gets out of the car.

"Rain, is that you?" says Jessy.

"Hey, Jessy. How are you this morning?" says Rain.

"How am I? I am fine. How are you? When did you get out of the hospital?" asks Jessy.

"What are you talking about get out of the hospital? I haven't been in the hospital," says Rain.

"Rain, you haven't been to your shop since June 29. They said you were burned almost to death in that fire. They said you probably weren't going to survive. I gotta say there is not a burn on you," says Jessy.

"Jessy, what are you talking about? Who is *they*? What do you mean I haven't been to my shop since June 29? It's Sunday, July 1," says Rain.

"Rain, it is July 11. You have not been to your shop in two and a half weeks. The gentleman running your shop said you were in that fire in Summersfield, and Kenneth was with you. Why you two were there at all is a mystery," says Jessy.

"Summersfield? Was this fire in a house owned by people called Brenner? You say Kenneth was with me? Was he burned as well?" asks Rain.

"I don't think they were called Brenner. Their last name was Shailes. Kenneth is supposedly in the hospital like I thought you were," says Jessy.

"Marlene, hey, Marlene," calls Rain.

Rain turns around to talk with Marlene, but she is not there.

"Marlene. Where the hell did she go?" says Rain.

"Rain, who are you talking to?" says Jessy.

"Marlene. You saw her. She was standing right at the back of me. You saw her when you pulled in, right?" says Rain.

"Rain, I didn't see anyone, just you," says Jessy.

"This is nuts. I have to get to my shop and see what is going on. Do you know what hospital Kenneth is supposedly in?" says Rain.

"I'm pretty sure he is at Bryers Hill. That is where I thought you were," says Jessy.

"One other thing. This fire—was it on Doctors Way Road?" asks Rain.

"No, it was on Bender Turn Road, not too far from here," says Jessy.

"You've got to be kidding me. That is Marlene's house, and her last name is Shailes," says Rain.

Rain turns and looks at his house. Marlene is standing in the doorway, looking at him.

"Jessy, look at my door. Do you see her?" says Rain.

Jessy looks at the door to Rain's house. He looks and sees no one.

"What are you talking about? There is no one there," says Jessy.

Rain is looking right at Marlene. She starts to laugh at him.

"Jessy, thank you for stopping by. I have to figure some things out. You should be going," says Rain.

"All right, Rain. I hope you figure things out," says Jessy.

"Yeah, me too," says Rain.

Jessy gets into his car and drives away. Rain stares at Marlene in the doorway. She laughs at Rain and then backs into the house out of sight. Rain runs around the house to his armory shed. He unlocks it and looks in to see it is empty. He backs out, and Marlene is laughing at him from the kitchen. He can see her in the sliding glass doorway. The door is open, but the screen door is closed.

"What is going on, Marlene?" asks Rain.

Rain walks toward the porch slowly. He walks up onto the porch and faces Marlene, who is standing inside the screen door.

"A little confused, Rain? You should come in and have some breakfast. I'll explain things for you," says Marlene.

Rain opens the screen door and walks in. Marlene backs from him, gesturing her left arm out toward the table, which is set and adorned with pancakes, bacon, eggs, milk, orange juice, and toast. Rain looks at the table, stunned to see it prepared, looking and smelling delicious.

"Sit, your chair is waiting for you," says Marlene.

Rain sits, and Marlene sits in the chair kitty-corner to him.

"Eat," she says.

"I have no appetite, however, my curiosity is fully aroused. I am awake, correct?" says Rain.

"Yes, you are awake," says Marlene.

"Somehow, you have had me in a sleep or a trance for a very long time. I figured that out, but that's about all I can figure out. The rest is just so outlandish. The dream—is any of it real? The demons, the cult, my friends. What is going on? Are you real? What is the point of all this?" says Rain.

Marlene leans in close to Rain and talks quietly.

"Rain, they need you. They want to sacrifice you because you are a very valuable mortal. The more valuable you are, the longer they need to prepare you before they sacrifice you. They want your friend Smoke too. You two are very valuable. What that means is that if they prepare you correctly and sacrifice you in the proper way, they will get the maximum youth from your sacrifice. Your sacrifice will mean a full lifetime granted to the one who sacrifices you. Smoke too. They need to keep you subdued for at least a month to prepare your soul to be devoured by them. They are half way there." Says Marlene.

"I've got to stop you right there. I can't even believe I am hearing this demonic sacrificial bullshit. If they are halfway there, then that is all they are going to get because it's over now," says Rain.

Rain gets up and starts to leave the kitchen.

"Rain, wait, it is not over. They are waiting for you. They are all over the place, and you don't know who they are. They have been doing this for centuries. They have seen and heard it all. They always get their intended prey," says Marlene.

"Well, let them come and try to get me," says Rain.

"Rain, Rain, don't go. They will find you, and they will kill you. Even if they don't get the full youth that you are good for, you are still a very valuable catch. They will kill you if they think you are getting away," says Marlene.

"You know what, Marlene, your car is in the driveway. I want you to get in your car and drive somewhere far from here, and don't come back. You hear me? Get the fuck out of here before I throw you the fuck out of here," says Rain.

"Rain, don't throw me out. Please. Rain," says Marlene.

Rain pushes Marlene out the front door toward and all the way to and in her car.

"Rain, you will be helpless, you will be blind without me. Rain, please don't push me away," says Marlene.

Rain shuts her car door and walks to his car, starting it up. He tries to back up and can't. He pulls forward and backs around Marlene's car. As he is passing by her, he yells through the windows.

"I do have a question for you. How is it that Jessy did not see you? Are you really some sort of demon bitch? Are you invisible to everyone except me? I must be in a dream still," says Rain.

"Rain, if I do not do what they say, they will kill me. You have to believe me. I do love you. I loved you from the first time we started dating," says Marlene.

"As far as I can remember, we have only been dating for a month," says Rain.

"Yes, Rain. We have been dating for a little longer than a month," says Marlene.

"When I get back, you better be gone or have some fantastic answers for me," says Rain.

Rain backs out and speeds down the road.

"Rain, Rain!" yells Marlene.

Marlene gets out of her car and yells for Rain, running on his front yard, but he speeds away. Marlene falls in the front yard, crying. Rain is driving toward his gun shop like he does every morning, so he just drives that way like normal. He gets to his shop twenty-five minutes later and drives through the parking lot. It is Sunday, so no one is around, and his shop is always closed on Sundays. He sits debating to himself if he should go in and look around, but he has this crazy thought that is sticking in his mind and he has to check it out. He has not seen Ajaunta outside of one brief moment since they graduated high school, but he did see her in his dream or dreams. He saw her house and remembers how to get there. He is dying to see if her house is really there and if it is burned. He remembers her boys and girls were burned in the fire and that demon lizard ate them. He cannot resist the curiosity. He starts to drive to the location he remembers from his dreams. He looks in the center console of his car to see if his phone is there, and it is not.

"Damn. It must be in the house," he says out loud.

Rain drives on, and for the first time since he broke ties with his best friend Smoke, he really wishes Smoke was with him now. Meanwhile, back at Rain's house, Marlene stands up and regains her composure. Her crying face immediately turns deadly serious as Rain drives out of sight. She pulls her car into the garage and closes the garage door. She walks into the house, closing the front door behind her.

Chapter 9

It's All Right, My Dear

Rain is driving toward Ajaunta's house. When he gets into the town of Summersfield, he is a little lost. He can picture Ajaunta's house, and he knows it is on Doctors Way Road, but he can't remember how to get to Doctors Way Road. He drives around for thirty minutes, for the most part lost, but finally, he finds Doctors Way Road. When he drives around the corner and turns onto Doctors Way Road, he can instantly see the house has been burned right to the ground. He pulls into the driveway and looks from his car for a few moments. He gets out and walks to the perimeter of the house. It has been completely burned with very little other than the foundation left. He walks around, kicking the ashes, trying to remember anything he can from his dream. He can see metal remnants of what was probably the chairs the kids were tied to. He tries to remember more as a jogger runs up the driveway.

"Did you know the Brenners?" says the jogger.

Rain is a little startled and turns to see the jogger behind him.

"I did know Ajaunta. We were in the same class together from fourth grade until we graduated high school. She was a beautiful girl. I'm sure her family was wonderful one," says Rain.

"Yeah, they were a nice family. This fire was a tragedy," says the jogger.

"Was everyone killed in this fire? All four kids and both parents?" says Rain.

"You know that is the sixty-four-million-dollar question," says the jogger.

"Why do you say that?" says Rain.

"Well, everyone thinks the whole family was killed in the fire, but there are no remains of any of the Brenners. The whole house was pretty much incinerated, but still there should have been remains of bones and teeth. There are no remains of any of the family here. Both their cars were here, and none of the family has been seen or heard of since the fire. Everyone believes the whole family was killed in the fire," says the jogger.

"When was the fire?" says Rain.

"It's been four days now since the fire," says the jogger.

"Wow, well, I had heard about the fire, and I wanted to come out and see. Ajaunta was a very special girl, and I wanted to pay my respects," says Rain.

"Well, it was nice meeting you. Good day," says the jogger.

The jogger starts to head out on his jog.

"You too. Oh, I have a question for you before you go. Do you know if there was anyone else involved in the fire? Were there any other fatalities, or was it just the Brenners?" asks Rain.

"As far as everyone knows, it was just the Brenners," says the jogger.

"Thank you. Have a good jog," says Rain.

The jogger takes off, and Rain looks at the woods behind the house. He walks around in the center of the house, avoiding the stairway into the cellar, which is full of partially burned timbers and debris. He kicks around twisted melted metal parts and odds and ends left in the ash when he notices something. He bends down and moves some debris to side. There are more debris under it, which he moves to the side, exposing a very large footprint in the ash that resembles that of a lizard, which sends chills down Rain's spine. This really creeps him out, and he stands looking around like one of those hell lizards is going to pop out of the center of the house. He heads back to his car and starts it up. He sits in his driver's seat, talking to himself. "Well, what now, Rain? Do I go to Bryers Hill Hospital and see if Smoke is there, or do I go to Marlene's house and see what is going on there?" Rain does not even know where Bryers Hill Hospital is, so he decides to go to Marlene's house to do a little more investigating into this mystery he is now a part of. Rain heads back to Lilston. He stops by drive-through for a quick bite of fast food, and then he is back on the road. He is heading to Marlene's house, and when he gets there, the first thing that surprises him are the For Sale signs in the front yard. There are a few cars parked in the driveway that he does not recognize, and he pulls in behind them. He gets out of his car and heads toward the front door. A woman walks out talking to a man and woman. Rain is walking up the front step when the realtor addresses him.

"Sir, can I help you?" says the realtor.

"Yeah. I was wondering if you know the Shaileses—you know, the people who live here?" says Rain.

"I'm sorry, sir, the Farneitis had lived here. The house is for sale now, and I am with clients right now. You can have a walk through and look at the house if you would like. Here, let me give you my card, and you can call me tomorrow if you would like," she says.

"Are you sure the people who had lived here were not Mr. and Mrs. Shailes? I swear I was here, well, I guess it was in the last month at any rate. I'm sorry, don't mind me. It has been a very confusing day for me. Can I ask you when did this house go on the market?" asks Rain.

"It's only been up for sale for about two weeks now, maybe a little more. I can tell you this—there is a lot of interest in this house. It will surely sell fast, and the Meyers here seem to be very interested in it. I will have more information for you tomorrow," she says.

"Oh, thank you. I am not interested in buying the house. Thank you," says Rain.

Rain heads to his car and gets in. He scratches his head trying to figure out how he ever got into this mess.

Meanwhile, right after Rain had left this morning, Marlene had walked back into his house. She walks into the kitchen, looking at her phone, when cold chills run up and down her spine. She looks up to see Glamfury standing in the kitchen. He is six feet two inches tall with dark hair and dark eyes. He wears a leather trench coat that does not zip or button up the front. It is open with a high collar that extends up as high as his head and rounds away from his head. This odd trench coat allows for his brownish-red leather pants with black stitch and his sparkly dark purple shirt to be seen. It looks like he wears heavy eye shadow. He has a very gothic look about him, which some girls do find very attractive.

"Glamfury, I am sorry. He will come back. He will be back within the hour," says Marlene.

"Shh, shh, shh. It's all right, my dear. You are right. He will be back. He will be back a lot sooner than you may think," says Glamfury.

Glamfury approaches Marlene and runs his fingers through her hair. He holds her shoulders with both his hands. Marlene gets noticeably shaken and starts to whimper. She is a very beautiful woman with a world-class smile. She has perfect teeth, long, wavy dark brown hair, brown eyes, and a curvy body men have fought over many times in her life.

"Shh, shh, shh, like I said, it's all right, my dear," says Glamfury.

"Glamfury, he will be back. He will be back very soon. Men always come back to me—they always do. I did everything I was supposed to do. I seduced him and fed him the food just the way you had said. Everything was going according to plan, but he woke up from his dream this morning, and he remembered things. He remembered things that drove him away from me, away from my touch. You have to believe me, no matter what happens now, he will come back and he will be mine again. We only have two weeks to go. Please, Glamfury, please," says Marlene.

"I had told you what a difficult preparation this would be. Men like Stormy are hard to seduce, but you had said there is no man on earth you could not seduce, did you not?" says Glamfury.

"Yes, that is true, and I did. You said once he had eaten the tainted food, all I would have to do was feed him twice a day and he would never regain cognition. I was right there with him for two and a half weeks, and he is strong. I had to love him every day, which was very enjoyable and exhausting. So why did he wake up this morning? He was fully aware, and what were the images he was remembering? How did he know about his friend Smoke and Ajaunta? How did he know? How did he remember these images, and yet he seemed not to remember being with me? He said they got me—did he mean you? Were you setting me up from the start? There is no man ever who just forget about loving me. What about the food? I fed him twice a day just as I was supposed to," says Marlene.

Glamfury is holding Marlene by her shoulders with a stern look on his face. He is unwavering, and Marlene is getting very scared. Her heart is starting to beat faster and faster, and she starts to feel nauseated.

"Glamfury, please. Please, Glamfury, I did everything I was supposed to do. I don't know what went wrong," she says.

"Shh, shh, shh, it's all right, my dear," says Glamfury.

Glamfury wraps his arms around Marlene and hugs her close to his chest. She starts to cry. He raises his right hand to hold the back of her head to his chest. He looks to see a beautiful woman walking in from the living room into the kitchen. She is wearing a purple toga. It has gold trim that wraps up over her left shoulder. Its length is down to her knees and slit up both legs to her waist. She walks up behind Marlene, and Glamfury watches as she raises her hands. Her eyes start to sparkle like lightning is flashing in her deep blue eyes. Her fingernails start to grow like talons, and she pulls the toga, dropping it off her shoulder, exposing her nude body. Glamfury shakes his head up and down. Marlene starts to talk to Glamfury, unaware anyone is behind her. The woman thrusts all the talons on both her hands into the lower back of Marlene, penetrating her muscle and internal organs. Marlene tilts her head back, screaming. Glamfury holds her stomach to his. She pushes as hard as she can to break free from Glamfury's embrace, but he is too strong for her. The woman behind Marlene starts to glow with circles of light flowing from Marlene into the woman's fingers and up her arms and shoulders and down her body. The woman starts to laugh. She starts to breath heavily, while Marlene writhes and starts to scream as loud as she can. The woman behind her is actually sucking the blood out of Marlene's body, and you can see her skin and flesh start to shrink from the loss of fluid in her body. Marlene's screams grow fainter and weaker as her body shrinks and she begs for her life.

"Glamfury, I only wanted to be yours. I always wanted to be yours. Why would you do this to me? Why would you not use me for whatever you wanted? I would do anything for you," says Marlene.

The woman behind Marlene leans up to her shriveling head and whispers in her ear.

"Because he has already had you a hundred times over, my sweet, and your soul was as easy as any to seduce. Your beauty will nourish mine for twenty years. I thank you," says the woman.

She steps back from Marlene, drawing the last of her bodily fluids. Marlene falls back with her mouth wide open, literally skin and bones. The woman pulls her talons from the decrepit body of Marlene and laughs, aging in reverse right in front of Glamfury. She does not look old at all to begin with. Glamfury throws Marlene's corpse to the side of the kitchen. He watches with wide eyes as this beautiful blond-haired, blue-eyed beauty roughly forty years old starts to transform slightly but noticeably when you are watching. Her calf muscles, thigh muscles, hamstrings, buttocks, stomach muscles, neck, and muscles in both arms start to tighten, becoming leaner, more slender. Her skin starts to tighten and look more rosy. Her smile tightens, and her teeth become whiter and brighter. She laughs looking over her arms and legs. She rubs her breasts, which have become firmer and a little plumper. She rubs her stomach and runs her hands down her legs, bending right down, touching her toes, showing off her new flexibility. She stands with a wide smile, raising her arms, showing off her new body to Glamfury. She looks like a teenager stepping into adulthood with perfect skin, shiny hair, and all the right curves. Glamfury holds out his arms like he wants a hug from her, and she walks into his arms with that great smile. She walks right into his kiss, and quickly she starts to moan, which becomes an openmouthed scream with blood dripping from her mouth. Glamfury pulls back as far as he can from her with her tongue in his teeth. Glamfury releases her tongue, pulling back from her having bitten his top and bottom cuspid teeth on the right side of his mouth right through her tongue, causing her to bleed a lot. Glamfury pulls back with blood trickling down the side of his mouth, looking up with closed eyes and the look of overwhelming satisfaction as he savors the fresh blood in his mouth. The woman laughs, and Glamfury watches as her tongue heals in seconds.

"Ahhhhhh," sighs Glamfury.

"The feel and taste of fresh youth. There is no better orgasm," says Glamfury.

The woman grabs his groin with her right hand and then both, causing Glamfury to grow instantly.

"There are so many great orgasms that youth provides for us," says the woman.

"Yes, there are, my dear, many more indeed," says Glamfury.

She kisses him passionately. She runs her hands under his leather coat, dropping it off his back. He grabs her hands tightly, breathing in deeply like he is catching his breath.

"Everything is on schedule? Everything is still going according to plan? You have this under control, right?" says Glamfury.

"We got this floozy pretending to be Marlene just as I said we would, did we not?" says the woman.

"Yes," says Glamfury.

"We are about to make love on Rain's kitchen table just as I said we would, are we not?" says the woman.

Glamfury starts to laugh.

"Yes," he says.

"Rain is not here, Smoke is not here, and I know where they are going. I know where they are going to be," says the woman.

"Are you sure it is going to play out like that?" says Glamfury.

"I am positive, and I guarantee Rain will be mine for the next two weeks until he is ready for sacrifice. Smoke is your problem," says the woman.

"Oh, I have just the answer for Smoke. Meet Bailey," says Glamfury.

She is still holding Glamfury around his waist, and he holds out his left arm toward the doorway leading into the living room. She looks to see a beautiful woman in her midthirties walking into the kitchen. She is wearing a micro bikini with a little extra weight on her legs. A noticeable love handle on both sides of her lower back but still very busty and very beautiful. Bailey walks right up to Glamfury's mistress and puts her hands on her cheeks and kisses her deeply openmouthed with lots of tongue. The blond-haired woman swears the kiss lasts for ten minutes before their lip lock is released.

"Oh, Glamfury, I see what you mean," says the woman.

The girls lie on the kitchen table. Glamfury can be heard laughing outside of Rain's house. No one is there to hear it.

Chapter 10

Back to the Log Cabin

Rain leaves Marlene's house—well, the house he thought was Marlene's house. He drives back toward his house, thinking to himself, *I cannot believe I did not go into my shop this morning. I better get over there and check it out.* Rain drives to his shop and goes in. He remembers his armory shed at home had been emptied, or at least it looked like it had been. He wants to see what his shop looks like. He goes in, and it looks exactly the way he had hoped. Everything is right where it is supposed to be. Obviously, he has a lot more weapons and ammunition here than he has at home. He gets his favorite .357 Magnums and a double shoulder holster. He loads a whole duffel bag full of speed clips so he has plenty of ammunition. He grabs a few tactical fighting knives, and he even grabs an M16 rifle with lots of ammunition. Now he feels indestructible. He gets in his car and thinks, *You know what, there is one more thing I better check out. That log cabin. I wonder if it is even there or if it's just woods.* Rain drives toward the Fright Woods. He goes solely from the visions in his dreams driving there and making it there late in the afternoon.

"Goddamn, this Sunday feels like a whole month," he says to himself while driving.

He says it out loud again getting out of his car, stretching his legs. This time, he drove right up to the log cabin, and unbelievably, it is here and it is gorgeous. Immediately upon getting out of his car, he can hear chanting from behind the log cabin. It takes him right back to his dream, and chills run up and down his back. He puts two knives in sheaths on his belt and puts as many speed clips in his pockets as he can. His shoulder harness is on and holding his favorite pistols, and he notices Smoke's BMW is parked far to the left of the cabin near the woods. He draws his right-hand pistol and heads around the cabin just as he did chasing after Ajaunta in his dream. He gets around the cabin, and there is Smoke on the sacrificial rock held by ropes just as Ajaunta's husband was in his dream. Rain hesitates not a second charging the men or demons or whatever they are wearing the same coconut masks with vines hanging from them. He draws both his Magnums and fires at the man holding the knife first. Then he shoots the four holding the ropes. They all fall to the ground with lethal gunshot wounds.

"Rain, Rain, is that you? Thank god," says Smoke.

There are a dozen or so people in dark brown cloaks with hoods covering their faces, and they start to chant.

"Stormy Rain Clouds. Stormy Rain Clouds. Stormy Rain Clouds." Then they start to chant, "Kenneth Royden Phillips. Kenneth Royden Phillips. Kenneth Royden Phillips."

Rain can see Smoke has been stabbed in the gut and helps him to a sitting position. He and Smoke get the ropes off his wrists and ankles, and Rain gives Smoke one of his .357s.

"Are you OK?" says Rain.

"Yeah, that fucker with the knife stabbed me, but he did not hit any major organs. It looks bad and hurts like hell, but I'll be all right. Let's give these demonic cult motherfuckers an express lane to hell," says Smoke.

Rain steps to the left side of the rock and gets ready to blast away. Smoke goes to the right, and just before they both start shooting, they notice the air between them, and the cult members start to ripple like they are looking at water. A man rises from the earth between Rain, Smoke, and the cult members. The man holds up his right index finger, waving it side to side.

"No, no, gentlemen. These disciples are personal favorites of mine and not to be harmed by you," says the man.

Rain and Smoke look at each other.

"Who are you?" asks Rain.

The man does not say a word and sinks into the earth. The air starts to ripple heavily so they cannot see the cult members. Rain and Smoke start to fire blindly. It seems the rippling air, which looks like water, seems to be absorbing the bullets. Both men fire all six shots, and Rain tosses a few speed clips to Smoke. They reload, and the rippling slows and the air clears. There are no cult members anymore. They look around, and it is just them. They both hear screaming from inside the log cabin.

"Ajaunta!" yells Smoke.

"What? Is Ajaunta here?" asks Rain.

"Yes, I came to save her from the Egengyns," says Smoke.

"The Egengyns. Those evil slimy motherfuckers. How did they get here in America? That's right, they always used those hallucinogens. That's why I had those crazy dreams and thoughts. We killed them all in Jamaica. How did they get here?" says Rain.

"Apparently, we did not kill them all. We must have missed some of them in Egypt. I guess they found the leader they were looking for, and now they have a cult following here in America," says Smoke.

They hear Ajaunta scream.

"Those fuckers are dead," says Rain.

Rain and Smoke charge the log cabin. Rain runs up onto the deck and opens the sliding glass door. He scans the large open room of the cabin. It is beautiful with nice furnishings. It's mainly a wide open room with a kitchen to the right, bathrooms to the far corner, and there is a stairway leading to a large loft above the kitchen. Rain can hear Ajaunta struggling from up in the loft. He runs up the stairs gun first, and Smoke is following. They see Ajaunta lying on a king-size bed with two masked men holding her arms and one straddling her, ripping the shirt from her body.

"Die, motherfuckers!" yells Rain.

Rain shoots the man on Ajaunta. He shoots the man to her left, and Smoke shoots the man to her right. Rain pushes the man off Ajaunta onto the floor and sees her ankles are tied to the bed with ropes. Ajaunta is crying and screaming hysterically. Rain grabs her arms, realizing she does not even have her eyes open.

"Ajaunta, Ajaunta. It's me. It's Rain. We got them. Calm down. We got them all. Calm down. I'm going to get you out of here. Calm down. Smoke, untie her ankles," says Rain.

He does. Ajaunta opens her eyes.

"Rain. Stormy Rain, is it really you?" says Ajaunta.

"Yes, I am here. Smoke is here too. We're getting you out of here. They won't hurt you anymore," says Rain.

"Rain, they killed my husband. They killed my kids. They burned them, they killed them," says Ajaunta.

Ajaunta cries, and Rain hugs her tight. He stands, reaching under her legs, lifting her off the bed, and she cries into his shoulder, holding him around the neck.

"Smoke, let's get out of here. Make sure the coast is clear to our cars. I parked not too far from you. Ajaunta and I are right behind you," says Rain.

Rain follows Smoke down the stairs, carrying Ajaunta. They get out onto the porch of the log cabin heading toward their cars, and there between them and their cars is the man they saw earlier with a beautiful blond-haired, blue-eyed beauty to his right and a voluptuous brunet to his left. Both women wear micro bikinis covered in diaphanous togas. The girls are very distracting, but Rain and Smoke are professionals. Smoke walks down the stairs, pointing his fully loaded gun at the man.

"You must be the god the Egengyns were always praying to and talking about. Sorry, we missed you. I won't miss you this time," says Smoke.

Smoke fires all six shots in as few seconds. When the smoke clears, he has already reloaded, and the man and the blond-haired girl are gone. The brunet is lying on the ground with two bullet holes in her chest. Smoke can see she is breathing heavily and most likely she is dying. He walks up to her, pointing his gun at her. Rain walks up behind Smoke, still carrying Ajaunta.

"Shoot her, Smoke. Put a bullet in her fucking head," says Rain.

Smoke looks down, pointing his gun at her head.

"Bailey. Bailey Sue," says Smoke.

Smoke falls to his knees beside her. His arms go limp, and his eyes start to tear up, thinking she is going to die. Tears are running down her temples from the corners of her eyes.

"Smoke, how did I get here? Where am I? Smoke, did you shoot me? Why did you shoot me?" says Bailey.

She barely leans her head forward seeing she has been shot twice in the chest.

"Smoke, I'm dying. I don't want to die. Why did you shoot me?" says Bailey.

"Bailey, how did you get here? You were with very bad people," says Smoke.

"I don't know, Smoke. I don't know how, but they made me have sex with them. They made me do things, and I didn't know I was doing it until just now. It's like I was in a trance or something," says Bailey.

She starts to cry hard.

"Smoke, please don't let me die. I don't want to die, not like this," says Bailey.

Rain walks up beside Smoke, who is kneeling beside Bailey. Rain points his gun right at her head.

"No, Rain. Leave her be. I know her. She was my lover," says Smoke.

"Kill her, Smoke. You know better. There's no telling what kind of crazy drugs they used on her, not to mention you already shot her twice. Let's get the fuck out of here," says Rain.

"All right, Rain, Mr. Know-It-All, shoot Ajaunta in the head, and then I will shoot Bailey in the head," says Smoke.

"All right, you made your point," says Rain.

Rain walks to the other side of Bailey and sets Ajaunta on her feet. Rain kneels to his knees beside Bailey. He holsters his gun. Smoke gives him his other gun, and Ajaunta kneels beside Rain. Rain looks Bailey over and looks at Smoke.

"Let's sit her up. So far as I can tell, the shots did not hit any vitals. Bailey, we're going to sit you up, all right? Now, obviously, you are in pain, but what I want you to tell me is if you feel any heavy pounding of your heart or if you feel like there is mass moving around inside your chest, OK?" says Rain.

Bailey shakes her head up and down. Rain grabs her left arm and shoulder, and Smoke grabs her right arm and shoulder. They help sit her up. The bullet hole to her left side is just under her collar bone, and the bullet to her right chest is just above the collar bone. They can clearly see both shots have gone clean through her. Rain touches the blood from the entry and exit wounds and rubs it between his fingers.

"Well, Bailey, looks like I have some good news for you. It does not look like your lungs have been hit at all. Looks like you have nothing more than flesh wounds. You should see a doctor and get these wounds thoroughly cleaned and stitched. Smoke, let's get these wounds covered and stop the bleeding." Smoke gets a med kit, which is in the trunk of his BMW. He takes his shirt off and tears it into pieces. He sprays the cloth with antibiotic spray, and they cover her wounds. He has medical tape, and they bandage her pretty good for the short term.

"I'm going to be OK? I'm not going to die?" says Bailey.

"You're going to be OK, Bailey. I tell you what, Smoke, we have seen some shit in our life, and it's coming back to haunt us," says Rain.

"Don't say it, Rain. I don't want to hear it anymore," says Smoke.

Rain leans back, sitting on the grass, exhaling like this is the longest day of his life.

"Rain, how did you know I was here? You saved me," says Ajaunta.

"All I can say is I had this dream. I don't even know if it was one long dream or a whole bunch of dreams. I saw Smoke. I saw the woman I had just started dating. I saw you and your family. I saw this log cabin. I saw all this in a dream, and somehow, it brought me here. Smoke, how did you get here?" says Rain.

"It's almost like you, Rain. I had these dreams. I saw this log cabin. I saw a house not too far from your house. You and I were in the house, and there was this beautiful woman in the front yard. I know this is going to sound crazy, but we were upstairs, and she was in the front yard, and this monster, I don't know, like demon lizard rose up from the ground and ate her," says Smoke.

"Yes, I had that dream to except you turned out to be some sort of demon and you were killing me," says Rain.

"I said I did not want to hear that anymore, Rain," says Smoke.

"I'm serious that was a dream I had. That's when I woke up and started to trace back all the places I saw in my dreams. I went to your house, Ajaunta," says Rain.

"My house," she says.

"Yes, and I saw your husband sacrificed right here where they were trying to sacrifice Smoke. I saw your boys and girls burned in your house. They were burned, and then this demon lizard rose from the ground and ate them. I swear these are dreams I was having, but I don't know if it was actually your house. Hell, I don't even know if it was actually your family. Like I said, it's all dreams, and I don't know what is real and what is not," says Rain.

"Well, in my dreams, this man comes to me and seduces me. He has wonderful sex with me. I fall in love with him in my dreams, and I can't wait to get back to sleep because the love is so powerful, it's so good, and it feels so real. I started to see him in real life, and I got scared. Now my family is dead," says Ajaunta.

"Oh my god! That is happening to me," says Bailey.

"It's the man who was here," both girls say in unison.

"Who?" Rain and Smoke say in unison.

"Glamfury," the girls say in unison.

"I'm getting a little nervous. I want to get out of here," says Bailey.

"Me too," says Ajaunta.

"Wait, that is his name—Glamfury?" says Rain.

"Yes," say the girls.

"Well, now we have something to go on. We have to look up the name Glamfury and see what or who he is," says Rain.

"I want to get out of here," says Bailey.

"Smoke, I don't want to take Bailey to the hospital because of all the bullshit we will have to deal with—the police, the bullshit questions, etc.," says Rain.

"I know. I don't want to deal with that either," says Smoke.

"Can't you guys do it? Can't you put antibacterial stuff on me and clean the wounds and stitch me up?" says Bailey.

"I don't want to go back to my house. I just don't know what is going on there. I have been dating this girl for I don't even know how long, maybe a month, but she has to be involved in this somehow. Who knows what is waiting for me at my house? These fucking Egengyns, and this guy Glamfury, he must be their leader or their god. I bet my house is booby-trapped or under surveillance. I don't think we should go there. Smoke, what about you? Where are you living now?" says Rain.

"I actually have a house in Liesnell. I've lived there for almost a year now. It should be safe there. Come on, I'll take Bailey with me, you take Ajaunta, and we will go to my house. We can rest and try to figure out what is going on," says Smoke.

They all agree that sounds good and get into the cars and head for Smoke's house.

Chapter 11

Smoke's House

Driving back to his house, Smoke can tell Bailey is in a lot of discomfort.

"Hurts, doesn't it?" says Smoke.

"Yeah. It hurts a lot," says Bailey.

"When we get home, Rain and I will fix you up good as new," says Smoke.

"I hope so," says Bailey.

"I have all the things we need to clean your wounds and stitch you up. I apologize now because it's gonna hurt a lot," says Smoke.

"Not as much as being shot," says Bailey.

"I apologize for that too. I did not know it was you. I was trying for the man. If he is in fact the one the Egengyns consider their god, then Rain and I have hunted him before, and he evaded us. We never did find or see him until today if in fact that is who I am thinking of, and if so, he is one evil man. That is why I did not hesitate to shoot at him. I tried to put him down immediately, and I will do the same if I ever see him again. Now I know what he looks like," says Smoke.

Bailey leans back in her chair, looking out the window, and Smoke can tell she is fighting the pain.

"We are almost there," says Smoke.

Rain is following behind Smoke with Ajaunta in his car. He looks over to see Ajaunta, and it's like he is in a dream again.

"So that guy that appeared in the front yard, the one Smoke shot at, the one you called Glamfury, you have seen him before? You have talked with him?" says Rain.

"I have these dreams. He is in them. He always comes to me in some fantastic way. He is always dressed so handsomely. He is so charming. When I first started seeing him in my dreams, it was like in the 1800s. I was wearing these big full dresses, and we were in these huge mansions dancing and drinking and dining with lots of people. He would sweep me off my feet and walk me up these big wide stairs into a bedroom that was beautiful. He would then seduce me and make love with me. I kept having these dreams, and the time period would work up to the present day. The last dream I remember with him in it was a little over a week or two ago, and he made love with me in the present time. The next day after that dream, I saw him in real life," says Ajaunta.

"That must have been creepy," says Rain.

"It was, it was very creepy, but he seemed not to notice me, and I could not resist making contact with him. I have to admit I was so attracted to him. I found him irresistible. In my dreams, he was my perfect lover, and I found out in real life he was too. Now my family is dead," says Ajaunta.

Ajaunta goes silent, and Rain can see the anguish in her face.

"You remember Smoke and I went into the service right out of high school?" says Rain.

"Yeah, we all remember," says Ajaunta.

"Well, Smoke, as I am sure you remember, is an adventure seeker. He needs to be on the edge. When we got in the service, he found out about this special program for adventurous young men and women. Very few are actually accepted into the program, but Smoke and I were. We were sent all over the world hunting down the most elusive and cunning of criminals. This included the most dangerous of evildoers. There was and possibly still is this group of mercenaries called the Egengyns. They are not loyal to any government. They only follow the leadership of their god. They hunt, kill, steal, and take whatever their god desires. These Egengyns have enemies on all sides. They are hunted by all governments because they have killed and taken the brides and wealth of all sides. No one knows how they are funded or where this god of theirs comes from. Smoke and I found a group of these Egengyns in Egypt. We killed most of them, and the few that escaped us, we tracked to Jamaica. We killed them all, so we thought. We never did find their leader, the one they call their god, but I think this Glamfury, as you say his name is, I think this is the god of the Egengyns. It's almost myth how the leader of this group has always eluded capture. There are no pictures, and he has never been seen. I think we saw him today," says Rain.

Rain looks over at Ajaunta, and she is not even paying attention to him. She is sleeping in the passenger seat.

"Well, we are going to find out soon enough if this Glamfury is the god of the Egengyns," says Rain.

Rain follows Smoke to his house in Liesnell, and they all go into his house. Smoke has a surprising amount of medical supplies, and Bailey and Ajaunta are shocked how efficient and knowledgeable both Rain and Smoke are at cleaning her gunshot wounds, applying antibacterial suave, stitching, and bandaging her. They work on her in the kitchen. She is more than happy to let the two men work on her while she sits in her bra stained with blood. Rain and Smoke wash her front and back with moist cloths, and she loves the attention the men give her. When they finish, Smoke brings her a large T-shirt and some sweatpants. She goes into the bathroom and gets rid of the bra and puts on the sweatpants and T-shirt. She walks into the living room, looking at the large cathedral ceiling with its large chandelier light set to a warm dim setting. The large gray couch is eight feet long in the form of a horseshoe facing the wall with a sixty-four-inch flat-screen TV on it. The carpet is golden brown deep shag, which feels so good under Bailey's feet. There is a very large picture window to the right back side of the couch, and she walks to the window, looking out. She cannot see anything outside because it is late now. Ajaunta and Rain are sitting on the couch talking, and Smoke walks in with a drink for Bailey. Smoke and Bailey sit on the couch.

"How long have you had this house? I can't believe you live, what, only about an hour from my house and you never told me," says Rain.

"Yeah, well, I thought you didn't want to see me anymore," says Smoke.

"No. I just don't want to be dragged into firefights, fistfights, and just plain fights anymore," says Rain.

"I've been here a little over a year now. I'm getting too old for all the fighting too, but it looks like the fighting is not done with us," says Smoke.

"I'm afraid you are right. I still can't figure out how this all began. I can't remember anything from the past week or even the past month. All I remember is parts of this dream or multiple dreams. I remember this girl Marlene whom I was very attracted to, and we started dating. We started to get serious with each other, and the first night we were intimate, we were attacked by three guys. Smoke, they were the three guys from Willsdus. You remember those guys?" says Rain.

"The guys in the parking lot? The ones mad because we were dating Shelly and Stacy?" says Smoke.

"Yes, those three guys. Well, they attacked Marlene and me, hitting us with a baseball bat, and you came in and killed them. This was a dream, right? This did not really happen, did it? Because I can't tell. I actually thought it happened for real," says Rain.

"No, Rain, I have not been to your house in over five years. Not since you said to never come back, remember?" says Smoke.

"Well, anyway, the dream goes on and on and on. I don't know when it started, and I'm having trouble figuring out when it stopped. What about you, Smoke, how did you get to the log cabin today? How did they get you on that rock ready to be killed?" asks Rain.

"It was a well-laid trap. Hold on a second, let me show you," says Smoke.

Smoke gets up and walks into the kitchen and walks back with an envelope. He hands it to Rain. Rain opens the letter and reads it out loud.

"'You thought you had me in Jamaica. You killed a lot of my followers. You killed a lot of my courtesans, but you never got close to me. Well, the time has come to return the favor. Your friend for life and your lover are mine. Follow the map and be here by noon to witness their sacrifice,'" reads Rain.

Rain unfolds another piece of paper, which is a map to the log cabin.

"So you went to the cabin to rescue me and Bailey? Bailey is your lover? It is nice to meet you, Bailey. I wish we had met under better circumstances. I am a little surprised you never told me about Bailey," says Rain.

"That is because of me. I asked Smoke to keep our relations between the two of us. We are lovers and have been since Guatemala," says Bailey.

"Oh my god! I knew I had seen you before. That's right, I remember you from the barracks held by the Eagle Sky Militia. So Smoke got you into America? Are you two married?" says Rain.

"She married someone else," says Smoke.

"I see. So you went to the cabin to rescue me and Bailey, and, what, they captured you?" says Rain.

"I went there and parked on the side of the log cabin. I got out of my car, and the next thing I remember, I'm tied up on this rock, and then you showed up. You ended up rescuing me just like old times, and then we heard Ajaunta. So, Ajaunta, how did you get there?" says Smoke.

"I had been seeing Glamfury in my dreams. I saw him in real life a few weeks ago. He called me and said he was going to kill my husband and my kids if I did not go out there. I went out there, and they killed my husband on that rock. They burned my house with my kids in it. I don't remember going to my house, but I remember seeing my kids being burned and eaten by some demon lizard." Ajaunta starts to cry.

"The next thing I remember, those men, or whatever they were, they were attacking me, tearing off my clothes in that bed. I have no idea how long I was there. Then you two showed up and saved me," says Ajaunta.

"Bailey, how did you get there?" asks Smoke.

"I was having dreams of the same guy the same way Ajaunta was. He was seducing me in my dreams. I loved him. Then I saw him in real life. Soon after that, my husband and two kids were gone. I don't know what happened to them. I got a letter with a map telling me to go to the log cabin, and I had been there for maybe a month or two, I can't tell how long. I don't know what is dream or real as well. I stay hopeful that my husband and two kids are still alive, but I have not seen them in who knows how long," says Bailey.

"Well, all this dream stuff is driving me crazy. There has to be some real explanation to what is going on here. I think it has to have something to do with the Egengyns and their god, Glamfury. Come with me, I may have some things that may help us out here," says Smoke.

Rain, Ajaunta, and Bailey follow Smoke down a spiral stairway leading down into the cellar. This is a very nice wide stairway spiraling down with thick carpeted stairs into a beautiful well-furnished carpeted cellar. There are nice couches and a bar down here. There is a doorway leading into another room. Smoke goes in and comes back out a few moments later. He has some books with him.

"Smoke, you still have our records. Good man," says Rain.

"Yeah, and you remember this gem?" says Smoke.

Smoke tosses a thick book to Rain.

"Holy shit, Smoke. I am glad you have this. I forgot all about this. How did you keep this from the colonel?" says Rain.

"Well, they can't take what they don't know about," says Smoke.

"In this case, I am glad they did not know. Let's see here," says Rain.

Rain opens the thick book. It looks like a huge diary.

"What do you have there?" asks Ajaunta.

"Smoke and I were given orders to go to Egypt. That is where the Egengyns had what they thought was a safe place to be. They were safe until Smoke and I got there," says Rain.

"You went there to kill them? Just like the Eagle Sky Militia?" asks Bailey.

"That's what we do," says Smoke.

"So I guess you did not get them?" says Ajaunta.

"About a dozen of them got away. We tracked them to Jamaica, where we thought we had finished them off. Their leader and their god, Glamfury, is one slippery bastard," says Rain.

"Yeah, I don't know how he did that thing at the log cabin today. He made the air look like water, and I had him dead in my sights. I shot all six shots, and there is no way I missed. When the air cleared, he was gone with that blond-haired girl. How he did that creepy voodoo magic, I'll never know," says Smoke.

"Yeah, they were gone, and that is where we found you, Bailey. Who was that blond-haired girl with you?" says Rain.

"I swear I don't remember much. It was like when I saw you guys at the cabin. I was waking from a dream. I remember just pieces, and I never knew the girl before. She was someone making love with me and Glamfury. She was probably being seduced just as I was for Glamfury's pleasure," says Bailey.

"So what I want to know is how is this guy getting into our dreams? How is he manipulating our dreams and then we are seeing him in real life? Maybe this book will have some answers," says Rain.

"I don't get how he is in my dreams and I fall in love with him and then I see him in real life and I can't resist him. So why is he coming into my dreams as a loving beautiful man and then in real life causing death and destruction? Why the double personality? Why the deceit?" says Ajaunta.

"Yeah, why is he like that? Any ideas?" says Bailey.

"I don't know. It sure is not making any sense," says Smoke.

"You remember when we were in Egypt? Remember the cellar under the barracks, the place we called hellhole?" says Rain.

"Yeah, I remember that place. Holy shit, that's right, those weird coconut shells with vines hanging from them just like the ones they were wearing at the cabin today. I can't believe I forgot about them. They were hanging on the walls. That's where I found that book you are holding," says Smoke.

"Well, you remember in the barracks, we ran into those men or demons or whatever they were, and we killed them. They were wearing these mask vine things. You remember that is where I said, 'This is it.' That's where you and I started to go our separate ways," says Rain.

"Yeah, I remember, Rain. That's where you freaked out, and I promised to never talk about what we had seen there. Well, here we are facing those nonhuman things again."

"Well, we thought we got them all in Jamaica, but we did not. Here they come again. I thought I left this life behind, but it's coming for us. It won't let us go until they are dead or we are dead," says Rain.

"Are we going to have this argument again? I told you then and I'll tell you again. We have to stay on the attack. We have to hunt them or they will hunt us, it's that simple," says Smoke.

"I know you are right, but I don't know how we will survive this one," says Rain.

"Yeah, well, we better think of something," says Smoke.

Bailey has moved to a lying position on the couch and has been drifting to sleep. Ajaunta has lain down as well with her head on a pillow on Rain's leg.

"Looks like the girls are falling asleep," says Smoke.

"Yup, this couch sure is comfortable," says Rain.

Smoke rubs Bailey's shoulder a little.

"I'm going to bed. You want to stay here or come with me?" says Smoke.

Bailey shakes her head and gets up with Smoke, and they head to his bedroom. Rain stays on the couch in the dimly lit room, reading through the book they had gotten in Egypt, while Ajaunta sleeps comfortably by his side.

Chapter 12

Egypt

Rain and Smoke are on a plane very high in the sky. They are the only two in the back of the dark plane. They are dressed in black, and a red light flashes. They both get up as a lift in the back of the plane opens, and the two men jump out the back of the plane. Their black clothing makes them virtually invisible in the dark background of night. They are very streamlined with very little gear on their bodies. They dive headfirst at the ground, holding their arms and legs tight to their bodies, speeding as fast as gravity will pull them. They wear helmets connected to a smooth durable fabric fitting their bodies snug in one piece designed to slice through the air with as little friction as possible. They fly faster and faster at the ground like bullets. They have no parachutes, and they seem to be diving to their immediate deaths. They are heading at the ground somewhere south of Minya, north of Asyut and west of the Nile River where lush forest meets the desert in Egypt. This uninhabited part of Egypt is a place known to be sanctuary for the Egengyns. As the two get closer and closer to the ground, they open their arms and legs. The suits they are wearing stretch from the tip of their toes to tips of their fingers, giving them a complete surface area, making them look like human kites. As they approach the ground and open up their arms and legs, this gives them lift, and they literally glide on the air horizontally with the ground, and they tilt their bodies at a forty-five-degree angle, slowing their speed until they land on the ground at a speed comfortable for them to run. They land looking very similar to ducks but more controlled. They unzip their suits, roll them up, and head to the forest not far away under the cover of night, which is fading fast into dawn. They get into the woods wearing tan camouflage, and they have modified M16s with lots of ammunition and secondary weapons like knives.

"Listen, Smoke, I have no idea how you got me here in Egypt hunting a bunch of devil worshipers. I'm getting tired of this bullshit. This is it I am done after this if we survive. Fucking devil worshipers in the goddamn desert. This is not what I want to spend my life doing. I mean it, Smoke. If we survive this, it is the last mission for me. I'm through," says Rain.

"Yeah, yeah, yeah, you've been saying that. Right now, let's keep our heads on straight and get the job done. I'm taking the east entrance, you take the west. We eliminate the last of the Egengyns, and then we will talk about future missions," says Smoke.

"I'm serious, Smoke. I am talking with Colonel Sanbers after this mission, and that is it. I'm letting him know this is going to be my last mission. Chasing after a bunch of devil worshipers is it. That's where I draw the line. Shit, even if we kill them all, we still have fifty miles through a foreign country to travel just to get to our evacuation site. You keep getting me into these bullshit situations," says Rain.

"Rain, you are a professional. Shut your mouth and move," says Smoke.

Smoke heads through the lush forest to the east. Rain heads to the west with his gun ready. Moving silently through the forest, they look and listen for enemies. There is a pretty big building that is only one story tall. It looks like a big building made out of dried mud with doorways cut right out of the walls. Windows with no screens or glass. There are no doors, just doorways. Rain moves around the building with no signs of people at all. He stops by a tree and scans the area. The sun is breaking the horizon, so visibility is becoming better. There is nothing just silence. He moves up to the doorway and leans his back against the wall. Taking a deep breath, he turns into the doorway, pointing his weapon ready for action. There is nothing. He moves into the structure, which seems to be a solid dried mud dwelling. There are tables and chairs and a few other furnishings, but not much else for Rain to notice as he searches the building. He walks through the structure, which seems to be vacant, finally running into Smoke near the center of the structure.

"Did you see anything? Anything at all?" asks Rain.

"Nothing. What about you?" says Smoke.

"Nothing. Looks like this place is abandoned," says Rain.

"It can't be. They have to be here. Stay sharp. These Egengyns are crafty bastards. They have to be here somewhere," says Smoke.

They quietly search when Rain notices a metal ring in the floor. He taps Smoke on the shoulder, pointing out the ring, which he grabs and realizes it lifts a doorway leading underground. Smoke readies his gun, while Rain slowly lifts on the wooden hatch leading down a stairway into the earth. When Rain lifts the hatch, they can hear chanting coming from below. Smoke looks down, seeing nothing, and heads down into the unknown. Rain follows behind him, closing the hatch behind them. The wooden ladder leads to a passage dug right out of the earth. They follow to a very large room where about twenty people are kneeling in the center of the room wearing red-and-brown cloaks that completely cover their bodies. There are about a dozen very large men over six feet tall each standing around the outer walls of the room, and they are wearing coconut masks covering their heads with vines running from the bottom of the masks to their knees. There are torches on the walls illuminating the large round room, and there is a man standing at a podium in the front of the room. The man addresses his disciples covered in red cloaks with gold trim and very elaborate stitching throughout the cloaks. The man speaking has his face covered, so Rain and Smoke cannot see him. There are hallways that exit behind where the man at the podium is. These passageways must lead outside because Rain and Smoke can feel a fairly strong flow of air blowing from where they are out into the large room.

"Rise, my followers. Stand and ready yourselves," says the man at the podium.

"Well, let's not fuck around. Time to fuck them up. You ready?" says Rain.

"Let's hit them," says Smoke.

Rain and Smoke calmly ready their guns and walk into the room, firing their personalized M16 rifles. They have their guns set to semiautomatic and start with the people in the center of the room. Quickly, the large humanoids wearing the masks standing around the outside walls of this large circular room move toward Smoke and Rain.

They calmly shoot them, watching as the creatures that obviously are not human start to break apart and crumble like dry dirt as they are shot. It does not take long for Rain and Smoke to shoot down the masked creatures and kill the followers in the center of the room. The whole time, the man at the front standing at the podium is laughing. Rain and Smoke reload looking at each other and the final man standing at the podium who is still laughing. They point and ready their guns.

"Boys and their toys. Ha, ha, ha," says the man, pointing his index finger at Rain and Smoke.

"Let's see how you like these toys, scumbag," says Smoke.

The two of them start to shoot. The man does not flinch; he does not move. Rain and Smoke both walk toward him, firing a steady stream of hot lead, blasting holes in the dirt wall behind the man. They both walk right up to him, and when then get to him, the robe he is wearing falls to the ground. They walk around the podium, and Smoke uses his gun to pick up the robe. He looks to Rain.

"What the fuck? How did he do that?" says Smoke.

Rain looks around at all the dead Egengyns in the center of the room. Then he looks at the masks and vines around the outer walls, which are all that are left of whatever those things they shot were. Smoke looks at the podium, and there is a door opening up, exposing a small shelf or cabinet. There is a large book in here, and he grabs it.

"Look, Rain, a book," says Smoke.

"You keep that book. I mean, put it somewhere safe and you hold on to it. Don't turn it in to the colonel. It may have a lot of valuable information that we may need in the future," says Rain.

"You got it. What do you suspect those things around the walls were?" says Smoke.

"I don't know. This guy here we shot, where the fuck is he? Goddamn devil worshipers. It's freaky shit like this that freaks me out. Where the fuck is he? We put at least forty rounds in that bastard. I know he's dead, but where is he?" says Rain.

"It's goddamn creepy Egypt voodoo devil magic," says Smoke.

"Yeah, it's gonna come back to haunt us, you watch. That's it, let's get the fuck out of here, and I'm done with this shit," says Rain.

"Yeah, I've heard that before. You can't quit, you live for the fight. Without the fight, you've got nothing. You'll shrivel up and die without the service—you need it," says Smoke.

"Not anymore, I don't. It's time to settle down, get a house, and live. You too, Smoke. We are getting too old for this shit. This is a young man's game, and we've seen our game. Come on, let's get out of here and go home. That was the last of the Egengyns. We've done our part," says Rain.

Smoke puts the book in a pocket on the outside of his right leg. They both reload and start to head out the passageways behind where the podium is. Just as they get around the wall and out of sight of the carnage, they hear strange noises. They look at each other and take a few steps back to see what is causing this odd noise. All the bodies in the center of the room are rolling into the center of the room. The vines attached to the masks act like legs standing, and the coconut masks are high above the vines. They walk over to the bodies, removing the robes and tossing them away from the nude bodies. The vines straddle a body and bend, lowering the coconut down over the head of a body, which is animated, and it comes to life. The first body stands and faces the two men, and then one after another stand, and they are all coming back to life. Rain looks at Smoke.

"Now that is some creepy Egyptian voodoo magic," says Rain.

Rain and Smoke start firing blasting holes in the coconut shells, blasting them to bits, and the bodies fall, crumbling like dried dirt. They blast all the bodies, and the ground starts to shake like an earthquake. Rain and Smoke are trying to keep their balance, but they fall to the ground. The center of the room starts to fall like it is sinking, and the men try to climb upward, not being drawn into the sinking hole. The hole sinks and sinks, and they cannot avoid falling down. They know if they fall to the bottom, they will be sucked into the earth, and just before they fall deep into the hole, the earth stops sinking, allowing them to climb up to the outer rim around the outside of the room. Rain notices a shelf that has been exposed in the wall, and he walks to it. Sitting on the shelf is another book similar to the one Smoke got from the podium, but this one is bigger and cannot be opened. There is what seems to be dried lava around the binding of the book, holding it shut, and it is very hard. Rain uses the strap from his gun to tie around the book and to his belt. The passageways leading behind the podium have been caved in, and they cannot exit this way. They head back the way they came, but before they get to the ladder going up into the building, two demonic humanoid creatures emerge from the center of the room, rising from the earth, blood red with thick strong muscles, long claws, and long beaks like toucans. Rain and Smoke see them and start shooting. They blast the demons to bits and get out of there as fast as they can. When they get up the ladder into the structure, they hear laughing all around them, but they have no idea where it is coming from.

"Where is it coming from? Where is he? It's that guy that was at the podium. How is he still alive?" says Rain.

"I don't know, but I'm a little freaked out at this point. Come on, let's get out of here," says Smoke.

They start to leave the structure, and just as they leave the building to head back into the jungle, Rain kicks something with his boot, which gets his attention. He looks down to see a very strange object. It actually looks like a piece of lava, and for some reason, Rain picks it up and puts it in his pocket. The laughing continues, but the men ignore it and head toward their rendezvous. They have many miles of forest and then many miles of desert to cross to get to the Nile River, where a military escort is waiting to take them back home. They have two days to make it back, which they can easily do. Fortunately, this part of Egypt is not inhabited, so they should make it to the Nile with no problem. The laughter stops as they make their way and changes to a sinister voice.

"You can run, but you cannot hide. I know where you are, and I know where you will be. You can never hide from me. When the time is right, you will be mine. You did not finish the job you came to finish. You can never finish the job. You can never end me."

The voice changes back to laugher, which fades, and is gone. Rain stops and looks around the horizon.

"Then come finish it. What are you waiting for? I am right here. Come finish it. Well, I am waiting for you, come on!" yells Rain.

Smoke grabs Rain by the shoulders.

"Come on, Rain, let's get out of here. Forget about it. Let's get to the boat. There is time for that guy later, come on," says Smoke.

Rain and Smoke are exceptionally well conditioned. They can travel fifty miles in the heat of a desert with minimal water, which is the situation they are in. They have studied their route and know where they are going. There is nearly thirty-five miles of forest to traverse and then about fifteen miles of desert. Their training is about to come in very handy, and they head out to make their rendezvous on the Nile.

They make it to the Nile with no problem by early evening the next day. Once on the ship, they are scolded by the commanding officer.

"Colonel Sanbers, what are you doing here?" asks Rain.

"You two were supposed to eliminate all the Egengyns. What happened? Why did you let them all escape?" says Sanbers.

"Sir, we eliminated them all—all of them," says Smoke.

"I don't think so. Explain this to me," says Colonel Sanbers.

He goes on to show both Rain and Smoke images of a dozen men leaving the structure and escaping on foot into the forest.

"Yes, that is right. The whole place is under surveillance, and they escaped. We watched them make their way to this airstrip, and now they are on this flight on their way to Jamaica. That is where you two are going to finish the job," says Sanbers.

Rain and Smoke look at each other.

"Sir, it is well known and it was explained to us that these Egengyns are devil worshipers, and I will tell you I put holes in them. You want me to go do it again, then I will," says Rain.

"Yes, you will, Master Sergeant, both of you will. Get below deck, get a hot square, and rest up because we are on our way to the Caribbean. You two have unfinished business," says Sanbers.

"Yes, sir," they say in unison.

Rain and Smoke go below deck to their bunks where they both still have the books they collected. Rain gets out the piece of lava, which looks like an arrowhead, but it's big, about four inches long with sharp edges and a design that looks natural and yet almost like a perfect sculpture of some sort.

"What is that you have?" asks Smoke.

"I don't know. It caught my eye, and I picked it up for some reason. Something tells me I need it for some reason. Look at this book I found. I can't open it. Here, check it out," says Rain.

Smoke looks at the book and tries to open it, but he can't.

"Well, maybe that piece of lava will help you open it. Here, you hold on to this book and I will hold on to this one. I think you were right—we should keep these. That voice freaked me out, and these books may come in handy for us someday. For right now, we better get a hot square and get some sleep. Something tells me Colonel Sanbers is gonna kick our ass tomorrow," says Smoke.

"Shit, you know he is. No doubt about that. Hide that book and I'll hide this one," says Rain.

"All right, see you in mess," says Smoke.

"Yup, I'll be right there," says Rain.

Smoke heads to his bunk, and Rain looks at his book, trying to figure if in any way the odd piece of lava he found fits the similar kind of lava holding the book shut. He maneuvers the lava piece around the book, twisting and turning it to see if the odd shapes fit together at all. He finds that the piece fits on the cover of the book with the point of the lava piece pointing diagonally toward the top right corner of the book. To his amazement, the piece of lava fits flush into the lava on the book. The book turns red hot, and flames burst from the book, causing Rain to drop it. This startles him, and he shakes free from his dream. He is sitting very comfortably on the end of the couch with a pillow on his left leg, and Ajaunta is sleeping with her head on the pillow. Rain looks to the arm of the couch, and the book he was reading before he fell asleep is still on the arm of the couch. "Holy shit, I forgot about that book," Rain says quietly to himself. He looks at the clock on the wall, seeing it is 5:45 a.m. "I have to go get that book," he says to himself.

Chapter 13

Still at Smoke's House

Rain gets up gently, quietly trying not to wake Ajaunta, which he does, but she falls back asleep. He gets his keys and heads out to his car. It is already light out, and he starts to head home. He knows if Smoke or the girls want to talk with him, they will call him. He still does not have his phone on him, so it has to be at his house, and he is less than an hour from home. He wants to find that book he found at the barracks in Egypt. He hid it at his house when he got back from Jamaica, and only Smoke knows he has it. He wants to read through it, something he has not done yet. Not only that, but also he wants to get back to his store to see if someone is actually running his store, saying that Rain (himself) is in the hospital. The traffic is light, and he makes very good time back to his house.

Driving into his driveway, he gets a little uneasy looking over his front yard and the front of his house. He gets out of his car and heads toward the front door. He gets chills as he reaches for the door handle. He pulls back, looking all around, feeling like someone is watching him. It seems like he is hearing eerie sounds, but he can't tell if it is just him thinking he is hearing it. "Fucking bullshit, this is my house."

He grabs the door handle, unlocks the door, and walks in. He walks through the living room toward the kitchen, and just before he walks into the kitchen, he looks at the couch against the wall and scratches his head. He walks over to the couch and looks under it. Sure enough, there is his phone, and he picks it up. He puts it in his pocket and heads into the kitchen, and in the corner of the kitchen is a door leading down a narrow stairway into his cellar. He goes down, and in the corner is a wooden box with a light sitting on it. It looks like a simple piece of furniture meant for a light or whatever to sit on it. Rain reaches down and under the front of the wooden square box. He pulls the front, which opens, exposing a safe inside. He knows the combination and opens the safe. Inside are his important documents and the book he collected and held on to ever since he found it in Egypt. He picks up the book, which is still sealed inside a ziplock bag. He sealed the book and the piece of lava in the bag for better preservation while they were on the boat in Egypt.

He unzips the bag, pulling the book from it, and now he hears laughing for real, loud laughing echoing through his house from the upstairs bedrooms to the first-floor living room and bedroom, the kitchen, and all the rooms down to the cellar, where he has just picked the book. Chills wiggle his whole body, and he remembers why he never opened the book and read through it before. First of all, when he put the key in the cover of the book where it fit perfectly, the book began to burn, burning his hands. He dropped the book, and the key broke free from the cover. He put the key and book in a ziplock bag and never opened the bag until now. When he got home from their mission in Jamaica, he put the sealed bag with the book and key in his safe. That is where it sat until now. That was over five years ago. Rain looks around, wondering if he is going crazy.

"What the fuck are you?" He looks around his cellar.

"This book has to have the answers I am looking for," he says out loud.

Rain puts the key into the cover like he did years before, only this time, he is prepared for the possibility of the book starting on fire. As soon as he puts the key in place, the book is swiped from his grip like someone grabbed the book from him. The book levitates waist high right in front of him, and he sees a man materialize right in front of him. The man is laughing. He is a few inches taller and heavier than Rain. He looks quite well-to-do and sturdy.

"Who are you? How did you get in my house?" says Rain.

"You still don't know who I am, do you? Of course, you don't, you clueless bastard. You still don't know what is going on," says the man.

"All right, what is going on? Tell me," says Rain.

"No, no, no, don't take the fun out of the game. You have to figure out what is going on before I feast on your youth—well, let me rephrase that, someone will feast on your soul," says the man.

"Yeah, I don't think so, asshole," says Rain.

Rain grabs the book, and it starts to burn in his hands, causing him to drop the book, which stops burning by the time it hits the floor.

"What the fuck is going on?" says Rain.

The man in front of Rain laughs loud.

"Now you are pissing me off. Laugh at this, bitch," says Rain.

Rain kicks the larger man with surprising force, sending him back against the wall. Rain is there in an instant, landing a right cross, left uppercut, right jab, breaking the man's nose. The man falls to his knees with blood streaming from his nose. Rain raises his right knee, crashing it into the left temple of the man, dropping him to his side. Rain gets ready to punch him some more when the man raises his left hand.

"Stop, stop. All right already. Please don't hit me anymore," says the man.

The man is talking through the blood flowing from his nose into his mouth. He sits against the wall. Rain takes a step back, and the man starts to laugh. Rain cannot believe his eyes as the man seems to levitate to his feet and float across the floor, standing right in front of him. He pulls his hand from his nose, which is clearly broken and deformed toward the right side of his face. Rain watches as his nose stops bleeding and heals completely. The man is standing in front of him like he was never struck at all.

"My turn," says the man.

The man punches Rain dead center his chest, and Rain flies backward. Rain did not feel a thing. It did not hurt at all, and he seems to be flying backward in slow motion. He can see the man approaching him, but he cannot move. The man punches Rain in the face, and this changes his trajectory. He is now flying backward but at a downward angle. Rain still cannot move, and he watches the man hop to his right foot and kick with his left leg. He kicks Rain on his lower back underneath his right rib cage, changing Rain's trajectory again. Now he is flying up the stairway at the closed cellar door. Rain still cannot move, and still he seems to be moving in slow motion. He can see himself approaching the door, but he cannot move.

Just as he is about to hit the door, reality hits him in real time. Rain crashes through the door, flying into the top row of cabinets in the kitchen. He falls to the ground with his nose gushing blood. His ribs on his lower back hurt so bad; it hurts to breathe. He is coughing blood at a scary rate from his nose, and the floor is splattered with way more of his blood than he cares to see. Rain struggles to get up, and he sees the man walking up the stairs. Rain heads out the glass door toward his armory shed. He can hear the man start to laugh as he tries to get into his shed, but as he grabs the door, the man kicks him from behind. The kick lands on Rain's right ribs again. He flies in slow motion toward the woods, unable to move. The man walks beside him, taunting him with laughter. Rain watches as he floats in slow motion horizontally with the ground. He watches the man walk right beside him and punch him in the face, changing his trajectory. The man moves to where Rain is going and waits for Rain, punching down, hitting Rain in the face again.

Rain hits the ground in real time, and like before, the pain now hits him. He crashes onto the ground headfirst with his nose broken to the left of his face and his right eye swelling almost shut. Blood is dripping from his nose, and Rain stands for the first time in his life, afraid he is about to be beaten to death. He cannot even believe that he, Stormy Rain Clouds, is running in fear, but that is what he is doing. He runs toward the woods, hoping he can lose this predator in the brush. Before he makes it to the woods, he is struck in the left leg, breaking his leg below his knee. This is the first extreme pain Rain feels, sending his heart into a beating race, throbbing pain throughout his body with every beat. Rain falls, screaming. The man picks Rain up by his hair.

"OK, OK, I am no match for you. You don't have to deform me anymore," says Rain.

The man kicks straight up Rain's groin. Rain cries gushing tears from his eyes, and the man simply lets go of his hair, and he falls limp to the ground. Rain tries to stand using his right arm to gain lift until the man kicks Rain's forearm, breaking it in half. Rain is crying not because of the pain. He is already past the point of feeling pain. His body is in complete shock, but he knows his body cannot heal from the damage being done to him. He knows he is dying; this is very scary to Rain, and he cannot stop his tears knowing this is how he is going to die.

"Stop. Why are you doing this to me?" cries Rain.

Rain struggles up to his good leg and hops, trying to get away, knowing he can't. The man walks beside him, studying him, searching for a part of Rain's body to crush and break. He kicks rain in the right thigh so hard he breaks Rain's thigh bone right in half. Before Rain falls to the ground, the man grabs his left arm and breaks his elbow over his knee. Rain falls to the ground, broken, unable to move in unimaginable pain all throughout his body. The man kneels beside Rain and slaps his cheek slowly but hard. Rain coughs as he tries to breathe splattering blood from his torn mouth. Some of his ribs have been broken and splintered into his lungs, causing more blood to spew as he tries to talk.

"Who are you? If you want to kill me, then just kill me. You want to torture me. Why?" says Rain.

The man grasps the book in his right hand and smacks Rain over the head with it.

"I don't want to torture you. I actually respect you a lot. You are the most valuable man I have ever met. Fortunately for me, you never knew what you had in this book. You never knew that by sealing this book and its key, you prevented me from knowing or finding its whereabouts. It has taken me five long years or longer now to track down this book. Because of that, I could not pursue my favorite activity, and that is sexual conquest. This book is mine. This book is a complete history of my life and all my personal conquests written by my personal hand. This book is magic to a mortal human like you, but you never knew that," says the man.

"So you are not mortal. You are the god of the Egengyns?" says Rain.

"Well, sort of. I am mortal, however, I have been granted eternal life by my god Lucifer. You see, in this book is a complete account of all the lives taken by me to extend my life. I take life and steal its youth. This, of course, extends my life indefinitely. As far as the Egengyns are concerned, I'll tell you a little secret. Most of the Egengyns are, were, and always will be nothing more than a bunch of illiterate, ignorant mercenaries that will kill and take life for any reason. Of course, I promised them eternal life, but only stupid people would believe in such things. Now I kill for a reason, and that is to extend my personal life, which was granted to me by my god Lucifer. He can grant such things I cannot," says the man.

"Are you the one they call Glamfury?" asks Rain.

The man smiles like the sound of his name is the sweetest music to his ears.

"I am Glamfury, but don't make me mad or I become Glamfurious," says Glamfury.

Rain can see Glamfury's head turn red. Short, thick, pointed horns extend from the left and right top side of his head. His eyes are a brilliant deep blue, contrasting beautifully with the deep red of his skin. Flames are about his head like he is on fire. The red and flames disappear, and the human man smiles, looking at Rain.

"Well, Rain, I have to say it was a pleasure playing with you. Now I have my book back and I can get back to my work. My work with you is done now, but I want you to know it was a true pleasure playing with you," says Glamfury.

Glamfury stands and starts to walk away. Rain watches, still unable to move. He can move, but the pain is excruciating. Rain tries to move and ends up coughing blood. It seems like every bone in his body is broken, and he struggles just to roll his head back and forth. Glamfury has walked out of sight, and Rain struggles to straighten his legs and arms. Glamfury walks back into view, calling Rain's attention.

"Oh, by the way, I said I did not want to torture you—that does not mean I do not want to kill you," says Glamfury.

Glamfury starts to laugh, and Rain watches him walk out of sight again. The ground between Rain and the woods starts to rumble and break apart. Rain can see the head of a huge lizard rising from the earth. It is flame red and looks just like the kind of lizard he saw eat Marlene at her house. It's the same kind of lizard he saw eat Ajaunta's kids in the fire. The lizard rises from the ground. It is huge and walks right out of the earth. It is walking toward the woods using its tongue to sniff the air. It walks in a circle, letting its tongue guide it to Rain, who can barely move. Rain tries to crawl. He tries to get up. He does everything he can to try and make his way back to his shed. He fights the pain, knowing if he does not get into his shed, it will eat him whole. Both his legs are broken. Both his arms are broken. Some of his ribs are broken, and he tries as hard as he can to get to the shed. There is just no way he can move fast enough. The lizard gets his scent, and it is heavy with blood. The lizard homes in, scooping Rain in its tongue, pulling him into its mouth. Rain screams being pulled to the teeth pointing toward the back of its mouth. It bites Rain, and the sticky tongue licks Rain's chest, pulling him deeper into its mouth. His arms and legs are crushed by the powerful bites, and his broken body is drawn to the gullet and swallowed. Rain's eyes start to burn as digestive juices start to break down the softer parts of his body. He is drowning in the stomach acid that is already beginning to digest his body. Before he loses consciousness, he can hear his name being called. It is a muffled sound, and he thinks heaven is calling him home.

"Rain, Rain, Rain."

He can hear his name being called louder and louder and louder. He feels his right ankle being grabbed, and he his pulled from the stomach of the lizard. He is pulled right out of its stomach and lands on the ground. Amazingly, he can stand up and sees the lizard lying dead on the ground. He turns to see Smoke standing there with a sword. Smoke grabs Rain by both his shoulders and starts to shake him.

"Rain, Rain, Rain. Come on, Rain, wake up," says Smoke.

Rain opens his eyes, taking a deep breath. He is all sweaty, and Smoke is shaking him. He looks around to see he is in a sitting position on the couch just the way he was when he fell asleep.

"Smoke, Smoke, I'm still in your house. I had another dream. Holy shit, Smoke. I can't tell what is real and what is dream anymore. Where is Ajaunta? She was sleeping right here beside me," says Rain.

"I don't know. Bailey is gone too. You were screaming in your sleep, and it woke me up. Bailey went to bed with me, and now she is gone, so is Ajaunta. I don't know where they went. You were having one hell of a nightmare. I never heard you make a sound in your sleep before, and we slept in some pretty scary war zones. Whatever you were dreaming about was so scary it woke me up," says Smoke.

"I saw him. I saw him in my dream," says Rain.

"Who?" says Smoke.

"Glamfury, the god of the Egengyns. He was the man you shot at, at the cabin. You remember the books we got at that barracks in Egypt? Those were his books, and he used me in my dream to find where I was keeping my book. Then when he found it, he kicked the shit out of me. He knows where it is. We have to get to my house. We have to go get the book before he gets it. I was reading the book you had. It was right here on the arm of the couch when I fell asleep. Where is it?" says Rain.

"I don't know. You had it. You don't think he was here. You don't think he got it?" says Smoke.

"I don't know, but we have to get to my house and see if my book is there. Come on, let's go," says Rain.

Chapter 14

Intimidation

"I don't like that fucker. He tried intimidating me in my dream, and he did. I don't like that shit. That's for wimps, not me. How did Ajaunta and Bailey both get out of here without either one of us waking up? We must be getting old," says Rain.

"Old and slow. It's still only three in the morning. I can't believe Bailey got up and left without saying a word. She must still be in a lot of discomfort from those gunshot wounds. If they did leave, how did they leave?" says Smoke.

Smoke walks into the kitchen.

"Are you shitting me?" says Smoke.

Smoke walks out the front door and looks for his car. He walks back to Rain, who is standing in the doorway.

"They took my car. Can you believe that shit? They took my car. Fucking bitches," says Smoke.

Rain turns off the lights and walks out, closing the door behind him.

"Come on, let's get to my house and see if my book is still there. I am the only one who knows the combination. Even if this guy can find the safe, he can't get into it. Come on," says Rain.

Smoke says, "Hold on a second." He runs into his house for a moment and runs back out, locking up behind him. He gets into Rain's car, and they head off into the night back to Rain's house.

"Where do you think the girls went to? I can't believe they would leave and not tell us. I can't believe they stole my car," says Smoke.

"Right now, we have to worry about this Glamfury guy. In my dream, he was bad. He was able to move crazy fast. I was defenseless against him. I keep seeing those demon lizards to. There are like three different kinds of them. Lizards, men that wear coconut masks—they have normal human bodies, but their heads are just skulls if you take the mask off them—and then there are these humanoid creatures with these huge bills on the front of their face like a huge toucan. Have you been having any strange dreams? Have you seen any of these creatures, or have you seen Glamfury in any of your dreams?" asks Rain as he drives through the night.

"I have been having bad dreams, but I really can't remember them. I know they are bad, and at times, it's like I keep trying to remember what was happening, but I can't ever remember. It's very strange how vividly you remember your dreams and then replay them and tell me about them. It's really weird how this guy seems to be controlling you in your dreams. Aren't you supposed to be the dominant person in your own dreams?" says Smoke.

"I don't know what the fuck is going on, but you have to help me figure out what is happening," says Rain.

"No problem, we will figure out what is going on," says Smoke.

"Did you ever read that book you got in Egypt? I think I read some of it in my dream last night, but I can't remember any of it. I can't remember any of it at all. I know I tried to read it when I first got it. You remember I found that piece of lava that I thought was a key to open the book?" says Rain.

"Yeah, I remember it," says Smoke.

"Well, one time, I was able to fit the key into the top of the book, and it started to burn. Fucking A. It started to burn. I dropped the book, and the key fell out of the cover, and the book stopped burning. I sealed the book and the key and put them in a safe in my house, so I never actually saw or read what was in the book. In my dream last night, Glamfury saw where I hid the book. He said because I put it in an airtight bag, he could not find it. In my dream, I took it out, and he homed right in on it. Did you ever read any of what was in the book you had?" asks Rain again.

Smoke rubs his face.

"I swear I read it. I thought I read it a few times, but I can't remember what it said at all. I wonder where it is now. Rain, where are you going?

Even though I can't see much of anything since it is so dark out, but where the hell are we?" says Smoke.

Rain leans forward, looking straight ahead, and he looks over at Smoke with a very puzzled look on his face.

"That's a good question. I don't know where the fuck we are. Am I lost? I don't even know where we are," says Rain.

Rain slows down, looking for a street sign or another road to gain his bearings. It is very dark out, and there are no streetlights, no signs, no nothing, just a straight road that they have been following for a while now. Rain slows down and puts his head out the window.

"Well, one thing is for sure, it sure is humid out here tonight," says Rain.

Literally two seconds after he says that, it starts to rain. It starts to rain hard, and they roll up the windows.

"I don't know where we are," says Rain.

"Well, drive on until we get somewhere. I mean, we can't be lost," says Smoke.

A huge hand or paw with long, thick, sharp talons slams the windshield and drags its nails across the glass, making the most horrific sounds, scaring the crap out of both of them.

"What the fuck was that?" says Rain.

"I don't know. It looked like a huge crocodile paw. How the hell can that be?" says Smoke.

The paw shatters the passenger window, grabbing Smoke by his right shoulder, digging its talons deep in his shoulder. He screams, grabbing at the talons, digging into his flesh, trying to pull them out.

"Rain, get it off me. Get it off me!" screams Smoke.

Rain opens the center console where he has a knife, and he starts stabbing the arm. He can hear a very large creature cry out when he stabs it. Unfortunately, it does not let go of Smoke; it pulls him right out the window in an instant.

"Raaaiiiiiiinnnnnnnnnnnnnnn!" yells Smoke as his voice sounds further and further away. Rain stops, gets out of his car, and runs around the car, yelling for his friend.

"Smoke, Smoke, where are you?" yells Rain.

"Rain, help me. Help me. It's got me, Rain!" cries Smoke.

The rain is pouring, and Rain can barely hear Smoke still crying out for him. Rain runs after the sound of Smoke calling for him. He runs right into the tall grass and into the woods. He is drenched from the wet foliage and the pouring rain. It is dark, and he cannot see a thing. He is slipping and falling, getting hit with branches and stepping in small pools of water. He is following the voice of Smoke, which seems pretty far away and getting further. Rain runs faster, trying to catch up with Smoke, when he runs face-first into a very thick branch, splitting his lip and knocking him down.

"Smoke!" cries Rain.

Rain rises to his knees, feeling his fattening lip. He can taste the blood that is dripping from his lip and bites torn cheek dangling in his mouth.

"Smoke!" he cries, feeling he let his friend die, feeling he did not do enough to save Smoke.

"Rain, Rain," calls Smoke.

Rain hears Smoke calling for him, and he is not far away. Rain gets up and runs toward the sound of his friend.

"Smoke, I am here, I am here. Smoke, where are you?" calls Rain.

Rain runs into a clearing, and he can see. He cannot see well, but he looks up, and even though it is raining, there are breaks in the clouds. The moon is out, and without the dense cover of tree branches and leaves, he can see fairly well. He can see that there is a large pond maybe seven or eight yards across. There is tall grass all around the pond and then forest around that.

"Smoke, Smoke!" yells Rain.

He can see the tall grass flattened where his friend was probably dragged into the pond. There are waves rippling from the center of the pond, and, of course, the raindrops are causing splashing all around. Rain looks at the center of the pond, calling for Smoke, who rises from the water. He is in the mouth of a huge crocodile—no, it's not a crocodile. The head looks like a crocodile and a big one, but its neck sits on shoulders, and the head faces forward. Its arms are humanoid except for the paws, which are crocodilian. It throws Smoke by flipping its head toward Rain, and he flies over Rain, landing just before the tree line. Rain runs to Smoke, helping him to a sitting position. Smoke screams in pain, and Rain can see his chest and stomach have been crushed. There are puncture wounds all about his chest, back, and legs. Smoke cries as Rain tries to help him up.

"No, Rain. I can't go on. The pain is too much. It crushed my ribs, and I can't breathe. Rain, run, go, get out of here," says Smoke.

"I'm not leaving you here to face that thing alone," says Rain.

"I can't make it, Rain. You still can. It got me. I can't outrun it," says Smoke.

"Then I will fight it," says Rain.

Rain hears its deep grumbling voice as it walks from the pond toward them. He looks at this huge humanoid crocodile. Its head is four feet long and very wide with lots of long sharp teeth. Its head looks at him as it walks like a human from the pond. It's huge, nearly seven feet tall. Its abdomen looks just like a crocodile, round and tough. Its legs are humanlike with huge talons for toes, just like its fingers are talons designed to tear, rip, and grab flesh. It even has a long, thick crocodile tail. It stands on the bank of the pond and grumbles, looking at Rain, who stands between Smoke and the creature, pointing his knife at it. Rain looks around to see if there is anything he can use. He is looking for a long stick he can use like a staff. He finds nothing, and the creature starts to walk at him.

"Come on, motherfucker. Come on," says Rain, flipping his knife from hand to hand. The creature raises its right hand, ready to swing at Rain, when Rain hears whistling—loud whistling coming from the woods. The creature steps back from Rain. It walks backward into the water and lowers into the pond under the water, out of sight.

"What is that? I hear it, but where is it coming from?" says Smoke.

"I don't know, but it scared that croc man back into the water," says Rain.

Rain is looking across the pond, scanning the tree line as good as he can in the rain and poor lighting, when he hears Smoke faintly calling his name.

"Yeah, Smoke, I'm right here," says Rain.

Rain turns around to see Glamfury has Smoke by the throat. He is holding Smoke above his head with his left arm. Smoke is too weak to fight back, and he holds Glamfury's wrist with his hands to keep as much pressure off his throat as possible. He is just barely able to breathe.

"Rain, have I told you how much I like playing with you? I'm serious, you are the best. This guy here is, well, what is his name? Ohhh, yeah, Smoke. He is just not as much fun as you are. I mean, look at this guy. There is no fight in him," says Glamfury.

Glamfury starts to crush Smoke's throat.

"Stop, stop, let him go. I'm the one you want to play with, right? Come on, here I am. Let him go and come play with me," says Rain.

"I don't think so," says Glamfury.

Glamfury starts to crush Smoke's throat. Rain draws his right arm back and throws his knife, striking Glamfury in his right eye. The knife penetrates hilt deep until the hilt is flush with Glamfury's brow. Glamfury falls backward, dropping Smoke.

"Smoke, Smoke," calls Rain.

Rain runs to Smoke, seeing he is still alive, and sits him up.

"So that is Glamfury. Well, now I've seen him twice. He has a hell of a grip," says Smoke.

"Yeah, that motherfucker is fast too," says Rain.

Rain and Smoke see Glamfury rise like his body is on a board to a standing position. He grabs the knife with his right hand and pulls it from his eyeball.

"Nice throw, Rain. That's a good arm you have," says Glamfury.

Glamfury throws the knife so fast neither of them can see him throw it. The knife enters Smoke's chest, cutting right through his heart. Rain pulls the knife out, but the damage is done.

"Rain, don't take no shit from this motherfucker. Fuck him up with all your strength," says Smoke.

Rain is holding Smoke, and he can feel Smoke's body go limp, losing its life. Rain leans him back in the rain and wet grass, knowing there is nothing he can do. Rain stands looking at Glamfury and swings his arm. Glamfury twists his body, watching to see the knife fly by him, but it does not. He looks back at Rain to see Rain thrust the knife into his left eye hilt deep. Rain pulls the knife out and thrusts it under his chin up into his brain. This causes Glamfury to quiver and gush blood from his throat and mouth as he makes disgusting gurgling sounds. Rain pulls the knife again and thrusts it into Glamfury's left temple hilt deep, and still, Glamfury does not fall. Rain pulls the knife out and steps back. He cannot believe Glamfury is still standing. Both his eyes have been destroyed, and his brain has been punctured four times. Rain looks to see Smoke lying dead in the wet grass, and this infuriates him. He steps at Glamfury and kicks him straight on. Glamfury catches Rain's foot with both hands and begins to laugh. Rain is in a pretty compromising position now. He is hopping on his right foot, wishing he did not kick at Glamfury. Rain looks at Glamfury and cannot believe what he sees. Glamfury has both eye sockets hollowed out with blood and puss running from them. There is a hole below his chin where he was stabbed. There is a hole in his left temple gushing blood and brain matter. The constant flow of rain makes his whole head look like it is constantly bleeding and gushing brains.

"You see, Rain, this is why I like you best. You are not like your friend there. You are a fighter. You will not give up. You will not die. You will do anything to protect your friends, and that is why I cannot kill them. I need to keep them alive so I can intimidate you," says Glamfury.

"There is no intimidating me. You may be faster, stronger, and better at fighting, but you will never intimidate me. That is not a part of me. So if your goal is to intimidate me, then you lose. If your goal is to kill me, then get on with it. Obviously, I can't hurt you. I have put holes in your head, and still you come back like nothing has happened to you. This is all just a dream, so quit fucking around, quit procrastinating, and do what you have to do," says Rain.

"Oh, no, this is no dream. I am hell on earth, and this is just the start of your pain. You and Smoke killed all my disciples, or did you forget about that? I'm not just going to kill you—I am going to torment you. I am going to break you down cell by cell, molecule by molecule. You will beg for death long before your pain is through. You will die a thousand deaths before I even think about killing you. You will watch your friends die over and over because that is what I do," says Glamfury.

Glamfury disappears, and Rain sits by his fallen friend. The scene is dark with heavy rain and just enough moonlight so he can see a little. Glamfury charges through the wet grass and is on Rain in an instant, grabbing him around the throat. Rain is pulled face-to-face with the eyeless representative from hell and raised in the air as Glamfury stands with Rain in his grasp. Glamfury waves his free hand toward the pond and then uses it to cover the hole under his chin. He whistles surprisingly loud. The water begins to swell as the croc man rises from the water. It walks in humanoid fashion until it reaches the land when it lowers to all fours and grabs the body of Smoke with its huge head. It chomps down on Smoke, dragging him back into the pond. Rain is held so tightly around the throat he cannot even call for his friend, who is dragged under the water. Glamfury laughs and tightens his grip around Rain's throat, choking the life out of him. Glamfury laughs louder and louder.

"This is nothing. This is nothing but playing in the rain," says Glamfury.

Glamfury laughs loud, holding Rain by the throat. He holds Rain up as high as he can, squeezing his throat until Rain falls unconscious.

Chapter 15

Will This Dream Ever End?

Glamfury throws Rain, and even though he is unconscious, it is like he is watching the scene from far away. He lands in the tall grass next to the edge of the pond. The impact with the ground, though awkward, is relatively soft because of the wet, muddy conditions. It is not a hard painful impact but still wakes him from his dream. Rain sits up in his bed. He feels his chest, head, and arms. He is not sweaty or breathing hard. He looks at the nightstand to the side of his bed, seeing it is 5:30 a.m. The morning sun is bringing its light into his room, which is limited, thanks to his curtains being closed. He stands up.

"Rain," says a female voice.

This startles him, and he turns to see a girl in his bed.

"What the fuck? What the fuck is this shit? How did you get here?" says Rain.

Rain is blown away to see Ajaunta sit up in his bed.

"How the hell did you get in my room? What the hell is going on here? This is a dream, isn't it? I am in a constant never-ending dream, aren't I?" says Rain.

"Rain, so am I. I don't know how I got here. The last thing I remember, I was with you and we were on a couch in Smoke's house. I fell asleep, and I was dreaming about that evil man. I can't resist him. I love him in my dreams. He seduces me, and I can't resist him. Why can't I resist him? He killed my husband and my kids. In my dreams, he seduces me, he loves me, and he kills you and Smoke. He has done this to me so many times now, and I can't stop him. Why is he doing this to me and to you?" says Ajaunta.

"First of all, we have to figure out how to get out of this never-ending dream. I mean, this can't be real. I have had like a month's worth of dreams without waking one time as far as I can tell. We have to wake up. We have to figure out how to get back to the real world and out of this dream," says Rain.

"How do we do that? Is everything still normal in the real world? Are my husband and children really alive and I'm just dreaming they are gone?" says Ajaunta.

"I don't know. I don't even know how I got back in my house, and here I am in my bed with you. Wait a minute—the book. I wonder if the book is still here. He found it in a past dream, but still he did not know how to get into the safe. I wonder if the book is still here," says Rain.

"I remember that from my dream—the book you and Smoke had talked about. I remember you were reading a book on the couch before I fell asleep. I had a dream where that man Glamfury held me by the throat, and he made me watch a snake man eat you and Smoke. Then he made me love him, and I could not resist him. He was laughing at me, and still I could not resist him," says Ajaunta.

Ajaunta starts to cry, and she runs to Rain, hugging him.

"Rain, I need you to get me out of this dream and back to my family," says Ajaunta.

Rain is instantly and uncontrollably excited as Ajaunta's nude body flush with his causes his excitement to rise until their genitals are touching. Ajaunta looks up, very attracted to Rain, and he looks down, and they stare at each other quietly for a moment. Rain slowly kisses her, and she closes her eyes. They both enjoy moments of relaxed lip sensation, holding each other as their blood warms their excited bodies. Their genitals swell in excitement as they unconsciously move to the bed and lie back slowly. Ajaunta wraps her legs around Rain as they kiss. Her nether regions become very wet as she squeezes, slides, and rubs all over Rain's excitement. She is lost in the kiss and reaches down with her right hand, moving Rain into her slippery excitement. She breathes heavily onto Rain's kiss as her excitement shoots through the stratosphere, and she does not want it to stop. She wraps her arms around Rain, loving his thrusts and movements. She loves his kisses and the way he squeezes her chest into his. She wraps her legs around his hips, squeezing, grinding, loving the excitement until she is out of breath. She relaxes with an uncontrollable smile, showing off her satisfaction. Her smile is unwavering as Rain continues strong and hard until his smile is as big as hers. They both lie breathing heavily, laughing with each other in unified gratification. Rain starts to get up, and Ajaunta grabs him.

"Wait, wait a minute, don't move. Not yet. It's going to make a mess when you pull out of me. I know because I could feel that big time," says Ajaunta.

"I have wanted to do that all my life, you know," says Rain.

"Well, that was good. My husband and I, we love each other, but we really don't love each other like that much anymore. I can't even remember the last time we—well, it's neither here nor there. It's just the way we have grown," says Ajaunta.

"It's not like we are kids anymore. I'm sure you remember the all-night sex marathons. You are the most beautiful woman I have ever seen in my life. I swear I just said that to you not too long ago. It must have been in a dream, I guess. Anyway, my point is if I were your husband, I would still be loving you physically. Why I never made you my girl, I don't know. You were the only girl I ever wanted to be with in my whole life—I mean, the only girl I ever wanted to marry, that is. Well, what do you think?" says Rain.

"What?" she asks.

"Do you think we can get up and make it to the bathroom attached to each other and not make a mess all over the place—you know, not leak all over?" says Rain.

Ajaunta laughs.

"I think we are too old to even try. You are just going to have to pull out of me, and whatever leaks all over leaks all over. I wonder if a girl can get pregnant in a dream because you certainly filled me up. I could feel that, and it was amazing," says Ajaunta.

Rain pulls out of Ajaunta and stands up.

"Augh. I can feel it," laughs Ajaunta.

Rain goes to the bathroom and comes back with a warm washcloth. She is still lying on the bed, and he hands the cloth to her. He watches as she washes off and gets up.

"What are you looking at?" she says.

"You, all of you. You are so beautiful," says Rain.

"I was beautiful in school. Now I have had four kids and I'm fat. Don't lie to me," says Ajaunta.

"Please, we are, what, forty-five, fifty years old. You will always be beautiful," says Rain.

Ajaunta sighs.

"Oh, Rain, come on and wash my fat ass for me," says Ajaunta.

"OK," says Rain.

Ajaunta runs a hot bath, and they talk in the bathroom while the tub fills. They get in forgetting about the situation they are in while they feel and caress each other in the warm water. They get out, dry off, and Rain finds some sweatpants and a shirt for Ajaunta to wear.

"Well, one thing is for sure, dream or not, I am starving. Do you have anything to eat around here?" says Ajaunta.

"I should. The refrigerator should be full. Help yourself to anything you like," says Rain.

"Are you hungry? Do you want me to make you anything?" says Ajaunta.

"Sure, there should be eggs, bacon, toast. I have to check something out that is bugging me," says Rain.

"What?" asks Ajaunta.

"You remember in that dream where we were on the couch and you fell asleep? I was reading the book that Smoke had," says Rain.

"Yeah, I remember," says Ajaunta.

"Smoke got that book from a barracks in Egypt. That was a book we got from the Egengyns. I got another book. I believe these books were somehow important to Glamfury. He came to me in one of my dreams and saw where I keep the book I have. He followed me in one of my dreams right to the book, but still he can't get into the safe. I need to make sure the book is still here. I have not read it yet. I have to go check it out," says Rain.

"OK, I will be in the kitchen," says Ajaunta.

"OK," says Rain.

Rain heads down into the cellar, while Ajaunta looks in the refrigerator. He feels a little nervous heading down into the cellar and looks around cautiously like he expects Glamfury to be waiting for him. Rain walks around, looking in the closet and behind the furniture just to make sure he is alone. He walks to the safe and opens it up. The book he is looking for is in the safe still sealed in the plastic bag just as he put it years ago. He sits on the couch and puts the book on the coffee table. He remembers the last time he figured out how to get the lava key into the cover of the book, it started on fire. Opening the bag, dropping the key and book from the bag, he looks them over, apprehensive as to whether he should try putting the key in the book. He tries to open the book, but the lava still has the book securely shut and it will not open. He can see exactly how to fit the key into the cover of the book, but he wants to set the book on something fireproof just in case it starts on fire. He has a metal shelf in his armory shed, so he carries the book and key up into the kitchen. Ajaunta is cooking eggs and steak.

"Damn, that smells good," says Rain.

"I hope you don't mind. I don't even know why, for some reason, eggs and steak sounded good to me," says Ajaunta.

"I don't mind at all. I will be back in a few minutes," says Rain.

"You found the book you were looking for?" says Ajaunta.

"Yes, I did. I need to check some things out," says Rain.

"All right, I will be here eating, hopefully not alone," says Ajaunta.

"I will be back in a few minutes. You know what, steak sounds pretty awesome right now. Make me one if you can," says Rain.

"OK," says Ajaunta.

"I'll be right back," says Rain.

Rain heads into his armory shed. He is very pleasantly surprised to see all his guns and ammunition are right where they are supposed to be. His workbench is metal, and he sits on his stool, setting the book on the metal bench. He fits the lava key into the cover, and the book starts on fire. Rain watches as flames rise from the book with no smoke. He puts his hands by the flames, and it sure is hot, much too hot for him to touch. He watches as the book burns, but the paper of the book is unharmed. Rain is mesmerized watching the flaming book. He waves his hands over and around the book, and it feels like normal fire, but there is no smoke. After a few minutes, the book starts to move and shake. The flames stop. The lava on the cover of the book has fallen over the corners of the book like melted wax. The key lifts from the book on three growing pieces of lava that look like stalagmites. It grows up about two inches, and the lava covering the book cover pops and snaps, breaking apart, and the key falls on the book. All the lava has broken apart. Rain picks up the book, and all the lava falls in pieces with only the key remaining intact. He can now see the book free of lava for the first time. The front and back cover is thick brown leather. The binding is very high quality, and the book is thick. The cover reads "Glamfury: Eternal Women." Rain opens the book, which is nine inches wide by thirteen inches high. It is very thick, and the pages are a type of cloth that seem to be very durable. Rain looks over the first page, but the penmanship is written in a language he cannot read. He flips through the pages, seeing it seems to be written in different languages. Near the end of the book, it is written in English, and just as he starts to read it, he hears Ajaunta call for him.

"Rain, your steak is ready. Come and get it if you want it while it's hot," she says.

He is starving, and he closes the book, putting it back in the bag along with the key. He seals it and heads to the kitchen. Ajaunta is eating steak and eggs.

"Goddamn, it smells good in here," says Rain.

He sets the book on the table and sits down to a fantastic breakfast. The two of them eat quietly enjoying eggs, steak, orange juice, toast, and jam. Ajaunta even made hash browns.

"Wow, you are a hell of a cook," says Rain.

"It kind of happens when you have four kids. It's automatic," says Ajaunta.

"Well, I sure do appreciate it. This is fantastic," says Rain.

"Thank you. Maybe you will have to make me orgasm in the morning more often now," says Ajaunta.

"I think that can be arranged," says Rain.

They laugh and devour their breakfast like they haven't eaten in days. Rain starts to do the dishes immediately after they eat. He does not like dishes left in his sink. Ajaunta helps him get the dishes washed and in the strainer.

"So were you able to look over that book at all? Is it what you were looking for?" says Ajaunta.

"Well, most of it is written in a foreign language or languages, but some of it near the end is in English. I did not really read through it that much. Just a quick glance. The cover is in English, but it looks like different languages are written in the book. It's really weird," says Rain.

"Well, I am going to sit down for a little bit. I stuffed myself," says Ajaunta.

"Yeah, me too," says Rain.

They go to the living room and sit down. Rain starts to look through the book, and Ajaunta sits next to him.

"Wow, that looks like a very old book," she says.

"I know. I wish I could read this." Rain flips through the pages. "You see, it looks like it is written in a different language here." Rain flips through more pages. "And this here is a different language too. It's like that all the way through until here, where it is written in English, you see?" says Rain.

"Yes, I see. It's very odd. I wonder if different people were writing in this book. There must have been. It looks like this book is hundreds of years old. Look at this cloth they use for paper. The writing must have been written with a quill or something like that. Then later in the book, it seems to have been written with a more modern writing utensil," says Ajaunta.

The room starts to shake. Ajaunta spreads her arms and legs on the couch.

"What was that?" says Ajaunta.

"I don't know. Here we go again," says Rain.

They both hear laughter throughout the living room, and the whole house starts to tilt from one side to the other. All the furniture start to slide from one side of the room to the other. Rain and Ajaunta are on the couch, riding it back and forth in the living room as it slides from one side of the room to the other. The front door swings open, and Smoke peeks in, holding on to the wall. He is soak and wet, and rain is pouring in the door. It sounds like a hurricane outside.

"Come on, guys, you have to get out of there. He's here. Glamfury is here. Get out of the house before it collapses on you. Come on, get out," says Smoke.

Just then, the door slams shut. Smoke dodges just in time not to lose his head, but he is not quick enough to pull his hands from the door edge, and the door slams shut, cutting off all eight of his fingers, and they fall on the floor. The house stops shaking. Ajaunta and Rain can hear Glamfury laugh as he rises from the center of the floor. Rain rises from the couch and tries to punch Glamfury right in the nose, but his whole body freezes stiff just inches before he makes contact with Glamfury.

"You just won't learn, will you, Rain? You are my toy, nothing more. What is this here? Well, take a look at this beautiful little honey," says Glamfury.

Glamfury slides onto the couch next to Ajaunta, rubbing his hand up her leg, abdomen, breast, neck, and down her arm.

"Rain, get him off me. Rain!" cries Ajaunta.

Rain is moving as fast as he can, but he is in slow motion, and there is nothing he can do. He tries to talk, but his words are just long slurs making no sense at all. Glamfury stands, picking Ajaunta up and putting her over his shoulder, slapping her ass, and smiling at Rain as he steps to the door. Rain can feel he is moving faster but cannot catch up with Glamfury.

"Don't worry, Rain, I will take good care of this little treat. Oh, did you want to say something?" says Glamfury.

Glamfury flicks his fingers at Rain, and he can move at normal speed.

"Let her go!" yells Rain. Glamfury jumps out the door into the darkness, and Rain can see neither of them anymore.

Chapter 16

Burial at Sea

Rain runs to the door and grabs the wall as his house tilts upward. He is hanging on to the wall by his doorframe as his house starts to tilt up in the air. Water starts to run into his house, filling it up. He holds on as water flows over him, and his house now seems to be standing on the back side of the house. The front door is where the roof usually is. His house starts to settle back to normal with water running in and out the door about knee high. He looks out the door wide-eyed to see his house is floating in the ocean, and there is a severe storm going on. As if that is not bad enough, his house is starting to sink. The water is swelling to enormous waves many times larger than his house. The wind is blowing furiously, and Rain is forced to jump into the ocean as his house is about to sink. Rain is a very good swimmer, but this is not a situation anyone would want to be in.

Rain uses his survival training by taking his pants off and tying the cuffs in knots and then raising the waist in the air and twisting it, creating a fairly effective life preserver, which he puts over his shoulders, allowing him to float with his head above the water. Still, the heavy wind and gusting waters are choking him and spinning him all about. He takes his shirt off and ties the cuffs together. He puts them under his arms and holds the bottom of the shirt above the water, creating an air bubble in the shirt, giving him added buoyancy. Rain knows many techniques by tying his pants and his shirt together, giving him a makeshift life preserver. That is all good and well, but the conditions here are much too severe. He cannot help but gulp large quantities of water every minute or so, and he will have to keep refilling his clothes with a new supply of air, which takes a lot of energy.

He does the best he can, and after an hour, he can already feel his body tired and weak. He is constantly gagging from the cold salt water, and his muscles are fatigued to the point where the swells and the currents pull him under. He is sinking with his arms above his head. His clothes are blown across the water, and he sinks with his eyes open, waiting as long as he can without instinctively having to breathe. He watches the cold dark water, and only his eyes have the strength to move. He feels the water crushing his body as he sinks deeper and deeper. He cannot believe he has not gulped for air yet.

Then he sees what he believes will be his last vision. He can see far off as a dark green serpent slithers effortlessly through the water toward him. It has wide fluorescent green eyes. It has fins that seem to waiver like a kite tail from the length of its back. It has arms instead of fins extending from the sides of its body, which at times extend, showing the webbed fingers, giving the serpent great maneuverability in the water. It flashes its large teeth, and Rain knows he has no chance. He watches as the serpent approaches him and in a flash is by him, catching him with one of its arms. Rain screams, not even realizing there is still air in his lungs, which is quickly expelled as the arm of the serpent has hooked fingers with very long, sharp, strong talons at the ends. Rain is hooked right under his right ribs, and the talons tear and break two of his ribs before the serpent breaks the surface of the water, throwing Rain high into the stormy air. He falls back, crashing into the sea like a doll flowing as the current sees fit.

The serpent swims by him, grabbing him by his left ankle, and breaks the surface of the water again, throwing Rain high into the air. Rain falls back to the sea, and the serpent breaches the surface, gliding by Rain in slow motion, swinging its tail like a bat right into him. Rain flies over the next huge swell, falling into the turbulent ocean. He hits the water with his eyes open. He can see the bubbles and hear the sounds of his body gulping for air. He has no strength to tread water; he is a toy being played with by this predator. He still has the sense of touch, and he can tell he has just been hit by a Mack Truck out here in the ocean. The light is bad, but he can see everything turn red, which is obviously his blood. His body is thrashed back and forth as his head breaches the water, and he has been bitten by a great white shark. He cannot see it because it hit him from the back, biting below his arms and just below his hips. This takes the serpent by surprise, and Rain can see the serpent swimming right at him very fast.

This is it, finally, thinks Rain, and he closes his eyes. He feels the rush of the water go by him, and then all seems to go quiet. He feels pleasant. He feels calm. His heart is not pounding anymore. His breathing is relaxed. The wind and turbulent current is not thrashing him anymore. He feels the sun warming his body. He feels the salt crystalizing on his skin. He touches his face and opens his eyes. Looking around, he can see he is still in the center of a stormy ocean, but he is on some sort of turtle shell. A very large turtle shell. He stands up, realizing about ten steps in any direction will take him to the end of the shell and back into the ocean. The ocean is swelling, and the waves are huge. For some reason, the shell he is on is calm and not affected by the stormy weather. Rain looks up to see a small ring in the clouds allowing the sun to shine down directly on him. He looks at his ribs to see they are healed. He feels his back, which was torn to pieces by the shark bite, and it is healed as well. He is standing there in his boxer shorts full of energy like nothing has happened at all.

He notices small creatures walking onto the shell from all around the edges, and lots of them. They look like crabs with two very heavy thick claws that look like they can clamp with great power. The odd thing is they walk on two legs like people. Their legs are bowed outward from the shell, and they look very awkward as they walk. It makes them look very cute. They stand about six inches tall and have shells like turtles, humanlike legs to walk on, and crab claws to clamp with. They have eyes that extend up on tentacles reminiscent of a snail. The eyes extend from a turtle head raised from the top of the shell. Rain finds this creature very interesting and bends down to study the closest one. He tries to touch it, seeing if it will hide its claws, head, and legs in its shell like a turtle. It does not. It clamps down on his finger with its claw, crushing it in intense pain.

Rain slams the creature down on the ground repeatedly, trying to rid the creature from his finger. More and more of these creatures are constantly creeping up from the water onto the shell and walking toward Rain. He is now crying because the pain in his finger is so great. He grabs it with his other hand and holds the legs as far from the claws as he can. He slams the heel of his foot as hard as he can three times, finally crushing the creature and releasing the claw from his finger. He stands completely surrounded by hundreds of them now, and he can see they have very small but sharp teeth, and they are flashing them at him. He can hear their claws clamping. He has nowhere to go, and they are on him. He has to move.

Rain takes a few long steps and dives back into the turbulent ocean. He turns to see all the small creatures racing toward the water and start to swim toward him. This is not as menacing as the large eyes that breach the water and look right at Rain. He quickly realizes it is one of these creatures only about sixteen feet long and can probably swallow Rain in a few bites. It starts to swim toward him using its long, thick tail. All the small creatures have the same tail, and they are swimming for Rain. Rain swims as fast as he can, but he is not moving; in fact, the current of the water is pushing him backward. The small creatures cannot catch Rain, but the big one clamps down on his right ankle, almost crushing his bone in agonizing pain. It pulls its large claw back, pulling Rain under the water. He gags, gulping glassfuls of water trying to swim toward the surface with his arms and free leg. He can barely see light as he is pulled downward in the darkening water. His lungs are full of water, and he cannot even try to breathe anymore. He feels his body go limp, and with his last sight, he sees dozens of dolphins swim by him.

He slowly turns his head, watching as the dolphins attack the large turtle, crab, snail, man. The dolphins ram it with their bottle-nose heads over and over until the creature lets go of Rain. The dolphins feast on all the little creatures, scooping them up in their mouths as they swim around. The large creature starts to swim into the depths to avoid all the dolphin attacks, and they push Rain to the surface, where he coughs water over and over, gasping and gulping for air. He catches his breath, but he is right back in the storm, and he will not last long in these conditions.

He sees Smoke standing on two dolphins and holding a leather strap attached to a third dolphin swimming in front of the two Smoke is standing on. They are riding down the huge swell right toward Rain, who cannot believe his eyes. The dolphins swim right by Rain. Smoke leans down, grabs Rain by the shoulder, and flips him up in the air. Like magic, Rain lands behind Smoke and is now standing on two dolphins right at the back of Smoke. They are riding dolphins down the wave, and they are going very fast. All of a sudden, Rain is having a blast.

"Smoke, what the hell is going on? Where the hell did you come from? Hell, where did you go? You've been in the ocean the whole time like me?" says Rain.

Still, the wind is thrashing the water all around, and the rain is pouring. The two yell through the wind and the rain.

"I don't know how, but all of a sudden, my fingers where cut off in the door, and I fell in the ocean. The next thing I know, I'm being eaten by some sort of shark man, and then these dolphins come by and start attacking it. Somehow, they got under my feet and lifted me up. They put reins in my hands, and I can barely hold on to them. Here, you take the reins. Let me stand at the back of you," says Smoke.

Smoke hands the reins to Rain, and the two switch from front to back, standing on the dolphins.

"Holy shit, I can actually steer them by pulling left or right," says Rain.

Rain can hear the voice behind him change. It gets deeper and sounds more menacing.

"Well, that is because I told them the only way they can breathe is if they obey the reins. Ha, ha, ha, ha, ha, ha, ha," says and laughs the odd voice.

Rain turns to see the man behind him is Glamfury. He looks down and sees the heads of the dolphins are Smoke, Ajaunta, and Bailey. They breach the water every few seconds to breathe.

"What have you done to my friends? You have turned them into dolphins?" says Rain.

"No, I have turned them into bait. They are serpent food just like you. Ha, ha, ha, ha, ha, ha, ha, ha, ha, ha," laughs Glamfury.

Glamfury floats backward and up into the dark rainy sky. Rain watches as he floats out of sight, and this brings his attention to the serpent following behind him, breaching the surface of the water every few seconds. It's the same serpent he saw a little while ago, and it's catching up to Rain and the dolphins. Rain grabs the reins and steers to the left. He pulls back on the middle rein so the three dolphins are closer together. The serpent is catching them and strikes at the dolphin with Smoke's head on it. Rain steers left, and the serpent misses with its strike.

"Come on, guys, we have to move fast or this thing is going to eat us," says Rain.

Rain turns to see the serpent has submerged, and he has no idea where it is. He turns his head facing forward to see it rise in the water in front of him. It has caught the middle front dolphin with Ajaunta's head in its mouth. The serpent's arms, which have really long talons at the ends, catch the other two dolphins, and it stops all three dolphins in an instant. Rain flies for fifteen feet before splashing into the turbulent see. He rises just as the swell passes by the serpent. Just before it goes out of sight, Rain sees it bite the dolphin in half with Ajaunta's head on it. Then it bites Bailey's head off the other dolphin.

"Smoke!" yells Rain as the dark sky and rainy air darkens more. The wind is blowing water in his face, and already he has lost his bearings. He is swept away with the current. His only thought now is how long can he hold on yet again. The constant pounding of the water on his body, the constant struggle of trying to stay afloat, the constant gagging and choking on the brackish water, the constant torment thinking he is going to die, thinking his friends are going to die or have died already, are driving him insane. He lies back in the water and relaxes. He lets his mind clear, and he just lies on the water. He starts to sink, and yet again he watches the water as his body falls into the cold dark. It is so much quieter here, so much more peaceful than on the surface where the wind is deafening and the splashing waves are always choking him. He falls, he sinks, he drifts like a rag doll in slow motion.

A hand the size of half a house reaches into the water and scoops Rain into its palm. Rain is lifted from the dark cold. As he gets nearer to the surface, the water is clearer and the sun is shining bright. He can see as he is lifted from the calm fresh water and laid on a warm sandy beach. He watches the hand and arm recede back into the crystal-blue water. Sitting up in the wet sand, the warm waves wash up to his legs and fall back into the ocean. He can see someone walking down the beach toward him. He stands, trying to see who it is.

"Smoke? Is that you? Smoke, it is you," says Rain.

"Smoke, I saw you killed again. This crazy dream will never end," says Rain.

Smoke starts to laugh. He digs his fingernails into the center of his forehead and pulls the skin down his face, neck, and off his shoulders.

"Glamfury, I should have known it would be you," says Rain.

Glamfury starts to laugh as his body starts to thicken and grow wider. The skin mimicking Smoke falls to the ground like rubber. Glamfury's skin is dark, almost black, and his fingers grow thick talons where his fingernails would be normally. His face and muscles grow wider, and he is still human looking but with a very demonic presence, which Rain can really sense.

"All right, Glamfury, I believe you have some sort of devil power about you. Is that what you have been waiting for from me? For me to admit you are some sort of servant of Lucifer himself? I mean, what are you waiting for? You want to kill me, so what are you waiting for? You keep killing me over and over, and just before I die, you bring me back. I can't fight you. I can't do anything to hurt you, so what are you waiting for? Why all the torment? Why the torture, or is that what you get off on? Maybe you can't kill me because this is all a dream? This is a dream, and even though it seems like weeks, I have only been asleep for a few hours, and I am going to wake up soon. Soon, I will be rid of this nightmare, and I probably won't even remember any of it, right?" says Rain.

Glamfury gets visibly mad; he screams into the blue sky.

"You think you can rid yourself of me? You think this is some dream where all you have to do is wake up and I am gone? I am going to torture you. I am going to kill you a hundred times over. I am going to kill your friends. I am going to torture everyone you know until I am satisfied. I am going to haunt you, beat you, and rip your guts out until you beg me to reach into your chest and rip your very soul from your being," says Glamfury.

Rain starts to laugh at Glamfury. He laughs hard, infuriating Glamfury.

"You are some sort of devil, all right, I get it. I don't get why you are after me. There is no reason why you should be after me. I am no devil worshiper. I am no doer of evil. It seems to me those are the types of people you should go for," says Rain.

Glamfury laughs. "That is why I like you the most, Rain. So confident, so strong in your beliefs, so righteous, so delicious. I am going to feast on your youth. You take for granted that when you and your accomplice attacked and killed my disciples, you drew first blood on my collection, giving me free rein on you and all your friends. They are all mine now courtesy of the great Rain and Smoke. I am going to torture you both, and all the lovers you two have had all your lives are mine. Ha, ha, ha! Ha, ha, ha, ha! Ha, ha, ha, ha! You are all mine," says Glamfury.

Glamfury extends his right arm, thrusting his fingers and thumb talons deep into Rain's chest. Rain has never felt such pain. He screams as Glamfury raises him high above his head and squeezes his fingers and thumb together, cracking ribs and cutting vital organs in Rain's chest. Glamfury draws Rain's face eyeball to eyeball with him.

"Rain, your time is near, but now is the time for Smoke to meet his maker, and his maker is not in the heavens. His maker is in hell. Ha, ha, ha! Ha, ha, ha, ha! Ha, ha, ha, ha!" laughs Glamfury.

Glamfury winds and throws Rain like he is a baseball. Rain flies out over the ocean, and the sky turns dark. The clouds thicken and roll in dark, followed by thunder and rain. Rain splashes into the dark swell, which seems a mile high. He is able to reach the surface and gags as the salt water burns his eyes and stings his throat. His chest is killing him, and he is having trouble breathing. The choking water fills his lungs. His arms are weak, and the damage done to his organs by Glamfury is making his struggle to hold on to life come to an end. The current thrashes his body back and forth. He sways to and fro with the current and is pulled under the large swell by a current. He screams underwater, watching the last air bubbles exit his mouth, and that is all. He goes calm, numb, sinking into the dark, and the light fades for the last time. He can hear his heart beating, and it is getting slower and slower and slower until Rain hears and sees no more.

Chapter 17

The House in the Woods

"Come on, Rain, she's in here. I know she is in here. He has her, and he said he was going to kill her," says Bailey.

Rain looks around. It's dark outside, and he has just parked his car in the driveway of a house he is not familiar with. He looks over to see Bailey getting out of the passenger seat of his car.

"Wait, wait! What is going on? Where are we? Who is in there? Who is going to be killed?" says Rain.

"Rain, have you been sleeping? Come on, he's got Ajaunta, remember? He took her from the couch right next to you. He told us if we weren't here by midnight, he was going to kill her, remember? Smoke is on his way. He said he was getting some serious firepower, and you were all ready to smash Glamfury's face in with your bare hands, remember?" says Bailey.

"Oh, yeah, that's right. Let's kill that fucker," says Rain.

Rain gets out of his car and looks at his watch. It reads 11:50 p.m. The house is a one-floor ranch with woods around the back and sides of the house. It sits only about fifteen feet from the road, and there is a walkway leading to the door in the center of the home. There are no lights on, and it looks empty, or everyone is sleeping.

"OK, we're here now. What do we do? Do we just go in?" asks Bailey.

"Come on, follow me," says Rain.

Rain instinctively reaches for his .357, but he does not have his shoulder harness on. He does have one survival knife hanging from his belt.

"No guns just one knife. No problem, I'll just have to gut that fucker. Come on, let's not even be quiet. Let's just attack," says Rain.

Rain walks up to the door, and it is locked. He kicks in the door violently, and it slams open. He walks into the dark living room.

"Come on out, Glamfury. We are here. This is what you wanted, right? Ajaunta, are you here? Ajaunta, where are you?" calls Rain.

Bailey walks into the kitchen and turns on the light. Rain turns on the light in the living room. He walks into the bedroom from the living room, and Ajaunta is tied to the bed and gagged. She is struggling to free herself. Rain unties her hands and removes the cloth tied around her head and mouth. Ajaunta has been crying. Her tears are dried to the sides of her face. She sits up, hugging Rain.

"Rain, he said he was going to kill me. He said he was going to torture me. He was touching me, Rain," says Ajaunta.

"Where did he go? Where is he?" asks Rain.

Bailey walks into the room and sits at the foot of the bed. She unties Ajaunta's feet and moves to the head of the bed. She hugs Ajaunta.

"It's all right, Ajaunta. We are here now. He can't get us when we are all together," says Bailey.

"I was sleeping with my head on Rain's lap, and he walked right in and took me away. We can't do anything against him. He is a monster," says Ajaunta.

"Yeah, we will see about that. He has to have a weakness. He thinks he can keep playing games with us. He thinks we are just a bunch of rats in his maze. He is going to find out we are not the average run-of-the-mill rats. He can't kill us. For some reason, he needs us alive, or we would be dead by now. He needs to separate us so he can play his mind games with us. We need to stay together from now on, and one of us always needs to be on guard. We need to find Smoke, and I bet Marlene is still alive too. We need to find them. The five of us are all a part of this crazy dream. We need to band together and face this demon in strength. That is what we need to do," says Rain.

Bailey and Ajaunta shake their heads up and down, agreeing with Rain.

"Rain, you are right. He went out that door right there," says Ajaunta.

Ajaunta points to a door that exits the bedroom to the woods outside. Rain looks out the door, and he hears a lot of men running in the woods, speaking a foreign language that he recognizes as Egyptian.

"Come on, girls, we need to get out of here. We need to get back to the car and get the fuck out of here now," says Rain.

"What about Smoke?" says Bailey.

"Smoke will be just fine. Let's get the fuck out of here. Glamfury has a lot of followers, and I think they are circling through the woods right now. Come on, let's get out of here," says Rain.

The girls get off the bed and head into the living room, and Rain is right behind them. Bailey opens the front door, and she is met with hundreds of gunshots. Her body shakes and twists from all the bullets shredding her. Rain wraps his arms around Ajaunta and pulls her to the floor, rolling up next to the couch. Bailey is held up as hundreds of bullets shred her entire body. Rain and Ajaunta are splattered with blood. Hunks of flesh and bone are torn from her body as minutes go by. The shooting finally stops, and Bailey falls backward, dead for over a minute now. She falls back, splattering more of her blood and flesh all over Rain and Ajaunta. Rain rolls toward the door, kicking it shut with his feet.

"Bailey. Look what they did to Bailey!" Ajaunta cries.

"Yeah, that was no Glamfury. That was the Egengyns. Looks like he has gotten his followers back or started a whole new order of followers, which Smoke and I will have to eradicate," says Rain.

"Are you and Smoke going to kill them all? Are you sure you can?" says Ajaunta.

"We did it once, we will do it again. That is why that evil fucker is after Smoke and me in the first place—because we killed all his followers. I bet we killed off all his power by killing his followers. That is why he is after Smoke and me. I am so sorry we dragged you into this, Ajaunta. I don't believe in all this demonic, satanic bullshit, but there is some sort of evil voodoo going on here. I just have to figure out how to fight that fucker. These scumbags outside now, they are nothing. But Glamfury, he is one motherfucker that I just can't figure. I know there is some reasonable explanation to what is going on. I just have not figured it out, and I will," says Rain.

Ajaunta hugs Rain.

"Rain, I don't know how or why life is the way it is, but I always did love you. I don't know why I never let you get close to me in school, but I always loved you, and if we are to die here tonight, I am glad I am with you," says Ajaunta.

"Don't worry, Ajaunta, we are not going to die here tonight," says Rain.

Bullets start to break the glass. The walls start to splinter and break away as a barrage of bullets start to shred the walls and windows. Rain and Ajaunta hug each other tight as debris fly all over the room. The lights, the TV, the paintings on the walls, and most of the furnishings start to break apart all over. Glass, pillow feathers, electronics, and wood splinters fill the air covering the two as hundreds and thousands of bullets shred the home. Rain holds Ajaunta's head close to his chest as she starts to panic from the noise and debris falling all over them. The noise is deafening, and amazingly, no bullets actually hit the two of them, but with all the debris falling all over them, it's hard for them not to think they have been shot. The gunfire starts to slow down. The debris is still falling all around. Rain looks up to see the air filled with debris. He looks and sees Bailey lying on the floor with her face facing him. Her eyes are still open, and the sight of her lifeless body looking at him is haunting. The bullets stop, and Ajaunta's crying is now heard.

"Shh, shh. It's all right, we are all right," says Rain.

Rain squeezes Ajaunta tight, kissing her cheek and forehead. The bullets start to fly again. They hear the shots ringing out, but none seem to be hitting the house.

"Now what? Won't they ever stop?" cries Ajaunta.

"I know that sound. That's not them. That is Smoke. Smoke, were in here!" yells Rain.

The door flies open, and Smoke runs in, tripping over Bailey's body. He falls on the ground not far from Rain and Ajaunta.

"What was that?" He looks to see Bailey dead on the floor. "Ahh, motherfuckers. Motherfuckers killed Bailey. I will kill them all." Smoke gets up and walks to the window, blasting out with his twenty-four-shot pump-action shotgun.

"Smoke, get down. Get down here, Smoke," says Rain.

The house starts to fill with debris as gunfire fills the air and the house is turned into Swiss cheese again.

"Get down here, Smoke, before some of that erratic gunfire gets you dead," says Rain.

Rain pulls on Smoke's pant leg, pulling him to the floor. Smoke throws a shoulder harness to Rain, and he puts it on.

"Glad to see you were thinking of me, buddy," says Rain.

Rain draws his .357s.

"Rain, as I was coming in the house, they were changing. They were changing into those toucan-billed demons we saw at the cabin," says Smoke.

The windows have been completely blown apart. There are holes throughout all the walls, and all the furnishings are scattered all over the floor and furniture. Ajaunta screams. Rain and Smoke look to see huge red toucan bills, arms, and chests start to enter into the house through the windows.

"Just like old times, Rain. Let's fuck them up," says Smoke.

Smoke slides on his arms and knees to the closest window, putting the muzzle of his shotgun under the bill of the demon trying to get into the window. He shoots, blasting a hole right up and through the bill. The demon backs away. Smoke stands and blasts, sending the demon back into the woods. Rain stands and walks toward the window on the other side of the room. A demon is climbing in the window. Rain shoots four holes in it, kicking it right in the head, sending it back into the darkness. Rain turns to another window, shooting at the demon that has almost made its way in. Smoke runs at it with a jump kick under its neck, sending it back out the window.

"You guys, the kitchen!" yells Ajaunta.

They turn to see a toucan demon walking into the living room. They both shoot, sending it back into the kitchen. Rain grabs Ajaunta by the hand, helping her up.

"Come on, Ajaunta, we have to get out of here. Come on, Smoke, we can't just sit in here," says Rain.

"I know. We have to get out of here. No reason to hold back. Let's charge right through them fuckers," says Smoke.

Smoke opens the front door to see a toucan demon stick a large spear right though his abdomen and raise him to the ceiling. Rain steps in, points both his guns at its head, and blasts holes in it. It falls, letting go of the spear. Rain slams the door shut.

"Get it out of me. Get it out of me, Rain," says Smoke.

"Damn it, Smoke. Hold on, this is gonna hurt," says Rain.

Rain grabs the spear and kicks up with his knee, breaking the spear near Smoke's stomach. He walks at the back of Smoke and pulls it from his abdomen.

"Aha, goddamn fuckers. Motherfucker, that fucking hurts," says Smoke.

Smoke dropped his shotgun, and he puts his bloody hand on Rain's shoulders, holding himself up.

"It looks worse than it is. I'll be all right," says Smoke.

"You sure? I don't have time to fix you up right now," says Rain.

"Rain, fuck them up. Get us out of here. I parked just at the end of the driveway. Get us to the car, and we can get out of here," says Smoke.

Ajaunta picks up the shotgun dropped on the floor and starts to fire. She is walking toward the bedroom door, blasting a demon.

"If you two are done socializing, we have some fucking demons to blast," says Ajaunta.

She shoots holes in the demon, sending it back into the bedroom, turning to smile at Rain and Smoke. She pumps the shotgun with intensity in her action, and the sound of the empty shell casings bouncing on the floor echoes through the room. They look at her, amazed at her initiative. The floor under Ajaunta erupts in splinters. Arms reach up, grabbing Ajaunta by her knees. She looks at Rain and Smoke with terror in her eyes. They look at her with their hearts gripped in fear. She is pulled down into the floor in the blink of an eye and gone.

"Ajaunta!" yells Rain. He dives on the floor, reaching into the dark hole. He can see nothing; he can hear nothing. "Ajaunta!" His scream echoes down the long dark tunnel leading to hell.

"Rain. Come on, Rain, they are coming," says Smoke.

Smoke grabs Rain by the shoulders and pulls him back from the hole leading into the unknown. The two of them curl up as the room erupts in a hail of gunfire yet again. Yet again, the room is full of debris, splinters, and furnishings are flying all over as bullets tear through the home again. There is one door that none of them have gone into yet, a second bedroom to the back corner of the living room.

"Come on, Rain, we have to get in there. Come on," says Smoke.

They crawl toward the door, and Rain reaches up, opening the door. It leads into another bedroom, and they crawl in, closing the door behind them. There is a bed in here along with dresser, nightstand, and a closet with sliding doors, which are open. They are both on the floor, leaning against the bed.

"Smoke, it's them, goddamn Egengyns. I told you I never wanted to go after no goddamn devil worshipers. Somehow, they can change between demon and human. It's not natural, it's not real. We have to figure out how to kill that Glamfury. Then they all die. How much you want to bet?" says Rain.

Rain feels the bed wiggle, and he pops his head up to look.

"Marlene, is that you? Marlene, you have been here the whole time?" says Rain.

Marlene is struggling and making faint muffled sounds through the gag tied around her mouth and head. Her arms and legs are tied to the bed, and she can barely move at all. Rain climbs on the bed and unties her. He removes the gag from her mouth.

"Rain, you have to get out of here. It's a trap," says Marlene.

"Yeah, we know. Too late to worry about that. We are here now. Let's figure out how to get out of here," says Rain.

Marlene slides to the side of the bed. Rain helps Smoke up to a sitting position on the bed. She can see the wound on Smoke's stomach.

"You're hurt bad," she says.

"It will be all right," he says.

It is very quiet. All the shots have stopped, and it seems like they have a moment of reprieve. Rain looks out the screen of the sliding door, and the sun is rising, casting light into the room.

"The sun is coming up. Maybe they have gone. Maybe we have survived," says Smoke.

"Something is not right. The sun is rising, but it shouldn't be. It has not been all night. Why is the sun rising?" says Rain.

"Who cares? Can we get out of here now?" says Marlene.

"Hold on, you two, stay right here. Let me check and see if the coast is clear," says Rain.

Rain opens the bedroom door cautiously. He peeks out. He looks around and moves into the living room. They hear him move around through all the debris in the living room, and he walks back into the bedroom.

"Come on, it looks like they have gone," says Rain.

Smoke tries to get up, and Marlene can see he is in a lot of pain. She helps him to his feet. Smoke looks up, hearing a sound he has heard many times before. It is the sound of a whistle being blown at one hundred times normal speed. It is the sound of terror, and Marlene hears it too. They look at Rain as the sound turns into a "whack." Rain takes a step forward, looking to his side, confused. He touches his lower right abdomen and looks at the blood on his hand. The sound comes again, and this time, blood splatters the faces of Smoke and Marlene as the bullet exits Rain's back, and he falls to the floor at the foot of the bed. Rain rolls to his side and moves toward the door, having no idea what he is doing. Smoke moves from the bed, grabbing Rain by his hand.

"Rain, get away from the door," says Smoke.

He pulls Rain away from the door as another shot penetrates Rain's chest, and another passes through his abdomen.

"Rain!" cries Smoke, pulling Rain to the corner of the room. Marlene kneels by him, crying. Rain looks at the blood on his hands. He looks at Smoke.

"I want you to know I would have never changed a thing. I would have never done anything differently than I did. I want you to know you were always my best friend. I would . . ."

Smoke and Marlene watch as Rain fades to eternity.

Chapter 18

Spiders

Rain sits up in a bright room. It is a glass box, and he has no idea where the light is coming from, but it is bright. He stands and can see Smoke and Marlene just on the other side of the glass. He starts pounding on the glass and yelling, "Smoke! Marlene!" He can see them both in the bedroom, and they are looking at his dead body. He pounds on the glass, calling to them, but they cannot hear him.

"Smoke, Marlene, I'm right here. Can't you hear me? Can't you see me?" yells Rain.

Rain bangs on the glass. He yells as loud as he can, but they cannot see or hear him. Rain is actually standing on the outside of the house, and he can see the toucan demons entering the house through the windows. Smoke gets the .357s from the floor, which Rain had dropped, and shoots the remaining bullets, which is not enough to stop more than the first two demons. Rain watches from the brightly lit glass room, yelling and banging on the glass. He watches as the demons walk in and capture Smoke and Marlene. They are carried out of the room and out of sight through the front of the house. The glass walls start to shatter, and the light in the room dims to the dark of night like the setting around the glass box. The glass shatters, and Rain bends down, covering his head with his arms, protecting himself from the shattering glass. He looks up to see a toucan demon swinging a large thick stick hitting him right in the head.

Rain sits up, rubbing his head on this beautiful midmorning day in the woods. He has an excruciating headache, which is very unlike him. He can hear his name is being called, but his head is killing him. He looks in front of him, seeing Smoke being pulled like there is a rope tied around his ankles.

"Rain!" yells Smoke, and Rain sees Smoke pulled very fast into the forest.

Rain hears his name being called again and looks to his left. Ajaunta is being pulled the same way, and she yells, "Rain!" In an instant, she is gone.

He hears his name called again and looks to his right, seeing Bailey and Marlene together both with their legs tied. They yell, "Rain!" and they are pulled into the forest.

Rain cannot make out what all their legs are tied with; it looks like a thick rope, but it is shiny, almost transparent. Rain stands up and can barely hear his name being called as his friends are dragged off through the forest. He looks around, having no idea where he is. The only thing he knows is that he is obviously in the woods. He searches for tracks and looks where Bailey and Marlene were. He can easily track the woods they have been dragged through. He follows the drag marks through the dirt and follows the broken plants easily. He looks for tracks to see if he can tell what is dragging his friends, but the tracks he finds are not human. No animal he is aware of makes these tracks, which makes him very uneasy. He hopes that all his friends are being taken to the same place, and he hopes he gets to them before harm does.

"Bailey! Marlene!" he yells, and he has to stop and kneel down because his head throbs and aches. He squeezes his head with both hands, trying to squeeze the pain out. He can feel the huge knot on his forehead where he was struck, causing a headache like he has never known. It hurts so bad it is hard for him to think. He lies on the ground, rolling around just trying to position his body in a way that is not excruciating. This is a debilitating pain, and he cannot even function. The pain seems to be getting worse, and he starts to cry because his brain is hurting like no pain he has ever known. "Ahh, come on!" he yells, and all of a sudden, he feels fine. He takes a deep breath and opens his eyes, seeing someone kneeling beside him.

"There, you see how easily I can take your pain away? I can bring it on just as easily as well," says Glamfury.

"Oh, great, what do you want?" says Rain, sitting up.

"I just want to see if all that survival training you had teaching you how to hunt and survive in the woods is going to be enough for you to save your friends. Smoke had the same training you had. So I wonder if the two of you can save the girls and yourselves before you all become ingested by my little pets. You see, this training seemed to help you two greatly in hunting my followers in Egypt and in Jamaica, but this time, you have a different adversary. Not only that, but also Ajaunta, your love, Marlene, your love, Smoke, and Bailey have all already been caught, and soon they will be eaten unless you get to them right quick. Ha, ha, ha. Ha, ha, ha. Ha, ha, ha," laughs Glamfury.

Glamfury floats backward through the woods out of sight. Rain stands up, feeling much better. He feels his forehead, and the knot is gone. He is all better like nothing ever happened. He gets right on the trail and follows the drag marks where Marlene and Bailey have been dragged through the woods. There are tall trees all around with plants taller than himself. There are lots of spiderweb that he keeps walking through, which is not uncommon in woods, but he definitely notices them becoming more and more numerous to the point where he is starting to wipe spiders from his person. This is really freaking him out because Rain is fine with spiders as long as they are not on him. He really gets freaked out when they are on him. He grabs a stick, which he uses to swipe at the webs before he walks through them. The trees and plants start to become more and more snared in the webs like the forest is becoming a lair of spiders, and he is starting to get seriously creeped out. He moves on, and webs start to cover the foliage like blankets. He rubs his hands on the webs and notices how lots of spiders converge on that location. He grabs a larger, thicker stick and sways it back and forth in front of him as he treks deeper into the labyrinth of webs.

"Marlene! Bailey! Smoke! Ajaunta!" he yells. The stick he uses to slice through the webs gets fat at the end, looking like cotton candy. He wipes the excess web on the trees he walks by. He keeps yelling for his friends, but the forest gets quieter and darker. The webs start to get so thick that the trees are completely held together by the webbing, which is now one huge web all around Rain. There are holes through the web taller than Rain, which is clearly a route for something or some things to travel through the web. He looks all around, realizing he is now completely surrounded by the web, and his stick is becoming pretty useless at this point as he now follows the routes already drawn in the web.

"Rain." He hears his name faintly being called. "Rain." The voice is coming from above him. He uses his stick to break through the web. He slices to a tree and clears the web all around and above him.

"Bailey, is that you? Bailey," calls Rain.

"Rain, I can't move. Rain, hurry, I can't move," says Bailey.

He can tell the voice is coming from above him and clears as much of the web away as he can. He can see a silhouette of what could be a body wrapped in a ball of web, and he can just reach it with his stick. He jumps, tapping the entombed body with his stick. It is held up by two thin but strong webs. He keeps jumping and tapping the ball of web.

"Rain, hurry. Rain, it hurts," says Bailey.

"I'm coming. I'm coming. Hold on, Bailey."

The mass starts to sway and swing back and forth, falling closer and closer to the ground. Rain can now reach one of the webs, holding it up with his stick, and he swings, breaking the web. The web cocoon falls, hitting the ground with one web still holding it in the air. Rain pulls his knife and cuts the web. The cocoon falls to the ground.

"Rain, hurry. Rain, it hurts," says Bailey's muffled voice.

"Hold on, Bailey, I've almost got you out. Hold on," says Rain.

Rain uses his knife to cut down the front of the web trap, and the web spreads open. Rain gasps and takes a step back as the inside of the web is full of spiders. They are small, only a little larger than a quarter. They fall onto the ground all around the body of Bailey. Rain covers his mouth, almost crying to what he sees, and the smell gags him.

"Rain, hurry. Rain, it hurts," says Bailey through her swollen mouth. Her eyes are swollen shut, and her entire body is swollen. She has been bitten thousands of times by the spiders, and her sense of feel is completely gone. Most her senses are gone at this point, and she is near death. There is nothing Rain can do for her, and he knows it. He can't believe she can even speak muffled and slurred though it is. He can't help but look over her body. There are spiders attached everywhere on her body. The spiders have injected her body with venom, which digests her body from within her skin, and now they are drawing the fluids from her body, nourishing their bodies. This sight is probably the most gory thing Rain has ever seen in his life. He cannot believe she is still alive. Rain is not squeamish at all, but he turns his head, almost vomiting to see Bailey like this.

"Rain, hurry. Rain, it hurts," she says, barely getting the words out of her swollen lips. Rain does not know if he should end it or not. He can't believe she can feel or think or understand. He stands and backs away. Spiders start coming for him as he touches and backs into the web behind him. The ground starts to crawl with thousands of spiders as Rain backs away from Bailey, who is clearly unable to move.

"Rain, hurry. Rain, it hurts," says Bailey.

"I'm sorry, Bailey," says Rain.

Rain steps in and cuts her throat with his knife. Her blood does not even look like blood. It looks like liquid honey with drops of blood in it. The spiders advance on the liquid that seeps from her slit throat and start to suck on the grotesque liquid, which almost makes Rain puke yet again. Rain runs past Bailey down the large hole, running through the web, easily outrunning the spiders in pursuit of him. He comes to a split where he can follow to the right or to the left. His choice is made for him when he hears Marlene scream down the right passage through the web.

"Marlene, is that you?" calls Rain.

"Rain. Hurry, Rain. Hurry!" says Marlene.

Rain can hear the fear in Marlene's scream, and he runs down the circular passage in the web.

"I'm coming, Marlene. I'm coming!" yells Rain.

"Rain, it's a spider, a huge spider. Hurry, Rain," says Marlene.

Rain runs through the web, which turns to the right and enters an open area. Marlene is off the ground about six feet with her arms and legs spun with web, which extend to trees to the sides of her. She is tied with the web, and she cannot break free. Rain runs to her and starts to beat the web with his stick, but the web bounces back and forth. He pulls his knife and jumps, being able to reach the webs that shackle her legs, but he cannot reach the webs holding her arms.

"Rain, behind you. Behind you!" screams Marlene.

Rain turns around to see the largest spider he has ever seen in his life, but it's not the size of the tarantula that freaks him out the most. It's the fact that it has the head of Smoke on it. It runs up to Rain and stops. Its legs stand a foot taller than Rain, and the head is some four feet taller yet. Rain looks up.

"Smoke, what the fuck? Is that you, Smoke?" says Rain.

The head of the tarantula leans down toward Rain.

"You always said I would be the death of you," says Smoke.

"Smoke, don't do this. You don't have to do this. I'll get you out of here," says Rain.

"I don't think so," says Smoke.

Smoke's head sits on shoulders, and normal human arms and hands extend from the shoulders. His shoulders sit atop the cephalothorax. There are three sets of spider legs on the cephalothorax, or midsection of the spider. The abdomen, or final section of the spider, is leg-free, but it splits down the middle and has two huge fangs at the rear instead of spinners, which will cut right through Rain if he is struck by them.

"Look at my hands, Rain. Look at them. They look normal, right? Check this out," says Smoke.

Smoke points his hands at Rain, and he shoots webbing from all eight of his fingertips. Rain dives to the side, avoiding the webs. Smoke continues with the webs until they catch Marlene's legs, and he pulls her toward him. Marlene screams.

"Rain, it's got me, it's got me!" screams Marlene.

She is now horizontal with the ground, and the tarantula stands tall on its spider legs and swings its abdomen underneath its entire body, coming up with its large fangs right into the back of Marlene. Its fangs dig through her ribs, into her chest, and she screams. Rain can see her body fattening as venom fills her chest and abdomen.

"Rain, it burns. It hurts, Rain!" she screams, and her screams fade as she loses consciousness.

"Smoke, what are you doing? Smoke, you are killing her," says Rain.

Smoke looks at Rain and smiles.

"No, Rain, I am eating her," says Smoke.

Smoke opens his mouth wide, and his teeth grow into pyramid-shaped sheers on the top and bottom. Rain watches as Smoke pulls Marlene to him and bites a huge chunk of flesh from her stomach. Her abdomen gushes a golden liquid mixed with blood. Smoke swallows the flesh whole, and Rain can see the chunk of flesh slide down his throat until it reaches the cephalothorax of the spider.

Rain looks around, thinking what to do. He looks at his stick and his knife. He pulls his belt and wraps it around the knife at the end of the stick. He wraps it tight and uses the buckle to secure the knife on the stick. Smoke is biting flesh from Marlene's body, which is softened by the venom injected in her. Smoke has walked up to her, and her body now lies on his arms. He strips the clothing from her. He bites the right breast right off her body, right down to her ribs, and Rain can see her flesh stripped from her bones as Smoke swallows the flesh whole. He pays Rain no attention as he bites the muscles on her right leg and strips them from her bones like a chicken wing.

Rain screams in disgust, thrusting the stick up into the throat of Smoke, who is paying him no attention at all. The blade of the knife digs right under Smoke's chin and sinks into the lower part of his brain. Smoke goes crazy, dropping Marlene's partially eaten body, which bounces on the webs that still hold her arms. Smoke grabs his throat and moves away from Rain. Rain pounces, thrusting the weapon up again, this time striking directly under Smoke's chin, and Rain thrusts the blade right up into Smoke's brain. Smoke raises his body out of the reach of Rain's blade. Rain thrusts repeatedly over and over, stabbing many times into the cephalothorax of Smoke, and this is very effective. Smoke has lost his thought process; he is simply moving and swaying in a reactionary state. Rain stabs and slices over and over, releasing the contents of the spider's insides, fortunate that Smoke does not have the wherewithal to make significant attacks of his own. Smoke slows and falls closer and closer to the ground as Rain stabs him over and over until the gigantic tarantula with Smoke's head falls to the ground dead.

Rain moves over to Marlene and pulls on her left leg. He can reach the webs holding her up by her arms with the knife at the end of the stick, and he cuts her down. Her right leg, the right side of her chest, and her abdomen have huge chunks of flesh bitten from her body, and she has already expired. Rain hugs her lifeless body as he lowers her to the ground, affected in a very traumatic way seeing her like this. Her insides have already begun to be digested, and the puke-like liquid seeping from the wounds on her body stink of bile, and Rain cries. Rain's mind and body are worn out and beat down. He cries, thinking he has let his best friends and his loves die. He cannot distinguish what is real and what is dream. He can't tell who he is anymore. He cries, and then he hears Ajaunta calling for him.

"Rain, Rain, where are you? Rain. Help, Rain!" cries Ajaunta.

Rain stands up and looks around the open space he is in. There are holes that run into the web all around him. The space he is in now is actually pretty big. He can see the sky in places through the web, which rises up the trees at least forty feet, and he can move around an area probably fifteen yards across. Ajaunta runs into the opening from one of the holes.

"Ajaunta, I'm here. I'm right here, Ajaunta."

She sees him and runs right to him. She grabs his hand, pulling him in the direction she is running.

"Come on, Rain, we have to get out of here," says Ajaunta.

"Where are we going?" says Rain.

"Away from them," says Ajaunta.

Rain looks where she is pointing, and he can see thousands, maybe tens of thousands of small spiders running after Ajaunta.

"Holy shit. Yes, yes, that way. Let's get the fuck out of here," says Rain.

They run toward a hole opposite from where Ajaunta ran into the opening, but they stop before entering because a huge tarantula with Smoke's head comes running from that hole and enters the opening. They head toward another whole to the right just to have another Smoke-headed tarantula block their way. A third Smoke-headed tarantula enters into the opening. Now they face three tarantulas towering over them. The larger tarantulas are walking toward them, pushing them back, as thousands and thousands of smaller spiders pour in from the hole that Ajaunta ran in from. The smaller spiders are darkening the floor and the web walls like a dark cloud as they move closer to the two, covering the entire web-enclosed room.

"Rain, there are too many of them. What are we going to do?" says Ajaunta.

Ajaunta starts to step on the smaller spiders, which are now starting to crawl up their legs.

"Well, they are not going to get me without a fight, I can tell you that. Come on, you fuckers. You want some of me? Come and get it," says Rain.

Ajaunta stands behind Rain, holding on to his stomach with her head buried in his back. She can't bear to watch what is going to happen. Rain charges the middle tarantula with his stick. There are so many spiders coming up behind them now that if they move back, they will be engulfed by the spiders in no time. Rain stabs upward at the middle tarantula with his stick. The spider blocks the stick with its arms.

"Nice one. Oh, nice try, Rain. Come on, you can do better than that. Oops, you missed. OK, my turn," says the middle tarantula.

It points its fingers and shoots web at the stick, catching it in sticky webbing. The spider pulls upward very hard. Rain holds on, being yanked into the air. Ajaunta holds on to Rain a little but loses her grip and falls to the ground as Rain is thrown upward and sticks in the web some ten feet in the air. Rain looks down to see the two outside tarantulas converge on Ajaunta, both swinging their abdomens under their legs and up. Ajaunta is stuck in her neck, her left rib cage, her stomach, and her right rib cage just under her breast. She freezes with the look of shock on her face, and Rain can see her body bulge from the venom being pumped into her body from the enormous tarantulas.

"No!" yells Rain, and he jumps from the web wall. He flies downward toward the tarantula in the middle with its back to him. He comes down with the stick like a spear and drives it right through the back of its head. This tarantula is smiling and watching Ajaunta get fat from the venom pumping into her body until Rain's knife drives right out its face, and it falls dying. Rain pulls the spear from its head and jumps at the tarantula to his right, driving the spear right through its head, killing it. The third tarantula pulls its fangs from Ajaunta's body and steps back, laughing. Rain pulls the spear from the head of the second tarantula and walks toward the third one. It backs from Rain, laughing.

"Ahh, oh, ooh, you are not mad, are you, Rain? I mean, that was not the love of your life we just pumped full of death, was it? Ohhh, maybe it was. My bad." The Smoke tarantula laughs.

"Oh, ahh, hurry, Rain, maybe you can save her. Hurry before all my offspring suck up her juices, and, oh, I bet her juices are sweet," laughs the tarantula.

Rain looks to see thousands of spiders engulf her body. He can't stop being drawn to take a closer look, and he sees all the little spiders have Smoke's head on them. They all have Smoke's head with fangs, and they are all biting Ajaunta, sucking the juice from underneath her skin. The venom pumped into Ajaunta is already digesting her body from within, and all the little spiders are nourishing themselves from this cocktail of muscle, blood, bone, and venom.

Rain freaks out, crying, "No." He draws back his spear and throws it at the last tarantula, hitting it dead center in its face. The spear flies right through the head of the tarantula and hits the web wall, shattering it like glass. The entire web wall all around starts to shatter and fall. Rain bends down and covers his head with his arms. His body is drenched in glass that seems to fall for minutes, and he can feel his arms, back, legs, and shoulders being cut by the falling glass. He can feel the blood oozing from his cut skin. The weight of the glass gets heavier and heavier, and no matter how still he remains, it matters not as he feels he is being killed by thousands of razor-like cuts from the glass. He can feel his body get cold and weak, and it seems like he falls asleep.

Chapter 19

Shattering Expectations

Rain is falling; he can't see anything. He can hear his voice screaming as he is falling. It seems like he is falling in a shaft, and he hears his screams echoing above and below him. He can see his reflection momentarily, and, wham, he falls into a very thick mirror. Crashing through the glass mirror, it cuts him badly, and still he is falling. He can see himself, and again he crashes through another mirror. He gets cut very badly and still falls into another mirror and another. He is now a bloody mess. His arms and face are bleeding as is his whole body. He is falling for yet another mirror, but this time, he does not crash through it; he bounces on the mirror, flopping a few times before coming to a bloody stop.

He can barely move, and he is in agonizing pain from all the deep cuts all over his body. He has never known fear like seeing all the blood drain from his body, and he does have the strength or the supplies needed to stop it. He lies there for a few moments, noticing the circular walls around him are mirror. His horror is maximized seeing his body torn, cut, sliced, and his clothing mostly torn and ripped from his body long ago. His flesh, his muscles, and his bones have all been sliced. He is a gory mess, and somehow, his eyes have been spared from being sliced by all the broken glass.

He looks up to see all the broken glass seemingly suspended in the air high above him. His eyes widen as the glass falls. He screams knowing this will shred his body. He can't move because all the muscles

140

in his body have been severed, so he waits to be ground up by the glass. He can hear all the glass hitting something and flowing away from him.

"Wow, that was close, huh, buddy?" says Smoke.

Rain opens his eyes to see Smoke standing above him. Smoke is holding part of the glass wall that was surrounding Rain. Smoke holds the glass above his head, and the glass that was going to fall on Rain is diverted to the side and falls into the dark unknown.

"Rain, get out of here. I can't hold this forever," says Smoke.

"Get out of here—where? I can't move," says Rain.

"There." Rain nods with his head since his hands and arms are holding up the glass wall. It is like an oval in the glass wall has been tilted in an upward position, and Smoke has it lying on his back just above Rain. Rain can see there is a passage leading into another room.

"Go on, Rain, crawl if you have to. Get in there so I can sew you up and we can get out of here," says Smoke.

Rain tries and manages to crawl into the next room, leaving a heavy trail of coagulating blood behind him. Smoke comes in behind him. Rain can see how Smoke pushes on the glass, and it pivots on two hinges, closing the tube that Rain was just in. Smoke walks into the room Rain is in now, and the glass tube seals shut. Rain looks around, seeing nothing. The room is completely empty, and it is silvery black with mirrored walls, so all he can see is himself and Smoke. Smoke starts to use a hook with a long dark thread to sew up the wounds on Rain. Rain's clothes have mostly been shredded and stick to his body in bloody clumps.

"Smoke, what are you doing?" says Rain.

"I'm putting you back to together, buddy," says Smoke.

Rain can feel the hook and thread being pulled through his flesh as Smoke sews him back together. It does not hurt as bad as you might think. Watching himself being stitched up is way worse than the actual pain. Rain can barely move his head, but he can see how badly cut his entire body is. His muscle, his bones, and his veins are exposed just everywhere on his body.

"Smoke, why are you stitching me? Look at me, there is no chance. I will die of blood loss. Look at me," says Rain.

"Oh, stop, you are going to be fine. I am going to stitch you up, and it will take a while, but you will be fine. You always thought I would be the death of you. Huh, you see here I am saving your life. See, I always told you I didn't want to hear that crap about me being the death of you," says Smoke.

Smoke just keeps stitching and stitching. It takes hours, and Rain loses consciousness while Smoke is stitching him up.

"Rain. Rain. Wake up, Rain. Come on, wake up. What are you doing?" says Smoke.

Rain sits up and looks around. Everything is black. He can see there is just nothing to see. He stands up, noticing his arms. He looks over his body, screaming in horror. His body is completely stitched up from his feet to the top of his head. It is a horrific sight—all the thread holding his flesh together. He makes Frankenstein look like a beauty queen. Rain holds out his hands and arms, looking them over, screaming into the air.

"What's the matter, Rain? Don't like what you see? You always thought I would be the death of you, but, no, I am actually your savior. Without me, you would be dead right now. I saved you, Rain," says Smoke.

"You should have let me die. Look at me, look at me," says Rain.

Rain can actually move and walk now, but his muscles have all been cut, ripped, and torn, so his movements are all decrepit. He just looks awkward, and there is no fluidity to his movements at all.

"What good is this, Smoke? What good is this at all? I cannot defend myself. I cannot make any significant contribution in any way. What good am I?" cries Rain.

Rain looks around, but Smoke is gone. The floor he is standing on drops like he is standing on a trapdoor. Rain falls, and he screams as he falls in what seems like slow motion. He strides with his legs like he is running. He swings with his arms like he is treading water, and still he falls for what seems like minutes with no sight of the bottom. He feels severe pain in his right leg going up through his hip and his torso. He feels pain in his left foot, both his arms, and suddenly, the pain is everywhere in his body. It is the worst pain he has ever felt in his life. He tries to look around, but he can't move his head. Now his head is in severe pain. He can't move his arms or his legs. He cries out in pain and fear not knowing what has happened to him. He can only see darkness, and like a switch has turned on the lights, he can see he is in a cylinder again.

Again the walls are mirrors, and he can see all around him. He has fallen into a pit with stakes rising up, and he has fallen on the stakes that have driven up all throughout his body. Seeing the way he has fallen on the stakes and seeing the way he is stuck scare him to death, and he screams, crying in fear and pain. He cannot move. His arms are out to his sides, and stakes are up through his legs, his torso, and even up through his head, so he can't spin his head around. He is stuck.

"Rain, Rain. Hold on, buddy, I'm gonna get you out of here. Hold on!" yells Smoke.

"Smoke, Smoke, is that you? Smoke, kill me. Kill me, Smoke!" cries Rain.

Rain can hear a chainsaw being started. He can hear the chainsaw cutting down trees.

"Smoke, what are you doing? Smoke, where are you? Smoke!" cries Rain.

Rain can't see Smoke, but he can see the stakes all around him start to sink out of sight until only the stakes he has fallen on are left.

"Don't you worry, buddy. I'm gonna get you out of here, and all this time you thought I was going to be the death of you. I'm gonna save you, buddy, hold on," says Smoke.

"No, Smoke. Don't save me. I don't need saving. I need to die now. It's my time. Let me pass to the afterlife," says Rain.

"I will hear none of that. I'm getting you out of here, buddy," says Smoke.

Rain hears the chainsaw cutting away, and the stake through his left foot starts to fall, pulling on his left foot, causing excruciating pain in his foot and leg. The same happens with the stake through his left arm. Rain screams in pain.

"Smoke, you are killing me. Smoke, stop!" cries Rain.

"Hold on, buddy, I almost got you out, hold on," says Smoke.

The stakes in his right arm fall. Rain feels like his body is being pulled apart as, one by one, the stakes are falling, pulling on his body. He can feel the weight of the stakes getting heavier and heavier. He can't believe his body does not rip apart, and then the last stake in his right arm falls. His body cannot bear the weight of the stakes anymore. He feels his body start to tear. He screams in horror as his groin tears right up through his stomach, up through his chest, up his neck, and his face splits right up the middle. His body falls backward, and he can see out both eyes as his body falls, slamming on the black floor with each half of his body still having wooden stakes in them.

"Oh, shit, Rain. Hold on, buddy. Hold on, I'm gonna make it better. I'm gonna save you," says Smoke.

Rain can move. He can look around with each eye, and he can see. He cannot speak. He can move his mouth, but there is only half a mouth and half a tongue incapable of speech. He can feel Smoke pulling the stakes from each half of his body, and the pain is unbearable, but he does not pass out; he endures the pain. He can lift each half of his head so he can see Smoke pulling the stakes from his body. He tries to cry, he tries to tell Smoke to kill him, but no words come out. He watches Smoke pull hook, thread, and sew the two halves of his body back together. Rain watches as Smoke puts his insides back in and sews from his groin, back up his torso, back up his head.

"And you thought I was going to be the death of you. Just hold on, buddy, I'm putting you back together. Hold on, buddy," says Smoke.

Rain watches as his intestines are put back in. His stomach is put back inside. Smoke sews from his groin up to his ribs.

"Hold on, buddy, we can't forget about your ass," says Smoke.

Smoke flips Rain onto his stomach. He can feel his back being sewn together all the way up to his neck, and he is flipped back onto his back. He watches as his beating heart and lungs are put into his chest, and Smoke sews his chest up. He sews up his neck and chin. He sews between his eyes, and Rain can now talk again.

"Smoke, this is not real. Smoke, what is going on? This is worse than a bad dream," says Rain.

"There, you see? You thought I was going to be the death of you. There, I have saved you, like, three times today already. You see, everything is all better now," says Smoke.

Smoke sits Rain up and pats him on his back. Rain looks down and screams in terror seeing he has been sewn back together with the right side of his body facing forward and the left side of his body facing backward.

"Ahhhhhh! Smoke, you sewed me back together with half of me facing forward and half of me facing backward. Smoke, what did you do?" cries Rain.

"Oh, shit. Rain, how did I do that? Oh, shit, Rain, hold on. I'm gonna fix you, buddy. Hold on," says Smoke.

Rain watches as Smoke stands up and starts a chainsaw.

"Smoke, what are you doing? Smoke, what are you doing?" cries Rain.

"Hold on, Rain. Now brace yourself. This is probably going to hurt a lot," says Smoke.

Rain looks up as Smoke comes down with the chainsaw dead center at the top of his head.

"Smoke!" cries Rain.

Rain feels all sweaty and excited. He raises his head to see Ajaunta underneath him. She is breathing heavily, and they are in the middle of passionate love. Her arms and legs are wrapped around his body, and she is grinding her loins into his. She starts to moan loudly, squeezing him tightly.

"Don't stop. Rain, don't stop now I'm almost there. Rain, what's the matter?" says Ajaunta.

Ajaunta opens her eyes, and her passion turns to horror. She screams loudly and looks over Rain, pushing him away from her. "Get off me. Get away from me!" she exclaims. She pushes Rain to the side, and he rolls to his back. Rain cannot move, but he can see Ajaunta stand up, and she is covered in blood. Rain can barely raise his head to look down his body, and again he is all cut and torn up, bleeding throughout his entire body. He screams seeing his mutilated body.

"Ajaunta, how did I get here? Ajaunta, help me," says Rain.

She screams, looking at his grotesque body.

"Rain, you got blood all over me. Rain, your blood is in my pussy. Ahh! Rain, there is blood in my mouth. What is wrong with you?" screams Ajaunta.

Ajaunta wipes the blood from her genitals and spits it from her mouth. She cries in disgust.

"Rain, you are so gross. This is the grossest thing I have ever seen in my life. I don't ever want to see you again. Ahh!" cries Ajaunta.

She screams and turns to run away. She turns to see Smoke standing right there in front of her.

"Well, we can't have you thinking Rain is the grossest thing ever. He loves you. He has loved you ever since he first saw you in fourth grade. We must have you looking and feeling just like he is. We'll fix this real quick," says Smoke.

Rain can barely raise his right arm up, and he reaches for Ajaunta. He can barely speak, and he calls for her.

"Ajaunta, get away from him. Smoke, what are you doing? Smoke, don't," says Rain.

Rain yells as loud as he can, but it is just whispers. He watches as Smoke starts to slash at Ajaunta's body. He has large knives in both hands, and he starts to slice her body from head to toe. Ajaunta starts to scream, defending herself with her arms, which are quickly bloodied and sliced very badly. Smoke moves very fast with accurate slicing motions, cutting her back, her abdomen, her breasts, her legs, her arms, her face, her rear, her cheeks, her lips, and even her ears. Ajaunta moves back away from Smoke, but he slices her body, and now she is a bloody mess. Her muscles are starting to be unable to support her weight. Her bones are showing in places, and she is crying in fear and pain. She moves back from Smoke until she is where he wants her, and he punches her right in the nose. She falls back on her back, lying right next to Rain. She looks over to Rain, who can barely move. Her body is sliced and bleeding just like Rain.

"Rain, why did he do this to me? Rain, we are going to die." She cries.

"Now, now, Ajaunta, don't cry. You two are the same now. Now it's time for you two to truly be one. After all, Rain has never loved anyone ever but you. You should make him happy, and girls love to be one with the men that love them, right? Come on, be together, you two," says Smoke.

Smoke raises his arms, pointing his right arm at Rain and his left arm at Ajaunta. He brings his arms together, and the two of them slide toward each other.

"Rain, what is he doing? Rain, make him stop!" cries Ajaunta.

"I can't move. I don't know what is happening," says Rain.

The two of them move closer together until Rain's right arm is touching Ajaunta's left arm. Their arms start to fuse together. The wounds on their arms act like lips sucking on the wound of the other person, and they draw together. Their arms pull together, and their bodies start to roll with all the slices on their bodies, acting like lips sucking and pulling them tight to each other. Rain rolls to his right and Ajaunta to her left as their bodies merge, becoming one. Ajaunta screams in horror.

"Rain, what is happening? Rain, what do we do?" cries Ajaunta.

"I don't know. I don't know," says Rain.

Ajaunta rolls to her left being lighter than Rain, who lies flat on the ground. She rolls up on him, and their bodies continue to fuse together. Her breasts fuse to his breast. Their stomachs fuse, and her genitals suck his genitals into hers. Their cuts feel like paper cuts as their bodies become one, which is painful. Their genitals become one, which confuses their senses, providing them with euphoric pleasure mixed with razor-sharp pain all at the same time. The fronts of their legs fuse together right to the tips of their toes. Their shoulders are slowly fusing together right up their necks to their chins.

"Rain, Rain, what is happening?" cries Ajaunta.

Rain cannot get out any words as their lips start to fuse. They can feel the tips of their tongues touch and grow into one another. Their noses touch and fuse, leaving their nostrils able to breathe. They cannot speak anymore, and their bodies completely fuse as their right arms fuse right to the tips of their fingers.

Smoke laughs. "Now that's the way two lovers should be—joined as one from head to toe." Smoke laughs and walks away. Their foreheads have fused together to their eyebrows so they can look around, but Rain cannot move. Ajaunta does not have the strength to move both of their bodies. They can only make snorting sounds through their nostrils since their mouths and tongues are fused together, so they look around, barely able to move. The room goes black as Smoke slams the door behind him.

Chapter 20

I'm Your Wife

"Wake up, Rain. Come on, get up. It's time to get up. You wanted me to wake you up early, remember? You have that important meeting with Mr. Rockwell this morning," says Ajaunta.

She shakes Rain by his shoulder. Rain breathes deeply. He hears the alarm clock and opens his eyes. Ajaunta has gotten out of bed, and she is standing over him. She leans over and shuts the alarm clock off. She sits on the bed next to Rain and kisses his cheek. Rain stretches his arms and legs, sprawling out under the covers. He reaches his arm around Ajaunta's waist and feels the soft nightgown she is wearing. He snaps to reality, sitting up.

"Ajaunta, is that you?" says Rain.

He reaches over and turns on the light sitting on the nightstand. It is 4:00 a.m. and still very dark outside.

"I knew you would not wake up. You never wake up this early. That is why you asked me to make sure you got up. It's time to get up," says Ajaunta.

Ajaunta stands and walks to her side of the bed and crawls back under the covers.

"Ajaunta, what the hell is going on? Why are you here? Where are we? Wait, this is my house, my bed. What are you doing here? Don't get me wrong, I have always wanted you in my bed, but how did you get here? When did you get here?" says Rain.

"What are you talking about, silly? We have been married for twenty-five years. I am your wife," says Ajaunta.

"My wife? Yeah, I wish," says Rain.

Rain gets up and walks to the dresser. He looks at the pictures of all the kids with him and Ajaunta on the dresser.

"Who are these kids with us?" says Rain.

"Rain, are you serious? Are you hurt or something? What is wrong with you?" says Ajaunta.

Ajaunta gets out of bed and walks up behind Rain. She puts her hand on his forehead and hugs him, looking at him in the mirror on the back of the dresser.

"What is wrong, Rain? You mean you don't remember our kids? That's Betsy. That there is Belinda. That's Gerard, Samantha, and Donald. Our kids, you remember? You wanted more, and I said five is enough. I know it's hard they have all moved out now. Sometimes I wish we could have more, but five is enough. Go on, get in the shower. I'll make you some bacon, eggs, toast, and coffee just the way you like go on. Oh, don't forget to shave this morning. You know Mr. Reynolds is a stickler on being presentable, and you have not shaved in weeks. I don't like it either. Shave it," says Ajaunta.

Rain goes to the bathroom, feeling his face. He has a thick beard, and he hates beards; they always itch him. He can't believe he even has a beard, so he shaves, which is very difficult when his beard is this heavy. He uses three new razors before he is done, and his face is killing him with razor cuts all over. He gets in the shower, and Ajaunta goes downstairs to make breakfast. Rain tries to remember his life with Ajaunta as the water falls on his face. He stands motionless trying to remember anything from his past, and he draws a blank. He can't remember Ajaunta; he can't remember his kids—nothing.

"Rain, I laid out your favorite suit on the bed to wear to your meeting this morning," says Ajaunta.

"All right, thank you, dear," says Rain.

Rain showers and dries off. Walking into the bedroom, he looks at the suit laid out on the bed for him to wear. It is very nice, and he holds it up to his body, looking at himself in the mirror. He puts it on and goes downstairs to a wonderful smell.

"Goddamn, that smells good," says Rain.

"Well, nothing special here, just bacon and eggs," says Ajaunta.

"I must be starving because that smells so good. I feel like I could eat a horse," says Rain.

"Well, dig in, here you go," says Ajaunta.

Ajaunta puts a plate in front of Rain, and he starts to eat. She steps at the back of him and brushes his shoulders with her hands.

"Gosh, I always knew the reason I married you. That is because you dress up so good. I have the most handsome husband in the whole world," says Ajaunta.

She kisses him on the cheek while he eats.

"Well, don't kiss me. Get some breakfast for yourself and eat with me," says Rain.

She makes a plate for herself and sits down to eat.

"You know I have to be honest with you. I don't know where I am going this morning. I don't know where I work. I mean, I work at—" Rain pauses. "I don't even know where I work. I don't remember our kids. I don't remember marrying you. I don't remember anything. How is that possible?" asks Rain.

"You work at Philburns Lending and Financial Consultation of Leesberry. You are the vice assistant to Chairman Rockwell. Rain, what is going on? You have been preparing for this meeting for weeks now. You are meeting with Mr. Rockwell himself, you know, the founder and owner. You are poised to become president of the Leesberry branch. Rain, this is a very important meeting. You are scaring me now. Do you have amnesia or something?" says Ajaunta.

"I think I do because I don't know anything about finance. I pay my bills, and that is all I know. I don't even remember wearing a suit before. I don't remember any Mr. Rockwell or any lending institution. I don't remember marrying you, and I don't remember any kids. This is driving me mad," says Rain.

Rain gets up after devouring his breakfast and starts to walk from the table when he falls to the ground. He tries to get up, but he can't. His vision is blurry, his muscles are weak, and he rolls to his back.

"Rain, Rain!" yells Ajaunta, leaning down to feel his face. She helps him to a sitting position.

"Rain, what is wrong with you? Come on, we need to get you back to bed. Come on, help me get you up," says Ajaunta.

She helps him to a standing position and puts his arm over her shoulder. She walks him to the stairs and up to their bedroom. She leans him back on the bed, and Rain can barely see as a figure walks behind Ajaunta and grabs her from behind. He can hear her scream, but he can't move. "Ajaunta!" he cries as his vision goes black.

Rain opens his eyes, feeling his face. It take a few seconds, but he realizes he is now waking, and he snaps awake just to find he is falling. He can feel the air blow by his face. His arms and legs drag behind him as he falls back first toward the earth. He has no idea how fast he is falling, but it is very fast. He screams, turning, facing, and seeing the ground approach fast, and he has no time to react as he falls face-first into the ground. He hears his neck break and many of the bones in his body crunch as his body slams into the ground, and he bounces four times before coming to a mangled stop. He twists, turns, and rolls until his arms and legs are twisted around his body and his head is backward on his neck. He can feel blood dripping from his nose. He can move his eyes around, but he cannot move any of the muscles in his body. He feels pain, but he can't tell where the pain is. It is like his whole body is just a big pain.

"Rain, Rain, help me. Rain, he's coming after me. Rain, help me!" cries Ajaunta.

He can hear his name being called. He knows it is Ajaunta, but he can't see her. Then he sees her running into his line of sight. She is running right toward him, calling for him.

"Rain, he is coming for me. Rain, don't let him get me. You said you would never let him get me. Rain, get up. Get up, Rain!" cries Ajaunta.

Rain can see Glamfury chasing Ajaunta, and he catches her. She fights, and he slaps her senseless as she tries to free herself from his grip.

"Glamfury, I will kill you. I will kill you!" yells Rain.

Glamfury walks to Rain, whose body is broken, twisted, and mangled. He kneels next to Rain and slaps him on his face.

"I told you, Rain. I told you I would kill you and all that you love, but this beauty; oh, this beauty here deserves a good fucking before I kill this one. Wow! Rain, you sure married a beautiful one, and I am so glad you did because now she is mine," says Glamfury.

Ajaunta is flopped on the ground with her face facing Rain. She looks at Rain with blood dripping from her mouth and her nose. Glamfury tears the clothing from her body, and she can't fight back anymore as he begins to savagely invade her. She looks at Rain, distancing her mind from her body.

"Rain, it's OK, Rain. I know there is nothing you can do. I knew what I was getting into when I married you. I knew there was probably only one real end for us. It's OK, Rain. I loved the time we had together, and I always loved you," says Ajaunta.

"No!" screams Rain, unable to move as he watches his love sway and move with the violations of her body. Rain watches as Glamfury slams his palm on Ajaunta's head. She is looking at him when her skull cracks and her brains squirt all over his face.

"No!" cries Rain, looking up as Glamfury slams his palm down on Rain's face.

Rain wakes up, sitting in a chair. His hands are tied behind him, and his ankles are tied to the legs of the chair. He struggles and shakes around but cannot free himself from the chair. Looking around, he can see he is in a room with a large mirror on the wall facing him. He gets the feeling people are watching him from the other side of the mirror.

"All right, are you having fun? Who is there? I know you are watching. Is this some kind of mad game you are playing? You plan on just leaving me here tied to this chair? Come on, show yourselves!" yells Rain.

He struggles to get out of the chair. The chair is very heavy and moves around, but he cannot tip or move the chair far at all. He struggles and struggles. He starts to have visions of all the scary images, demons, and monsters he has seen in his nightmares over the past days, weeks, months, or however long it has been; he has no idea. Rain struggles and struggles, wearing himself out, and he starts to laugh.

"All right, you win. You win!" he yells. "What do you want? What are you? What is this maze of hysteria I am in? What is this never-ending dreamworld I'm in?" says Rain.

Rain can see a door open to the left wall, and Ajaunta is shoved into the room. The door closes behind her. She is cut and bruised. She struggles to move toward Rain. He can see she has been beaten very badly. She crawls to the chair he is tied to and starts to untie his ankles. She grabs his legs and slowly raises to his lap.

"Rain, he beat me. He beat me, Rain. I want you to kill him. You have to kill him, or he is going to kill us and our kids. You have to kill him," says Ajaunta.

Ajaunta slowly moves to the back of the chair and unties his hands. Rain Stands and turns to Ajaunta, who falls. He catches her and cradles her in his arms. She is cut badly all over and breathing very shallowly.

"Rain, you have to get to him. You have to get to him before he gets our kids. He is going for them. He is going to kill our kids," says Ajaunta.

"What kids? What kids are you talking about?" says Rain.

"Our kids, Rain. Our five kids. We have been married for twenty-five years, Rain. I am your wife," says Ajaunta.

"Ajaunta, we were never married. We have no kids. What are you talking about? This is all just a dream, just a crazy hallucination made up from my dreams and my love of you. Somehow, this Glamfury is tapping into my subconscious and using it against me," says Rain.

"Save our kids," says Ajaunta.

Rain feels Ajaunta go weak. She goes limp and stops breathing. He sits down in the chair and hugs her lifeless body. He cries as he hugs her beaten and bloody body.

"Ajaunta, I love you. I have always loved you. What do you want? What do you want?" yells Rain.

The mirror on the wall starts to shake and widen until the whole wall is a mirror. It shakes back and forth until it shatters. Rain lowers his head, and he can feel the razor-sharp shards slice and cut his body as they fly by him. He hears laughter and slowly raises his head, seeing Glamfury standing in front of him, laughing. Rain can see his arms and sides have been severely cut by all the glass flying by him. There are many shards of glass stuck in Ajaunta's body, and he sets her on the ground.

"You're dead!" yells Rain, and he charges at Glamfury. As soon as Rain gets to where the mirror was, the entire area turns into a dark sea that Rain runs right into. Suddenly he, is sinking in a dark green ocean, and he can see a sea serpent swim by him. It looks very familiar. It looks like the one that was trying to eat him when he was buried at sea. It swims by him so fast he can't see where it goes. It swims by him and bites his foot, dragging him through the water at incredible speed. The pain is great as its teeth dig deep into his left foot. It swims toward the surface and throws Rain out of the water. He flies up and lands on the ground in heavy grass. It is nighttime and raining heavily.

"Rain, Rain, I need your help, Rain!" cries Smoke.

Rain looks over to his left side. He sees Smoke lying with his legs in the water. Rain crawls over to him. His left foot is killing him and bleeding badly from the bite of the serpent.

"Smoke, come on, buddy, let's get you out of the water," says Rain.

Rain grabs Smoke by his hands and pulls him from the water. Smoke cries in pain, and Rain realizes his legs are gone from the knees down.

"Smoke, what happened to your legs?" says Rain.

Rain sees the head of a crocodile breach the water, and he remembers the pond where he first saw this creature. As a matter of fact, this is the same pond, and Rain remembers this croc ate Smoke the last time they were here—at least he thinks it did.

"Smoke, come on, Smoke, get away from the water. Help me get you away from the water," says Rain.

Rain pulls Smoke as hard as he can away from the edge of the water, but he is not fast enough. The croc man leaps from the water, biting Smoke by his legs. "Rain!" yells Smoke as he is dragged into the pond. Rain holds on to Smoke being dragged into the pond himself. He is dragged underwater, where he watches as the croc man bites and twirls, breaking and ripping Smoke's body into pieces and swallowing them whole. Rain swims back to the shore of the pond and crawls back onto the wet grass, crying for his friend who has been eaten by the croc man. He yells into the falling rain.

"What is this hell? What is this nightmare? Will it ever end? Why is this still going on?" cries Rain.

He sees the crocodile breach the water again and move toward the shore where he is. It swims and then walks up on land, heading toward Rain. He gets up, limping on his bitten foot and moves toward the trees. He finds a thick, long stick, which he grabs and uses like a bat. He swings hard, hitting the croc man in the head, knocking it to its side. It does not fall; it swings its enormous head back at Rain very fast, and Rain bats it again harder. This time, it falls. Rain attacks, beating it repeatedly over the head. It retreats, crawling on its hands and knees toward the water, and sinks back into the dark pond water out of sight. Rain falls back, breathing heavily, when he hears his name being called.

"Rain, it's you. Rain, you are OK!" yells Ajaunta.

Ajaunta comes running from the trees to sit next to Rain.

"Ajaunta, I was here before. We were here before. I can't remember what happened. I thought the croc man got you. I thought it got you and Bailey and Smoke. It definitely got Smoke this time. I saw it. I saw it eat him," says Rain.

"Well, the croc man did not get me, but you did not save me from Glamfury, did you? The croc man didn't get me, but Glamfury did," says Ajaunta.

Ajaunta stands up, grabbing the stick Rain was using to bat the croc man with.

"Glamfury. What are you talking about? Glamfury is the one controlling this whole dream. He is the one masterminding this whole nightmare—he has to be," says Rain.

"No, Rain, he is not. You are. You are making this whole dream happen. You said you would protect me, and you lied. You said I would be safe with you all the time, and you lied. You said you would do everything to make me happy, and you lied," says Ajaunta.

"Ajaunta, what are you talking about? What are you saying?" says Rain.

"I am your wife, Rain," says Ajaunta.

Ajaunta swings the stick, hitting Rain over the head.

"I am your wife, your one true love, remember?" says Ajaunta.

She strikes him in the head with the stick again.

"You said you would never let anyone hurt me, and you lied," says Ajaunta.

She strikes him again.

Rain is bleeding from his head. He is holding up his arms, trying to protect himself from the strikes of Ajaunta, but she is beating him silly. She strikes him harder and faster, talking all the time, but he cannot make out what she is saying anymore. She is beating him into unconsciousness.

"Ajaunta, stop, stop. Ajaunta, you are killing me," says Rain.

Rain sees the stick come right at his bloodied face, and everything goes quiet; everything goes black.

Chapter 21

You Are Doing Fine, My Dear

Ajaunta wakes up and sits up in bed. She stretches her arms, breathing deeply. She gets out of bed and walks to the right side of the bed. Rain is sleeping, and she shakes his shoulder.

"Rain, Rain, wake up. Rain, wake up," she says a few times, shaking him, and he rolls over with a sigh, never coming close to waking up. She turns on the light, sitting on the nightstand, and this does not wake Rain up. She rubs his face, running her index finger across the age lines on his face. She touches his neck and rubs his chest, moving the covers to his abdomen. She looks at him so peacefully sleeping, and she pulls the covers back over him, tucking him in nice and snug. She walks to the bathroom, turning on the light, and looks in the mirror. She rubs her face, which has no age lines at all. She is the same age as Rain. He is actually three months older than she is. Rain still looks very good for someone who is forty-three years old, but Ajaunta looks like she is still fifteen. She turns to look at the full-length mirror on the door. She smiles, rubbing her body and running her hands through her long blond hair. Her blues eyes sparkle, and her teeth gleam. Her bra and panties cling snug to her body like a second skin, and her muscles are tone ready for action at a moment's notice. She walks out of the bathroom, turning off all the lights, and goes downstairs, leaving Rain sleeping in his bed. She goes downstairs and gets some orange juice and a sandwich from the refrigerator. Sitting on the couch in the living room, she eats and drinks her juice. The front door opens, and all she sees is darkness.

"What are you waiting for? Come on in. Don't you like what you see?" says Ajaunta.

She stands and bounces on her toes so her breasts bounce up and down for Glamfury, who walks into the living room.

"Oh, I do love what I see. How do you feel? Is it not exhilarating becoming young again?" says Glamfury.

"It is better than you said it would be. I feel strong, rambunctious, just full of energy. I want to fuck all night," says Ajaunta.

"Yes, my dear, we have all the time in the world for that, but that is not what I need right now. The book. Has he brought forth the book?" says Glamfury.

"Yes, just as you had asked. I forgot about the book, but I was actually looking at it with him earlier. Where did he put it? It has to be here somewhere," says Ajaunta.

"Find it. I need the book. I retrieved the other book from the home of Smoke earlier. Now, the second book, and I will be invincible again, and you shall be my queen. The book, where is the book?" says Glamfury.

"Hold on, I'm looking. Where did he put it?" says Ajaunta.

She rubs her head, trying to remember what Rain did with the book. She retraces her steps.

"OK, I remember. We were looking at the book right here on the couch when the house started to rock back and forth. So we were in a dream when we were looking at it," says Ajaunta.

"Well, that does not do me any good. The book must still be in the safe," says Glamfury.

His voice gets deeply mad, and Ajaunta feels fear race through her body.

"I'll go back to bed with him. I'll get in his dream and have him open the safe, no problem," says Ajaunta.

"You're damn right you will right now," says Glamfury in a very deep voice.

Ajaunta's demeanor quiets; her smile fades. She turns, heading back up the stairs.

"I need that book. Once I have the book, we torture him until his mind collapses in on itself. We continue to haunt his mind until he begs for death, until he puts the knife in my hands, thinking me cutting his heart out is his only salvation," says Glamfury.

"Bailey and Marlene are still mine, right? I get to take their youth like I did that blond floozy with you at the cabin, right, and the girl whose youth I stole when she was pretending to be Marlene, right?" says Ajaunta.

"Yes, my sweet. You get Rain to show me the combination to the safe. Then you keep him occupied in his dream. I will get the book and devour the soul of Smoke. Smoke is ready, and so is Bailey. Rain is still very strong. The strongest I have ever come across. You still need to love and torment him. You love him good, my sweet. You give him everything he desires physically. Give in to him. Let him know now that your family is dead and gone. He is your man. He is your strength, your only reason to live. I will continue to break him down. You are his weakness, and we need to use this against him. When I have devoured Smoke, I will come to you with Bailey, and we will love until she is weak and trapped in my embrace. Then you draw her life, you suck her youth, and you become my immortal queen. Ha, ha, ha, ha, ha, ha, ha. Take this and make him drink it when you get into bed with him." He hands her a vial with a blue liquid in it. "This will keep him in dream for half a day. This will make his mind weaker yet, and take these vials. You will need to pour these vials in his food for another week. He is strong. I expect we will need another week to break him down. Now go. You know what to do, my sweet," says Glamfury.

Ajaunta turns to go in the kitchen, and Glamfury fondles her ass.

"Oh, yeah, you are doing fine, my dear. You just keep doing what you are doing. You keep Rain in dream. You keep him guessing from one minute to the next. I love the part where you make him your husband and tell him you have five kids. Make him the president of a lending institution so he has a lot to lose. Oh, yeah, you are doing fine, my dear. As long as he can never keep things straight from one minute to the next, he will weaken, he will beg for death, he will freely give his strength to me to us. Now go," says Glamfury.

Glamfury turns and leaves the house. Ajaunta goes into the kitchen and puts the box of vials on top of the refrigerator. She holds the one vial in her hand, turning it up and down. She looks at it, thinking, *I don't know how this stuff does what it does, but it sure is cool the way I can get into other people's dreams. Time to go make the magic happen.* Ajaunta walks upstairs. She gets into bed with Rain. She pops the cork off the medium-size vial and takes a sip of the potion. She tilts Rain's head and drips the liquid into his mouth. His natural bodily functions instinctively drink the fluid, keeping him in a heightened dream state. Ajaunta sips the potion and pours more into his mouth three times until it is gone. She puts the cork back on the vial and tosses it into the air. The vial gently floats like a dandelion on the breeze until it touches the floor, sinking into it like it was liquid vanishing. Ajaunta pushes the covers down, exposing Rain's body. She rubs his chest, sliding her left leg over his groin and in between his legs. She runs her nose up his neck, reaching her arms and legs around him, gently squeezing him close to her. The potion is starting to take effect on her senses. Her eyes start to fall heavy. She gently kisses Rain on the neck and whispers in his ear.

Rain sits up fast like a terrible noise scared the crap out of him. He looks around, breathing deeply like he is scared out of his mind, but he has no idea why he is scared. He feels the intensely hot sun beating its searing hot rays into his skin. Looking around, he sees the dried and cracked earth with no vegetation for as far as he can see. "Now where the fuck am I?" he says out loud as he stands up. He takes off his shirt and ties it around his head. It is very clear that he has to do something fast. The heat is almost unbearable, and without water, he won't last but a few hours. He tries to figure the best way to go. Unfortunately, the sun is directly overhead. He has no way of making his bearings, so he starts to walk. Instantly, things get worse as he looks down, seeing he is barefoot. "Oh, this just keeps getting better." He sits down, taking his pants off. He rips his pants, wrapping the cloth around his feet, giving them some protection from the dry hot earth. He puts the pants, now shorts, back on, heading off into the desert. He hears his name being called.

"Rain, Rain. Help, Rain, help!" cries a voice.

Looking around, everything looks like a mirage. Everything looks like water vapor rising from the scorching earth.

"Rain, Rain, over here. Help me, Rain!" cries the voice.

Rain moves toward the sound, and he can see Ajaunta tied to the earth. Her arms and legs are stretched as far as they can be, and her body forms an X on the ground. He runs to her and starts to untie her hands that are tied to stakes.

"Hurry, Rain, hurry and untie me before they get to me," says Ajaunta.

Rain looks to see another body tied to stakes a few feet from Ajaunta. The body is nothing more than bones, and it is covered in ants. The ants are moving toward Ajaunta, and some of them are already on her. They are biting her and eating her flesh.

"Ouch, ouch. Hurry, Rain, it hurts. They are biting me," says Ajaunta.

Rain unties both her arms, and she sits up, frantically wiping the ants from her body, as is Rain. Rain looks closer to see the ants have the head of Smoke on them.

"Smoke, is that you, Smoke? What the hell?" says Rain.

The little ant with the head of Smoke on it looks up and laughs at Rain. Rain squishes it with his right hand.

"Goddamn Smoke ants. They are ants with the head of Smoke on them. One minute he is spiders, now he is ants. What the hell? This has to be a dream," says Rain.

"Rain, get me out of here. Untie me, Rain. They are biting me. They are going to eat me like they did Bailey. Hurry up, Smoke. They are biting and eating me," says Ajaunta.

Rain looks to see the earth moving when in fact it is many thousands of ants moving toward Ajaunta. He tries to untie her ankles, but he cannot untie the knots. In fact, there are no knots at all. The ropes are around her ankles and run through a hole in the stakes with no knots. They are one piece. He tries to pull the rope off her ankles, but they are too tight.

"Ajaunta, I cannot get them off you. I don't know what to do," says Rain.

He looks her over, and she is wearing nothing but her underwear. He stands and tries to pull the stakes from the ground. He tries over and over, but they do not budge.

"Rain, they are on me. Rain, they are biting me. They are eating me. Rain!" cries Ajaunta.

"Stand up, come on, stand up," says Rain.

Rain helps her stand up. Her legs are spread apart, and she can barely stand. This is not working either. The ants are on both of them and starting to race up her body and his. Rain has to jump up and down and furiously brushes off the biting ants. Ajaunta is screaming, and Rain can see her feet being stripped of flesh right to the bone. She screams and cries as the ants strip the flesh from her body right up her legs to her genitals when the ropes are severed from the biting ants. Ajaunta walks toward Rain on her legs, which are only bone. Slowly, her crotch is eaten away, and Rain can see her flesh eaten away up her abdomen.

"Rain, you said you would protect me. You said they would never get me. What do you call this, Rain? My tits are about to be eaten by ants. What do you call this, Rain?" says Ajaunta.

Rain backs away from her as she walks toward him. He is jumping, hopping, and wiping the ants from his legs.

"No, Ajaunta, I never wanted this to happen. I never wanted any of this. I always wanted to be with you and protect you. I failed you, Ajaunta. I failed," says Rain.

The ground shakes, and Rain falls to his back. Looking up, he sees the ants eating the flesh and insides of Ajaunta right up to the bottom of her breasts. She is bone from her feet to the bottom of her ribs. Her bra is snapped and falls from her body. She walks toward Rain, and suddenly, all the ants run away from the two of them and into holes in the ground.

"Is this what you wanted? Huh, Rain, is this what you wanted?" says Ajaunta.

She kicks him in the head with her right tibia bone. Rain blocks her repeated kicks with his arms.

"Ajaunta, stop. Stop it. They have gone. The ants they have gone away. You are still alive. I don't know how, but you are still alive," says Rain.

"Oh, you want some of this. Is that what you want, Rain? Is that it? You want some of this? Maybe you want some breast milk, huh?" says Ajaunta.

Ajaunta starts to squeeze her nipples, and they shoot breast milk at Rain like fire truck hoses. Thick powerful streams of breast milk flow on Rain, rolling him, tumbling him over and over on the desert ground.

"Ajaunta, stop. Stop, Ajaunta," says Rain.

Rain tries to block the streams of breast milk with his hands as Ajaunta squeezes over and over, spraying him with the milk. The ground shakes again, and up from the earth behind Ajaunta rises a huge ant. It is twelve feet tall and has the head of Smoke on it. Another ant rises from the earth to the right and to the left of both Ajaunta and Rain. Ajaunta freezes with a surprised look on her face. She looks up to the left and right.

"Rain, I have a bad feeling about this," says Ajaunta.

"No!" yells Rain as the ant at the back of Ajaunta swoops in with its head. The heads are exactly like the heads that were on the tarantulas. The teeth are pyramid shaped, creating sheers, and the ant bites Ajaunta's head clean off. Ajaunta falls neck first, landing right between Rain's legs. Her head would have hit him in the groin, but there is no head. There is only flesh from her neck to her arms and hands and to the bottom of her ribs; the rest of her is bone. "Ahh!" screams Rain, standing as the three huge Smoke-headed ants approach him. They stand in front of him and to the sides of him. They tower over him, and he has nothing to defend himself with.

"Oh, I get it, Smoke. You are going to eat me now, is that it? You couldn't get me as a spider, so you are going to get me as an ant. Oh, wait a few minutes from now, you will be, what, centipede man? Oh, no, I got it. You will be cricket man. That's a good one for you, Smoke. You should be cricket man. Enough with the hallucinations, Glamfury. I know this is you. I know this is you trying to look like Smoke. If you want to eat me, then eat me. Quit wasting my time and my dreams. Go for it. Do your worst," says Rain.

Rain holds out his arms and closes his eyes. He stands there for a few moments, waiting for it to be over. He feels the heat of the sun go away and the bright of the light lessens on his eyelids. He opens his eyes to see the landscape change before his very eyes. The sun rolls around the horizon, and the stars fill the night sky. Trees rise and grow, as does the grass and the sound of insects in the bush. Rain can hear Glamfury laughing, and he turns to see Glamfury walk up behind him. Glamfury slaps Rain on the back. You would think it is a friendly slap, but it knocks Rain violently to the ground. He sits, wiping the blood from his lip and his nose. He spits blood and stands, facing Glamfury.

"That's why I like you the best, Rain. You ain't no schmuck. You're no pushover. You can see your friends die, and it does not bother you at all. Hell, I could rape your love right in front of you, and it would not faze you one bit, would it?" says Glamfury.

Rain screams and throws a straight punch at Glamfury's face. Glamfury waves his right hand, and Rain is stopped just before his fist reaches Glamfury's nose. Glamfury walks to the side of Rain, who seems to be frozen in time.

"You see, Rain, you can never fight me. You cannot touch me if I do not wish it. It's just not fair, but I like you, Rain. I'm going to give you a chance. I'm going to let you in on a little secret. I am human. I can be hurt and killed like any other person you know. There is, however, a big difference between me and all other people. You want to know what that difference is? Well, funny you should ask," says Glamfury, looking at Rain, who is actually moving very slowly. "I have sold my soul to the devil. That's right, I have sold my soul to the devil. Now, many people have sold their souls to the devil in exchange for some sort of supernatural power here on earth. My power is very interesting indeed. I am going to tell you my power. I'm going to tell you because I like you, because I need something from you, which you had stolen from me, and you will give it back to me. You see, I can draw the youth from living people, and as that person dies, their soul is funneled into hell where Lucifer himself feeds on that soul, while I am energized with the youth of that person, giving me eternal life. Isn't that cool? Now you are something very special. You are very special indeed. You see, I have already lived for over half a century. That's right, respect your elders, Rain. With me being as old as I am, I need to consume more and more youth as I get older and older. A long time ago, I could drain the youth of a person and maintain my youth for, say, fifty years. Not anymore. Now I need to consume youth almost yearly. That's a lot of people, Rain, but there are special people. There are people who are just more fit than others spiritually, mentally, and physically. You are one of those persons. I could maintain my youth up to ten years with a person like you, but I can't just kill you, oh, no. You have to beg me to kill you. You have to plead with me to take your life. If I were to just kill you and consume your youth, I would get more-than-usual life from your youth, but with the proper preparation, I will get a decade of worry-free life from your youth. Now beg me to kill you. Plead with me to take your youth, or watch your friends die," says Glamfury.

Chapter 22

Cogitate

Rain sits up in his bed, looking to his right. It is dark and quiet. He lies back with his back very, very sore. He knows he has been sleeping way too long. He looks at the clock on the nightstand, seeing it is 3:15 a.m. Slowly he gets out of bed, stretching his arms, rubbing his neck, and bending over at his waist to stretch the back of his legs. He is sore all over and has a terrible headache. He has no idea how long he has been asleep, but he knows it has been a long time. He walks to the bathroom and rinses his face with cold water. He has a heavy beard and knows something is way off. He never goes more than a day or two without shaving, and he has at least a week's growth on his face. He shaves, and his body feels all sticky. He stinks, so he gets in the shower and thoroughly cleans his body with his shower gel. After washing his hair and rinsing off, he gets out of the shower, dries off, and puts the shorts he was wearing into the hamper. Walking into the bedroom nude, he hears someone crying in the hallway leading to the stairs. He puts on a new pair of shorts and walks into the hallway. He sees Ajaunta lying at the top of the stairs on her stomach, and she is crying.

"Ajaunta. Ajaunta, is that you?" says Rain.

Rain walks up and sits next to her, turning her to her back. She is nude and crying.

"Ajaunta, how did you get here on my stairs? Come on, let me get you some clothes," says Rain.

Rain walks to his bedroom and gets some sweatpants and a big T-shirt for her to wear. He turns to see she has walked to his bedroom and she puts on the clothes. She walks to the bed and sits down. Rain sits by her comforting her.

"Rain, he keeps coming to me in my dreams. He keeps loving me, and I can't resist him. I know he is not real. How can he be? But my family is gone. What happened to them? I can't free myself from him. I can't tell what is real and what is not anymore. I just want to die," says Ajaunta.

"Shh, shh, shh. Stop that," says Rain.

He hugs and comforts Ajaunta. He slowly rocks back and forth, sitting next to her, holding her in the dark. Rain thinks to himself, *Glamfury. He said he got the book. I finally got it open, but what happened to the book? Where is it? We were looking at it after we ate. We were on the couch, and the house sank in the ocean. Did he get the book? Was that even real?*

"Rain, I don't want to die. I don't want to give up, but I don't know what else to do," says Ajaunta.

"Shh, shh, it's time to make things right. It's time to give him what he wants," says Rain.

"Give him what he wants? What are you talking about? What does he want?" says Ajaunta.

"He wants you. He wants me to give you to him," says Rain.

"Rain, you are not going to give me to him, are you? I can't get away from him anyway. He takes me all the time, at least sexually he does in my dreams," says Ajaunta.

"It's not the sex he wants. It's your soul. He knows he can't have my soul. He knows I have always loved you, so to best hurt me, to weaken me, he needs you. By jerking you around in front of me like a bone in front of a dog, he thinks he can get to my soul. I know what I have to do. I know how to fight back. Come on, I have to check something," says Rain.

Rain gets up and heads downstairs. Ajaunta follows him down into the kitchen and down into the basement.

"Rain, what are you doing?" says Ajaunta.

"It's the book. It was always the book. That is his source of power. He needs the book," says Rain.

"What book? What book are you talking about?" says Ajaunta.

"Don't you remember we were looking at it before we were swept into the ocean? The biggest problem I have had all along is knowing whether I was in a dream or I was in reality. While in dream, we can't hurt him. While in dream, he can manipulate our surroundings. He can kill us over and over. He can rape us, mutilate us, eat us. He can emotionally destroy us in our dreams. In reality, he cannot. In reality, if he kills us, we die for real, and he gets nothing unless we are sacrificed properly. Without his book, he gets nothing, and I have the book. With the book, I can kill him and end this nightmare. I finally know the difference between reality and dream, and we are in reality right now. I know he does not have the book. I got the book out, and we looked it over, but that was in a dream. Now we are here in reality, so when I get the book, he has to come for it, and I will kill him. In reality, he is no match for me, like in dream, I am no match for him. Time to bring Glamfury to me. Time to end him," says Rain.

Rain bends down to the cabinet, pulling the front panel, exposing the safe. He turns the combination dial.

"Rain, I don't know. Are you sure you can handle him? Are you sure we are not in a dream right now? What if he is just waiting for you to get the book for him?" says Ajaunta.

Rain opens the safe, and, sure enough, there is the book still sealed in a large ziplock bag. Rain closes his safe and stands. He turns to Ajaunta, holding the book and key.

"He is waiting for me to get the book. He is waiting right now and just waiting for the right moment to make his move. What he did not plan on was Stormy Rain Clouds," says Rain.

"Rain, what are you going to do?" says Ajaunta.

"I am going to wait," says Rain.

Rain heads upstairs and up to his room. He puts the book on his dresser, never unsealing the bag. He starts to dress himself.

"Rain, what are you doing? I am scared. I don't want him to come here. What are you doing?" says Ajaunta.

Ajaunta gets close to Rain and hugs him. She tries to kiss him, but he ignores her. She kisses his neck. He gets dressed and heads back downstairs with the book. Ajaunta follows him.

"Where are you going? What are you doing?" asks Ajaunta.

Rain walks outside, looking in his driveway.

"I knew it. I knew your car would be here. Listen to me. Do you want to see your husband and your kids?" says Rain.

"Yes, there is nothing I want more," says Ajaunta.

"Then listen to me. Your husband was sacrificed in a dream. Your kids were eaten in a dream. They are still alive. They are at your home right now, wondering where you are. Go to them. Go to them right now," says Rain.

"Rain, I am scared. What if Glamfury comes for me? What if he kills me?" says Ajaunta.

She hugs Rain and starts to cry.

"Well, then I guess you die and you will never see your family again," says Rain.

He pushes Ajaunta from him and gets in his car. He starts it up and backs away, leaving Ajaunta standing dumfounded. She is stunned and runs after his car. She gets in the passenger seat before he leaves the driveway.

"Rain, I am scared. Take me home, please. You take me home. I feel safer with you," says Ajaunta.

"OK, but you are with me, and I have some things to do first. I am starting to figure this nightmare world out. This Glamfury has let me live too long. I know he could have killed me and he has missed his chance," says Rain, and he speeds off.

"Rain, where are we going?" asks Ajaunta.

"Listen, I am in no mood for chitchat. My life is on the line here. This motherfucker thinks he can fuck with me. He thinks he can wear me down and get me to beg him to kill me. Motherfucker is in for a big surprise. Motherfucker is dead already and does not even know it. He wants my killer instinct. He wants my superior intellect. He thinks he can use you to get to me. He is wrong," says Rain.

"Well, at least tell me where we are going?" says Ajaunta.

"We're going to get something to eat. I am starving," says Rain.

Rain drives to Sandy's, the all-night diner he and Smoke always used to meet at and talk while having coffee. Just before they get to the diner, it starts to rain outside. Rain parks and walks right into the diner, holding the book in his left hand.

"Hold on, Rain, wait for me," says Ajaunta.

Rain walks in, and he is so glad to see Renee greet him.

"Oh my god! It's Stormy Rain Clouds. Well, it sure is great to see you after all these years," says Renee.

Renee greets Rain and hugs him. She sees Ajaunta walk in behind Rain and gives her an inquisitive look. Ajaunta returns the look.

"What's the matter? Never seen a girl in sweatpants before?" says Ajaunta.

"Not one with Rain. The usual booth, Rain?" says Renee.

"Renee, I am so glad you are here. I can't believe you are here. I have to ask you a few things," says Rain.

Rain and Ajaunta follow Renee to a booth and are seated.

"Was I here, oh, a week or two ago? Did you talk with me recently?" asks Rain.

"What are you talking about, Rain? I have not seen you in, what, five years or so," says Renee.

"What about Smoke? Has he been here recently?" asks Rain.

"Not that I have seen," says Renee.

"Just as I figured," says Rain.

"Rain, is everything all right, sweetie?" says Renee.

That just kind of slipped out, and Renee notices a not-so-nice look from Ajaunta.

"So would you two like some coffee? Would you like menus?" says Renee.

"Actually, I would like some pancakes, eggs sunny side up, and bacon. I would like some coffee to go with it. Ajaunta, do you want anything to eat?" says Rain.

"I'll take a menu, please," says Ajaunta.

"Coming right up," says Renee.

She walks back to get some menus, and Ajaunta watches as Rain gets up and stops her to talk with her. He writes on a piece of paper and gives it to Renee. Then he comes back to the table and sits.

"What was that all about? She must be your girlfriend?" says Ajaunta.

"No. I just gave her Smoke's phone number. She is going to call him and have him come meet us here," says Rain.

"Smoke—you mean Kenneth," says Ajaunta.

"Yup, the same Kenneth who ate you as spiders, as ants, and who knows what else in the future dreams we may have," says Rain.

Renee comes back to the table and hands a menu to Ajaunta.

"Sorry, Rain, there was no answer at the number you gave me," says Renee.

Renee fills his coffee, and she fills a cup for Ajaunta. Ajaunta orders some breakfast, and Renee leaves the two of them alone. Ajaunta can see Rain is lost in heavy thought and hardly responds to her at all while he eats his breakfast. He eats like he has not eaten in days. He finishes long before she does and is ready to leave. He puts money on the table and does not even wait for her to finish. He is up, leaving the diner. Renee gives Rain a hug before he leaves, and Ajaunta follows behind him. It is still raining outside, and the sun is starting to break the horizon. Rain still holds the book close to him and drives off.

"So where are we going now?" asks Ajaunta.

"We are going to Smoke's house. You remember the house where you were sleeping with your head on my leg, and somehow, that bastard Glamfury took you without me even knowing it? Time to go back there. Time to get Smoke. Time to turn the tide on this Glamfury character," says Rain.

"I hope you are right," says Ajaunta.

Rain actually drives right to where he remembers Smoke's house is in Liesnell. He drives right to the house and pulls in the driveway.

"This is it. Look, there is Smoke's BMW right there. Come on, let's go get him," says Rain.

Ajaunta follows Rain to the front door, and he knocks. Smoke answers the door.

"Rain, is that you, buddy? Rain, it is you. Ajaunta. Oh my god, it is so good to see you two. I have so many things I have to talk to you two about. Come on in, come on in," says Smoke.

They follow Smoke into his living room where the horseshoe couch and plush rug are instantly memorable.

"Rain, I can't tell what is real and what is dream anymore. I can't even tell if I am awake anymore," says Smoke.

"Smoke, I have been having the same problem, but right now, we are awake. We are not in a dream right now. This is real, and it is time to turn the tide on Glamfury," says Rain.

"Who is Glamfury? Wait, is he the one tormenting me? Is he the one torturing me and not killing me? He is the god of the Egengyns, isn't he?" says Smoke.

"Yes, he is, and he is trying to steal our youth from us. By sending our souls to the devil, he maintains our youth. Do you still have the book you got in Egypt? You remember when we killed the Egengyns in that barracks and you found that book? Where is it?" says Rain.

"Ah, I don't know. Let me look. Hold on a second," says Smoke.

Rain and Ajaunta sit on the couch, while Smoke goes down into the basement. While they are sitting there, Bailey walks out from the bedroom with her hand in her hair. She is wearing just panties, and her hair is a mess. She is very beautiful and so sexy in her half-asleep state. She seems to not be at all concerned with her nakedness and sits on the couch. She lights a cigarette, finally noticing Rain and Ajaunta sitting at the other end of the couch. She points her right hand with lit cigarette in between her fingers at Rain and Ajaunta.

"I know you two. I have seen you two in my dreams. Is this a dream? You keep killing me over and over. Why? Why do you hate me so much? I don't even know you," says Bailey.

She is mainly pointing at Ajaunta.

"Me? I don't know you, but I have seen you in my dreams, and you keep dying. We all keep dying. It's this Glamfury guy. He keeps killing us all," says Ajaunta.

"No, it's you who keeps killing me. You have stabbed me. You have shot me, and you have pushed me off a cliff. You keep killing me, and there is this guy who keeps laughing while you kill me every time. He keeps fucking me in my dreams, and I can't stop him," says Bailey.

She starts to cry. Ajaunta moves over to her and hugs her. "He does the same to me. He keeps seducing me in different times. I am always wearing different clothes, and we are having wonderful times eating and dancing, and then he loves me and I can't stop him. I don't want to stop him and he loves me over and over. Then I see him in real life and he kills my family. I hate him, but I can't resist him," says Ajaunta, and the two girls cry while hugging each other.

Smoke comes back into the living room.

"Rain, it's gone. The book is gone. I think he took it, but I thought it was in a dream. I did not think it was real, but it's gone," says Smoke.

"I was afraid of that. Well, he needs this here," says Rain.

He holds up his book.

"Rain, you still have the book. Do you have the key with it?" asks Smoke.

"Yes, I do, and something tells me this god of the Egengyns needs this book to finish us off. Make no mistake, he intends to kill us all. We now have the upper hand. We are aware of him. We are in the real world now, and we are strong together. He can only hurt us in our dreams. This book has to have the answers to how he is getting into our dreams with us. I bet he cannot track us as long as the book is sealed. Once I unseal the book, I think he can track us down, but as long as we are awake, he knows he is no match for us. He needs to get us in our dreams to use his demonic power on us. I have seen the pages of the book. They are written in different languages from the past to the present. Smoke, we need to find someone who can help us translate what is written in this book. We need to find a multilingual person who also has knowledge about demonic cults. This is where it gets very difficult for us. I have no idea who can help us," says Rain.

Smoke takes a deep breath. He sits by Bailey and comforts her.

"He's right, Smoke. This guy keeps coming to me in my dreams. He keeps killing you, and he has this girl here kill me over and over. No offense, Ajaunta, but it is really creeping me out sitting next to you," says Bailey.

"I understand," says Ajaunta.

She moves over by Rain.

"He keeps tormenting me. I keep seeing you and Rain being killed over and over, and I can't stop it," says Smoke.

"OK, guys, who can help us understand the writing in this book? Have any of us seen anything in our dreams that can help us?" says Rain.

The four of them sit sorting through their recent dreams. They try and think of historians and multilingual persons that may be able to help them.

Chapter 23

Smoke's Escape

Smoke raises his head. "I've got it, you guys. I know who can help us. You guys? Where did you all go? Hey, guys, where are you?" says Smoke.

Smoke gets up from the couch. He is alone and walks through his whole house looking for his friends. There is no one here except him. He walks to the front yard and sees only his car is in the driveway. He hears Bailey crying and sees her crawling up the driveway toward his house. He runs toward her, and as he steps on the blacktop, it turns red hot. He has to back off into the grass because it burns his feet.

"Smoke, it burns. It burns, Smoke!" screams Bailey.

"Bailey, get off the blacktop. It's turning red hot, and I can't get on it without burning myself!" yells Smoke.

"Smoke, it's burning me. Smoke, help me!" cries Bailey.

Smoke runs onto the blacktop, and his bare feet burn. He grabs Bailey and lifts her off the blacktop, but her face sticks, and all the flesh is torn from her face and the front of her body as Smoke pulls her onto the grass. She screams in horrific pain as Smoke lays her on her back. Her flesh from the top of her forehead down her face, chest, stomach, and legs to her knees has been stripped and seared. Her flesh smells like roasted human, and Smoke nearly pukes at the sight and smell of his love charred, stripped of flesh, and nearly dead.

"Smoke, why did you let him burn me? Why, Smoke, why? You said you would protect me. You said I could come to America and I would have a good life. Why, Smoke? Why did you let this happen to me?" cries Bailey.

"Bailey, no, this is not real. This is a dream. How did we get back in a dream?" says Smoke.

Smoke picks her up and carries her back into his house. As he walks into the house, he hears the laughing of Glamfury. It is loud and echoing throughout the house.

"I know who you are, Glamfury," says Smoke.

"Ha, ha, ha, ha, ha. Been talking with your buddy Rain, have you? Well, I guess now that you know who I am, it is probably a good time to end your misery, don't you think? Looks like Bailey has all but been eliminated, unless you know how to replace burned flesh. Ha, ha, ha, ha, ha, ha, ha, ha, ha," laughs Glamfury.

Smoke carries Bailey into the living room, where he sees Rain and Ajaunta are sitting with their heads hanging down. They are sleeping on his couch. He lays Bailey down on the other side of the couch, but she holds on to him. He looks at her, holding back his scream. The flesh on her face is gone. Her eyes are bright white, and so are her teeth with the rest of her face moist coagulating blood, and it's one of the grossest things Smoke has ever seen. Her hair is matted all through her face and neck. Her breasts are skinless, and she reaches for him as he moves away from her.

"Bailey, I don't know what to do for you," says Smoke.

"Here, I will help you," says Glamfury.

He appears standing behind the couch. He swings a long hooked blade, which passes right through Bailey's neck. Her head does not move, and she still calls and reaches for Smoke. Smoke yells, "No!" Her head rolls forward and down her chest. Smoke instinctively reaches his hands out and catches her head in his hands. He holds her mutilated face up, seeing she is still looking at him and talking, but there is no sound coming from her mouth. Glamfury laughs from behind the couch, and Smoke throws Bailey's head at him, hitting him in the chest with it.

"Now that was not nice, Smoke. After all, she deserted you. She dumped you. She did not love you. Listen to her own words," says Glamfury.

He holds her head up by her hair in his left hand. Blood drips constantly from the bottom of her neck. She begins to speak, and Smoke can now hear her.

"Smoke, you bastard. Why did you let him cut my head off? Why did you let him burn me and strip the flesh from my body? Why, Smoke, why? I knew you were no good. That is why I left you. That is why I left you and found someone I truly loved. You were just a visa for me to get here to America. Now you bring me to your house so I can be killed. I never loved you, Smoke. I only used you to get to America," says Bailey's head.

"OK, OK, enough of that," says Glamfury.

He throws her head out the window while she is still talking. Her head screams as it crashes through the glass and out into the darkness.

"So you see, she never loved you. I was doing you a favor by killing her," says Glamfury.

Smoke starts to shake Rain and Ajaunta.

"Rain, wake up. Come on, Rain, wake up. Ajaunta, wake up. Come on, you guys, wake up. Why won't you wake up?" says Smoke.

Smoke takes a few steps back as Glamfury appears on the couch sitting between Rain and Ajaunta. He has his arms around the two of them.

"No, no, no, they are not going to help you, Smoke," says Glamfury.

Smoke runs out of the living room, hearing Glamfury's laugh throughout his house. Smoke goes to his bedroom, opening his gun safe and getting one of his lethal assault rifles.

"Come on, you fucker, I got something for you," says Smoke.

He heads back to the living room where Glamfury is standing with Rain in his left hand and Ajaunta in his right hand. They are both still sleeping, and he is holding them by the back of their necks. He holds them, and Smoke points right at Glamfury's head.

"I . . ."

Glamfury gets no more words out before Smoke fires. He fires automatically, shooting holes through the wall since Glamfury, Rain, and Ajaunta disappear. Smoke stops his fire. He hears noise in his bedroom. Slowly walking backward, he points his rifle, watching his bedroom, and he can see Glamfury standing in his room. He fires a single shot and sees Glamfury stagger. He fires another shot, and Glamfury falls. Glamfury tries to crawl out of sight, and Smoke fires two more shots. He can hear Ajaunta screaming from inside the bedroom. She is calling Rain's name, and Smoke moves toward the bedroom, opening the door with his rifle and looking in. He can see Ajaunta is on the bed.

"Smoke, Rain has been shot. Help him, Smoke, help him!" cries Ajaunta.

Smoke looks down to see Rain lying next to his bed, and he leans down beside him.

"Smoke, I just want you to know I would have never done anything differently. I will always be your best friend. I would never change anything we have done. I always knew you would be the death of me, and that is OK. I knew it would be this way, and I would have it no other way," says Rain.

"Rain. No! You don't understand. It's not like you think. It's not like you think," says Smoke.

He sets his rifle against the wall and tries to comfort Rain, but it is too late. Rain passes.

"Smoke, Smoke, Smoke," calls Ajaunta.

Smoke looks up as Ajaunta quietly calls his name. Glamfury has a knife to her throat. Ajaunta is lying on her hips with her hands on the bed and her arms extended. Glamfury is standing on the bed, straddling her, holding her hair with a very large knife at her throat.

"So now you have shot your best lifelong friend. That must suck. You actually killed him for me. Thank you. Let's see how you deal with this," says Glamfury.

Glamfury pulls the knife across the throat of Ajaunta. Smoke sees the blood slowly trickle from the slice on her throat. Glamfury pushes on the back of her neck, pulling on the top of her head, opening the wound wider and wider, and the blood starts to pour from her neck. He swipes the knife strong and hard from the back side of her neck, severing Ajaunta's neck.

"Need a little head?" laughs Glamfury.

He throws Ajaunta's head at Smoke. Smoke catches her head, and it is facing him while in his hands.

"Smoke, you let him kill me. You let him cut my head off. You shot Rain. You killed both of us. Why, Smoke, why?" says Ajaunta's head.

Smoke throws her head and grabs his rifle. Glamfury is still standing on the bed, laughing. Smoke points and fires a barrage of bullets, ripping holes throughout the back wall in his bedroom. Smoke screams while firing until his bullets are gone. Smoke is rising from the super heated muzzle of his rifle, and he throws his gun on the floor. Smoke looks to see Ajaunta's headless body on his bed. Rain is dead, lying on the floor by his bed, and Glamfury has vanished. Smoke gains his composure and grabs his rifle. He goes back to his gun storage and reloads his ammunition. He can hear Glamfury laughing throughout his house.

"You boys and your toys you will never learn. What good do you think that gun will do you? It has already killed Rain. You have shot me one hundred times with it already. Ha, ha, ha, ha, ha, ha, ha, ha," laughs Glamfury.

"Yeah, well, for some reason, you cannot be hurt while in my dreams. When I wake up and I have my gun, I don't think you will be showing yourself around me, or it will be lights out for you," says Smoke.

"Well, then let's test that theory. Time to wake up, Smoke. Time to meet your maker, and he's in hell waiting for you," says Glamfury.

The floor disappears, and Smoke falls. He is falling and falling with no sight of the ground. He has no idea where he is falling. He lands on his back right on a large boulder. This wakes him from his dream, and it is early morning. He is rushed by four men who look very familiar to him. They are very large men wearing coconut shells over their heads with vines from the bottom of the shell to their knees. They grab him by his arms and legs. They bind his limbs with rope and step back, pulling on the rope so he cannot escape the boulder he is lying on. There is a fifth man who is chanting some demonic gibberish with a very large knife in his hands. Smoke looks at him, yelling.

"No. I know what you are. You are not going to sacrifice me, you goddamn demon worshiper. You murderous Egengyns. I know what you are. We killed you once, we will kill you again!" yells Smoke.

Smoke struggles, pulling as hard as he can with his arms and legs. He puts up quite a struggle, but the men holding the ropes are very large and very strong. Smoke cannot escape. Smoke can see there are about two dozen men and women fully robed and chanting in the background. The man holding the knife approaches Smoke and raises the knife high with both hands. Smoke screams, calling the man every curse word in the book, struggling to break free of the ropes. The men pulling on the ropes pull a little lever built into the unique ropes that draw hooks at the ends of the ropes tied to Smoke's wrists and ankles. He screams as the metal hooks dig into his flesh, and the disciples pull hard, drawing blood, and Smoke no longer resists. He yells into the air, looking at the large man holding the knife, ready to thrust it into Smoke's chest.

"You won't kill me. Rain was right. Rain, you were right! They won't kill us in the dreamworld. They need to kill us in the real world to gain our youth. You won't kill me. You are nothing but a peon. Glamfury needs to kill me. He needs to sacrifice me to take my youth. He needs me to beg him to kill me. He needs me to grant him my soul. I have to plead with him, beg him. I have to supplicate my life to him, or he gets nothing—nothing, you hear me, you mindless freak!" yells Smoke.

Smoke laughs, and the men holding the ropes pull harder, causing great pain and a lot of blood to drip from his ankles and wrists.

"Yes, Smoke, he needs you to beg him to take your life. He needs you to tell him you freely give him your youth, but you don't have to do any of these. You can suffer forever. You can watch your friends die over and over. You have seen Bailey, Rain, and Ajaunta die how many times now? You tried to save them every time, but this time is different. You know you are not in the dreamworld, don't you? You know this is real. You know when Bailey dies, this time she dies for real. Are you knowingly going to sit by letting her and your best friends for life die for real?" says the man in the mask, holding the knife above Smoke's chest.

The man removes the coconut shell from his face, and it is Glamfury. "Glamfury!" yells Smoke.

"Yes, I am no disciple. I am the closest to a god you will ever see until you meet your maker, and that will be soon. You are going to die here on this rock very shortly, and how you die is entirely up to you. Will you die with dignity, or will you whimper, cry and watch as your loved ones are tortured before you die?" says Glamfury.

Glamfury waves his hands toward his disciples, who are fully covered in robes. The row of disciples splits, and two men holding Bailey by both her arms bring her toward Glamfury.

"Bailey, how did they get you here? Damn, Rain, you were right. You were right, Rain!" yells Smoke.

Smoke starts to laugh. He laughs louder and louder as the men pull tighter and tighter on the ropes, tearing his flesh, drawing more blood. Bailey is walked toward Glamfury, and he grabs her hair. He holds the knife to her throat. Bailey begs and pleads with Glamfury to let her go.

"You think this is funny? You know what happens when I slice her throat with this knife? Not only will she bleed out and die right before your eyes, but also her soul will go directly to Lucifer and her youth will be mine. Is that what you want? You are the one I want. I give you my word that when you grant me your youth, your soul, and your life, I will let her go free. I have no need for her. If you do not, then I will bleed her right in front of you," says Glamfury.

Smoke laughs louder yet.

"Rain, you were right. He is doing exactly what we thought he would do. He is so predictable. He is such a demonic douche. Ha, ha, ha, ha, ha, ha, ha, ha," laughs Smoke.

Glamfury gets ready to slice Bailey's throat when he hears sirens coming toward the cabin. They are coming from the dirt road leading to the cabin. They are getting louder and louder, closer and closer. The men and women in robes get antsy and start to move into the woods out of sight. Glamfury holds Bailey and starts to back toward the woods as the sirens get louder and louder. Smoke laughs.

"You're not going to make it, Glamfury. We are on to you. We know how you have been pulling us into dreams where you are present. We know you have been manipulating us to do and show you things in our dreams. We know you bring us out of the dreams into the real world where you expect to kill us. We are on to you, Glamfury!" yells Smoke.

Glamfury backs into the woods with Bailey. Cop cars come driving past the cabin into sight, and police officers exit from the three police cruisers that arrive. Two police officers exit from each car. They see Smoke held in place by the four large men holding on to the ropes. They draw their weapons, ordering the men to let go of the ropes. The men wearing the coconut shells over their heads with vines running down to their knees let go of the ropes and run off into the woods. The officers order them to stop, but they run into the woods out of sight. Rain and Ajaunta exit the back of one of the police cruisers and run to Smoke, pulling the hooks out of his ankles and wrists.

"Rain, you were right. How did he take us from the real world and get us into the dreamworld? That is the one thing I still can't figure. How did you know he was going to bring me here, and how did he get Bailey? He still has Bailey. He ran off into the woods with her. Where is he taking her? Do you think he is going to kill her?" says Smoke.

"No. He needs her to get to you. He will get us back in the dreamworld, I am sure of it. We have to be prepared. We have to be ready," says Rain.

"This is crazy. It seems like literally two minutes ago, we were sitting in my living room, and all of a sudden, we are in the dreamworld, and then I wake here on this rock, tied and ready to be sacrificed. This is totally bizarre. How is he doing it?" asks Smoke.

"I don't know yet. You remember how all our reports always told us how the Egengyns would use drugs that would make people hallucinate?" says Rain.

"Yeah," says Smoke.

"Well, I bet somehow we have been dosed with some of these drugs. This Glamfury must have a way of dosing us, and we have to figure it out and stop it. We have to find out what this drug or drugs are and how much of these drugs are in our system already. He has a way of drugging us. That is the only way I can think he is able to bounce us into the dreamworld. He must truly be some sort of servant to hell. That is how he is able to be with us in our dreams. Can either of you think of any way or any time he may have drugged you?" asks Rain.

Ajaunta and Smoke both look at Rain, shaking their heads no while pondering the question. The police wrap Smoke's ankles and wrists with bandages, and the three of them leave in the police cruisers.

Chapter 24

Shh, Shh, My Dear

The police take Smoke to the hospital, where his wounds are cleaned and stitched. All three of them give blood samples. They ask to have their blood checked for drugs or any unusual substances that may cause them to sleep or hallucinate. They will have to wait one to two weeks to get the results from their blood work. They have to fill out paperwork and answer many questions with the police. The police find their story about this Glamfury hard to believe, but they take the statements from Rain, Smoke, Ajaunta and log them into their system. Later that night, the three of them are returned back to Smoke's house. It has been a long exhausting day, and they sit on Smoke's couch, fearing the thought of sleep. Smoke leaves for a while and then comes back into the living room and sits.

"Rain, it is gone. The book is gone. I suppose you lost your book as well?" says Smoke.

"We were all sitting here trying to figure out who could help us translate and understand the book, remember? The next thing we know, we were in the dreamworld. He is one sneaky bastard, that Glamfury. He has had centuries to work on his dream magic. I remember somewhere he told me he has been alive for centuries," says Rain.

"I remember him telling me that in my dreams too. He always kills you, Bailey, Ajaunta, and even me in my dreams. He thinks he is wearing me down emotionally and I will beg him to kill me, but that will never happen," says Smoke.

"I know he does the same to me. Ajaunta, all he does is love you in your dreams. What is he after with you and the other girls he loves, I wonder?" says Rain.

"I don't know. Maybe he has killed my family. I still have not heard from them, and no one answers when I call any of their phones. They must be dead. Maybe he needs to love me to steal youth or health or something from my family. Why he only loves me in my dreams, I don't know," says Ajaunta.

"I have a feeling we are going to be seeing him soon. There is no way we can avoid sleeping. I wonder if he is already waiting for us," says Rain.

"Well, he has Bailey. I wonder if he plans on using her in my dream when I see him next. I wonder if he is somehow planning on bringing me out of dream into the real world where she is present. I bet he needs me in the real world with Bailey to use her to get to me. He can't kill us in our dreams, right? I mean, if he kills us in our dreams, we just wake up, right? That is how he keeps killing me and I'm still here because he kills me in my dreams and I wake up," says Smoke.

"I think you are right. He has killed me in my dreams, and I just wake up, I think? I don't actually know how it works. Do I just fade to another dream or just wake up? I don't know," says Rain.

"Well, I gotta tell ya I don't know either, but something tells me I am going to be seeing Glamfury and Bailey pretty soon. You knew he was going to try and sacrifice me in our last encounter. You even knew he was going to take me to the cabin. How does he get us from our dreams to places in the real world? Do you have any idea where is he going to take me or us next?" says Smoke.

"I don't know. I just went on a hunch last time, and I happened to be right. It was pretty amazing how Ajaunta, I, and the police made it to you in time. What do you think, Ajaunta? You have been very quiet," says Rain.

"I wonder if we are tied to each other when we fall asleep, will we be separated in our dreams, or will we be together in our dreams? More importantly, if my family is in fact dead, does that mean he does not need me anymore? Am I going to be killed or sacrificed?" says Ajaunta.

"You are going to be sacrificed just like the others, my dear," says Glamfury.

Glamfury walks into the living room. He has Bailey in front of him, and he has a knife to her throat. The three sitting on the couch turn to see Glamfury and Bailey walk into the living room. He is followed by tall men wearing coconut shells over their heads and vines hanging down to their knees. They are followed by men and women covered in robes. Rain, Smoke, and Ajaunta stand and back toward the wall heavily outnumbered and surrounded. Bailey is quietly sobbing with tears falling from her eyes.

"Smoke, he is going to kill me. He says he is going to kill me, Smoke," says Bailey.

"Shh, shh, my dear, this is not going to hurt at all," says Glamfury.

"Smoke, don't just stand there and just let him kill me. Fight for me. At least do something. Don't just let him kill me," says Bailey.

"Ahh!" yells Smoke.

Smoke charges over the couch. Rain follows suit and charges over the couch as well.

"If you're going to kill us, you're going to have a fight on your hands, you evil son of a bitch!" yells Smoke.

Smoke dives over the couch right for Bailey.

"Yeah!" yells Rain.

Rain is a step behind Smoke. Ajaunta steps back to the wall and stands there. Smoke and Rain see time start to slow, and their movements slow down, but they hear Glamfury talk in real time.

"You are starting to get it, aren't you?—what is going on, I mean. Well, not really. You see, playing with you two is so much fun. I have so many ways I can manipulate your minds, you have no idea. I can take you into dreamworld at any time, or vice versa, get it? Oh, sure, I have had the two of you drugged, but there is so much more than just the drugs, and by the way, your doctors will not be able to trace the drugs that are still present in your bloodstreams right now," says Glamfury.

Smoke and Rain see wires start to grow from the ceiling down toward Bailey, who is in slow motion as well. No matter how fast they try to run or move, it makes no difference because Glamfury is walking around them and talking to them, and they can only keep pace with him with their eyes. They try to talk, but their words are slurs and unrecognizable. Bailey sees the wires form like crystals that are growing from the ceiling toward her. She is getting very nervous, but she cannot move out of the way. She cannot talk in understandable language. Smoke and Rain can see she is starting to cry because she is afraid. Glamfury is laughing and walking in circles around them. He waves his hands at his disciples, and they all exit the room.

"That's right, boys. And look at this cutie over here. I believe I had the distinct privilege of putting her over my shoulder and feeling her all over with all of me, if you know what I mean. You remember that time I was in your house, Rain, and your house was sinking? I saved this beauty for you, and, of course, she repaid my generosity with all her warmth. Oh, what was that? Did you want to say something, Rain?" says Glamfury.

Glamfury waves his hands, and Rain is moving in real time again. He turns and runs toward Glamfury, who slams his fist down, hitting Rain on top of the head, and he slams into the ground. Glamfury picks Rain up and puts him standing by Smoke, and again they are in slow motion. Glamfury puts Ajaunta over his shoulder just as he did when he was in Rain's house. He walks in front of Rain and Smoke and pats Ajaunta on her ass and rubs it.

"Oh, by the way, I keep Ajaunta alive because she is one great piece of ass. You have been so busy thinking about me and what I am doing you have not even noticed how I have restored some of her youth. Isn't she gorgeous? I will get tired of her, but for now, oh, yeah, I'm gonna go fuck her hard. As for you two, let me ask you something. You do know this is real. This is not a dream. Bailey is going to die right here in front of you two unless you stop those wires before they grow down to her neck and suck her dry of all her blood. While you two try and figure out how to save this little girl here, I will be fucking this little girl here," says Glamfury.

Glamfury is rubbing Ajaunta's ass and laughing at Rain and Smoke.

"You motherfucker!" yells Rain, but his words are nothing but slurs.

Glamfury walks out the front door with Ajaunta over his shoulder. Rain and Smoke can now move their heads in real time so they can talk, but their bodies are still in slow motion. Bailey can talk and move her head as well.

"You guys, I can't move. Those wires are coming for me. Help me, guys, help me," says Bailey.

"Rain, what are we going to do?" says Smoke.

"Smoke, has he done this to you before? Make your body move in slow motion like this? He has done this to me in my dreams, and I don't know how to break free from this slow motion," says Rain.

"Yes, he has done this to me a lot, and he has killed all of you while I watched, but never outside of a dream. We have to get Bailey before those wires get to her," says Smoke.

Bailey looks up, and the wires start to crystalize faster, growing faster and faster, reaching down to her neck. She calls for the guys, who, like her, are unable to move. They all watch as the wires grow down to each side of Bailey's neck and needles grow out the ends of the wires, which insert into her neck. Bailey starts to cry as she sees her blood being sucked from her body up through the wires into the ceiling.

"You guys, you guys, what's it doing? It's sucking my blood out. You guys stop it!" cries Bailey.

She cries, not being able to do anything but watch as her blood is being drawn from her body. Glamfury walks back into the living room by himself. He walks up behind Bailey, who is crying.

"Shh, shh, my dear. Yes, my dear, you are dying. It will all be over soon. Fortunately for you, it will be quite painless. You will just be gone. Of course, when you get to where your soul is going, well, that is a different story. There, your pain will just be beginning. Ha, ha, ha, ha. Ha, ha, ha, ha. Ha, ha, ha, ha," laughs Glamfury.

Glamfury turns to face the doorway leading into the living room.

"Come, my dear. Come on, don't be shy. Show off your new accessories to the boys. Come on, Ajaunta, that's my girl, come on," says Glamfury.

He waves his hands toward the doorway. Rain and Smoke see Ajaunta walking into the living room, but Bailey has her back to the door and cannot see her.

"Fight him, Ajaunta. Fight him!" yells Rain.

Ajaunta cries.

"Rain, I can't stop. I can't fight him, Rain. I don't know what he is doing to me. He did something to me, and I can't stop. Rain, help me, help me!" cries Ajaunta.

She is walking toward the back of Bailey. Ajaunta is wearing a see-through toga that is lavender in color, and Glamfury swipes the cloth over her shoulder, dropping it from her nude body.

"That's it, my dear, that's it," says Glamfury.

Rain and Smoke see Bailey start to lower her head as the draining of her blood is draining her energy and life. Glamfury points his hands at the ceiling, and ropes grow from the ceiling, which he uses to tie Bailey's wrists. These ropes hold her up as she goes unconscious. Glamfury waves Ajaunta toward the back of Bailey. He points at the ceiling, and two more tubes start to crystalize and grow from the ceiling down toward Ajaunta. The tubes grow down and enter into the neck of Ajaunta, and blood starts to flow down the tubes into Ajaunta. She closes her eyes and sways like she is in a trance.

"Hurry, my dear, the time is now. You haven't much time. Suck her, my dear. Drain her! Steal her!" says Glamfury.

Rain and Smoke watch as huge talons grow from the fingertips of Ajaunta. Her eyes start to glimmer and sparkle like lightning is circling in her eyes. She walks up behind Bailey.

"Ajaunta!" yell the men.

Ajaunta is unresponsive.

"Ajaunta, fight it. Fight it, Ajaunta. Don't let him into your mind. Fight him!" yells Rain.

Ajaunta walks up behind Bailey. The talons on her fingers look deadly, and she thrusts them into the back of Bailey. Bailey is unconscious, but the pain of having her back penetrated by all ten of Ajaunta's talons wakes her, and she screams weakly. Rain and Smoke watch as the tubes from Bailey's neck draw back toward the ceiling. The last of the blood in the tubes flow into Ajaunta's neck, and then the tubes draw back from her into the ceiling. Ajaunta is now sucking what blood is left in Bailey's body directly into her syringe like talons. Rain and Smoke are powerless to do anything but watch. They watch as Bailey is sucked dry of all her blood. Her body shrinks and deflates right before their eyes. Her muscles shrivel to her bones, and her face ages one hundred years. Her skin dries and tightens like it is aged on the desert floor.

"No! Bailey!" cries Smoke.

Glamfury swipes his hands at the ropes holding up Bailey's corpse, and they sever, dropping her body to the floor. Rain and Smoke watch as Ajaunta's body firms and tightens. Her breasts lift, and her stomach thins. Her cheeks look less droopy and become more rosy in color. Her eyes and teeth become noticeably brighter. Glamfury walks up behind her, wrapping his arms around her, cupping her breasts with his hands.

"Now that's what I am talking about," he says, looking to Rain and Smoke.

Ajaunta holds her hands up, looking at the dangerous weapons her fingers and thumbs are. They start to transform. She watches the hard nail like talons wither, dry, and flake off, falling from her hands until her natural fingers and thumbs are revealed in their new healthy, younger form. Glamfury turns her facing him, and he hugs her close to him. He kisses her, biting right through her tongue with his teeth. Blood seeps from their lips, dripping down both their necks.

"You gross motherfucker. I'm going to kill you!" yells Rain.

"You're dead, motherfucker!" yells Smoke.

Glamfury ignores both of them. He waves his hand toward them, and they can no longer speak in normal time. They are back to being so slow; their words are slurs. Glamfury leans back, laughing with a mouthful of blood. He holds his head up tilted back, gurgling blood, which drips from his mouth down his neck. Ajaunta wipes the blood from her lips and chin and smiles at Rain and Smoke as she exits the way she came in. Rain and Smoke obviously notice the younger, firmer-looking buttocks and legs of Ajaunta as she exits. Glamfury turns to the men.

"Well, looks like you two have a corpse here to bury. Believe me when I tell you this is real, and by now, this one here is already in hell," says Glamfury.

Glamfury kicks the corpse on the floor. He stands in between Rain and Smoke, putting his hands on their shoulders.

"Now listen to me, you two. You are next, but there is no hurry. You two are very special, very special indeed. You two will make my master very happy, and the youth I will gain from the two of you will hold me for decades. So I am going to leave you two with this corpse here, and you decide if you are going to give in to my wishes, or do I keep killing those you love like Bailey here and, what was her name, oh, yeah, Marlene. Must I bleed her in front of you as well? So when you two are ready to beg me to kill you, when you are ready to freely give me your youth, you just call my name. I am never far from you. If you make me wait too long, I will simply move to those you love, and they will be mine. Any questions? I did not think so. Well, time to go get me some old lady with young ass, oh, yeah," says Glamfury.

He laughs as he walks out of the living room. Just as he exits, he waves his hand at Rain and Smoke, and they both fall to the ground, able to move in normal time.

"That motherfucker. How does he do that? How are we supposed to fight him? Is there nothing we can do? Why are we so powerless?

How does he freeze us in time like that? Motherfucker, I am fucking pissed. I can't believe I am saying this, but I think it's time to find God," says Smoke.

Smoke kneels by Bailey's shriveled corpse, which lies behind his couch.

"I am so sorry, Bailey. There was nothing I could do, nothing," says Smoke.

Rain stands looking determined even though he feels outmatched at every turn. He knows there has to be a weakness. There has to be a way of overcoming these seemingly overwhelming odds stacked against him and Smoke.

"Don't give up, Smoke. We have to keep thinking. We are overlooking something, and it's usually something that is so easy, something that is so simple. We are not thinking about our enemy the way we need to be thinking about him. He is a devil worshiper. He has dark magic on his side. Maybe you are right saying we need to find God. Maybe God is our salvation in this situation," says Rain.

Smoke stands up. "Did I just hear you say God is our salvation? Rain, you just said God is our salvation. Now I have heard everything," says Smoke.

"Yup. These are some very unusual times, my friend, very unusual times," says Rain.

Chapter 25

The House of God

"Come on, we have to go get Marlene. We have to go get her before Glamfury gets her and calls us into a trap—a trap where we will only watch her die," says Rain.

Smoke follows Rain out to his car, and they drive off.

"You do have your handy pistols, right?" says Smoke.

Rain lifts his sport jacket, showing he has both his guns. Smoke smiles, looking in the back seat where he put his rifle and a few pistols covered with a blanket.

"So we are going to get Marlene?" says Smoke.

"Yup. Then we are going to see God," says Rain.

"What are you talking about? Going to see God? Since when are you spiritual?" says Smoke.

"Since I broke ties with you. I have had to make some changes," says Rain.

"Well, that is some big changes. Rain, a churchgoer? Come on, that does not even compute," says Smoke.

"Well, we are going to get Marlene, and then we are going to see Father Furnham," says Rain.

"Whatever you say, Rain. Whatever you say. We are in real world, not dreamworld, right? I can't even be sure anymore. It's like he just pulls us at any time into dream or out of dream. What if he pulls us into a dream before we get Marlene?" says Smoke.

"Let's hope we get to her before we are pulled into a dream. We will know because if we are pulled into a dream, her house will not be her house. If we get her at her house, then we are in the real world, and I am pretty sure we are in the real world right now," says Rain.

Rain drives for a little over an hour, getting to Marlene's house very early in the morning. The sky is starting to brighten with heavy cloud cover threatening rain. Smoke stays in the car and watches Rain run to the front door and knock. After a few minutes, the door opens, and Rain enters the house. Smoke sits in the car for a while and then gets out and stretches his legs. A few minutes go by, and he hears Rain and a girl arguing as they exit the front door.

"It's OK, Mom. I will be fine. It's OK, Dad," says Marlene.

She closes the door and zips up her sweater.

"I thought I told you I would call you. I told you I needed some time away from you, remember?" says Marlene.

"Yeah, I do remember, but some crazy shit has been going on ever since that night—crazy shit that somehow involves you," says Rain.

"Hey, I know you—I mean, I don't know you, but I have seen you in my dreams," says Marlene.

She approaches the car, addressing Smoke, and he nods to her. They all get in the car, and Marlene gets in the back. Rain starts up the car and backs out of the driveway and drives off.

"OK, listen, Rain, I have to admit some crazy shit has been going on with me. I have been having crazy dreams—I mean, some crazy shit. This guy comes to me in my dreams, and he, well, he fucks the shit out of me, and it's great. I wake up craving this guy like he is real or something. Then just yesterday, I see this guy at the supermarket, and it is him. It's the guy fucking me in my dreams. Rain, this freaked me out. What the fuck is going on? You know who he is? Is that what you were saying to me at my house?" says Marlene.

"Yes, that is what I was saying to you. This guy Glamfury is trying to steal our youth for himself, and our souls go to the devil. He has threatened to take your life unless Smoke and I give in to him. By giving in, I mean sacrifice ourselves, which is not going to happen," says Rain.

"That's where I know you from. You are the guy who killed those men in Rain's house. The night Rain and I almost actually made love for the first time. I don't think we will ever get to that—the making love part, I mean," says Marlene.

"Yup, that's me. I am Smoke. Nice to meet you. I am not sure about something. When we met, was that for real, or was that a dream?" says Smoke.

Smoke reaches back to shake hands with Marlene, but she ignores him.

"Yeah, yeah. So where are we going? Do you have a plan to deal with this dream maniac?" says Marlene.

"As a matter of fact, I do. We are going to see Father Furnham," says Rain.

"Father Furnham? You are taking us to church? Well, I guess it can't hurt. Why not?" says Marlene.

"All right, here we are. Come on, we are going to see Father Furnham," says Rain.

Rain parks and gets out of the car. Smoke and Marlene follow him up onto the porch. There are two very large pillars, and they walk between them to the large doors entering the church. Rain opens the door to the left and walks in. The morning light shines through the stained glass windows. They walk down the red carpet in between the pews toward the podium where Father Furnham gives his sermons.

"Father Furnham. Father Furnham," calls Rain.

Father Furnham walks out from a door and up to the podium.

"Rain, how nice to see you. It is very early in the morning, but what a pleasant surprise. I see you have friends with you," says Father Furnham.

"Yes, Father. This here is Smoke, and behind me is Marlene," says Rain.

Marlene walks out from behind Rain.

"No, it cannot be. I have seen you. You are in league with Lucifer himself. You are not welcome in the house of God," says Father Furnham.

Father Furnham picks a Bible from within the podium and prays with it held to his heart. Marlene starts to laugh. Rain and Smoke look at her confused.

"Marlene, you are in on this devilry with Glamfury? So that is how I was drugged. It was you," says Rain.

Marlene laughs. "Yes, it was me all along right from the start. I was grooming you, drugging you and softening your mind, shaping your soul, and molding your vitality, which will bring me decades of youth," says Marlene.

"Out! Out of the house of God. With the power of my Lord in heaven, I command you out of the house of God," says Father Furnham.

Marlene laughs.

"You have got to be joking with that God talk," says Marlene.

She laughs.

"You have got to be joking," says Marlene.

She laughs louder yet.

"Everyone knows God does not walk among the mortals, so stop with your God talk, Father Furnham," says Marlene.

"No, God does not walk among us just as Lucifer does not walk among us, but just as Lucifer has his demons and his succubus walk with us, God has his saints to walk with us," says Father Furnham.

Rain and Smoke start to back away from Marlene, who laughs. They see Father Furnham start to emanate warm golden rays of light, and he grows in height. He walks toward Marlene.

"Touché, Father, but I think you are still outmatched, and where do you two think you are going? Ah, ah, ah, stop right there," says Marlene.

She turns to Rain and Smoke, who are backing toward the door. Marlene starts to laugh, and the doors leading into the congregation room slam shut. The windows shining their warm light darken like black paint is poured over them. Father Furnham gasps as he looks around.

"No, you are not welcome in the house of God. You cannot enter," says Father Furnham.

The doors leading into the congregation room open, and Glamfury walks through them. Rain and Smoke head back behind Father Furnham. Glamfury walks in with the doors slamming shut behind him.

"Oh, shit. Are we in a dream, or is this real?" asks Smoke.

"Shit, I really thought we were in the real world, but I don't know," says Rain.

Marlene laughs and walks behind Glamfury, who approaches Father Furnham. Rain and Smoke watch in awe as Father Furnham grows to nine feet in height. He radiates a golden glow, which illuminates the church like a huge candle.

"I have been expecting you, Azmander Bernardious Yvonnst," says Father Furnham.

Glamfury stops dead in his tracks. Marlene walks into his back.

"I am surprised, Father. I have not heard that name called upon me in over five hundred years. My deepest respect goes to one as cultured as yourself," says Glamfury.

Glamfury bends at his hips, lowering his head to his knees, waving his right hand in an arch to his side, showing his greatest compliment to Father Furnham.

"This is not a compliment, nor is it a sign of mutual respect. This is your eviction notice. This is your passport to hell. You are no longer welcome among the living. No longer will you gain youth from the innocence you kill. No longer will Lucifer get souls for free. God has sent his angels to deal with the scourge plaguing our world, and time for you to be banished from the living forever," says Father Furnham.

"You better be careful, Father. I am no ordinary demon, and you are not my equal," says Glamfury.

Father Furnham opens his Bible and starts to read from the book. The stained glass windows start to lighten, and the sun starts to shine through. Glamfury covers his eyes with his hands and cringes in fear. He gasps in seeming pain as Father Furnham reads from the book louder and stronger. Glamfury wilts to his knees, crying.

"Stop! Stop! You are killing me!" yells Glamfury.

Marlene looks concerned and rubs his back.

"My lord, what is wrong? My lord," says Marlene.

Glamfury rises to his feet, laughing.

Father Furnham reads louder, more intensely, and Glamfury laughs.

"Yes, Father, yes. Read it out loud. Read it, Father!" says Glamfury.

Father Furnham glows golden as his words ring out in the congregation room. Glamfury grabs Marlene by her left wrists and swings her between himself and Father Furnham. Glamfury starts to grow in height, matching the nine feet of Father Furnham. Glamfury starts to emanate a red hue, which shines, meeting up with the golden glow from Father Furnham.

"My master, surely these words are not affecting you the way you would make it seem?" says Marlene, looking up to Glamfury.

"No, they are not, my sweet. Time to put an end to this hilarity," says Glamfury.

"What are we going to do?" says Marlene.

"Well, my sweet, you are going to have a significant part in the end of Father Furnham," says Glamfury.

"Shall I seduce the father for you? Will that work while he is reading from a Bible?" says Marlene.

"No, my sweet, it will not," says Glamfury.

Glamfury pulls her left arm out straight and bites the muscle just at her elbow, ripping it from her forearm with his teeth. Marlene screams in pain. She falls to her knees, crying, as blood drips from Glamfury's mouth. He bites again and again, ripping the muscle from below her elbow down her forearms, exposing her bloody bones connected at her elbow. Blood drips from her arm, staining the floor. Marlene screams in pain.

"What are you doing? What are you doing?" cries Marlene.

"Sorry, my dear, time for you to be of real use. I love this part. Are you ready?" says Glamfury.

"Ready for what? You bit the flesh from my arm!" cries Marlene.

Glamfury bends her elbow the wrong way until it snaps. Marlene screams a horrific cry until she passes out. Glamfury wrestles her arm back and forth, violently twisting and wrenching until the sinew, tendons, bone, and flesh give way and her elbow separates. He drops her body, leaving her on the floor.

"Ah, yes, just what I was looking for," says Glamfury.

He inspects her bloody arm, running his free hand up and down it. Her arm starts to transform like it is being magically honed into an arm-length spear. The bone at the end becomes very sharp and whitens as all the blood and flesh melt back down her arm.

"Ah, yes, this will do just fine," says Glamfury.

He interlocks the fingers on her hand with his and faces Father Furnham, who still reads from the Bible. Glamfury steps toward Father, thrusting his arm forward, and the pointed bone of Marlene's ripped-off arm enters his chest. Glamfury thrusts it all the way through to the wrist. Father Furnham takes a step back, dropping his Bible. He stares at the hand, which starts to move. The fingers open; talons grow from the fingernails. They bend and grasp at his chest, digging into his flesh, pulling the palm of her hand flush to his chest. Father Furnham pulls at the hand, trying to pull it from his chest.

"Wake, my dear, wake," says Glamfury.

Glamfury waves his arms and hands over Marlene, who wakes and stands. She walks behind Father Furnham and touches her severed elbow like she knows it will reform. Father Furnham starts to gasp and scream as his coat and shirt are ripped from his body by Glamfury. Marlene starts to convulse and shake as skin, flesh, and blood start to rip from Father Furnham's back. It runs like molten flesh down her arm and reforms the muscles ripped from her arm. The sinew, tendons, flesh, and skin reform all the way to her elbow until her arm is reformed, and Marlene laughs, waking from her daze with a new arm. Father Furnham is standing with his arms stretched out, the flesh on his back gone, and his ribs and internal organs exposed from the back. Marlene opens her hand, still sticking out of the Father's chest, and clinches her fist. She laughs and pulls her arm out of him, holding it up, laughing, and looking at it all bloody. She can see Father Furnham's spine, and she grabs it with her bloody arm and rips it from his back. It pulls from his hips, and she grabs it with both hands, yanking on it, which pulls from the base of his skull. Father Furnham falls spineless with moments left to live. Marlene is now looking at Rain and Smoke, laughing and swinging a spine in her hands. She laughs as Rain and Smoke back away from her. Glamfury rolls the body of Father Furnham to his stomach and grasps the visible heart, pulling it from his body. He holds the bloody organ up, which pumps the last drops of blood from it, spilling onto the floor.

"My master, take this soul as your own. It still beats. It still fights for life even torn from its body. Its youth is mine. Its soul is yours," says Glamfury.

Glamfury bites into the beating heart, tearing the muscle with his teeth. He chews and laughs, holding the heart up in the air. Blood drips down his arm. Marlene holds his arm, licking the blood from his arm. The floor starts to sway and roll like waves on the ocean. Rain and Smoke stumble back and forth as the floor starts to crack and pull apart. They move back toward the wall of the church as the floor falls in a circle around Glamfury and Marlene. Rain and Smoke watch as mist and superheated steam rise into the church. The atmosphere darkens and feels like a sauna. Glamfury laughs, holding the heart high in the air.

"Yes, my lord in hell, yes. The heart of a true believer. This heart will strengthen your rule. This heart shall increase my lifespan tenfold," says Glamfury.

Glamfury laughs as lightning the colors of red and purple rise from the violet mist. The lightning scorches the church all around as it runs along the walls and ceiling. Rain and Smoke crouch down against the wall, hoping not to be struck by the electrical bolts that move around until they find their way to the feet of Glamfury, and he shakes as the lightning seems to strengthen him. The lighting moves to Marlene, and she shakes and twitches as the lighting melts her skin and cooks her flesh. She screams briefly as her eyes explode and her body ignites like a torch. Glamfury laughs as Marlene shakes and burns beside him until she falls at his feet, a charred body steaming with flames slowly fading away, leaving her charred corpse. Glamfury laughs, looking at Rain and Smoke. He holds his hands out, palms up, and fire rises from his palms, and he laughs.

"Yes, yes, you see me grow stronger as the years go by. As time goes by, my lord makes me impervious to death. He makes me the ultimate human being, and I serve him. I bring souls to him. And what does your God in heaven do? He watches, he sits by and lets the most faithful to him be stolen from him—stolen from him to rot in hell to be tortured forever. My god makes me immortal. He makes me impervious," says Glamfury.

Rain stands with only about four feet of floor until the ground beneath sinks right to the depths of hell.

"He makes you impervious, huh? Well, let's see how you like this!" yells Rain.

Rain pulls his pistols from their holsters under his arms and pulls the triggers as fast as he can. Glamfury steps back as the bullets make subtle holes in the front of his head while blasting the back of his head away as his skull shatters from the exiting bullets. He is hit with six consecutive bullets, stumbling him backward until he falls into the abyss.

"Nice shooting, Rain. That's how you do it," says Smoke.

They walk around the edge of the room, looking down, but all they see is the rising mist. It is very hot, and already they are sweating heavily from the heat. They cannot see anything other than the mist, which seems to evaporate as soon as it reaches the floor.

"How deep do you think this goes?" asks Smoke.

"I don't know. Probably all the way to hell," says Rain.

They walk around to the doors leading out of the church and try to leave, but the doors will not open.

"Oh, great. I don't like this. I got a real bad feeling. I think the worst is about to come," says Smoke.

"I think you are right," says Rain.

Chapter 26

Rise of Lucifer's Servant

Rain and Smoke twist, turn, push, and pull on the door handles, trying to get out of the church, but the doors will not budge. They turn, laying their backs against the wall as creepy sounds and wisps of hell mist blow from the reddish-purple abyss. The hair on their neck stands. Chills fill their veins.

"We have been in some life-threatening situations before, but I will honestly say to you now, I have never been afraid ever in my life until now. I have never been afraid to die, but this is some seriously scary shit. Dreamworld or not, this is fucked up," says Smoke.

Laughter fills the church. The center portion of the room, which is still intact, starts to buckle and falls into the abyss. The sound of bubbling lava rises from the deep with a wave of heat, causing the men to sweat. The laughter gets louder, and the mist expands, exposing a large head, which rises up. Sharp black horns break the mist, first thickening as they become visible, turning red as the large head of Lucifer rises high into the church. Molten lava runs down his neck, shoulders, arms, and torso into the mist, which conceals the rest of this very intimidating lord of hell. He looks exactly as Rain and Smoke would expect—a solid red hulk slamming his hands on either side of the floor still intact around the outside of the congregation room. He lowers his head to the tiny humans still leaning against the wall, terrified their lives are about to end. Lucifer rams his head right at them, stabbing his horns into the wall on either side of Rain and Smoke.

"Well, Smoke, this is what you always wanted, isn't it? I mean, what greater challenge than Lucifer himself right here in front of us? No better way to go out than taking on the lord of hell," says Rain.

"Damn right, buddy," says Smoke.

Like the two of them are reading each other's minds, they attack the devil simultaneously, punching him in the face over and over. Lucifer laughs as the two of them punch him with all their might. They punch him in his eyes and on his mouth. They uppercut his throat. They punch him over and over and can't even break his skin. The devil laughs at them until they exhaust themselves.

"I guess us mortal men just aren't enough to take on Lucifer hand to face," says Smoke.

Lucifer laughs still with his horns stuck in the wall and his face a few feet from the men.

"What are you waiting for, death breath? What's the hold up? You want us, here we are. Why don't you horn us or burn us or whatever? I grow tired of your taunting, fake dreams, and idol threats. We are men, real men, and you can't scare real men. If you want to kill us, then do it now and quit wasting our time," says Smoke.

"Now that's what I like to hear, Smoke. Real talk from my lifelong friend. Yeah, devil, do your worst and be done with it," says Rain.

Rain and Smoke stand firm, awaiting their fate. Lucifer pulls back from the men, rising into the air. He swipes his right arm and hand across the top of the lava surrounding him, which the men cannot see underneath the hell mist. The lava splatters across the wall and the men, burning the wall and searing their flesh. They dance around, trying to rid the burning lava from their skin. The devil laughs.

"Kill you? There is no rush. I get to watch you suffer for eternity, but I only get fleeting moments where I can torment the living and watch them writhe in pain," says Lucifer.

Laughing, he splatters the men with more lava, watching them frantically wipe the burning lava from their skin as they cry in pain.

"What the heaven, Rain? Did you not bring us to a church on purpose? Is God not supposed to help us in this situation? Are we so bad he would let us go to hell? Maybe he would let you and me go to hell, but what about Father Furnham? How does God let his own servant be killed by the devil, in a church no less?" says Smoke.

"God does not show himself. He does not protect you. Nothing can save you now," says Lucifer.

He points his fingers at the men. Large thick talons grow from his fingertips, and he stabs each man right through the center of his chest. They both scream in pain as Lucifer lifts them in the air and dips them in the boiling lava. They scream as their skin sears and their flesh cooks. Lucifer laughs as they cry in pain, losing their ability to move and their life fading away. Before they die, Lucifer bites off their legs and arms. He chews them, crunching their bones and swallowing. Rain watches as the lower half of Smoke's torso is bit off and chewed. Lucifer tosses the rest of Smoke in his mouth, chewing and crunching his body down bones and all. "No!" yells Rain, watching Smoke's body sliced and mashed in between Lucifer's teeth as he chews openmouthed.

Lucifer bites Rain's torso in two, and he watches his lower body being chewed, mashed, and swallowed. The rest of his body is put into Lucifer's mouth. Rain watches as the teeth come down, splitting his skull in two, but it does not break apart. He can feel his entire body being cut, mashed, and chewed. He even feels the saliva of the lord of hell mixed with his own blood wash his body as he is funneled to the throat and swallowed. It feels like he is falling as the top half of his body is held together by torn muscles and bones. Rain is submerged in the burning acidic stomach of the devil.

This is where the pain really starts for Rain. He feels his skin, eyes, and even his throat burn from the stomach juices starting to digest his body. He is completely grossed out as he instinctively tries to breath and gulps large quantities of stomach acid, which burns him from the inside out. He is burning on the outside and inside of his body, but he does not drown; he does not die. He can even smell the bile he is submerged in. He feels like he is on a ride that he has no control over as his body is plummeted to the next phase of digestion. Like he is on a fast track, he is tumbled, twisted, and turned. He speeds through parts of Lucifer's digestive tract, and he slows through parts that squeeze him. He cannot see, but he can feel his body is dissolving from the digestive acids. He cannot believe he has not drowned as he keeps gulping for air and swallowing disgusting digestive juices into his body. He is thrust forward and stopped over and over until he is squirted out of the anus of Lucifer and plops in a huge pile of hell feces on the ground.

At this point, he is a crushed skull with neck, shoulders, and midsection of his torso still intact barely. His left eye pops from the digestive juices, and he looks around, crying from his remaining eye. His body is chewed and held together by what he can only describe as flesh strings. His bones are broken and sticking out in all directions, and he is lying in a pile of crap emitting the worst stench he has ever smelled. He can see the remains of Smoke all around him. Smoke has been chewed and digested into little pieces scattered throughout the feces. Rain cannot speak, but he can whimper and make crying noises, which is all he can do. He can feel his hair being grabbed, and he senses he is being lifted in the air. He is dropped on the top of the feces with a smack as he lands on top of all the crap. His one eye looks around, trying to see what is happening. Glamfury comes into view, placing a chair in front of Rain, and he sits down.

"This has to be as low as it gets, huh, Rain? I mean, what kind of superbad karma must you have to be nothing? Nothing but an eyeball stuck in a broken skull lying in a pile of shit. A pile of shit that has your digested friend all around you. Yuck! You have to be the lowest I have ever seen, and believe me, I have seen the lowest. There is an out for you, though. You can say, 'Glamfury, please take my youth.' Just say, 'Glamfury, I beg of you to take my youth and grow stronger from it. It is mine to give, and I give it all to you.' That is all you have to do, and all your pain is over. No more of your friends will be tortured or molested. No more of your friends and lovers have to die. What was that? Did you want to say something? Oh, oh, hold on, allow me," says Glamfury.

Glamfury gets up from his chair and approaches Rain. He covers his mouth and nose, and just before he touches Rain, he pulls his hand back. He appears to not want to touch the filth that is all over Rain.

"Hold on a second," says Glamfury.

He shakes his right hand, and a handkerchief appears in his hand.

"Ah, that is a little better. Now listen, Rain. I am going to pull you from the filth you are in and put you back together enough to speak. If I do not like what you say, you are going right back in to rot, and you can stay there, unable to move, unable to die for an eternity. Oh, yes, I can make that happen, so think before you speak," says Glamfury.

Glamfury puts the handkerchief over Rain's head, and it covers his eye so he cannot see. The handkerchief is pulled, and Rain is sitting on a beach chair on a warm sandy beach with lots of beautiful women swimming in the ocean and sunbathing on the beach. Rain looks down to see his arms are gone from the shoulders down, and his legs are gone from just below his hips. Glamfury is sitting next to him.

"I figure you will be facing reality and the fact that you are mine. You have to give in to me, or I will simply torture you forever. I put you here to show you I can create any setting. I was quite sure you would find the view a pleasurable one—a view that you would say was pretty great before you parted with the world," says Glamfury.

Rain cannot stand or walk. He could roll out of the chair, but there is no real sense in that. He looks around at all the beautiful women, many of whom happily parade topless.

"Yeah, this is a pretty great view. I don't know what your game is, but I am pretty sure you can't just leave me in a pile of shit for eternity. I don't know how you keep getting me into this dreamworld, but there is a way out, and I will find it. I will discover the secret you manage to hide because there is one. There is some illusion at work here. There is an explanation. I will find it, and I will get to you. After all, Smoke and I just faced the lord of hell, and here I am still alive on a nice warm beach watching all these beautiful women running around. You can't be that bad," says Rain.

Glamfury laughs.

"Of course, you did not. That was me and a pretty good imitation since you believe you were truly eaten by my lord Satan. That which you saw was the vision most people have of him. Believe me, he is much worse, and that is the way he likes it. So back to our situation at hand. I need for you to simply submit. I need for you to verbally tell me to take your soul. I need you to verbally tell me to kill you. Just say, 'Glamfury, I am yours. You can have my youth. You can have my soul, my life.' That is all you have to do and your worries are over. I will kill no more of your friends and loved ones. Just do that and it's over," says Glamfury.

"Go to hell," says Rain.

Glamfury sits on his chair, facing Rain. He lowers his head and rubs his face. He laughs, looking up and standing up.

"Yup, that is why I like you so much, Rain. The more you struggle, the harder you resist, the more valuable you are. Make no mistake, you will be mine. I guess you need some more of your friends to die and go to hell before you do like Marlene. Remember I said I would bleed her in front of you. Time for you to say good-bye to Marlene," says Glamfury.

A loud scream disturbs Rain from his sleep. He rolls over on his couch and sits up. Hearing faint cries and screams, he gets up and walks to the kitchen. He sees the back of a woman with her fingers in the back of another woman, and behind both woman stands Glamfury, who smiles at Rain. "What the fuck!" yells Rain. Ajaunta turns her head to see Rain standing behind her.

"Rain, how did you get here? Well, this is awkward," says Ajaunta.

She looks to Glamfury, and he laughs with a big smile on his face.

"Ajaunta, what the hell are you doing? Is that Marlene? What are you doing to her?" says Rain.

Rain watches as Marlene is drained of blood through the fingertips of Ajaunta. She pulls her fingers from Marlene's back, dripping blood from her syringe like talons. Glamfury throws Marlene's shriveled body against the wall, and she falls dead to the kitchen floor. He grabs Ajaunta, kissing her, biting her tongue, and drinking blood from her mouth. Rain bends to see Marlene has passed and in a horrific way. He is overcome with hurt, anger, and grief.

"What have you done? You evil people. You have killed Marlene. I will kill you for that!" yells Rain.

Rain grabs his shoulder holster that is lying on the floor by the couch with both his pistols in it. He grabs them both, putting one in his waistline.

"No, no, no, he has his guns. Glamfury, he has his guns. I am not strong enough!" yells Ajaunta.

"Now, hold on, Rain. Hold on, son. You don't want to just start shooting up the place," says Glamfury.

Rain points his gun with both hands at the two of them. Glamfury grabs Ajaunta and holds her in front of him as Rain starts to shoot. He shoots all six shots in what seems like two seconds. Ajaunta screams as the holes drip blood from her chest and breasts. She looks to Glamfury with teary eyes. Rain throws his gun and grabs the other gun, shooting just as fast. Glamfury holds Ajaunta like a shield, and she is punctured with twelve bullet holes. She looks to Glamfury like she wants to say something, but her life is fading. She cannot breathe. She cannot speak. She just fades to death.

"Sorry, my dear. I guess Rain does not love you as much as I do," says Glamfury.

He kisses Ajaunta, and she passes to hell before he pulls his lips from hers. He throws her body on the floor next to Marlene.

"Well, you have gone and done it now, Rain. I mean, killing is nothing new for you, but I have to admit, I did not think you would kill your only love—the only true love you ever had, as said by yourself," says Glamfury.

Rain pulls the trigger over and over, but the gun is empty. He throws the gun, being swept with emotion. His eyes water as he lowers to both girls dead on the floor.

"That's right, Rain Ajaunta killed Marlene, and you killed Ajaunta. They are both rotting, screaming, and being tortured for eternity in hell right now. All thanks to you. That a boy, well done. What do you think? Are you ready to give your youth and your soul to me now? Are you ready to end the suffering and death of all your friends?" says Glamfury.

Rain looks at Glamfury with rage in his eyes. "I will kill you!" he yells as he charges at Glamfury. Glamfury throws a left hook, hitting Rain in the left side of his face. Rain's whole body follows his head as it is veered toward the living room from the punch. He is in slow motion, and Glamfury clobbers him over and over with punches, which redirect the trajectory in which Rain flies.

"You will never learn, will you? You stupid stubborn man," says Glamfury.

Glamfury grips his hands together and swings them both into Rain's back. He slams into the ground hard yet still in slow motion. Glamfury kicks him with his right foot, and Rain flies in real speed into the wall and falls to the ground, dropping back into slow motion. Glamfury lifts him by his throat and punches him in the face, crushing his nose and breaking six of his teeth. Rain falls to his hands and knees in real time, spitting tooth and blood, breathing hard and feeling pain in his stomach, back, and, of course, his face.

"What are you waiting for? Kill me. You just want to torture me? You just want to continue with this dream? Do your worst, you wannabe servant of hell," says Rain.

Rain starts to laugh. Glamfury has his back to Rain and turns with a step, kicking Rain across the face with his right foot, sending Rain in slow motion. His whole body follows his head, which is almost kicked right off. He flies into the wall and falls to the ground again, regaining real time as he rolls in utter pain.

"You think I like doing this?" says Glamfury.

Glamfury raises his right foot, stomping on Rain's ribs, crushing them. Rain screams in pain.

"You think I want to mutilate you?" says Glamfury.

Glamfury grabs Rain by his right ankle and swings his whole body in an arch, slamming him back to the floor. Rain hits his head on the ceiling, and he hears many of his bones break as he is slammed with incredible force on the floor. Some of his teeth even break free and fall from his mouth. Rain can't move; he can't speak. He can barely breathe, and yet he taunts Glamfury by laughing with what little breath he can muster.

"That's right, Rain, laugh it up. You laugh good now because the fun is just beginning," says Glamfury.

Chapter 27

The Hebtarian Mission

Rain curls up into a ball by the wall. His ears are ringing from the explosion that sent Smoke and him flying from the street into the alley they are now. He hugs his M16 rifle like it was a pillow as dirt and debris settle from the air. They are covered in a shower of dirt, and Smoke shakes Rain by his shoulder. His words are muffled, and Rain can barely hear him.

"Come on. Come on, Rain, we have to move. We have to get out of here. Come on!" yells Smoke.

Rain gets up groggy and dazed from the explosion. He runs behind Smoke to the back side of the houses. The back yards are all fenced in. There are dogs barking. There are even children running around, hopping the fences, running from the explosions. Rain ducks down as an explosion a few houses down explodes, and again the sky is raining dirt. Parts of wooden fences, parts of doghouses, and parts of human bodies land in the yard. All the fences to the north have been flattened by the explosion for many houses. Rain can hear people crying and screaming. He sees a young boy running from a house holding the hand of his little sister. They are running away from a large man holding a machine gun, and the man fires, killing the children in their steps.

"Motherfuckers!" yells Smoke.

Smoke gets up and walks right at the man, firing his automatic machine gun. The man shakes in his shoes as he is riddled with bullets until he falls dead. Two more men run from the house to be shot down by Smoke in the same fashion. Rain gets up and follows Smoke. A man is walked out from the back sliding glass door where the children were running from. There is a man behind him holding a gun to his head, and he is shouting to Smoke. Smoke shouts back, and Rain takes a knee, aiming his rifle at the assailant. The man shouts in a foreign language, and Smoke shouts in English, of course. While the two men shout, Rain takes the shot, shooting out the assailant's right eye, and he falls dead. Smoke turns to look at Rain.

"Damn, that is a nice shot, Rain. Come on, let's kill all these fucking Hebtarians," says Smoke.

"Smoke, you take the back. I am cutting back to Main Street. There can't be but a couple of dozen of them, right? How these thugs could take over a whole town is disgusting. Time to fuck up some thug," says Rain.

"All right, you take Main Street. I'll take the back. We will come together at the end of the block," says Smoke.

Smoke turns and starts firing. Rain heads along the house toward the street. He gets to the end of the house and sees a man in the street shoot a woman who is running from him. Rain puts the man's head in his crosshairs and puts a single bullet in it, dropping the man. He walks to the end of the house and drops to his knees, looking for bad guys. Two men run from a house across the street to the fallen man in the street, and Rain points his gun, putting them in his sights. For some reason, Rain hesitates, dropping his gun and tilting his head with the distinct feeling of déjà vu. He remembers shooting them. He remembers running down the street, shooting many more men exiting from houses, and meeting up with Smoke. The wall above his head explodes from gunfire. The two men in the street have noticed Rain, who raises his rifle and shoots them with pinpoint accuracy. He runs from house to house, shooting the Hebtarian gunmen. Screams of men, women, and children are heard all around as the gunmen are running through the houses and shooting anyone who does not follow their commands. Rain is picking them off from the street, and Smoke is doing the same from the back of the houses down this street. They meet up at the end of the street, completing most of their mission so far.

"How does this happen? Huh, Smoke? How can things get so bad that gunmen run wild through neighborhoods shooting people, and for what? I can tell you this—these are the guys I like shooting. These are the missions I like. Let's fuck 'em all up," says Rain.

"Roger that, buddy. We have cleared Lear Street and St. Mearls Street. All we have left is Main Street. Their leader is holed up in the town hall. I bet they have gunmen protecting it from the surrounding buildings. We better be real careful on this part. Rain, hey, Rain, what is the matter, buddy? What is it?" says Smoke.

Rain has his head slanted down with his thumb on his cheek and his fingers on his forehead like he is in deep thought. He is having another déjà vu. He remembers storming the town hall with Smoke, shooting numerous gunmen and the leader of the Hebtarians. He remembers dozens of citizens that he and Smoke had set free.

"Does this not seem very familiar to you? Does it not seem like we have already done this before? I remember you and I killed all the Hebtarians and all the people thanking us. Don't you remember?" says Rain.

"I don't know what you are talking about. At any rate, we have to get in there and save the hostages. Any Hebtarians that get in the way are dead. That is our mission, and we are nearing the end of it. You said yourself killing these bastards was the kind of mission you liked," says Smoke.

Rain shakes his head, clearing his mind. He then points out where the defending Hebtarian gunmen are stationed in the building leading to the town hall. He and Smoke snipe the unsuspecting gunmen and enter the town hall, where dozens are held hostage by less than a dozen Hebtarians and their leader. Rain remembers the scene and where all the hostages and Hebtarians are in the town hall. He instructs Smoke on entering from the rear of the building, and he will enter from the front. They will attack simultaneously and clear the Hebtarians with precise shots. That is the plan. They synchronize their watches, and Smoke heads to the rear of the building. Rain waits exactly five minutes and enters the front of the building. Immediately he sees a female hostage standing in the lobby. She is gagged, and her hands are tied at her back. Rain thinks, *I don't remember this,* as the face of the girl explodes outward from the bullet exiting the front of her face. She falls, and Rain touches his face, looking at his fingers, seeing he has been splattered by blood from the girl. He can feel the muzzle of a gun to the right side of his head and a man shouting instructions to him in a foreign language.

He does not understand what the man is saying, but he knows to raise his hands in submission, or else he will face the same fate as the girl he just watched fall. His rifle is taken from him, and his arms are quickly pulled behind his back and secured. Two more men run up behind Rain, and he is escorted by three men to the elevators in the lobby. He is taken up two floors, where he is taken to the leader of the Hebtarians. This is a large room where two to three dozen hostages are gagged and tied on their knees. Gunmen are standing at the windows, and the leader is sitting on a desk.

"Ah, yes, the Americans are here. Where is the other one?" says the man sitting on the desk. He is speaking in English. Rain looks around, thinking, *Is he talking to me?"*

"Yes, I am talking to you. Where is the other one? Ah, pardon me. Let me make our introduction. I am Lyiam, and, yes, I am in charge here. You are Rain, yes? Or are you Smoke? You two are famous, didn't you know? We all know of the fearless unstoppable duo Rain and Smoke. We are going to do our best to stop the two of you here and now. So where is the other one? Well, no matter," says Lyiam.

Just as Lyiam finishes what he is saying, the elevator doors open, and Smoke is brought into the room.

"Ah, yes, this must be Smoke. Now we have the two of you. Let us get started," says Lyiam.

He speaks in a foreign language, and Smoke is forced down to his knees. A man is brought from the hostages and put on his knees in front of Rain and Smoke. The leader says something, and the man is shot in the back of the head, falling forward. Rain and Smoke cringe, being helpless and knowing things are going to get a lot worse. The man is dragged away, and a beautiful young woman is brought and put to her knees in front of Rain and Smoke.

"That was just to let you know that everyone here"—Lyiam gestures with his right hand to the hostages—"is going to face the same fate as that young man just did unless you answer my questions," says Lyiam.

"I don't know any of these people. Don't think I give a fuck about any of them. I came here to kill you, plain and simple. So you win, you got us. You might as well kill me now and let them go because I will tell you nothing," says Rain.

"Oh, yes, you are definitely, Rain. You know what, Rain, I believe you," says Lyiam.

Lyiam looks at one of his gunmen and points at Rain. The gunman walks up, putting a pistol beside Rain's right ear, and pulls the trigger. Smoke closes his eyes as his face is splattered with Rain's blood.

"Rain!" yells Smoke as he watches Rain fall beside him.

Rain watches Smoke as he falls in slow motion to the floor. He hits the floor flush and hard, but he feels little. He can tell his body bounces a few times before he comes to a stop, and he can see Smoke yelling his name. Smoke seems to be calling his name in slow motion, and Rain responds. He tries to get up and does, but it is very slow. He tries to use his arms, but he can't; his hands are still tied behind his back. He says, "Smoke," and he can hear it sounds like he is talking very slow. He is able to bend at his stomach and rise to his knees. Turning his head and looking around, he can see all kinds of gunmen laughing and pointing at him. One of the gunmen walks up and cuts the binding on his wrists. The man laughs, pointing at Rain's head. Rain feels the side of his head with his fingers, and he can tell he is hurt bad by the moist feeling of his fingers. Looking at his hand, he can see all the blood on his fingers. He feels the side of his head again to try and figure how bad it really is, and half of the left side of his head is gone. He starts to cry seeing all the gunmen are laughing harder at him. They are all pointing their fingers at Rain and laughing hysterically.

"Stop laughing. This is serious. Stop laughing at me," says Rain.

He raises his right knee and puts his hands on his right leg. Pushing up from his right leg, he is able to stand to the amazement of those watching. The gunmen laugh like this is the funniest thing they have ever seen. They barely push Rain, and he falls to the ground. He struggles but is able to get back up and stagger around. The gunmen form a circle and push Rain around, holding him up so they can play with him like cats playing with their catch. Half of Rain's head is blown out, and they can't believe he is still alive. Rain is aware but barely. He is not aware that he is going to die soon. He finally realizes he needs to fight back, so he pulls one of his tactical knives from its sheath. He gets in an offensive stance and faces one of the gunmen. The gunmen cannot stop laughing. You would think they have never had this much fun ever in their lives. Rain makes a swift lethal stab at the heart of the man in front of him. At least he thinks he does. He is actually very slow, and the man is laughing hysterically at Rain. The man catches his hand, takes the knife from him, and stabs Rain on the top of the head with the knife. He backs from Rain, laughing harder as all the gunmen laugh so hard now they are almost falling over. They all back away from Rain, giving him plenty of room because they want to watch him and see what he will do.

Smoke cries from his knees, "Rain!" Rain can feel the knife is stuck in the top of his head, and he tries to grab it, but he cannot function correctly. He tries to grab the knife, but he can only raise his arms about shoulder high, and he stumbles around like Frankenstein. The gunmen including Lyiam are laughing so hard they are crying. One of the gunmen walks up to Rain and wiggles the knife sticking out of the top of his head. He taunts Rain, and the gunmen laugh. Rain tries to grab the man, but he simply moves, staying at the back of Rain. The man slaps Rain on the left side of his head with a huge cork, and it sticks in the side of his head. This gives the gunmen even more laughter as Rain stumbles in circles with a knife sticking out the top of his head and a cork in the left side of his head.

"These are the great American mercenaries sent to kill us," says Lyiam.

Lyiam raises his hands, and the laughter quiets. Lyiam walks to Rain, grabbing him by his shoulder.

"One thing is for sure. Only Americans can walk around alive with a knife sticking out of the top of their head and a cork stuck in the side of their head, holding their brains in place," says Lyiam.

Lyiam parades Rain around in front of his men. The gunmen bust out in laughter.

"Stop laughing at me," says Rain.

Rain's voice is a slowed, slurred voice, and the gunmen laugh harder yet. Lyiam raises his arm.

"Wait a minute, he can speak. Hey, can you speak?" says Lyiam.

Lyiam speaks to Rain, tapping the knife on top of his head.

"I can speak," says Rain.

The gunmen laugh hysterically.

"Wait a minute, everyone, the retard can speak. That means he can understand. Hell, maybe he can reason," says Lyiam.

Lyiam shouts a command to his men.

Some of them draw their weapons and point them at the hostages.

"No!" yells Smoke. He stands and is quickly dropped back to his knees by a gunman hitting him violently on the back of his left leg with the butt of his rifle.

"Let the hostages go. You have us, and we are what you want. You want to kill us, then kill us. No need to kill innocent women, men, and children," says Smoke.

Smoke has his head pulled back, and he is secured by the gunman.

"Ah, that is where you are wrong, my American adversary. I say we see if Rain here is willing to answer my questions yet. I want to see if Rain here is willing sacrifice his life and your life for all these innocent women, men, and children. You hear me, Rain? You understand me, Rain? Tell me, Rain, tell me you freely give your youth to me. Beg me to kill you, or I will start shooting," says Lyiam.

Lyiam is now holding Rain by the back of his head. Rain fumbles and slurs, but no real words are said. Lyiam shouts a few commands, and four of the hostages are shot in the head. The rest of the hostages start to scream, cry, and beg for their lives.

"You want more of them to die? Huh, Rain? I will kill them all unless you beg me to kill you, unless you tell me I can have your youth. What is it going to be, Rain?" says Lyiam.

Lyiam shouts more commands to his men, and six more of the hostages are shot in the head. The remaining hostages are hysterical, but there is nothing they can do. They are on their knees with their legs and arms bound, and gunmen surround them. Smoke cries and struggles through being punched and hit in the back. He struggles to his feet, and two gunmen grab him from behind.

"Ah, so the famous Smoke, killer of Wantego Aberous Fernmente, killer of the Wind-shadow. Yes, we are well aware of who you and Rain are. We have been waiting for you two, and the leading bosses of the Underworld will pay very nicely for you two—for just your heads, that is. Hell, we can even put holes in your heads, and they will still bring a great bounty," says Lyiam.

Lyiam commands the gunmen holding Smoke to put him on his knees in front of Rain, and they do. Smoke looks to Rain.

"Don't do it, Rain. Don't give in to them. If we are to die here and now, then that is our fate. We had a good run, buddy. I would have never changed a thing," says Smoke.

The gunmen put the muzzles of their rifles to the sides of Smoke's head.

"Give me your youth, Rain. Beg me to kill you or watch as Smoke's head is turned into Swiss cheese," says Lyiam.

Rain struggles and tries to get away, but he has no strength. He has no speed, and Lyiam easily holds Rain in place with one hand. Lyiam nods his head to his gunmen, and all three of them fire. Smoke's head splinters, fractures, and splatters all of them with blood, bone, and brain. Rain cries, and the gunmen laugh at him. Smoke remains on his knees, but he passes very quickly. The gunman at the back of him kicks his corpse, and he falls forward. Lyiam shouts more commands, and the gunmen point their guns at the remaining hostages. One by one, they are raised to a standing position and shot in the head just a few feet from Rain. This happens six times, and Lyiam just gives the order to have the remaining hostages shot. The gunmen unload with automatic machine gun fire, leaving everyone dead except Rain.

"Give me your youth, Rain. Beg me to kill you!" shouts Lyiam.

Lyiam points at Smoke and snaps his finger. One of the gunmen unsheathes what looks like a machete, a very shiny, sharp machete, and he starts to saw Smoke's head off. Within a few moments, Smoke's head holes, and all has been severed and raised in the air in front of Rain.

"You want to end up like this? Huh, Rain? You want your head cut off and sold to the highest bidder? You are going to die, but die with some dignity. That is a big thing for Americans, right, to die with dignity? Give me your youth. Beg me to kill you!" shouts Lyiam.

Rain remains silent. Lyiam snaps his finger at some of his gunmen. The one holding the machete hands Smoke's head to another. Lyiam snaps his fingers and steps away from Rain. The gunman holding the machete swings very hard. Rain sees the room start to circle as his head rolls to the side of his body and rolls as it falls to the ground. When his head hits the ground, everything goes black.

Chapter 28

Head Games

A loud whistle wakes Rain. He opens his eyes to see a foot coming right at his face. He tries to block the kick, but he cannot feel his hands or his arms. He is kicked right in the face. He is spinning, and this is the worst for Rain. If there is one kind of sickness he is susceptible to, it is dizziness or motion sickness. He is spinning very fast, and his stomach is already feeling queasy. He hits the ground hard and rolls. He is rolling so fast he cannot fix his vision on anything. Before he can focus his vision, he is kicked again and again. He is rolling very fast, and no matter how hard he tries, he cannot get his arms or legs to respond. He feels like he is going to throw up, and finally, he rolls to a stop. He tries to push himself up, but his arms and legs do not work. He looks around, seeing he is flush with the grass. He is kicked on the back of the head, and he is rolling again. He is kicked and flies through the air. Before he hits the ground, he is kicked again hard and flies through the air in the opposite direction. He is kicked over and over, going back and forth, rolling all over the place. He can feel his skull is cracked, and at times, he swears his skull breaks and softens. It feels like his skull is fractured throughout, but somehow, it stays together as he rolls and bounces on the evenly cut grass. He can hear crowds of people all around cheering as he is kicked and hits a net, rolling to a stop. He is picked up.

"Hey, hey!" he yells, trying to get the attention of the person who places him back on the ground. The person runs a few yards away from him and charges him, kicking him very hard, and he flies. "No!" yells

Rain as he flies through the air and feels like he is going to throw up. This is the worst he can feel. He hits the ground and rolls. He actually tries vomiting as he is rolling, but nothing exits his mouth. He keeps being kicked, he keeps rolling, he keeps feeling like he is vomiting, and he has no control. It is a never-ending cycle of nauseous misery that he is caught in. He finally gets a moment of reprieve. He is able to focus on a man who holds him to his face.

"Come on, Rain, give me your youth. Beg me to kill you. This misery you are feeling, it can all be over. Just beg me to kill you," says the man.

Rain looks around and, for the first time, realizes he is nothing more than a head. He has no body. "Ah!" he cries.

"Where is my body? How am I alive? Where is my body?" cries Rain.

The man laughs.

"You have no body. You are just a head—a head that feels nothing but pain. End your pain, end it now. Just beg me to kill you, and I will end the suffering for you. If you don't beg me to kill you, your suffering will only get worse," says the man.

"Put me back together. Where is my body?" cries Rain.

Rain hears a whistle, and the man runs. Rain is pulled over and behind the man's head and thrown very far before hitting the ground and being kicked again. Rain will not submit, and for hours, he is kicked back and forth, thrown around, kneed, stomped, crushed, slapped, bounced, and sat on. The man who was talking to Rain earlier picks him up again.

"Well, are you ready to die? Have you had enough being kicked in the face? You are nothing. You are a bloody skull rolling around. End your suffering, or the pain and suffering will get worse. Make your decision," says the man.

Rain says nothing, and he hears a whistle. The man takes a few steps, and Rain is tossed into the air. He can see a foot coming at him as he falls to the ground, and he is kicked very hard. He can feel he is flying high and far. He is caught and squeezed tight. Back and forth, he moves with the movements of the runner.

"Hey, hey!" yells Rain.

The runner gets hit very hard and falls to the ground. Rain gets slapped very hard in the face and is tossed to someone else, who places him on the ground. Rain yells and cries, trying to get the attention of one of the dozens of players running around him, but no one responds. He is hut from one person to another person and handed to another person and thrown to another person for hours. He is kicked, punted, slammed on the ground, and kicked. He spins, wobbles, tumbles, bounces, soars, and sails. Still he feels like he is going to vomit. He feels like every bone in his body has been broken, and he does not even know where his body is. He knows he is only a head. All he is, is a head, and still he aches and feels pain throughout his entire body. He constantly feels like he is going to vomit, but he does not. He is thrown and spins so fast that he feels nausea, combined with headache, and it is the worst feeling in the world.

"Stop, stop. Please, someone, stop this. Please, someone, put my head back on my body. Someone!" cries Rain.

No one is responding to him for hours. Finally, someone does talk to him.

"Rain, how are you feeling, buddy? You don't look so good. You look kinda green, not brown like a football should be. You look like you are sick, but then again, where's your body?" laughs the man. "You ready to give in yet? Come on, Rain, beg me to take your youth from you. I will put it to good use. Plead with me to kill you. I will take your youth, and it will be put to good use. It's not doing you any good. You are miserably stuck in eternity. I might add that this is the way it is going to stay until you beg me to kill you, until you plead with me to take your youth and add it to mine. It is only a matter of time until you beg me to kill you, so why wait? Why put yourself through a constant miserable struggle that will only get worse and worse?" says the man.

"Never," says Rain.

"OK. Here we go. Are you ready?" says the man.

Rain is put down on a tee. He is looking straight ahead from ground level, and he knows what is coming. He waits, he anticipates, and a few moments later, he is kicked off very hard. He tumbles through the air very fast, flying and spinning, until he is caught and ran back the way he just flew from. The sick feeling in his stomach is always worse when he is placed on the ground and sits idle. He opens his eyes and just wants to puke. He wants to puke this miserable feeling away, but it just continues. He is hut from one man to another and thrown, spinning very fast through the air, until he is caught and slammed on the ground again. He is picked up and placed on the ground, and the strong feeling of wanting to vomit takes him again and again and again for hours.

"All right, Rain, I can end this terrible feeling for you right now. Beg me to kill you. Come on, Rain, beg me." The man shakes Rain. "Come on, Rain, beg me to kill you. Nothing, huh? All right, if you thought you were feeling sick so far, you have felt nothing yet. Here we go. Get ready to feel sick for real," says the man.

The man tosses Rain straight up in the air. He can see the lighting has changed, and there is a ceiling very high up with rows of lights. Rain is hit from behind and flies to the left side. He is grabbed and thrown to the ground very fast, smashing his face on the hardwood floor. He is thrown again and again, smashing his face over and over on the floor. Within seconds, he feels his face has been smashed to the point that every bone in his face has been broken and his nose flattened flush with his face. His tongue is bloodied, all his teeth are broken, and yet his face holds together as he is thrown from person to person and slammed into the floor over and over. He is thrown upward into the air, spinning, with his head aching like it has been squeezed in a vise from every angle. As if the pain is not enough, here comes the feeling of being sick to his stomach all over again. His face is burned from passing through a net very fast, and he hears crowds of people cheering all around him. He cannot see anything because he is constantly thrown into the ground, smashing his head from every angle. When he is not bouncing or hitting something, he is spinning so fast he cannot focus his vision. He is thrown back and forth. He is burned from scraping, skidding, and bouncing on wood floors and glass backboards. Again he is slapped in the face over and over. He is thrown, bounced, smacked, slammed, and poked. Every once in a while, he tries yelling, he tries screaming, but no one listens. No one responds. No one acknowledges he is even there. The constant smashing and pounding, the constant nausea, the constant motion are driving Rain to mental breakdown. All he can do is cry, and he cries out loud.

"Rain, I am here to help you, buddy. I can end this suffering for you. All life has left for you is misery. You have to end it. You have to end it now, and the only way you can do that is to beg me to kill you. Beg me to take your youth and put it to good use. I can do that for you. Do you want me to end your misery?" says the man.

"Who the fuck are you? Where is my body?" says Rain.

"All right, Rain, I see you have not had enough. I see you just don't get it. It only gets worse. Bye-bye," says the unfamiliar man.

Rain is thrown high in the air and starts to fall back down. He is hit with incredible force and flies at insane speed into the ground and bounces up. He is hit even harder and flies back the way he just came from. He spins many times faster than he has been spinning in earlier events. He has no time to dwell on the sickness in his stomach. Now his face feels like it is being sanded off. He hits the ground, bouncing up with incredible force, speed, and a pain. The pain is simply transferred from his chin to the back of his head, from his ear to his eye, and so on, all around his head over and over. He slows for a moment just to be thrown face-first into the ground a few times and then thrown up in the air so he can start the burning, skidding, bouncing pain that continues for hours. Rain gets a moment where he is tossed up and down. He is tossed and bounces on the ground and rolls to the hands of a person who picks him up. Rain is crying.

"Rain, are you seriously crying? Why are you crying? Don't you like this? I mean, I can end all this horror for you. You know you are just a head, right? There is nothing you can do except be thrown, smashed, kicked, punted, dribbled, hit, slapped, smacked, sat on, spit on, and discarded. I mean, it is over for you. Let me end this bullshit for you. Beg me to kill you, and it is all over. Otherwise, you are nothing more than an object for everyone to abuse. What is it going to be? Want me to end this for you?" says the man.

"Go to hell and leave me be," says Rain.

"No problem, sir. Let the fun begin," says the man.

Rain is thrown on the table and bounces to be caught over and over. He can't stop crying as his brain is shaken around in his broken skull. He can feel his head cave and shrink as he is hit incredibly hard and hits the table, bouncing and spinning faster than ever. He flies up, and the spinning motion curves his trajectory back to the table, where he bounces again and immediately is whacked with a paddle. He feels his skull shrink, he feels his brain spinning, he feels his skull cracking, and he feels absolute fear not knowing how long he will have to endure this horror. Somehow, his head stays together. It feels like his skin and hair should be gone from skidding on the table at incredible speed over and over, feeling like his head is constantly being bashed in, like his nose, lips, teeth, and cheeks should be bloody, crushed, and swollen.

"Stop, stop, stop. I can't take this anymore. Stop already. Stop this torment. Stop it!" yells Rain.

He cries over and over. He is thrown and caught by a hand, which closes around his entire head.

"OK, Rain, enough is enough. Beg me to kill you. Tell me to take your youth. Do it now," says the unfamiliar man.

"Who are you? What do you want? Go away. Leave me alone," says Rain.

"You just don't get it, do you? You just don't want to learn. No problem. You will give in. You will cave soon enough," says the man.

Rain is slammed on the table. He can see a very sharp stick coming at his head very fast. It withdraws and comes at him again, threatening to pierce him right between his eyes. The stick charges his face several times and then sticks him right between the eyes. Rain rolls very fast and slams into a wall. He is hit from all sides of his head, ricocheting all around. He rolls, being constantly hit with very hard balls, breaking his skull. The pain he has felt so far has been great, but this is by far the worst pain yet. It is like his head is being slammed into a brick wall, and he remains conscious through the pounding and excruciating pain, which is a constant. He rolls to a stop and sees a pointed stick coming right at his right eye. It almost strikes him and withdraws. Rain cries, "No!" as the stick charges him and strikes him right in the eye. Rain can feel his eye explode as he rolls and strikes another very hard ball. He rolls to a stop, crying, unable to open his right eye. He is struck again and again, hitting other balls very hard, and his head is pounding. His left eye is struck and explodes from the impact. Now he is blind and can only feel this excruciating pounding in his head. He is picked up and set back down.

"Now what? What is going on? Someone, please stop this. I can't see, and the pain is too great. Please stop this!" cries Rain.

He is struck in the right ear and loses his hearing from that ear. He slams hard into balls, and the pain continues. Rain cries as he is slammed into balls over and over, and his head pounds in pain. His left ear is struck, and now he is completely deaf, dumb, and blind. His only feeling now is pain. He is picked up, and his eyes reform. His hearing is restored, but still his brain is in throbbing, pounding pain. The unfamiliar man looks at Rain but does not say a word. He sighs and puts his thumb over Rain's mouth. He punctures Rain's eyes with his index and middle finger. Rain cries with no sound. Rain feels like he is growing, and he is swung back and thrown very fast. He spins and slides on the smooth glazed hardwood, slamming into pins. He bounces all around, feeling his skull crack. His stomach sickness continues as he continues to spin and bounce off hard objects. He rolls down a long tunnel and up a chute into the hands of someone who swings and throws him again. This goes on for hours. Time is like a blur to Rain. It feels like days, weeks, and months have gone by. The whole time he is nothing but a head being used as the ball in all kinds of sporting events. His pain is continuous. A never-ending headache and motion sickness. A constant feeling of nausea and stomach sickness. The embarrassment of being slapped, poked, punched, kicked, slammed, thrown, and sat on. Rain thinks to himself many times, *Will this never end? Is this hell? Is this the torture that the souls of people in hell must endure for eternity?*

"No, Rain, this is not hell. This is not the kind of torture souls must endure for eternity. This is just the warm-up for you. This is just the beginning for you. This is just my way of welcoming you," says the man.

Rain cannot see, but he can hear the words, and now he recognizes the voice of Glamfury. Ran can feel his head being slammed onto his neck. He opens his eyes and looks down to see his head has been slammed onto his body, and once again, he is whole. His eyes have healed, and he no longer is in pain. All he can see is blackness. There is no ground he is standing on. There is nothing to grab. He is alone in space, yet he can walk. He can breathe, but there is nothing here; it is just him in space. He hears laughter behind him and turns to see Glamfury laughing.

"Rain, you are amazing. You are the most stubborn. You are the most determined. You are, by far, going to be my greatest conquest of youth yet to date. You may be the greatest capsule of youth of all time. Do you realize you have been kicked, punched, thrown, slammed, hit, punted, spit on, sat on, and farted on by just about every athlete on earth for the past two years? Still you won't accept your fate. Still you think you are holding out for something. Still you think your life is yours. I admire you, Rain. I love you. You are awesome, but make no mistake about it. The longer you fight, the longer you hold out, the more intense, the greater the youth, the longer and stronger my life becomes because of you, and unfortunately for you, there is only one outcome. That is right, right as rain, Rain. You are going to hell. There is nothing you can do about it. You can prolong your destiny. You can hold out, but it is only a matter of time before your soul will go to Satan. Your youth will be mine, so hold out as long as you like. Hold out for decades, and remember, the longer you hold out, the longer my longevity becomes," says Glamfury.

Glamfury runs at Rain. Rain tries to run, but there is no ground; he is suspended in space. He can move his arms and his legs, but he goes nowhere. He feels fear as Glamfury charges at him and kicks him in the stomach. Rain flies backward in an arched position led by his back. He watches Glamfury get smaller as he flies away, breaking through sheets of glass. He can see all the shiny shards of glass floating in space as he flies backward, breaking through many sheets of glass.

Chapter 29

The Sibian Surprise

Rain can feel his back is being shredded by all the glass he is flying through. He can feel coolness all over his back. He is obviously bleeding very severely, and he slams into the ground. He rolls to a stop on his stomach, and he cannot move. He closes his eyes.

"Rain. Rain, wake up. Come on, it is almost daybreak. We have to get moving. Come on, we have to go," says Smoke, shaking Rain from his sleep.

Rain opens his eyes.

"Smoke, is that you? My back, how is my back?" says Rain.

"What are you talking about? Your back is fine. Get up, we have to go," says Smoke.

"My back is shredded from all the glass I was flying through. It's torn to bits. I know it is," says Rain.

"You must have been having a bad dream. You and your dreams. Your back is fine. We have to get going so we can catch the Sibians off guard. Come on, get up," says Smoke.

Rain sits up. He was sleeping on his stomach, which is very unusual for him. He sits up and feels his back, noticing he is fine. He is wearing black clothing stitched with holsters for tactical knives in his shirt and pants. He can see his favorite M16 rifle leaning against a tree very close to him and grabs it, checking for ammunition and making sure the safety is on.

"Holy shit, I had a horrible dream last night," says Rain.

"Yeah, well, no time to worry about that right now. We have to go get those Sibians, rescue the governor's children, and get the hell out of here," says Smoke.

"Roger that, buddy. Let's go," says Rain.

They get up and move silently through the lush forest. The sun has not even shown itself in the sky and already the steam is rising from the forest floor. Smoke stops, pointing his arm to the right, and Rain heads in that direction. They can hear men shouting in an unfamiliar language, giving away their location. Smoke and Rain head toward the talking men as the light of day is overtaking the forest, announcing the coming of the sun. Rain can see a well-armed man leaning against a tree, smoking a cigarette, and he approaches behind him very quietly. Rain makes a faint whistle, and the man turns to look. What he sees is Rain thrusting a very large knife into his throat, cutting his windpipe. The man struggles for a few moments, unable to move because Rain grabs his arms. He cannot scream or make a sound because of the knife in his throat. The man slowly loses his life, and Rain pulls him into the forest.

Rain looks through the sights on his gun, scanning the entire building. The homelike structure is built right into a rocky hillside. There are large trees all around and gunmen standing at most of them. The sun is throwing rays of light, which are starting to creep through the dense foliage of the jungle. Steam hovers and dances in the creeping sunlight, making its way to the ground. Smoke and Rain can hear a man shouting from within the home, and the men outside the house are shouting back and forth. The house has windows with no panes of glass and doorways with no doors. It is rotting in lots of places with mosses and grasses growing on the roof.

Rain looks through his sights into the windows, but he sees no one inside the house. He can hear the one man still yelling from within the house. The five men outside the house all turn, pointing their guns away from Rain, and he knows to take advantage of this. Rain shoots the closest man to him in the head and then the next closest and the next. His rifle is so silent no one hears a single shot. The two other men fall from well-placed bullets from Smoke. Again, not a single shot is heard. The man inside the house is still yelling and walks to the front door, seeing all his men dying on the ground. He yells in English.

"Ah, the Americans must be here. You must be here to save the kids, right? Well, there are no kids. The surprise is on you. Fucking gringos. Oh, wait a minute, what do we have here? I'm sorry, gringos, maybe there are some kids in here. Hold on a minute," says the Sibian.

The man steps into the house and then reappears in the doorway holding a young boy in front of him with a gun to the boy's head.

"Is this what you are here for? Huh, gringos? Show yourselves or I shoot this one first. I'm not fooling around. You try and shoot me, and I will kill this one here, and the others are in a trap that will spring and kill them all if I fall. Come on, gringos, show yourselves," says the Sibian.

Smoke walks toward the man, holding his arms in the air.

"You, just you? I know there are more of you. Come on, all of you, show yourselves," says the Sibian.

"Listen, there is no way out for you. You don't have to kill the kids. You are not getting any ransom. You are only escaping here with your life if you let them go. Otherwise, you will die," says Smoke.

Rain has the man in his sights. He can put a bullet right between the man's eyes, but he hesitates. Rain is well camouflaged and hidden in the trees. The man holding the child looks right at Rain like he is looking right into his eyes. His face turns red; his eyes glow red and black. Horns sprout from his head, and flames burn from his head. The man smiles and laughs. Rain is startled and falls back. He gets up, looking back through his sights, and the man is gone. The doorway is empty, and Smoke is still standing with his arms in the air. Rain gets up and heads for Smoke.

"Smoke, they are Egengyns. They are devil worshipers. He is the leader," says Rain, walking toward Smoke.

Smoke has his attention taken by the fallen men all around him who start to get up. Smoke points his gun and starts shooting them. Rain advances from the forest and starts shooting them as well. The fallen men start to get up, and Rain or Smoke shoot another hole in their head, dropping them to the ground again. The fallen men keep getting up after every new hole blasted in them.

"What the fuck? This is some fucked-up shit. How do they keep getting up?" says Smoke.

"I don't know. Fuck them, we have to get the kids," says Rain.

They run into the house. The first room is decrepit, damp, and dark. They explore deeper into the home, realizing the house is built right into the hillside. There is barely enough light for them to see, but they are able to search all the rooms in the house. It is empty.

"What the fuck? Where did they go?" says Smoke.

Rain notices a metal ring in the floor, which he pulls, exposing a tunnel leading down.

"Oh, shit, this reminds me of the home in Egypt we raided, the one where we met up with Glamfury, the god of the Egengyns, remember?" says Rain.

"What are you talking about? There you go with that word *Egengyns* again, and what are you talking about Egypt? We have never been to Egypt. Who is Glamfury? Come on, Rain, time to focus. There is no telling what we are going to find down this tunnel. Let's get down there and save the governor's children. You ready?" says Smoke.

Rain shakes his head.

"What do you mean you don't remember Egypt? Where are we? I don't remember this house or this jungle. We have done over a dozen missions, and we just about killed all the Egengyns except that bastard they call their god, the one haunting our dreams, the one the girls called Glamfury, remember? You do remember, right?" says Rain.

"Rain, get your head on, man. This is only our second mission. We are in Peru, buddy. The Sibians have the governor's children, and they say they are going to kill them unless the governor pays one million per child—that's six million, Rain. We are here to get them out, remember?" says Smoke.

Rain looks down the passage leading to the underground. He looks up at Smoke.

"I don't remember this. I don't know what is down there. I don't remember what happens," says Rain.

"Well, where would the fun be if you knew what was down there? As far as what happens, well, we are going to kill them all except for the kids. Now wake the fuck up and let's go," says Smoke.

Smoke slings his gun over his shoulder and moves down the ladder into the underground. Rain follows. They get off the ladder in a very damp cave. They follow toward the sound of water and the rippling reflections on the wall of the cave. They can hear two girls weeping as they make their way through the cave, which winds to the right. They are poised with guns raised. The sound of water splashing and dripping gets louder, and the girls weeping gets louder as they make their way to a large opening in the cave. Smoke leans down to the left side of the opening and Rain to the right. The cave opens into a very large cavern with a large pond-size pool of water taking up the back side of the cavern. Smoke and Rain look around, trying to see where the source of light is coming from, and there are holes in the dirt and tree root ceiling leading up some forty of fifty feet to the jungle floor. Light is seeping its way into the cavern from here. Also the pond of water flows out a tunnel in the back of the cave, which leads outside.

"Do you see anyone?" asks Smoke.

"No, only the two girls tied to those wooden poles. I wonder how they got out there in the first place," says Rain.

"I know that is weird the way there are two mounds of land out in the middle of that water like that. I wonder who tied them up to those posts. Well, this smells like a trap if ever I have smelled one. No point in lingering. Time to spring it. You ready, buddy?" says Smoke.

"Oh, I hear ya. Let's get some," says Rain.

They get up and start walking very alertly toward the girls, who are out some five yards in the pool of water. Each girl is on a mound of earth where she is tied to a telephone pole-size post rising from the ground about six feet in the air.

"Is that—oh my god, it is. It's Shelly and Stacy, the girls we dated from Willsdus," says Smoke.

"It's a trap. It's a trap," says Rain.

"Of course, it's a trap. Now let's get the girls out of here. Shelly, Stacy, is that you?" says Smoke.

"Oh my god, Smoke. Stop, don't come any closer!" cries Shelly.

A head starts to rise from the water to Shelly's left side, and one starts to rise from the left side of Stacy as well.

"What that fuck is that?" yells Smoke.

Smoke points his gun. The creatures rise from the water, dark green, almost black in color. Their heads are humanoid with oversized eyes and nostrils that close like sea lion noses. Their teeth are deadly, sharp and large. From the neck down, they look completely outlandish. Their necks lead to a shoulder that completely circles their body, and from there, they have ten tentacles like those of an octopus, only human sized. At the ends of the tentacles are barbed hooks, which the creatures can use to capture prey and draw them in. The midsection of their bodies under the tentacles are much like a humanoid torso that lead to a very strong muscular tail fin like a bass. They can use their tentacles much like arms and legs to move on land with. It looks like they have the ability to breathe air, and they have gills underneath their shoulder and tentacles on either side of their torso so they can probably breathe in the water as well. The creature to the left swings a tentacle at Shelly and hooks her left shoulder. She screams in pain as the creature pulls, slicing her chest from her left shoulder down across her right breast. It is trying to pull her to it, but she is tied very tight to the pole, and her flesh is painfully sliced. Smoke yells, unloading automatic machine gun fire on the creature, filling it with hot lead. It very quickly descends into the water, leaving Shelly bleeding and crying. Rain shoots the other creature heading toward Stacy, and it descends into the water as well.

"I'm coming. I'm going to get you out of there, Stacy. Hold on!" yells Smoke.

"Smoke, no. Don't, Smoke. It's a trap. They are trying to get you into the water—that is what they want!" yells Rain.

A creature raises from the water very close to the shore where Smoke is about to enter, and Smoke looks up, seeing it is nearly ten feet tall standing on the tentacles. Smoke and Rain both fire on the creature, and it falls back into the water. Tentacles shoot from the water, hooking Smoke in three different places. He looks at Rain, and for a moment, they know. Smoke is pulled into the water and gone.

"Smoke, Smoke!" yells Rain.

Rain watches the ripples on the water slowly fade away, and Smoke is raised out of the water, gasping for air. He is held up by three tentacles, and three more tentacles spring from the water, slapping hooks into Smoke. All the tentacles pull him in different directions, and his body is pulled apart with chunks of flesh and bone raining into the pond. The pond starts to boil with activity as lots of very large fish start to eat the pieces of flesh raining into the pond. Stacy and Shelly scream and cry as two more of those large creatures rise from the water and hook the girls with their tentacles. Rain shoots them, and they fall back into the water only after pulling and ripping flesh from the girls. Again tentacles spring from the water, hooking the girls, ripping their flesh, and slicing them to death. The girls scream as the tentacles whip them from the water and hook them over and over. Rain shoots them, but there is nothing he can do. He realizes there are many more than just two of those large octobass creatures. Within minutes, the girls have been sliced to death. Large chunks of their flesh ripped from their bodies and flung into the water, where quickly their flesh is eaten by the large fish in the water. The girls hang at the wooden poles with blood seeping from their gouged flesh. Tentacles whip from all around the mounds of earth, hooking what is left of the girls, ripping them apart and pulling their torn bodies into the water.

"No!" cries Rain as he watches the churning water. Slowly the churning slows and stops. Rain looks around all alone in the cavern, not believing Smoke, Shelly, and Stacy are gone. *This is not real. This can't be real. I don't remember any Sibians or any governor's children that we rescued. What is this?* thinks Rain to himself. He looks around, noticing hooks on the cave walls. Hanging from the hooks are hollowed-out coconut shells with long vines hanging to the ground. He hears faint noise from the tunnel leading into the cave and notices the men he and Smoke had shot many times in front of the house have made their way into the tunnel where Rain is now. He backs to the water's edge, bending to his knee with his rifle ready. He refrains from shooting right away and watches the men walking like zombies. There are six of them, and they walk to the coconut shells and put them over their heads. They turn and face Rain. He now remembers the men holding Ajaunta's husband and Smoke at the sacrificial rock behind the house in the woods. "Egengyns, you're Egengyns, not Sibians. You're devil worshippers, and Glamfury is your god." Rain hears dripping water behind him and laughter. He turns to see Glamfury rising from the water in between the mounds of earth.

"You are finally here with us, Rain. You did not think your friends were dead, did you? So sorry, here, let me bring them back for you," says Glamfury.

Glamfury raises his hands upward. Shelly and Stacy rise from the water in front of the mound of earth they were on. Their bodies look like they have been put back together with superglue. They are torn and shredded. Blood is running down their bodies, and they look limp and weak.

"Rain, why did you let them kill us?" says Shelly.

"Yeah, why, Rain? Why did you let those fish eat us?" says Stacy.

"No. No. This is not real. This is a dream," says Rain.

Smoke starts to emerge from the water, walking up to the land where Rain is. His body is all torn and bleeding. His arms hang and his head droops like he has no energy or strength in his muscles.

"So I cannot kill you and get all your youth unless you beg me to kill you, unless you command me to take your youth and put it to good use by adding to the longevity of my life here on earth. What if Smoke were to kill you? What if he were to kill you right here in front of me? I wonder if I get all your youth in this case. Let us see." Glamfury laughs.

"You always said I would be the death of you, Rain. You always said I would kill you," says Smoke.

Smoke raises the rifle still hanging from his shoulder.

"Smoke, come on, buddy. What has he done to you? Come on, Smoke, this is not you," says Rain.

Smoke slowly raises his rifle and points it at Rain. He pulls the trigger, unleashing automatic gunfire, shredding Rain to bits, and Rain falls to his side. Rain can see his blood run over his eyes, and everything turns red and then black.

Chapter 30

Horror House

"Smoke, no!" yells Rain, sitting up in his bed. He is sweating and breathing hard. It is dark, and he cannot see much.

"Rain, what are you doing?" says a female voice.

Rain reaches over and feels a woman lying under the covers beside him. He reaches over and turns on the light on the nightstand.

"Rain, what are you doing?" she says.

Rain turns and sees Marlene lying beside him.

"Marlene. This is a dream. This is all one never-ending dream," says Rain.

Marlene sits up, and Rain just about jumps out of the bed. He gasps, covering his mouth, and backs out of the bed hurriedly.

"What, Rain? What is the matter? You don't like the way I look? This is all because of you, Rain. This is all your fault. The pain I feel every day, the horror I must endure every day—it is all because of you, Rain," says Marlene.

Rain can't take his hands from his mouth. She has been stripped of skin and flesh from her nose up and over her skull. From below her jaw to the right side of her body, she has been stripped of skin, and large chunks of flesh seem to have been bitten from her body. She moves off the bed and stands in just her panties. Her left leg has been stripped of skin and chunks of flesh bitten from her leg muscles. Rain backs to the wall as she steps toward him. She is as grotesque a sight as Rain has ever seen.

"What's the matter, Rain? You don't like what you see? This is all your fault, Rain. This is all your fault. All you have to do is give in to Glamfury. Tell him to take your youth. Tell him to kill you and my pain will be over. Stop my pain, Rain," says Marlene.

"No. This is not real. You are not real. Stay back. Stay away from me," says Rain.

He moves to the top of the stairway outside his bedroom, and Marlene slowly follows behind him.

"Go away from me. Stay away from me," says Rain.

Rain runs down the stairs into the kitchen. His motion is halted immediately upon entering the kitchen. He sees Ajaunta standing in the doorway leading to the living room. She has her hands on her stomach. She is bleeding from multiple holes in her stomach and chest. She raises her hands, looking at the blood on them. She points her hands toward Rain and looks at him.

"Why, Rain? Why did you kill me? You shot me, Rain. You killed me. You condemned me to an eternity of torture, an eternity of pain and death. Why, Rain? Why would you do this to me? I thought you loved me," says Ajaunta.

Glamfury walks up behind Ajaunta from the living room. He is laughing, and he squeezes Ajaunta from behind her. He grabs her breasts with his hands and sticks his fingers in the bullet holes on her body. He then sucks the blood off his fingers, savoring the taste of Ajaunta's blood in his mouth.

"Let her go. Release her from your hell, you sick fuck," says Rain.

"Why, Rain? Why would you let him torture me, rape me, eat me forever? Why, Rain?" cries Ajaunta.

Glamfury pulls her head to her left and bites a huge chunk of flesh from the right side of her neck. Blood squirts all over Glamfury's face. It splatters the wall as he rips the flesh from her neck. Ajaunta goes weak, and Glamfury throws her body to the floor. He chews the flesh, filling his mouth, and swallows. The flesh hanging outside of his mouth he pushes into his mouth and continues to chew, smiling and humming, "Mmmmmmmmm."

"You sick motherfucker. I will kill you!" yells Rain.

He charges Glamfury and dives headfirst at him. Glamfury laughs and disappears. Rain dives right into the living room and tucks his head under his shoulder, rolling to his back and feet. He stands with his momentum, taking him right into Bailey, who is standing with her wrists tied with rope. The rope leads to the ceiling, and Bailey cannot move. There are syringes in either side of her neck connected to tubes leading into the ceiling. Blood is being drained from her body and running through the tubes into the ceiling and coming down from the ceiling near the door. Glamfury is standing there holding the tubes, and the blood is dripping into his mouth. He is smiling, drinking the blood and letting it drip all over his face.

"Rain, why would you let him drink my life? Why, Rain, why would you let him drink me forever? He is killing me, Rain. He is killing me over and over and over. Please make him stop. Please beg him to kill you," says Bailey.

"I will stop him, Bailey. Don't you worry, I will stop him right now," says Rain.

He charges Glamfury, and Glamfury waves his right hand, stranding Rain in slow motion. Rain is moving as fast as he can. Unfortunately, he is barely moving at all in real time. Glamfury laughs. He puts the tubes in his mouth and sucks real hard on them. Rain can see Bailey start to shrink like her body is being sucked inward.

"Rain, stop him. Stop him, Rain. It hurts," says Bailey, and she starts to cry.

"It hurts, Rain. It hurts," she says.

Rain can see sections of her body shrink inward as Glamfury sucks on the tubes. He sucks hard, filling his mouth with blood and then pulling the tubes from his mouth, letting the drips of blood drip all over him and the floor. He swallows with blood dripping down his chin and neck. Glamfury laughs and sucks real hard on the tubes. Rain can see Bailey's stomach shrink inward as she screams and cries. Glamfury swallows a huge mouthful of blood, wiping his lips with a loud "Ahh." Bailey's stomach shrinks until her hips pull up to the bottom of her rib cage. She cries.

"Rain, he's killing me. Rain, he's killing me." She cries.

"Damn, she is so good. You want some, Rain?" says Glamfury.

Glamfury holds the tubes toward Rain, and blood drips from them. Rain tries to yell, he tries to talk, but in slow motion, faint sounds are all that can be heard from him.

"Oh, well, that is OK, Rain. More for me," says Glamfury.

Glamfury takes a deep breath. Bailey looks at Rain and starts to weep. Rain can do nothing, yet tears fall from his eyes in real time as

Glamfury sucks on the tubes hard. Rain can see Bailey's left leg shrink right down to the bone. Glamfury swallows and takes another deep breath. He sucks hard again, and Bailey's right legs shrinks to nothing but skin and bone for real. The clothing she was wearing falls to the floor except the shirt, which still hangs from her shoulders. She is now nothing but breasts, shoulders, and a head. She is still alive, and Rain cries as Glamfury sucks on the tubes, and her breasts shrink inward. Her neck sucks down to her windpipe, and the flesh on her skull shrinks. Her body goes lifeless, and her bones are pulled up to her skull. Her bones dangle on the ropes, and Glamfury sucks the last of the blood her body has. He lets go of the tubes, and her bones fall and stop just before hitting the ground.

"And here we go," says Glamfury.

Glamfury takes a few steps toward Bailey's remains, kicking them. Rain falls into real time as Glamfury kicks her remains, and they fly into the bedroom next to the living room. Rain gets up.

"I'm going to kill you, motherfucker," says Rain.

Rain yells, and he dives on Glamfury. Glamfury disappears, and Rain falls on the ground. The door opens to darkness, and lightning lights the outside as Smoke walks into the living room. The front door slams behind him. Rain gets up.

"Smoke. What has happened to you? Smoke, what the hell, Smoke?" says Rain.

Smoke walks toward Rain. His body is shredded and gouged. Pieces of flesh are torn from his body, and blood is dripping all over the floor. His rifle is hanging from his shoulder, and his head hangs like he cannot lift it up.

"Smoke, we're gonna get you some help, buddy. We are gonna fix you up like we always do," says Rain.

Rain slowly backs toward the kitchen and away from Smoke, who slowly advances like a zombie.

"Rain, you always said I would be the death of you. Remember, Rain? You always said I would be the death of you. I think it is time to make good on your request," says Smoke.

Smoke slowly reaches for his gun. It is obvious his body is not working up to snuff. He gets hold of his rifle and points it at Rain. Rain attacks and grabs the gun, pulling it from Smoke, who falls on the living room floor. Rain is startled as three men walk from the bedroom where Bailey's remains were kicked.

"What the fuck?" says Rain.

He backs toward the kitchen as Randy, Kevin, and Melveroykel walk from the bedroom into the living room. Their throats have been slit, and blood squirts and drains from their wounds.

"I told you it was not over, Rain. I told you," says Melveroykel.

Smoke gets up from the floor. Randy and Kevin both have knives in their hands, and they start to stab Smoke over and over.

"Rain, help me. Rain, help me. They are killing me, Rain!" cries Smoke.

Smoke tries to defend himself, but he is just not fast enough. He is stabbed in the stomach, chest, throat, back, and neck. Rain moves to help, and Melveroykel jumps in his path with a knife in his hand. He flips the knife back and forth between his hands.

"Where do you think you are going? Huh, Rain? Think you are going to help Ken, or is it Smoke? I think you are too late. Ken will be dying soon," says Melveroykel.

Randy stabs downward with his knife into the lower neck of Smoke, and Kevin does the same on the other side of Smoke's neck. They push, and Smoke falls to his knees. He then falls forward as Randy and Kevin hold on to the knives and turn to face Rain. Rain yells and pulls the trigger, unloading many tens of rounds into each of the men. They fall apparently dead. Rain checks his ammunition, realizing he has used it all on the three men. He throws the rifle on the couch, hearing noise coming from the bedroom. He looks to see Shelly and Stacy walking from the bedroom into the living room. They are cut, gouged, and severely deformed, walking with limps and blood dripping all over. Their heads are drooping, and their feet drag on the floor.

"Rain, why did you let the octobass men kill us? Why, Rain? Why did you not save us?" says Shelly.

"Why did you not sacrifice yourself? You could have saved us all this pain by just giving in and letting us live. Now we are doomed to be tortured, beaten, murdered, eaten, and brutalized for eternity, and it is all your fault," says Stacy.

"Yes, Rain, you could have saved us all. You still can. Just beg him to kill you. If he kills you, then our pain and suffering will come to an end. I would do it for you, buddy. Please stop the pain for us," says Smoke.

Randy, Kevin, and Melveroykel stand up with blood gushing from the bullet holes in their bodies. They start to walk toward Rain. Bailey walks from the bedroom into the living room. The skin on her head is shriveled to her skull. Her eyes seem huge in her shrunken eye sockets and incredibly white. Her bones are covered with just skin, and she walks toward Rain with the others.

"No, no, stop this. This is not my fault. You all stop this. This is not my fault!" cries Rain.

He backs into the kitchen where he is grabbed from behind by Ajaunta. This startles him, and he turns, violently throwing her against the refrigerator. She holds out her arms to Rain with tears forming in her eyes.

"I thought you loved me, Rain. I thought you would do anything for me. Please, Rain. Please, just stop the pain. Stop the never-ending torture," says Ajaunta.

Rain is startled again as Marlene approaches him from his left side and tries to hug him. She is so grotesque with the top of her skull skinned. Her lips are fine, but from her neck down the right side of her body, it has been skinned with huge chunks of flesh bitten from her body. She looks so horrific with one side of her chest busty and beautiful and the other side of her chest skinned and gruesome.

"Come on, Rain, kiss me. I love you, Rain. I thought you loved me too," says Marlene.

"Yes, kiss me too, Rain. I thought you loved me," says Ajaunta.

Both the girls are walking toward Rain.

Smoke, the other three men, and Bailey walk into the kitchen toward Rain. Rain backs toward the stairway leading into the basement followed by what seems to be live corpses.

"Go away. Leave me alone. Go to hell, where you all belong," says Rain.

He goes into the stairway leading into his cellar, closing the door behind him. He cannot lock the door from the inside, and soon enough, the handle starts to turn from the kitchen. The door is pulled open, and Rain holds the handle, pulling it shut.

"Go away. Leave me alone!" yells Rain.

"You cannot hide from us. We are going wherever you go," says Smoke.

Smoke is pulling on the door handle, but Rain is far stronger and holds the door shut. Rain hears loud noise coming from his basement and looks down the stairs. It is dark, and he flips the light on. He can see the floor of the basement is starting to break apart. The floor is falling and being blown away like somehow the house is a mile in the sky. "What the hell!" yells Rain.

"Yes, that is right, Rain. You won't give in. You won't sacrifice yourself so the rest of us can live, so we are bringing hell to you. That's right. If we are to be tormented and tortured in hell forever, then we are bringing hell to you so you can join in the fun!" yells Smoke.

Smoke yells from the other side of the door, and Rain can hear him laughing. The whole floor of his basement has fallen out, and sure enough, it looks like hell is below. Red hot lava swirling around and a loud hell wind is becoming deafening. More and more of the basement is falling into the hell fire, and now his basement is gone. The stairs leading up to where Rain is are starting to fall one by one into the abyss of hell. All the stairs fall into hell, and now Rain is hanging on to the door handle. He can feel the heat blowing across his body. He instantly starts to sweat, and his hands are losing grip on the door handle.

"Rain, do you give in? Do you want me to kill you and take your youth? If not, I am afraid Lucifer himself is coming for you. There is nothing I can do to stop him. All I can do is take your youth and kill you if you so desire," says Glamfury.

Rain sees no one, but he knows the voice is Glamfury.

"Never. I will never willingly give my youth to you. I will never beg you to kill me. Never!" yells Rain.

Rain's hands slip from the door handle. He screams as he is taken by the hell wind and flies toward hell. He is falling, and his hair is being whipped all over by the strong wind and heat. He is falling, getting closer and closer to the boiling, burning lava. He falls in with barely a splash of the thick hot lava. His flesh is instantly seared. He feels extreme pain for only a second. His eyes pop, and he feels like he has fallen asleep. Within seconds, his body is sucked under the surface of the molten rock.

Chapter 31

The Burning Abyss

Rain can feel he is being lifted up though the magma. He is solid like his body has been petrified. Actually, his body is charred like burned timber. He has no eyes, so he cannot see. His ears and all his skin is burned and crusty. He hears and feels barely the torrent of molten rock flowing over his crusty body. He is lifted to the surface where he now hears the rush of superheated wind blowing by. His body is stiff with his arms straight out to his sides and his legs straight down. He can feel he is being stood up on his feet, and he feels knocking on his head. Glamfury is hitting him with a hell hammer, knocking the charred flesh from his body. Rain's burned flesh falls off, uncovering fresh new flesh and skin underneath. Glamfury puts a long syringe into Rain's eye sockets and blows, filling his eyes, and Rain can see again. Rain can now move his head and neck. He watches as Glamfury chisels the charred flesh from his body, exposing the new flesh, and within minutes, Rain is good as new. He looks around to see he and Glamfury are standing on a large rock with streams of lava flowing very fast all around them. The wind is blowing almost hard enough to blow them over. It is very hot, and Rain is sweating.

"So why would you drop me into hell and then bring me out? Why not let me char and burn forever?" asks Rain.

"Like I have said before, I like you, Rain. You are going to be my greatest conquest of youth possibly ever. I can't just let you rot forever. I need to harvest your youth first. You are smart. You are stubborn. You are tenacious, but you will be mine," says Glamfury.

"You don't scare me. You don't intimidate me. You don't control me. Why don't you just let me go and move on? I am a total loss to you—a complete loss of time and energy. Given enough time, I will figure out how to destroy you. I will figure out how to put an end to this never-ending nightmare," says Rain.

Glamfury laughs and rises in the hell wind. He points behind Rain, yelling, "Tell that to him!"

Rain turns to see a gigantic lava man walking right toward him. It is walking waist high in the lava, and the top half of its body is at least fifteen feet high. "Oh, shit," says Rain with nowhere to go. The rock he is on is maybe six feet wide and about ten feet long. There is nowhere for him to go unless he jumps into the flowing lava. The lava man approaches and reaches its massive right arm into the lava, pulling a hardened lava club from the molten soup. It approaches and swings the club like a bat hitting Rain in the stomach. He flies, having the wind knocked out of him. He waits to fall into the lava to be burned to death again, but he falls on what seems to be sand. It is very hot but soft, and he rolls to a stop. He can see the lava man is walking toward him from an ocean of lava. Rain turns to see a forest behind him, a forest that is on fire, and there is heavy smoke all around, choking him. He runs into the forest, dodging and ducking the flames and falling debris. He sees animals that are burning and dying on the forest floor. He sees animals falling from the trees on fire, and the screams and cries of the dying are all around. Everything is on fire, and he runs deeper into the forest. Soon, he cannot see through all the smoke, and he runs into someone falling on them. Rain sits up to see he has run into Smoke.

"Rain, is that you, buddy? I have been looking all over for you. Somehow, we were separated. Come on, I found the way out. Oh, I found this and figured you would like it back. Hopefully we can avoid all the Egengyns. They are everywhere. Come on, follow me," says Smoke.

Smoke gets up and hands Rain his shoulder harness with both his favorite pistols fully loaded. Rain follows, covering his eyes and putting on his shoulder harness.

"Smoke, there is this huge lava man coming after me," says Rain.

"Don't worry, he can't go out of the lava. He can't come into the forest," says Smoke.

"Forest? Aren't we in hell?" asks Rain.

"We are not in hell, but this is much closer than I ever want to be to hell," says Smoke.

"I saw Glamfury. He burned me in the lava and then brought me back. This is some sort of trap or a game for him. He is trying to get something from us. The books. Gee, I can't even remember. I think he already got the books from us. Damn, it's just like one long dream that's broken up into a whole bunch of small little dreams but somehow combined into one long nightmare. Are you with me, or are you trying to find your own way through the nightmares you are in?" says Rain.

"I don't know. I think he has us all turned around and upside down. I have seen you and the girls killed at least ten times by now. I don't know what his game is, but I am tired of it," says Smoke.

"Me too. We have to figure out how to kill that guy," says Rain.

"First, we have to figure out how to get out of this place—this place I call pre-hell—and we have to get back home," says Smoke.

"You said you found the way out. You have been here before? I don't ever remember being here," says Rain.

Smoke bends down, and Rain kneels beside him. All the trees are on fire, and there is heavy smoke all around. They find it hard to breathe and are coughing a lot. Everything around them is burning, and it is amazing how loud fire is. They have been yelling just to hear each other, and the fire pulls and pushes the wind around them. Smoke points to a mountain that rises in the forest with a cave leading into it.

"You see there? That's the way out. I know it is. I don't know what or where it leads to, but I know it's the way out because all the Egengyns are standing around the entrance," says Smoke.

"Oh, yeah, I see them. Goddamn coconut shell-wearing, vine-hanging, devil-worshipping zombies," says Rain.

"Yeah, you have run into them too, I see," says Smoke.

"Yeah. I say we just charge them and shoot the fuck out of them, but they don't die. They keep getting back up," says Rain.

"That's the only thing that makes me hesitate. Like I said, I don't know what is in that cave, but it has to be the way out of this place. What do you think? You think we should just charge them and go in?" asks Smoke.

"I think it's better than sitting in this flame-infested forest watching everything around us burn to death. Time to shoot some more of those fucking devil worshippers," says Rain.

Rain stands, drawing his pistols, and Smoke stands with his rifle. They shake their heads at each other and approach the half-dozen Egengyns standing on the outside of the cave. They look like the Egengyns in the back of the cabin that were holding on to Ajaunta's husband when he was sacrificed. Rain and Smoke walk right at the devil worshippers, shooting holes in their heads. They are all shot and fall apparently dead as Rain and Smoke walk up and past them. They enter the cave and instantly notice the air is much fresher and much easier to breathe. They walk deeper into the cave, noticing it gets larger and larger the further they walk. The air hits them in the face as it passes them on its way out into the burning forest. They are glad the Egengyns do not follow them into the cave. The cave opens to a large cavern. They walk a ledge that that runs along the wall. A good forty feet below them, an underground stream runs deeper into this underground world. The air is warm and fresh. The water is crystal clear and running fast. The most amazing thing is that there is light here. There are trees and large plant life along the water's edge, and it is like there is a fluorescent light emanating from all the plant life. It seems to be a fluorescent green-lit day with a green sun hiding behind a wall of earth that is the ceiling. They walk along the ledge, and slowly it winds down to the water's edge. They both sip water from the stream, realizing it is pure and fresh. The water flows fast, and if they enter, they will surely be swept away by the current.

"This is odd. It seems like the water flows deeper into the earth. I don't see any way out, not yet anyway," says Smoke.

"This is too comfortable," says Rain.

"What do you mean?" says Smoke.

"I mean, the water is fresh. The air is fresh. No one is dying or screaming. This is a trap. This is a horrible trap, and we are in it," says Rain.

"Hey, look there," says Smoke.

Rain walks beside Smoke and looks into the stream where Smoke is pointing. There are five fluorescent green lights swimming around in the water. The lights swim fast and in circles, going out of view and then coming back into view. The lights swim closer and closer to the surface. Smoke's curiosity gets the best of him, and he moves closer to the water. He bends down, getting closer to the stream, trying to see what the lights are.

"Smoke, get back. This is the trap I was telling you about. I know it is," says Rain.

"I know you are right, Rain, but I have to know what it is," says Smoke.

One of the lights swims up in the center of the stream and breaks the surface of the water.

"Bailey!" yells Smoke.

"Holy shit, Rain, it's Bailey," says Smoke.

A second light breaches the surface, and the sight of Ajaunta draws Rain to the water's edge. The two girls smile and laugh. They hug each other, while Rain and Smoke watch speechless. Marlene rises behind the two girls and hugs them both. Now the three of them laugh and play as Stacy and Shelly rise up, and the five girls twirl, hug, and play in the warm water. Rain and Smoke are mesmerized watching the nude girls frolic in the water. The girls have long flowing hair, and their big smiles captivate the men. They swim effortlessly, rising up from the water and swimming deep out of sight. The girls twirl and jump in the water like dolphins. Rain and Smoke look at each other, noticing the girls are a type of mermaid. They are completely human all the way down to their knees, where their legs join, ending in a powerful tail fin, enabling the girls to swim with ease. Bailey swims up to the bank, reaching her hand out to Smoke. She has the most beautiful smile, and Smoke reaches for her hand. Bailey pulls her hand back, shaking her head back and forth.

"No, no, you can't come in unless you take your clothes off," she says.

Stacy and Shelly swim up next to Bailey, smiling.

"Come on, Smoke, come on in. We want to play with you," they say.

Marlene and Ajaunta swim up, calling Rain to come in too. Smoke has already put his gun down, and he is taking his clothes off.

"Smoke, what are you doing? Smoke, this is a trap. It has to be. It is way too good to be true. Smoke, don't do it," says Rain.

Smoke pays little attention to Rain as he has already stripped down and is reaching for Bailey's hand.

"Smoke, don't do it!" shouts Rain.

Rain reaches for Smoke, but Smoke grabs Bailey's hand, and she pulls him into the warm water. Instantly, the current washes him downstream. Rain runs along the bank of the stream, and the girls swim with Smoke. Rain calls and shouts to Smoke as he watches the girls swim around Smoke, dipping him in the water and rubbing all over him. Smoke is smiling and laughing and playing like a schoolboy on the playground. The girls tickle Smoke and throw him in the air. Smoke laughs and hugs the girls close to him. Smoke calls for Rain to jump in as he is continually rushed downstream with the flow of the water. Rain runs along the bank until the bank ends, and he watches as Smoke flows downstream with the girls.

"Smoke!" yells Rain.

Rain stands there for a second, and then a feeling of fear rushes his body. His veins fill with heated blood. He feels he has just watched his best friend flow away in the water for the last time. Rain raises his hands, yelling.

"Smoke, come back!"

From behind and upstream from Rain comes Ajaunta swimming fast, and he never sees her. She breaches the water very fast and grabs Rain's arm. He is pulled into the water where he starts to flow downstream with the current. Rain breaks the surface, breathing the fresh air, and Ajaunta rises before him as beautiful as ever. Shelly swims up behind him and Marlene to his side.

"You can't be wearing clothes in here. We want you naked," says Ajaunta.

The girls undress Rain in seconds and tickle his body. He smiles, flowing downstream, and the girls swim all around him, rubbing against him and touching him all over. Rain hugs them close to him when he faces them, and like they were moistened in oil, they slip from his grasp and swim away. The feelings and sensations of the girls tickling, rubbing, and flowing downstream with Rain are intoxicating. He smiles, laughs, and plays with the girls until they all flow over a small waterfall into a pond of warm water. Smoke is here swimming and playing with the other girls. Smoke watches as Rain flows over the waterfall just as he did a few minutes ago.

"Rain, is this great? The water is warm. The girls are warm and wet. What could be better?" says Smoke.

Smoke laughs out loud as the girl swim by him, tickling and rubbing all over him.

"Yeah, this is great," says Rain.

Rain is pulled underwater and sees perfectly in the warm crystal-clear water. Ajaunta swims straight for him, and she is beautiful. She swims up and hugs Rain, giving him a warm kiss, and they kiss for what seems hours suspended in the warm clear water. Ajaunta gives a kick with her tail fin, and the two of them breach the water. Rain takes a breath of fresh air. She slips right through his grasp and sinks back into the water. Rain smiles as Marlene slides up his legs and chest into his grasp. He does not get a word out before she locks his lips in a wonderful kiss that seems to last for hours. With a whip of her tail fin, she is lost in the depths of the pond. Rain looks down to see the green lights sink deep into the water until they are out of sight.

"Rain, what did I tell you? This is great. Isn't this great?" says Smoke.

Rain looks over behind him to where Smoke is, and the two of them tread water, for the first time having a moment where their senses are not invigorated by the girls.

"Yeah, Smoke, it is great, but where are we? I thought this was the way out," says Rain.

"Oh, yeah. I don't know where we are," says Smoke.

The two of them look around, and they see the waterfall that drains into the pond. The pond seems to be completely surrounded by a rock and earth dome, but they cannot see the walls that well. There is light, but it is a dim fluorescent green light that comes from the cave leading back the way they entered. They cannot see too far at all. They realize there is no exit, and they cannot get back up the waterfall. They are trapped.

"How do you think we get out of here? You think the water drains out through a tunnel? I can't see above us. I wonder if this cave leads up and out," says Smoke.

"I don't know, but I sure am starting to get a bad feeling. What happened to the girls?" says Rain.

Rain and Smoke look down into the water, looking for the girls, and they see the fluorescent green lights swimming up from the depths.

"Ah, there they are," says Smoke.

The girls breach the water in a circle around the guys. The girls are facing the walls, and they all breathe fire from their mouths like flamethrowers. Rain and Smoke are scared straight as the flames ignite torches on the walls, illuminating the entire pond and the walls and rocks around the edge of the pond. Now Rain and Smoke see what is left of men who have been in this pond before them. There are skulls, rib cages, leg bones, arm bones, and spines of countless victims strewn all around the edge of the pond. This does not scare Rain and Smoke as much as the sight of what the girls become. Bailey breaches the water in front of Smoke, and she opens her mouth about three times the size Smoke would have thought possible. She gives a screeching scream, sending chills up and down Smoke's spine. She exposes terrifying flesh-ripping teeth, and gills open and expand on either side of her neck. She transforms from the most beautiful woman to a horrific flesh-eating monster. This scares Smoke, and he screams. Rain cannot see her on the other side of Smoke, and it matters not. His attention is taken by Ajaunta, who rises before him and exposes her teeth and gills, sending spine-tingling chills through his body with her frightful scream.

All the girls circle Smoke, and one by one, they swim in and take a huge bite out of his body. Smoke screams as he is pushed away from Rain. Rain can see the water bubble, churn, and turn red. The girls bite the muscle from Smoke first, biting and ripping his biceps from his body, his leg muscles, and then they bite his stomach, tearing just the meaty fleshy part that hold his innards in place. Within minutes, the internal organs of Smoke's body are floating on the surface, and Smoke's cries for help come to a stop. Rain keeps swimming toward Smoke to try and help him, but the girls keep pushing him away, and Rain cannot catch up. Smoke floats lifeless on the surface, and Rain still cannot catch up with him. Rain can see the girls are biting away what flesh is left on his bones. They bite, rip, and tear the flesh from his body and swim away, engulfing the flesh like sharks.

Rain tries and tries to catch up with Smoke, but now he is a corpse that has been stripped of flesh. Rain swims, getting caught in the digestive tract of Smoke. Rain lifts the intestines, realizing what they are, and screams, frantically trying to rid it from around his neck. Rain swims backward and hits something. He turns to see Ajaunta open her mouth, exposing her terrifying teeth and gills on the side of her neck. He is attacked from behind and below as the other girls start stripping the flesh from his body with their sharp teeth. Rain tries to fight them. He tries to get away from them, but they are too fast. They are perfectly designed to strip the flesh from their prey, and Rain has no chance. He fights, but they target his muscles first, and quickly, he is unable to even move. All he can do is shake and bob up and down as the girls very quickly strip the nourishing flesh from his body. Rain takes one last look around the walls surrounding the pond, seeing all the bones decorating the walls. He sees the bones of Smoke thrown from the pond by the girls, and his eyes close, knowing his bones will be next to adorn the walls.

Chapter 32

Cats in the Basement

The crack of thunder shakes the room. Rain is woken from his sleep, and the hard pounding rain is easily heard. Rain sits up on the side of his bed. He bends forward, resting his elbows on his knees and his head in his hands. He feels exhausted from sleeping. The rain is pelting his house, and the window reveals watery shadows that move on his bedroom walls. Rain gets up with a loud moan like he is one hundred years old and walks to the window. He loves to watch the rain even when it is dark outside, and he can barely see.

"Are you OK, honey?" says a woman.

Rain turns to look at his bed. It is dark in his room, and he cannot see anyone in his bed, but someone is there.

"Who is there?" he asks.

"What are you talking about? Who else would be in our bed?" says Ajaunta.

"I don't know. Aren't you going to go make something to eat?" says Rain.

"At this time in the morning? I don't think so. If you are hungry, go make something yourself," she says.

"Well, you are in on this, right? I mean, you have to keep me subdued. You have to keep me under your spell," says Rain.

"What the hell are you talking about?" she says.

"Nothing. Go back to sleep. I need to check some things," says Rain.

Rain walks out of the bedroom and closes the door behind him. He walks to the kitchen and drinks from a gallon of milk in the refrigerator. He walks down into the basement and opens his safe. The book he was hoping would be there is sealed in a plastic bag. He picks up the bag and its contents. He walks over to a couch and sits, putting the bag on the coffee table in front of him. He rubs his forehead with a sigh. He opens the bag and puts the lava key in place on the book cover. The book starts to burn, and the lava holding the book closed melts like wax. A rush of air blows by and opens the book. It flips through some pages and then a lot of pages and stops. Rain can hear laughter, and he looks around.

"So this is what you are after, right? This is what you need, isn't it? Here it is come, take it, and leave me be," says Rain.

Rain can hear a faint noise—the noise he suspects a ghost would make—and he sees a ghost walking from his left side. It is wispy in appearance and grows stronger in color until in front of Rain when the life of Glamfury takes form and shape. Glamfury sits in a chair.

"That there is a complete account of all my sexual conquests for about the past seven hundred years. Yup, that is right, I was actually born in 1324. The reason a lot of the language written in that book is of different languages is the different places I have lived in the different centuries. I have always killed the husbands of the women I have met and seduced throughout the centuries. Of course, that is after I have consumed the youth of the women. You and your killer friend Smoke have presented me with a most terrific dilemma. Until you two have come along, I have been limited to the husbands of women I have seduced. So I thought. Now you and Smoke, by stealing my books, the two of you have introduced me to a whole new set of boundaries that I can draw victims from. Of course, they are friends and loved ones of you two." Glamfury laughs.

"Whatever. You have your book. Now take it and go leave me my friends and loved ones be, or trust me, I will kill you," says Rain.

Glamfury stands and holds up his right hand. The book on the coffee table flies up into his hand.

"It goes without saying you have no idea what you are up against. You will be mine. You are only delaying the inevitable. So until the time comes that you beg me to kill you, until the time comes that you tell me to send your soul to hell, until the time comes that your youth is strengthening my life, let the torture continue," says Glamfury.

Glamfury sinks into the floor with the book. Rain can hear him laughing even after he is gone. The couch Rain is sitting on reclines back like a La-Z-Boy chair. Wires stretch up from the couch, restraining Rain's wrists and ankles. Rain struggles to break free, but the wires just cut into his ankles and wrists. The harder he struggles, the deeper the wires cut into his flesh. He can see two tubes stretching down from the ceiling toward his ankles. They go out of sight below the couch and then reappear with scalpels. Rain can lift his head so he can see his whole body. The scalpels cut the pajama bottoms Rain is wearing and his shorts underneath. Now Rain lies nude on the couch with his arms and legs secured. The tubes bring the scalpels to his feet, and Rain tries to move his feet away from them. The wires squeeze tight, holding his ankles and wrists secure.

Rain screams and yells for help as the scalpels start to cut his skin from the base of his toes straight up his ankles and shins. The scalpels cut just deep enough to slice his skin, but it is excruciatingly painful. Rain screams all the cusswords he can think of and cries as the tubes suck the scalpels into them, and pincers appear. The pincers grab his skin on the left side of the slice, and two more tubes grow from the ceiling with pincers on them as well. They grab his skin on the right side of the slice, and the pincers pull opposite each other, pulling the skin from Rain's legs. Rain screams in horror as he watches himself being skinned all the way up to his knees. The pincers are sucked into the tubes, and the scalpels reappear. They cut around his knees, and all the skin from his knees down are removed. Where his legs touch the couch is so painful words cannot describe. Rain cries in pain. The scalpels are sucked back into the tubes, and the pincers return. Rain watches as the pincers move down to his toes, and Rain's eyes expand as they grab the toenail of his big toes, and simultaneously, the pincers slowly pull harder and harder. Rain starts to scream as his toenails are slowly pulled until they rip right off his toes. Rain cries, screaming every combination of cusswords he can think of. The pincers continue pulling the toenails from each of his toes until all the nails from his toes are gone. Rain continues to cry as the pincers very delicately peel the remaining skin from his heel, the bottom of his foot, and around his toes. The exposed flesh from his knees down hurts just from exposure to air. Rain can see the blood not gushing from his legs but slowly seeping from the exposed muscle below his knees.

Rain hears the swinging of doors and raises his head to see the entire floorboard of his basement is just one small animal door after another, and cats start to pour into his basement. "No, no, no, no!" cries Rain as cats start to jump on the couch. Slowly they notice the smell and get closer and closer to his legs. Rain yells and scream, trying to shoo the cats away, but they start to lick the blood from his legs, and Rain screams in pain.

The tubes return to his knees with scalpels ready, and they cut the skin from his knees right up to his pelvis. The pincers return and peel the skin from his legs as more cats move in to lick the blood from his legs. Rain cannot believe the pain he is in. He shakes his head back and forth violently, trying to knock himself out. The pain is so great he cannot believe he can take it without going unconscious. The cats start to bite. They start to chew the bloody meaty flesh from his legs. Rain thrashes his hips up and down as violently as he can, trying to scare the cats away from him. Wires wrap around his hips, holding him tight to the couch, and the cats line the inside of his legs. They line the outside of his legs to his hips, chewing the flesh from his body. Rain cries, and the scalpels start to cut along the outer sides of his abdomen and along his underarms. Rain cries more as the pincers return and peel the skin from his abdomen and chest. More cats join in the feast, and Rain watches as the cats chew and purr. The tubes return with scalpels, and Rain is skinned from his neck down his arms. His whole body is now skinned, and the cats line his entire body, chewing all the muscle from his body.

"Rain. Rain, is that you screaming? Is that you down here? Rain, are you down here?" says Ajaunta.

Ajaunta walks down the stairs, seeing Rain on the couch. She covers her mouth with her hands, but the sight of Rain skinned and most the muscle eaten away by the cats causes her to vomit. She runs to the couch, kicking at the cats, and the cats run into the little animal doorways leading out of the basement. Ajaunta covers her mouth, not knowing what to say. She has not a clue what to do. Most the muscle on Rain's legs has been eaten, his stomach muscles too. She can see his digestive tract still intact. She can see his liver pulsating, and his stomach, his kidneys too. She can see his lungs below his ribs and his genitals still intact and other than his head, the only part of his body not skinned or eaten away.

"Rain, you are still alive. You are OK? We can get you to a hospital. You can heal there. I am going to call 911. Don't move, I will be right back," says Ajaunta.

"Ajaunta, wait. Wait. Cut the wires. Cut the wires holding my wrists, ankles, and waist," says Rain.

"How? How am I going to cut them?" she asks.

"Over there in that tool box. There are some pliers that have sharp edges. You can use them to cut the wires," says Rain.

"OK," says Ajaunta.

She walks over to the tool chest. She opens the top drawer. She looks through the tools and does not find pliers. She opens the second drawer and does not find the pliers. She opens the third drawer and finds a pair of pliers that will cut the wires. She runs back to the couch and starts to cut the wires at Rain's ankles. Rain can see the tubes grow from the ceiling and approach Ajaunta from her back.

"Ajaunta, look out. Look out behind you, the tubes," says Rain.

Ajaunta turns to see tubes that quickly wrap around her wrists and pull them toward the ceiling. She screams as her arms are pulled apart and up. She is suspended by the tubes holding her up by her wrists. She kicks and runs suspended in the air, but she cannot break free.

"Rain, what is going on? Rain, what is happening?" she cries.

"Ajaunta, break free. I don't know how, but you have to break free!" yells Rain.

Rain and Ajaunta see tubes grow from the ceiling, one in front of her and one in the back. She is wearing a very big T-shirt, which she sleeps in that covers her to almost her knees, and the tubes grow down and up under the shirt she is wearing. Ajaunta starts to scream and kick violently.

"Rain, they are going in me. They are going in the front and in the back. Rain!" cries Ajaunta.

She kicks, screams, and cries. Rain can see blood dripping down her legs slowly and then gushing down to her feet and dripping onto the floor. The cats start to run into the basement from the animal doorways. They start to lick the blood on the carpet. More and more cats run in, and they line around Rain's body and start to chew and eat the muscle from his body. The tubes that are in Ajaunta retreat from her and expose themselves from under her long T-shirt. They now have scalpels at the ends of them, and they cut down the shoulders and

arms of her T-shirt, and it falls to the ground. The scalpels have cut
her insides, which are bleeding from her genitals and down her legs.
The scalpels move up to her neck and cut around her neck just under
her chin. Ajaunta is scared to death and crying, but she does not move
for fear of having her throat cut. The scalpels cut around her neck and
then down her shoulders and arms. Rain is screaming, calling Glamfury
every cussword he can think of. Rain begs Glamfury to stop this, but
there is no sight or sound from Glamfury. Two dozen tubes with pincers
grow from the ceiling, a dozen for each of Ajaunta's arms, and they each
grab a piece of skin.

"What are they doing, Rain? What are they doing?" cries Ajaunta.

"Ajaunta, don't look. Don't look, Ajaunta. Close your eyes," says Rain.

The pincers pull amazingly fast, and in a few seconds, they have
completely skinned Ajaunta from her neck down her entire body. The
pincers raise Ajaunta's skin in the air, and Rain has never been creeped
out the way he is seeing Ajaunta's skin minus Ajaunta. Ajaunta cries
hysterically seeing her bloody flesh with no skin. The wires that hold
her in the air pull back, and she falls to the ground. Ajaunta barely stays
conscious from the excruciating pain and is attacked by dozens of cats
that now have a craving for the taste of human blood and flesh. Ajaunta
falls to her back, screaming in pain. The cats attack her ferociously and
fight among each other for rights to chew on Ajaunta's flesh. More and
more cats flow in from the animal doors, and Ajaunta is covered in
cats. All Rain can see is cats writhing all about, and he knows Ajaunta
is underneath them. Rain can hear with exceptional clarity the cats
chewing and gnawing the flesh from Ajaunta's bones. Ajaunta has gone
silent, and Rain thinks she has passed.

One by one, cats that have had their fill back away from the ravenous
pack. They hop up on the couch where Rain cannot reach them and lick
the blood from their paws and faces. Rain screams and cries, forgetting
the cats are chewing the flesh from his bones as well. Within moments,
Rain has cats all around him, purring with full bellies from gorging
themselves with the flesh of Rain and Ajaunta. Rain can do nothing as
he looks down and sees the cats have chewed most the flesh from his
body from his neck down to his toes. Rain's digestive tract has been left
in place along with all his major organs, which still beat and move with
life. The wires holding Rain secure let him go and retreat back into the
couch. Rain sits up and swats the cats in his reach. The cats hiss and

run through the animal doors as Rain starts to hit them with force and anger. Rain gets up and moves even though he is nothing more than bones with his major organs still attached to his bones, and his head is intact from his chin up. Rain kicks the cats off Ajaunta, and he can see she is the same as him, only she has her bony hands covering her eyes.

"Ajaunta. Ajaunta, are you still alive?" says Rain.

"Rain, is that you? Rain, what is going on?" says Ajaunta.

Rain bends down and picks Ajaunta from the floor and stands her next to him. She opens her eyes and sees they are both bones with their major organs attached to their bones with sinew and tendons. Both their heads are intact from the necks up. Ajaunta screams in horror.

"Rain, what have they done to us? How are we alive?" screams Ajaunta.

"I don't know. I don't know."

"Rain, you said you would protect me. You said you would never let anyone hurt me. What the hell is this? You bastard!" yells Ajaunta.

She starts to beat Rain over the head with her right arm and hand, which is nothing more than bones.

"Rain, you liar. I hate you. Look what they have done to us!" yells Ajaunta.

She kicks and punches Rain. Their bones clank as they come in contact with each other.

"Ajaunta, come on, stop it. Stop it, Ajaunta!" yells Rain.

Rain backs from Ajaunta as she hits him repeatedly with her arms and kicks him with her legs. Rain is backed into the wall and grabs her with his hands. They look crazy with their heads intact and their digestive tracts held to their bones by tendons and their major organs still beating and working normally. Their genitals are still intact as well. The rest of them is just bone with drips of blood on them. Ajaunta starts to cry.

"Rain, I can't take this anymore. I want this to end. I am going to beg him to kill me, Rain. I don't care anymore. I just want this to end," sobs Ajaunta.

"No, Ajaunta, you can't. Don't beg him to kill you. What we are suffering through now is nothing compared to what is waiting for us if we give in to him. Trust me," says Rain.

"Rain, have you not had enough? This is not ending. He won't let us be. He won't let us rest. He won't let us have any peace. Look at me,

Rain. I am nothing but bones and a head. I can't take this anymore," cries Ajaunta.

Rain tries to hug Ajaunta, and she slams him over the head with her bony arm. She swings her arm over and over, hitting him harder and harder.

Suddenly, Ajaunta's voice turns very deep and very loud like it is being spoken through very loud speakers.

"Give in, Rain."

She slams him over his head.

"Beg him to kill you, Rain."

She slams him over his head, and his body crushes from the impact.

"Plead with him on your knees, Rain."

She slams him, and his body crushes more.

"Spare all the lives of your friends and loved ones, Rain."

She slams him over his head, and his bones are crushed into themselves. Rain is dazed and discombobulated as Ajaunta slams him over the head. He crushes more and more until he has been crushed down to one foot tall.

"I am sorry, Rain. I am sorry for my weakness, but I can't take it anymore. Give in to him, Rain. You have to give in to him. Finish what he has started," says Ajaunta.

She starts to walk away and up the stairs toward the kitchen.

"Wait, Ajaunta, wait. Where are you going?" yells Rain.

He runs after her, but he cannot climb up the stairs because of his size. Ajaunta walks up the stairs and into the kitchen, closing the door behind her.

Chapter 33

Sticky Situation

Rain struggles trying to climb the stairs, and he actually gets up about two of them, and he realizes he just is not going to have the strength to get up the rest of the stairs. He sits on the edge of the stair, looking around his basement, thinking about how differently everything looks when you are only one foot tall. It is like the whole world is suddenly a very different world. He looks around, and his head rises as if his nose were leading the way somewhere. He can smell the aroma of a freshly cooked dinner. He rubs his stomach and looks at his digestive tract that mostly hangs just below his ribs and is attached to his spine. His butt is still intact, and, yes, his genitals are still intact, which are just hanging around. Rain stands on the stair, raising his head in the air, sniffing, trying to see where the aroma is coming from. It must be coming from the other side of the couch. Rain climbs down by hanging from the stair, falling to the next lower stair, and repeats the process until he is on the basement floor. He runs around the couch, and what a neat sight watching him run. He is just bones, digestive tract, genitals, and head.

The coffee table in front of the couch has a second shelf, which sits only a foot above the ground. Rain walks up to it, and there is a complete meal placed. There is a plate already prepared, and Rain walks up, led by his nose. There is a big juicy steak seared to perfection with potatoes and long steaming green beans on a plate, a big glass of milk, and even a salad in a plate beside the main course. Rain licks his lips, and his stomach starts to pulsate. He cannot believe how hungry he is all of a sudden. He knows better, but he cannot resist this deliciously smelling dinner. He cuts into the steak, and the inside is pink and juicy. He bites into the perfectly cooked steak, and that is it. He sits at the chair that has been created just for him and eats the steak, potatoes, and green beans. He drinks the milk and even eats the salad.

Rain eats the most satisfying meal of his life and sits in the chair, leaning back after devouring the meal. He looks at his stretched stomach and feels good. He feels better than he has felt in a long time. He feels strong, he feels happy, and he feels revitalized. He feels tingly all over and looks down his arms and legs, seeing the flesh of his body is returning. He stands and watches the flesh grow back on his body from his genitals and just below his chin until he is whole again. He can't help but smile, and looking at the opposite end of the table where his dinner was set, he notices clothing laid out. He walks over and puts on the blue jeans and T-shirt, which fit him surprisingly well. Rain smiles, thinking, *This is the best I have felt in a long time.*

Immediately after thinking that, he hears the swaying of a door and chills run up and down his spine. He turns to see a cat has entered from one of the animal doors still lining the basement walls. The cat sees Rain and is frozen in a stance that Rain is well aware of. "Nice kitty," says Rain, who looks at himself, quickly realizing he may be thought of as dinner. The cat does not move and then very slowly starts to move toward Rain with its eyes fixed on him. "Oh shit!" Rain looks at his dinner plate at the other side of the coffee table. He thinks for one second, *Can I get to it in time?* and goes for it. Rain is only a few long steps from his dinner plate, and as soon as he starts to run, so does the cat. Rain gets to his steak knife and grabs it just as the cat reaches him and swipes its paw at him. The cat catches Rain with two of its claws, which dig into his lower right side. The cat draws him to its mouth and bites into Rain's left shoulder, causing multiple painful wounds. Rain swings hard, stabbing the left side of the cat's face. The cat lets go of Rain and swipes the knife from its face. Rain rolls under the coffee table.

"Rain. Hey, Rain, are you down here, buddy?" yells Smoke.

Rain can hear Smoke calling for him, and Rain can see Smoke's feet as he walks into the cellar from the stairs.

"I'm here, Smoke, I'm here!" yells Rain.

Rain gets out from under the coffee table on the other side of where the cat is, and the cat runs around the coffee table lightning fast, pursuing Rain.

"Smoke, I'm here. Smoke, I'm here!" yells Rain.

Smoke does not hear Rain, and he does not see Rain, but he sees the cat running around the coffee table. Rain runs as fast as he can, waving, looking, and trying to get the attention of Smoke. The cat is just about on him when Rain's feet stop dead in their tracks, and he falls face-first on something soft and gooey. Rain falls, and his left arm sticks palm up at a forty-five-degree angle down from his shoulder. His right arm hits the gooey softness and sticks palm down to the upper right side of his shoulder. His face hits and sinks slightly into the sticky gooeyness. He tries to lift his face, and it is sucked right back down with the entire right side of his face and most of his mouth stuck in the stickum. The cat is on him in a second and bites down on Rain just above his hips. The cat's teeth penetrate into his sides like stakes, causing a lot of pain. Rain's muffled screams barely get out through his mostly closed and glued mouth. Smoke sees Rain fall, and he sees the cat bit into him. "Shoo, get out of here," says Smoke.

He waves his hands, trying to get the cat to run away, and it does not. Smoke hits the cat on the side, and the cat hisses with Rain still in its mouth.

"All right, I ain't playing no more. Get the fuck off him, cat!" says Smoke.

Smoke hits the cat with force, and the cat holds on to Rain, hissing loudly, not letting go of its prey.

"Get the fuck off him, I said," says Smoke.

Smoke pounds down on the cat's back with a fist, and the cat releases Rain, faces Smoke with a loud hiss, and swings its claws at Smoke. Smoke is very surprised by this fearless move by the cat and actually backs up a step.

"What? Are you fucking kidding me? You are going to stand up to me and try to face me? You are going to hiss at me like you are a lion or something? Are you for real, cat?" says Smoke.

This pisses Smoke off, and he takes a step at the cat, kicking it like a football on a tee. The cat flies fast, slamming into the wall hard. The cat falls on the floor and does not move. Smoke takes a lunging step and kicks the cat like it was a soccer ball, and the cat flies across the basement into the wall again. The cat falls and does not move. Smoke can swear he feels and hears bones break with this last kick.

"Fucking cat," says Smoke.

He turns to see Rain lying face-first on the floor. Smoke bends down to the floor and inspects the area where Rain has fallen. It is strange looking. The carpet seems to have been cut out in a one-foot-by-one-foot section and filled in with some sort of glue or soft cementum.

"Rain, hey, buddy, can you hear me? What have you got yourself into? How did you get to be so small?" asks Smoke.

Rain struggles to move. He wiggles back and forth, but the more he struggles, the more stuck he gets. He pulls as hard as he can to get out of the glue and is pulled back into it stuck worse yet. His mouth is mostly stuck to the gooey glue, and his words are nothing more than muffled sounds. His eyes tear and shed many teardrops, and he can see Smoke looking at him, but he cannot communicate with him. Smoke inspects the area and gets up. He walks out of sight, and Rain gets nervous. Smoke returns with a utility knife.

"Hold on, Rain. I'm going to get you out of there, buddy. Let me get this stuff you are stuck in up and off the floor. Then we will figure out how to get you out of there. Hold on, buddy," says Smoke.

Smoke cuts the carpet outside where the glue is and is able to pick up the section with the floorboard beneath. He can pick up a two-foot-by-two-foot section and hold it up. He is looking at Rain, trying to figure out how to get him out of the gooey substance. Rain can't help but try to pull himself from the trap and just gets weaker and more stuck.

"Hold on, buddy. I'm gonna pull you out of there, OK? Hold on, Rain. Here we go," says Smoke.

Smoke grabs a hold of Rain and pulls him from the trap.

"Oooohhhhhh! Well, that did not work out as planned," says Smoke.

Smoke laughs even though the horror of what he has done is right before his eyes. Instead of pulling Rain from the trap, what happened was the flesh from the right side of Rain's face all the way down his body that is in contact with the stickum stays stuck in the glue. Rain's skin and flesh rips from his body, and Smoke stops pulling when all the flesh from the front of Rain's body down to his hips has been ripped from his body. Rain's hands and forearms are still stuck in the glue, but a lot of the flesh from the front of his body is ripped from his bones. Rain can speak now.

"Aaaajjjjhhhhhhhaaaa! Smoke, what are you doing? You're killing me!" yells Rain.

"Well, maybe you were right. I guess I will be the death of you. Don't worry, buddy, I'm gonna fix you up. I'm gonna get you out of there. Hold on, buddy," says Smoke.

Smoke sets the floorboard with Rain on it on the coffee table and walks away. Rain feels his body slide around on his flesh with his blood acting as a lubricant. The problem that Rain faces now is the portions of his body not stuck in the glue slide until it comes in contact with the glue and become stuck. So Rain is now stuck worse in the stickum.

"Don't worry, Rain, I'm gonna get you out of there. Don't worry, buddy, I'm here," says Smoke, who can't stop chuckling.

Again, Rain has his mobility and motion limited because of being stuck. He struggles and wiggles, wearing himself out. Smoke can't help but laugh seeing Rain struggle in the gooey substance. Rain hears hammering and can move his face just enough to see Smoke is hammering nails into the corners of the board, nailing it to the coffee table. Smoke nails it down and uses the utility knife to cut out a section around Rain. He picks the section with Rain on it and stands Rain on his feet on the coffee table. Rain is able to stand, but he cannot move.

"Smoke, don't leave me like this. I can't move. I am going to fall forward or backward because I can't move," says Rain.

"I know, buddy. I'm trying to figure out how to get you out of that glue. Then I'm going to have to sew you back together again," says Smoke.

"No more sewing. Last time, you sewed me back together backward!" yells Rain.

"Yeah, well, I can't just let you bleed to death. Gosh, this sucks. I don't know what to do. I guess I can cut the board around you very close to you and then chisel the glue away. I just don't know if I will have the patience for that," says Smoke.

Smoke picks Rain up and delicately cuts very close to Rain. He takes his time and very carefully cuts the glue between Rain and the wood. This is very time consuming and tedious work, but Smoke takes his time to get his best friend in the world somewhat free from the glue trap. Smoke cuts away the wood, and now Rain can move; however, the whole front of his body is covered in this sticky, gooey sap. The skin and flesh from his face down to his hips is torn, ripped, and just a bloody mess. His hands are intact, and his muscles are intact enough where he can move, though it is painful because of his ripped flesh, plus the sticky goo pulls his flesh whenever he moves. Anything Rain touches sticks to him. He cannot wipe, peel, or pull the stickum from himself because it is simply too sticky. Anytime he touches himself, he has to struggle to pull his hands or fingers away from the stickum all over himself.

"Smoke, what am I going to do? I can't get it off. What am I going to do, Smoke?" cries Rain.

"Hold on, Rain, I got just the thing, or you have just the thing. Don't you have Goo Away in your gun shed? I know you do. I know I have seen it in there before," says Smoke.

"Yeah, I do. I guess it's worth a shot," says Rain.

"Hold on, let me find something I can put you on, and I will take you to the shed. Hold on," says Smoke.

Rain watches as Smoke runs up the stairs.

"Smoke, hey, Smoke, where are you going? Don't go up there without me, Smoke. Wait! Smoke!" yells Rain.

Smoke runs up the stairs and closes the door behind him. Rain shakes his shoulders and holds up his hands in awe, in disbelief that Smoke just left him down there. Rain starts to feel chills run up and down his spine like he did earlier. Rain looks all around; he knows danger is close, he just knows it. He can see the cat that Smoke had kicked slowly walking around the side of the couch, and it sees Rain on the coffee table. The cat freezes when it sees Rain. Its eyes fixed on Rain, and Rain knows he is in serious trouble. He is about to be cat food unless Smoke gets back here quick. The cat squats on its hind legs and starts to wiggle slowly but noticeably. Rain knows the cat is about to make its charge on him. Rain does not wait for the cat to attack. He turns and runs toward the other end of the coffee table. The cat springs forward, jumping onto the coffee table. Rain is surprisingly fast considering the front of his body is a torn bloody mess. Rain gets to the end of the coffee table and just jumps as hard as he can with no idea what is going to happen.

It just so happens that there are four pillows on the floor, and Rain lands on one that is positioned in an upward position. It is soft with a lot of give, and Rain rolls down the pillow but not very far. The cat is right behind him and lands on the pillow as well. The pillow rises very fast from the weight of Rain and the cat. Rain is catapulted away. He flies up and fast. He screams as his flesh flaps in the wind. Rain flies and hits face-first on the wall and sticks. The stickum holds his flesh to the wall, but his head and front of his body down to his hips falls back. His forearms and hands still stay stuck to the wall along with his hips and legs, but the rest of his body falls back, creating an L form from the wall. Rain screams as the pain is intense, and slowly, his flesh rips from where it is still attached to his body. The cat jumps and catches the flapping part of Rain's body with its right claws. The cat holds on as Rain's flesh is torn from his right arms and hand right off. The cat dangles from Rain's body, which is tearing. The flesh from his body is torn from his left arm. Rain screams as the flesh from the front of his body is now tearing from his hips, and it tears faster and faster down his legs until all the flesh from the front of his body has been torn from his bones. The flesh of Rain's body that is attached to the stickum sticks on the wall. The cat bites Rain and runs for the animal doorway leading out of the cellar.

"Where do you think you are going?" says Smoke.

Smoke reaches down and grabs the cat by the back of the neck, raising it in the air. The cat gives a screaming hiss, sending chills up and down the spines of both Rain and Smoke. Rain is dropped from the cat's mouth and falls to the floor. The cat then violently digs the claws on both its front and back paws into the wrist and arm of Smoke. This is very painful, and Smoke frantically shakes and whips his arm back and forth, trying to rid the cat from him. The cat digs its claws deeper into Smoke's flesh and bites its teeth into his flesh, causing a lot of pain and drawing a lot of blood from Smoke. Smoke yells, calling the cat all kinds of curse words, and starts to slam the cat into the wall with such great force that you can hear bones breaking in the cat. Smoke slams the cat into the wall and into the staircase and into beams until the cat is thrown from his hand. Blood is splattered all over the basement walls, the furniture, and the floor. Smoke looks at his arm in disbelief to the amount of damage the cat has done to his hand and arm. He is bleeding severely and needs a lot of stitching. Seeing this sends rage through Smoke, and he runs at the cat, kicking it as hard as he can. He chases after the cat, kicking it again and again, and somehow, the cat manages to run through one of the animal doorways out of sight. Smoke is dripping blood all over and pulls his shirt off, wrapping it around his arm and hand. He falls back on the couch, letting his heart slow down. He has forgotten all about Rain, whom he sees lying on the floor next to one of the animal doorways. Rain has the muscles in the front of his body so badly torn and ripped apart that he cannot move now. He can still speak, but he is in shock and just stares at the ceiling. Smoke looks around and sees the flesh of Rain's body stuck to the wall. Most the flesh except a small portion on the front of Rain's face is gone from the front of his body, and what is still attached to his bones is ripped, torn, and just as horrific a sight as you could imagine.

"Hey, buddy, I'm glad I got here just in time to save you. Can you believe what that fucking cat did to me? Fucking A. Let's get you and your flesh from the wall and figure out how to put you back together," says Smoke.

Smoke gets up. He reaches down for Rain, and in an instant, that same cat pops out from the animal doorway. It slaps its paw down on Rain, digging its claws into him, and pulls Rain into the doorway out of sight.

"No!" yells Smoke.

Rain is put into the cat's mouth, and he can tell the cat is running with him, but everything is black; he cannot see anything. The cat runs from within the house through another small animal doorway to the outside woods and stops by a tree. Rain is still in such bad shape that he cannot move. He is in shock but not completely unaware. He is aware enough to see the cat's mouth open wide, showing its sharp deadly teeth. The cat bites down on Rain's skull, and everything goes black and silent.

Chapter 34

Skin Crawlers

Rain feels excruciating pain in his left leg. He can hear his bones being broken. He can hear the horrific sound of the cat's teeth crunching his bones and chewing his flesh. He opens his eyes and sees his body being drawn into the cat's mouth. It chews and crunches his legs and then his hips with the rest of Rain's body hanging out of its mouth. Rain has not enough strength to move, but he feels and hears the horrific sound of his body being eaten while he is still alive. His torso is pulled into the cat's mouth and chewed and then his chest, arms, and head are pulled into the cat's mouth. Rain is bathed in his blood mixed with the cat's saliva as he is chewed, mashed, and moved from side to side in the cat's mouth. His body is never chewed into pieces; it remains as one held together by what muscle and tendons are left on his body. The cat seems to swallow his legs and still chews his torso. It swallows and chews his chest and arms and then it crunches his head and he is swallowed entirely. Rain remembers being eaten by Lucifer or Glamfury acting like Lucifer. The thing that really freaks him out is the smell and taste, which he cannot get rid of. Of course, the fact that he is still alive is just all-out crazy.

Rain already thinks ahead to flowing through the digestive tract of the cat, but something different happens this time. He is suddenly and quickly sucked back the way he came. He is hurled out of the cat's mouth and splats on the grassy ground. Rain is a warm pile of mush basted in bile, not able to move, stinking and steaming, smelling of rot gut in the truest sense. His face is killing him. It feels like his skin has been sanded; in fact, he feels like that all over, not to mention all his bones have been broken and are sticking out of the mush pile that he is. His skull is crushed, and his left eye has been chewed and burst a long time ago. His right eye is still intact, and his skull sits on top of the pile of bloody bile. Rain can't cry, but he feels the emotion of crying. He can't speak because his throat, mouth, and tongue are all badly damaged. The only thing he can do is move his eye side to side, up and down. He hears laughter and sees Glamfury walking toward him. The cat sees Glamfury approach, and it runs away. Glamfury laughs and walks up to Rain, clapping his hands. He bends down, squatting on his toes, looking at the chewed partially digested remains of Rain.

"Whew, aren't you a disgusting mess? I can remember when you were just a piece of shit. Now you aren't even that anymore. Now you are just a stinky pile of cat barf. Seems like you are getting worse and worse. How much worse could it possibly get? I can't stand to see you like this, Rain. I mean, you are such a good-looking guy. You have so much going for you. How does someone as talented, as masculine, and as well-to-do as you end up like this? I can't take this. I have to do something about this. I have to do all I can to make sure you get back on your feet and get back on the right track. So I tell you what I am going to do. I am going to snap my fingers just like this," says Glamfury.

Glamfury snaps his thumb and middle finger. Rain feels his whole body start to tingle, but not in a painful way. He can feel his body is fusing. His bones are moving back together. His muscles are coming back together and attaching to his bones. His eye is filling and growing back to its normal size in its eye socket. His flesh is reforming, and his skin is covering his muscles. Rain is rising from the pile of mush into the man he is. Glamfury throws clothes that land on Rain, and he puts them on. Rain leans against the tree closest to him and takes a deep breath.

"Feels good to be whole again, doesn't it? Feels good to be alive, doesn't it? Listen, Rain, I can and will destroy you over and over for eternity. It does not have to be this way. You can end all this suffering you are going through by just begging me to kill you. Beg me to take your youth for myself and send your soul to hell. Listen, don't listen to what everyone always says about hell. You have to look at the benefits, like, hey, there is no winter in hell. That's right, it is always warm. I will tell you something else that is a misnomer. Souls do not feel pain. That is right. I will torture you forever and you are feeling the pain, right? In hell, you will never feel physical pain. You will never feel exhaustion or fatigue. You will never want in hell because all your needs are taken care of before you need them. So come on, what do you say? You ready to embrace your destiny? You ready to be a part of me? Come on, Rain, beg me. Beg me to kill you. Come on," says Glamfury.

Glamfury takes a deep breath, watching Rain, who sits leaning against the tree. Rain is distant and not paying Glamfury any attention at all. Rain is looking at the ground with a blank stare on his face, completely emotionless.

"OK, let the games continue," says Glamfury.

Glamfury stands and snaps his fingers. He takes a few steps backward while blowing over the palms of his hands toward Rain. Rain looks up as a cool gusts of wind blow by him, followed by a stronger gust, blowing leaves, twigs, grass, and a whole bunch of dirt on Rain. Rain sits up as Glamfury walks out of sight into the woods. Rain can hear him laugh even after he is out of sight. Rain's arms start to itch like the dirt was made out of fiberglass. He rubs his arms, and they start to burn.

"What the fuck!" he yells.

Rain stands up and looks at his arms. He brings his right forearm close to his eyes and looks closely at the horror he now faces. There are very tiny things that he has never seen before growing from his skin. It is like the dirt that was blown on Rain has deposited some sort of parasites that have burrowed into the pores of his skin, and now they are growing from within his skin. They grow out from his skin like a tubeworm, and then a horrific head emerges with two tiny eyes and a mouth with one row of razor-sharp teeth on top and on bottom. Once it grows just a fraction of an inch, it arches back to the skin like a slinky and bites into Rain's skin, swallowing the tiny morsel. The parasite then repeats this action until it has bitten all the skin around where it is growing from. The parasite eventually bites deep enough into the skin to cause blood to emerge, creating a blood-filled moat around its base. The head of the parasite then sucks the nutrient-rich blood, turning itself red like a mosquito filling its belly. Once it has drawn enough blood, it becomes stiff, standing straight up, and splits four times, causing all four sections of the parasite to fall like a bridge over the moat of blood. Teeth from the parasite's mouth act like tiny hooks, which dig into Rain's skin and pull that section of the parasite to the new section of skin. The base of the parasite flops away from the tooth holding it to the skin, and a tiny proboscis drills into Rain's skin, starting the process all over again, only now the one-quarter part of the parasite starts to grow to a full-grown parasite with full set of teeth and two eyes. This happens in less than a minute. There are sections of parasites that flop over, and there is no more skin for it to hook onto. The skin has already been consumed, and in these cases, the parasites fall off and die. Rain watches the full process, and already both his forearms have been turned red with his blood. This is again an excruciating experience for Rain. He tries to pull the parasites from him, but they are too small. He grabs a bunch of them at a time and pulls them from his arm, but in most cases, he breaks them or digs so deep into his flesh that the pain is too much to bear.

"What the fuck! What kind of hell is this? Come on, Rain, wake up. Wake up!" cries Rain.

Rain yells and starts to run through the woods. He smacks himself in the head over and over, yelling and screaming, trying to wake himself up from what he thinks is a horrible dream. He takes off his shirt and rips it in half, wrapping it around his wrist as tight as he can trying to squish the little parasites. He covers them and ties his shirt as tight as he can, causing a lot of pain to himself. He cannot see them anymore and, for a second, hopes this will stop the expansion of the parasites through his skin. He watches for a minuets and then is terribly demoralized as the parasites keep spreading through his skin. They are now halfway through the palms of his hands and nearing his fingers, making his hands mostly unusable because of the pain of having the skin chewed off them. His arms up past his elbows have been chewed free of skin, and blood drips from his hands as he frantically runs through the woods. Every branch, bush, or even leaf that he brushes against is an excruciating experience that gets worse and more painful with every new foliage that he brushes against.

Rain can hear water in the woods and runs toward it. He runs to a small lake and runs right into it, holding his arms in the water, hoping he can drown the parasites. He hopes they will fall off, jump off, or better yet, die. Unfortunately for Rain, what actually happens is that fish are attracted to the scent of his blood, and within seconds, lots of small fish are biting tiny chunks of flesh from his arms. He raises his arms with scores of tiny fish attached to his arms, sucking the blood from him. Rain cries and swipes them off, noticing that most the skin from his hands are now gone. Rain cries in pain.

Overwhelming fear consumes him as he walks from the water to shore with his arms in the air. He looks to see all the skin of his arms up to his shoulders has now been eaten away. His arms are a bloody mess, and the exposure to air is a pain that words cannot describe. Rain falls to his ass, crying, holding his arms high in the air. The parasites seem to be working faster and faster. His shoulders are now eaten free of skin, and the parasites are working their way down his chest and up his neck. He can feel them eating his skin. He cannot touch anything. He can't use his hands because the pain is too great, and he feels his face disappear as the parasites work their way up his face over his nose, around his eyes, and over the top of his skull. Rain can only cry, and the tears cause his blood red cheeks acute pain as they fall down and from his face. His hair would fall off, but it sticks to the blood of his head. Rain cries louder and louder as the skin crawlers work down his back to his buttocks, and there is nothing he can do to escape the pain, which grows worse and worse by the minute. Rain has had the skin from the top of his head down below his hips now eaten away.

The scent of his blood and the cries of his weakened body are traveling through the woods, attracting predators. Rain sits as the skin crawlers work all the way down to his feet. Barely conscious, only his buttocks and heels of his feet touch the ground. He can barely move, slightly turning his head back and forth as the pain limits his every movement. He watches as a wolf walks down the water's edge toward his left side. To the right side of him, a bear walks. Massive eagles, hawks, and vultures land in the trees above him. Even large fish swim as close to the water's edge as possible. Rain sees all these animals move in closer and closer to him, and he wishes they would end his pain.

"What's that, buddy? You want me to end your pain? Come on, beg me. Beg me to kill you. I can end this pain, and you will be reborn. You will be able to live forever and see all the world through me. Come on, beg me," says Glamfury.

Glamfury walks up behind Rain and sits to his right side. He slaps Rain on his bloody shoulder, splattering blood. Rain cries weakly as the pain is so great it draws his strength.

"You can kill me, but you can never have my soul. You can never have my youth. My strength will always be mine and mine alone. That is that. So kill me if you will or get the hell away from me, you scum," says Rain.

Glamfury stands up and takes a few steps toward the water. He turns to look at Rain. Rain is already looking like jerky. His muscles are deep blood red. Most the blood on his flesh has coagulated, and flies cover his body. His eyes and teeth are bright white in contrast to the almost black-red of his skinless flesh. Rain sits with his arms held in the air, just waiting for whatever is going to happen to happen. It is clear he cannot do much of anything but wait for destiny to take its toll. Glamfury looks to the left, right, and up in the air. He sees all the animals waiting for dinner. He waves his hands at them, and they run away or take to flight or swim away.

"All this time you thought they were going to eat you, didn't you? Well, I think the animals had to go find shelter. You see, the animals, they know when a storm is coming, and I think one is coming now," says Glamfury.

Glamfury walks up and past Rain, slapping his shoulder as he walks by. Rain is bathed in pain literally as the wind picks up, and Glamfury walks by into the woods, laughing. The wind picks up, and thunderclouds blow in overhead. The wind gets stronger, blowing twigs, leaves, and grass around, which stick to Rain's glutinous flesh. The pain is so great he cannot believe he does not pass out. Things only get worse as it starts to rain. It rains slowly at first and gets harder and harder with bigger and bigger drops of rain. The pain covers his whole body, and he leans back, exhausted. Rain looks up at the drops of rain falling from the sky, his eyes opening and shutting like a fast-frame shutter on a camera. He can see the drops of rain falling in slow motion, and it feels like each drop of rain that lands on his body explodes in a flash of pain, drowning all his senses. Rain closes his eyes; he envisions his body as it is rained on. He sees electrical charges of pain race throughout his body in purple, red, and blue. Rain embraces the pain. He feels every drop of rain, causing acute pain wherever it lands on his exposed flesh. He raises his arms above his head and lays them on the ground like he knows something drastic is going to happen. A large tentacle extends from the water and wraps around Rain's legs. It pulls Rain into the water in an instant. The tentacle sinks into the darkening depths, pulling Rain down. Rain watches as the water gets darker and darker until he sees nothing and pain is the only sense he is afforded.

Rain breaches the water. The sun is shining, the waves are big, and he is laughing and smiling.

"Rain, come on, Rain. I bet you can't catch me!" yells Ajaunta.

Rain swims as fast as he can to reach the shore. Ajaunta is running up the beach in her bright yellow two-piece swimsuit. Rain instinctively runs as fast as he can to catch the gorgeous girl. He catches up to her and wraps his arms around her stomach, lifting her and twirling both of them in circles as the two of them laugh. He sets her down and holds her stomach as she laughs.

"OK, Rain, you caught me. Now what are you going to do with me?" says Ajaunta.

Rain falls back on the sand with a good hold of Ajaunta. She laughs as she falls on him, and he rolls her to her back and starts kissing her. Ajaunta cups her hands on Rain's cheeks and gently pushes him back as she passionately kisses his lips.

"Rain, do you love me?" she asks.

"You know I love you. You don't ever have to ask that," says Rain.

"Would you do something for me?" she asks.

"Anything," says Rain.

"Would you die for me?" she asks.

"What kind of question is that? I say we grow old and die together," says Rain.

"I like that thought, but things are not going to work out like that for us. There is this guy, and he keeps coming to me in my dreams. He loves me all the time, and I can't get away from him. He says I have to get you to submit to him or he is going to stop loving me and start torturing me. Rain, I'm scared. I don't know what to do. He said you would know exactly what I am talking about," says Ajaunta.

"I don't know what you are talking about. All I know is that I am going to love you now and until the end of time. That is what we are going to do. Now stop worrying about this," says Rain.

Rain stands, and Ajaunta backs away from him. She starts to cry.

"Rain, he said if I did not get you to beg him to kill you, he was going to start torturing me right away. Rain, I'm scared he is going to start torturing me," says Ajaunta.

She backs away from Rain as he walks toward her. She looks at her arms and holds them up. She starts to cry.

"Rain, it's happening. It's happening," she says.

The sky starts to darken from the clouds rolling in. Rain can see the skin on Ajaunta start to turn red from her blood as the skin crawlers start to eat her away. She cries, calling Rain's name. Cracks of thunder deafen the sky, and lightning spiderwebs its way across the heavens. Heavy large drops of rain fall from the sky. Rain watches as a large tentacle reaches from the water, wrapping around Ajaunta and pulls her into the depths. Rain runs after Ajaunta, yelling, "No!" He trips and falls face-first into the sand. Rain opens his eyes, lying on his back, and the heavy rain is pelting intense pain throughout his body. He looks down, seeing his body is deep blood red and he has no skin. He holds his hands and arms above him, and he screams in agony.

Chapter 35

The Gates of Hell

Thunder splits the sky, startling Rain from his sleep. He was sleeping against a tree, sitting inside a thick rubbery poncho specifically designed to keep you dry during heavy thunderstorms. It is amazing Rain was able to sleep at all. The rain is pouring, and Rain lifts the top of the poncho, looking out to see it is still raining very hard. There is tall grass all around way taller than Smoke and Rain. Smoke walks through the drenched grass, and Rain can barely see him. It is obviously the middle of the night here somewhere in Vietnam.

"Rain, fuck this. I can't wait anymore. This rain is never going to stop. We have to go find Wicks and Smoulder," says Smoke.

"I can't stand this either. Wicks was the one who taught me how to shoot. I don't know how it's possible for any tunnels to not be completely flooded in this deluge, but I say we go take a look," says Rain.

"All right, put your poncho away and let's go. We're going to get wet, but fuck it. I need to know what has happened to them. If they are still alive, we need to get to them quick. I heard the Egengyns are some kind of devil worshippers. If that is true, then Wicks and Smoulder are probably dead already," says Smoke.

"Fucking devil worshippers. Scum of the earth. They better pray to their devil god that Wicks and Smoulder are all right," says Rain.

Rain folds his poncho and puts it away. He checks his gun and shoulders it. Smoke knows the look of Rain when he is serious, and

Smoke knows to stay clear of Rain when he is mad. This is when Smoke likes following Rain because fireworks are about to happen.

"You got the location on your GPS?" asks Smoke.

"Yeah, it is less than a mile from here. Stay on my ass and let's go get some," says Rain.

Rain heads through the tall grass, and Smoke follows close behind him. The rain is pouring, and soon they are walking in water that gets deeper and deeper. The water is up to their shoulders, and they walk out of the grass into a slow-flowing stream. The current is not strong enough to sweep them away, and they cross the fifteen-foot waterway until they reach the other side and enter into the tall grass again. The water gets shallower and shallower, and they walk up a bank out of the grass into the lush forest, which gives them a little protection from the heavily falling rain. They walk for about fifteen minutes, and Rain bends down by a tree. Smoke bends down behind him. Rain pulls some binoculars from his backpack and looks through them. He points in the dark and hands the binoculars to Smoke. Smoke looks through them, and they are night-vision capable. Smoke can see an entrance into the side of a hill, which seems to have been dug out by humans.

"That's it, Rain. That must be the cave where the Egengyns have taken Wicks and Smoulder," says Smoke.

"That's it. According to my GPS, they should be in there. Those devil-worshipping Egengyns will never hear us coming. We should hit them, get our men out, and get the fuck out of here. You ready?" says Rain.

"You head to the left, and I'll take the right," says Smoke.

They head through the forest to their respective side, checking for traps in the dark rainy forest. They meet up on either side of the cave and bend down. They look in and see nothing. The ground mounds upward, and the cave has been dug out of the earth. Heavy foliage, heavy rain, and darkness make the setting eerie, creepy, and the unknown causes Rain's and Smoke's hearts to pump adrenalin through their veins, which they both love. They use hand signals and enter the cave. It is dark, but the light of a fire glows yellow and red. The fire is very deep in the cave, and they move slowly toward it with their military rifles ready. They can see the fire ahead and move toward it. There is no one around, but Rain follows his GPS right to the clothing of Wicks and

Smoulder. All their gear is laid on the floor, including knives and rifles. Rain feels the pant cuff where the tiny transmitter is located.

"Well, here it is. This is their clothing, all right," says Rain.

"Goddamn, we are too late. Where are they?" says Smoke.

They look around. Not only are the men they are looking for not here, but also no one is here. They do hear faint voices and look around until they find a hole in the floor, which leads down to another cave. They look down and head down toward the voices they hear. Rain drops down first and then Smoke. They cautiously move through the cave around a bend, which leads to a large room, which has a large boulder in the middle of the room. Torches on the walls give off a surprising amount of light. They can see Wicks lying against the far wall, and his heart has been cut from his chest. Smoulder is lying on the boulder, and four very tall men wearing coconut shells over their heads have ropes tied to his wrists and ankles. The tall men have vines hanging from the coconut shells to their knees. There is one man near a fire on the ground that is at the head of the man, screaming on the boulder. This man holds a knife, and he is speaking in a language Rain and Smoke do not understand. The man raises the knife with both hands and stands over Smoulder like he is going to thrust the knife into his chest. Rain and Smoke do not hesitate; they enter the large cave and start firing on the men holding the ropes. The coconut shells explode, and the men are thrown back against the cave walls from the barrage of bullets. The man holding the knife holds out his hands.

"Stop!" yells the man.

Rain and Smoke have killed the four men holding the ropes, and Smoulder falls from the boulder, moving toward Rain and Smoke. Rain and Smoke ready their rifles aimed right at the man still holding the knife, but they do not fire.

"This man here, this man has something that belongs to me. Give me what is mine, and I will let you go unharmed. Return my belonging or suffer the wrath of hell," says the man.

"Suffer this," says Rain.

Rain pulls the trigger, unleashing rapid fire on the man. The man sinks or falls like he is nothing more than vapor. His clothing and the knife fall to the ground. Rain and Smoke go to investigate the ground, and there is no sign of the man.

"What the fuck is this shit? How the hell is he just gone like that? I don't like this. I don't ever want to be chasing no devil worshippers again, you hear me, Smoke? Fuck this bullshit. I shoot this man, and he, what, just disappears. What the fuck?" says Rain.

"Never mind that right now. Get over here and help me with Smoulder," says Smoke.

Rain walks over and helps Smoke get Smoulder to his feet. Rain uses his rifle to move the coconut shell from one of the men.

"What the fuck! Smoke, come look at this," says Rain.

Smoke walks over, and they all look to see the man has no face. It is just a skull in the coconut shell. They inspect the other three men and find the same.

"Come on, Rain, fuck this. We need to get Smoulder to his clothing. Come on," says Smoke.

Smoke helps Smoulder to the hole leading up to the next level where his clothing is. Rain looks the devil worshippers over, scratching his head. He walks over and takes the knife the man who disappeared was holding. He puts the knife in his backpack. Rain and Smoke help Smoulder up to the next level, and then they follow up. Smoulder gets dressed in his gear, which is still intact including his weapons.

"Smoke, did you see those men? They had no faces. They had no eyes, no noses or ears. What the fuck were they?" says Rain.

"Those were the Egengyns. You heard of them, right?" says Smoulder.

"They are real? We have heard of them, but I thought it was all fairy tale—you know, devil worshippers cutting out people's hearts, eating them, and living forever. What a bunch of shit," says Smoke.

"Yeah, tell me what you saw down there. They cut out Wicks's heart, and they were just about to cut out mine. It was the knife that one guy was using. It has some sort of power. It has some sort of regenerative power. It restores youth—at least that is what the myth says," says Smoulder.

"Where did you hear all this stuff about these Egengyns and this knife? You mean this knife here?" says Rain.

Rain pulls the knife from his backpack and shows it to Smoulder.

"Yup, that's the knife. I saw it with my own eyes. When that guy, the one they call their god, cut the heart out of Wicks, it started to glow, and just before he stabbed the knife into Wicks's heart, the knife created lightning that shot from the blade and seared Wicks's flesh. It cut his bones and exposed his heart. The knife then stabbed Wicks in his heart, and that man, that god, pulled the heart from his chest and ate it while it was still on the knife. He ate it all. Then they tied my ankles and wrists. You two know the rest," says Smoulder.

"Fuck. I am going to hunt that fucker down. I am going to fill that fucker full of hot lead. I am going to cut his throat. I will break every bone in that fucker's body. I will do whatever I have to do. Wicks may have taught you how to shoot, but he was my teacher, he was my friend. He was my hero. I will avenge Wicks," says Smoke.

"Me too," says Rain.

"He was my partner. I will chase that fucker to the gates of hell," says Smoulder.

Smoulder is happy to see his rifle is undamaged and still loaded. He slaps in his magazine hard.

"Ready to go. How about you two?" says Smoulder.

"Ready," says Smoke.

"Follow me. Let's get out of here," says Rain.

The three of them start to leave the cave when laughter rings out. They hold their rifles, ready to defend themselves. They have no idea where the laughter is coming from, but it is loud and echoes throughout the cave.

"I thought I heard someone say they would chase me to the gates of hell. I can accommodate that," echoes a voice through the cave.

"It's him. It's that guy they call their god, the one who ate Wicks's heart," says Smoulder.

Arms reach out from the soft muddy earth wall. They reach around Smoulder and put him in a full nelson hold. Rain and Smoke face their rifles at Smoulder but do not fire because the man is behind Smoulder.

"Drop the rifle or I will break your neck," says the man.

Smoulder drops his rifle.

"Shoot him. Shoot this fucker right now," says Smoulder.

"Yes, shoot. Shoot and see what happens," says the man.

Rain and Smoke look at each other, not pulling the trigger. They do not chance possibly shooting their friend.

"You hesitated. Good. Let's see what the gates of hell look like, shall we?" says the man.

Smoulder is pulled backward by the man. They fall into the wall and down. Very strong gusts of wind blow Rain and Smoke into the opening in the wall. They are falling behind Smoulder, who is still held by the mysterious man. They can see they are falling toward a yellowish-red light. It is getting very hot, and they are sweating. Smoulder reaches for Rain and Smoke, who fall behind him.

"Shoot him. Shoot him!" yells Smoulder.

The cave they are falling through opens up. They are all now in a free fall toward red hot molten lava. The cavern seems miles across, but not that deep as Smoulder and the man crash on what seems to be metal gates high above the lava. They roll off the gate and come to a stop on land. The man stands with a secure hold on Smoulder. Rain and Smoke crash on the ground and manage to stand and face their rifles at Smoulder and the man. It is very hot, and very hot winds are blowing every which way. The man backs toward the tall metal gate that is closed. Rain and Smoke follow closely.

"Stop. Stop right there and don't come any closer. This is the end of the line for Smoulder, but you two may still rise to talk about seeing the gates of hell," says the man.

The man holds Smoulder with his left hand and slowly waves his right arm toward the very tall gates behind them. The gates swing open with the sounds of rusty metal rubbing against itself. The man laughs as the gates slowly swing open. Smoulder looks at Rain and Smoke with a very sad look on his face.

"Rain, Smoke, you two need to live. You two need to move on. It is on me to make sure this hell ends here. It is on me to make sure the hell, the torture, the murder, and the mayhem that has plagued me and all my loved ones end here. Only I can stop this hell from entering your world and ruining your lives. Rain, Smoke, go, go now, and you will be taken back home. You can go back. Just walk back to where you fell, and you will be swept back up to our world. Go, go back now," says Smoulder.

"No, Smoulder. I am going to put a bullet right in this freak's face. Just duck, Smoulder. It's an easy shot," says Smoke.

"Yes, Smoulder, we got this guy dead in our sights," says Rain.

"No, you guys do not understand. This is where I have to make a stand. This is where I end this nightmare, or it will continue with you two, and I cannot let that happen. Please understand this is the only way. Glamfury, you will keep your word, right? This ends here, right?" says Smoulder.

Rain and Smoke look at each other, confused as to what is going on. They are ready to act, ready to shoot, ready for anything except what happens. Glamfury is laughing and lets go of Smoulder.

"Glamfury, take my youth. Please take my youth and send my soul to Lucifer. It is time for me to be one with you. Glamfury, I beg of you, kill me. Kill me!" says Smoulder.

Glamfury starts to grow. His head transforms from a very handsome man to that of a horrid beast with flame red skin and large sharp teeth. His arms and body grow very muscular. His fingers grow into strong pointed digits. Glamfury, now four feet taller than Smoulder is and behind him, looks every bit the humanoid beast from hell that he is. He reaches his arms around Smoulder's chest and digs his digits into Smoulder's sternum. Smoulder looks at Rain and Smoke with a sad, terrified look on his face.

"This is the only way," says Smoulder.

Glamfury pulls his arms apart, ripping Smoulder's rib cage from his body. His ribs fly behind the two of them through the gates of hell and assumedly into hell. Smoulder stands there with his inner chest exposed. Glamfury reaches around with his right hand, grabbing Smoulder's beating heart.

"No!" yells Rain and Smoke.

Smoulder looks at them, saying, "It's all right, it's all right."

Glamfury rips the heart from Smoulder's chest and holds it above his head, laughing. Glamfury puts the heart in his mouth and chews it. Rain and Smoke watch as a wispy outline of Smoulder floats from his body. His soul blows past the gates into hell. Glamfury slams his right fist down on Smoulder's head, and his body explodes into pieces, which fly past the gates into hell. Glamfury laughs.

"No!" yells Smoke.

Smoke walks toward the beast, firing his rifle. Automatic rifle fire shreds the beast. Smoke fires continually until he has exhausted all his ammunition, leaving the chest of this beast shredded, dropping bits of flesh and bleeding profusely. Smoke lowers his gun and reloads a new magazine. Rain walks up beside Smoke, and the two of them watch as this beast laughs. It looks down, and its chest starts to reform, healing at an incredible rate. Rain and Smoke watch. Smoke points his rifle, ready to shoot again. Rain puts his hand on Smoke.

"Smoke, wait, let me try this," says Rain.

Rain pulls the knife he collected earlier. He pulls the knife and raises it in the air. The knife starts to glow. Flashes of lightning start to flow up and down the knife. Rain can feel the energy surging into his hand, making him feel stronger, making him feel good. The beast sees Rain hold up the knife.

"Give me the knife, human. Give me the knife, and you and your friend go back to your homes on the world above. That knife is mine, and it belongs to me. Give me the knife," says Glamfury.

"I'll give it to you, all right," says Rain.

Rain charges the beast, and the knife starts to emanate lightning. The beast starts to fly back into hell through the gates. It reaches out with both arms grabbing the gates. Rain runs right up to it and stabs it in the gut. He uses both hands to pull the knife up through the center of its rib cage. The beast screams in pain.

"No. Stop, you do not know what you are doing. You do not possess the power to kill me. Not even with the soul knife. Stop!" yells Glamfury.

The beast form of Glamfury starts to fade away and shrinks down to the human that Glamfury is. Rain pulls the knife, holding it, facing Glamfury, who transforms right before him. Glamfury stands holding the gates with his hands and arms out to his sides. Rain points the knife at him, and lighting shoots from the knife, searing Glamfury's flesh where it touches him. Glamfury screams in burning, agonizing pain. Rain puts the knife in his belt. He reaches his hands in Glamfury's sternum and rips his rib cage from the front of his body. This exposes Glamfury's beating heart. Glamfury holds the gates of hell with both hands. He is seriously weakened, and his head droops downward. He looks up at Rain.

"You do not know what you are doing, human. You do not have the power to defeat me. You cannot possess the power of the soul knife and use it against me," says Glamfury.

"And yet," says Rain.

Rain pulls the knife. He stabs it into Glamfury's beating heart. Glamfury opens his mouth with screams of his dying breath, hurting the ears of both Rain and Smoke. Superheated hell air starts to blow harder and harder, blowing Rain and Smoke toward the gates of hell. Glamfury holds on with his dying hands as his body is blown toward hell. Glamfury holds on as hard as he can with the knife stuck in his heart. He starts to glow red, blue, purple, and yellow, like lighting is flowing through his body. Smoke grabs hold of Rain, who is almost pulled into the gates of hell.

"Come on, Rain, we have to fight the wind. We have to fight our way back to where we landed in this place. Come on, it is our only chance," says Smoke.

Smoke and Rain watch as Glamfury is still holding on. He is still screaming a death scream that is deafening and killing their ears. Glamfury's body starts to break apart, and bloody chunks of his flesh blow into hell. He screams, yelling, "No!" as his hands loose grip on the gates, and his body flies into hell. Rain and Smoke watch as Glamfury falls into the unknown and out of sight. The gates of hell slam shut, and the wind goes away.

"Come on, Rain, follow me. We have to get back to the exact spot where we landed when we fell in this place. Trust me," says Smoke.

The two of them walk back to where they landed, and sure enough, they vanish.

Chapter 36

Hell's Giant

Rain steps out of his car into the pouring rain. It is nearly midnight on this Tuesday night, and Rain wipes the rain from his jacket as he walks into Sandy's restaurant. He takes off his jacket, passing Renee on the way to the table where he and Smoke always meet to have coffee.

"Hi, Rain, I will be at your table in just a minute with a coffee for you," says Renee.

"Oh, thank you, Renee," says Rain.

Rain walks to the table and sits opposite Smoke, who is already sitting and sipping his coffee.

"They found him," says Smoke.

Smoke pulls a very thick file from a duffel bag and places it on the table in front of Rain. Rain picks it up and flips through the pages. Renee sets a cup in front of Rain and fills it with coffee.

"Thank you," says Rain.

Renee smiles and moves on to service other customers.

"Smoke, this is the leader of the Egengyns, those fucking devil worshippers," says Rain.

"That's right. We missed him in South America. They say he has ties to the Caribbean, but he has fled to the Sudan, and that is where we are going. We are going to get that fucker," says Smoke.

Rain rubs his head, having memories of killing Glamfury at the gates of hell. He sees memories of Glamfury taking Ajaunta from his home when his whole house was lost at sea. He has memories of

Glamfury freezing both him and Smoke in his home when Bailey was caught and the blood was sucked from her body. These visions come quick, and they are short. He remembers himself along with Smoke, Ajaunta, and Bailey sitting in Smoke's living room on that horseshoe-shaped couch.

"Smoke, we have run into this guy a lot of times already. Don't you remember? I killed him at the gates of hell. I killed him with his soul knife, and he fell into hell. He is not coming back from that. Don't you remember?" says Rain.

"Rain, what are you talking about? I don't remember any of that. We killed a bunch of his henchmen in that cave in South America, but their leader got away, remember? All I know is we have been called back. I know we are still on leave, but we can go get him. If we don't, they will probably send Wicks and Smoulder," says Smoke.

"They do send Wicks and Smoulder, and we could not save them, remember? Don't you remember? Ah, I can't take this anymore. No, I am not going after this guy. No more devil worshippers for me, Smoke. Just simple bad guys. Fuck these mind-altering, dream-creating, never-dying devil worshippers. I keep living horror over and over. Fuck this bullshit. No, I am not going after them," says Rain.

Rain puts his jacket on and leaves the diner. Smoke stays in his seat, talking as Rain walks out.

"Rain, where are you going? Rain, you can't say no. Rain, don't make me go without you. Rain, you are my partner. You are the only one I trust to have my back when the shit hits the fan. Rain, come back," says Smoke.

Rain walks out into the pouring rain. He is halfway to his car when Smoke reaches the door of the diner.

"Rain, how can you let this monster go? How can you walk away and let him continue to kill people? Devil worshipper or not, we are the only ones who can get him. We are the only ones who can kill him," says Smoke.

"We can't kill him, Smoke. Don't you get it? He has been playing us from the start. I don't know how or why, but we can't do anything against him. I don't even think he is real. I don't think any of this is real. This is all one big dream. It is a never-ending nightmare, and I have to figure out how to end it. I have to figure out how to kill this guy, and it's not going to happen by you and me traveling to some remote part of the world. We have been doing that for far too long already. This guy is playing us for some reason that benefits him, not us, and I have to figure out what his end game is before it is too late for me, you, and all our loved ones. He is playing us, Smoke, don't you get it?" says Rain.

Rain turns to go to his car. He is standing in the pouring rain and is soaked to the bone. He hears Smoke scream and turns to see Smoke trying to leave the diner. Smoke is pounding on what seems to be an invisible barrier. Rain can tell Smoke is calling to him, but his words are muffled by the barrier. The ground around the diner erupts in eight places with huge tentacles growing upward. They are like octopus tentacles that grow up and over the diner. Rain calls to Smoke and runs toward his friend. Before he reaches the diner, the tentacles grab hold of the diner and crush it, pulling it into the ground. Smoke calls for Rain as the diner is pulled into the ground and into the depths of hell. Rain crawls on his hands and knees to the edge of the pit, watching the diner falling into the earth. He can see the diner fall out of view into the darkness of the earth. Rain rolls to his back, lying on the pavement being pelted by the pouring rain. He screams and yells into the rainy dark sky.

"Why can I not stop this? How long is this nightmare to last? How long will it take me to figure out this puzzle, this riddle, this maze of dreamwork that has baffled my mind and yanks at my soul? What is this?" yells Rain into the rainy sky with his eyes closed.

"You can stop this. This is no nightmare, no puzzle, no riddle, or maze. This is the taking of one's youth so another can live on. This is the stealing of one's soul so the master of hell can endure forever. This is the way it is, the way it will be, and the destiny that is in store for you. The sooner you accept your fate, the sooner your hell here will end," says a very deep voice coming from the pit sinking into the earth.

Rain rolls to his hands and knees, feeling the ground beneath him shake. He hears loud crashes in the earth as a giant Glamfury starts to rise from the pit. He is as large as the pit will allow. Rain stands and walks backward down the road as Glamfury slams his hands on the ground outside the pit. He hauls his twenty-foot body out of the pit and stands, looking down at Rain.

"This is some sort of game. This is a dream. There is no way this is real. If you were going to kill me, you would have done it by now!" yells Rain.

"I have told you time and time again. I am going to kill you, but you are going to beg me to kill you first. You will beg me to send your soul right to Lucifer. I will have your youth, and your soul will be feasted on by the world's true savior, for he and he alone shall rule earth forever," says Glamfury.

"If you can only kill me if I beg you to do so, then it will never happen. If you are going to kill me, then kill me. If not, then leave me be!" yells Rain.

Glamfury screams, making fists and flexing his muscles. He bends down, swinging his right hand at Rain, catching him in the palm of his hand. He stands, holding Rain in his hand.

"You don't want to beg me to kill you. Then suffer, little man," says Glamfury.

Glamfury throws Rain toward a building across the street. Rain slams into the thick glass windows, breaking through and landing in the lobby of the building. He rolls across the floor, coming to a stop as he crashes into a solid wall. There is a stairway winding up the side of the lobby above him. Rain rolls to his stomach in severe pain. His arms, chest, face, and legs have been severely cut by the glass, and he is bleeding a lot. He is quite sure he has broken bones and struggles to get to his hands and knees. The huge hand and arm of Glamfury breaks through the glass into the lobby, grabbing hold of Rain. Rain is pulled into the rainy street where Glamfury laughs at him and throws him across the street the other way into another building where Rain suffers more horrific cuts and broken bones. Rain already cannot move. His body is broken all over, and he is grabbed again. Glamfury holds Rain in the palm of his hand, and the rain washes his blood down his body, and it drips to the road below.

"You want some more? I can end your pain and suffering. I can put a stop to all this, or I can continue. The longer you hold out, the longer you resist, the more souls and youth you bring to me," says Glamfury.

Glamfury lifts his left hand to his right. Rain opens his bloody eyes and can see Renee is held tight in Glamfury's left hand.

"Rain, what is this? Rain, this can't be real. Are we actually being held by a giant? What is going on, Rain?" cries Renee.

"No!" yells Rain.

Glamfury laughs and throws Rain onto the road below. Rain hits hard, landing on his face. He can hear and feel his bones break as he tumbles a few feet to a stop with his mangled body twisted all about. He sees the giant Glamfury walking down the road with Renee in his hand, and she is screaming. Rain cannot speak; he is so badly broken. He cannot move, and the rain washes the blood from his ripped and torn body into the storm drain on the side of the road. All Rain can do is watch as Glamfury walks out of sight with Renee in his possession.

Rain can hear the siren of an ambulance approaching, but he cannot see it. The siren and vehicle park close behind Rain, and two medical personnel approach. Rain is a twisted clump of flesh and bone and still unable to move. He finally sees the people, who pick him from the street and place him on a gurney. They unfold his body and lay it flat on the bed, which is extremely painful, and Rain cries in pain.

"He is still awake. How can he still be conscious?" asks one of the medical persons.

"I don't know. There is no time to waste. Let's get him in the ambulance and to the hospital immediately," says the other person.

They strap Rain down and wheel him onto the ambulance. The ambulance speeds to the hospital. Rain, for some reason, can speak now that he is lying flat on a bed, and the two medical people are working on him.

"Where are you taking me? Are you taking me to the hospital? Am I going to be all right?" asks Rain.

"Yes, sir, we are going to do everything we possibly can to make sure you are OK. Just relax and stay calm. We are going to give you some anesthesia to ease the pain," says the man.

The ambulance races to the hospital. Rain is wheeled into the hospital where there are two doctors already waiting. All the clothing was cut from Rain while he was riding in the ambulance and the two doctors look him over.

"Why is this man still conscious?" asks the doctor.

"I don't know, doctor. We administered enough anesthesia to knock out an elephant," says the EMT.

"Look at this poor soul. His bones are all broken and sticking out all over the place. I'm surprised he has not died of blood loss alone, and yet he is still conscious," says the other doctor.

"Yes, there is no time to waste. We must rush him to the surgical center room 108 on the eighth floor. Hurry," says the doctor.

"Yes, sir," say the EMTs.

The gurney Rain is on is rushed to the elevator.

"Hey, wait a minute. The eighth floor. That does not sound right. Am I going to be all right? How am I still awake? Aren't I supposed to be asleep or something?" says Rain.

"Don't worry, sir, you are in the best possible hands with the surgeons here at Hells High Riptorian Medical Center," says the EMT.

"What? What did you say? Where am I?" screams Rain.

The EMTs secure Rain to the gurney with straps as he is wheeled into room 108. There are four surgeons in the room wearing surgical clothing. Rain is looking around and begging them not to touch him, but he has no strength to get up or fight back as the doctors unstrap him and look over his broken body. Rain's ribs are broken and sticking out of his flesh along with leg bones and arm bones. His head is cracked and split diagonally between his eyes, so his face is not aligned or symmetric at all. He is a bloody, gory mess. Rain can hear this laughing, and he knows the sound of the laughter. He looks out the window to the right of him, and he can see the giant Glamfury looking in the windows and he is laughing.

Rain hears the sound of a handsaw, and he looks to see a doctor with a small handheld saw. He puts the spinning blade to Rain's hip and cuts into Rain's muscle. He runs the saw right down the top front of Rain's right leg. Rain screams in excruciating pain as the saw burns like a torch as his muscle is cut right down the center of his leg. Rain screams and cries as the doctors grab the flesh on either side of his leg and pull the flesh to the sides of his bone that is broken. His flesh is hooked and held apart as the doctors grab Rain's bones and physically pull, push, and adjust his bones until it is aligned and back together as one. The doctors then grab a small torch and some putty, which they use to solder Rain's bone back together with. The pain is overwhelming, but Rain stays conscious as the doctors unhook his flesh and then sew the muscle back together. Rain is breathing heavily and crying out in pain. Rain is yelling at the doctors, calling them every curse word he can think of, but the doctors ignore him and start to cut the muscle on his other leg the same way. They repeat this process on his lower legs as well as on his arms. Rain cannot move as his flesh is cut and pulled from his bones. He can only cry out in pain as his bones are moved back into place and soldered back together. Rain can only watch with his crooked eyes as the doctors grab both sides of his skull and push until his face is correctly aligned, and they solder his face diagonally from his forehead down between his eyes and over his left cheek. Rain has endured all this pain, and he has stayed awake while the doctors spend hours and hours putting his bones back together and sewing his flesh back together. Now Rain is back together, and his body looks like a rag doll that has been sewed together all over, and Rain is starting to fade to unconsciousness.

"Oh, no, doctor, he needs blood. He needs blood fast or he will die," says the nurse.

"Hurry, everyone, get him blood now," says the doctor.

Rain is just about to lose consciousness, but he sees all the doctors turn to him. They all have syringes full of blood, and they stick him in his main arteries—in his neck, in his arms, and in his legs. The doctors repeat this three times, and Rain can feel his strength coming back. Rain is actually starting to feel stronger and better than he has ever felt before.

"What have you doctors done? I feel great," says Rain.

Rain sits up, and the doctors back a few steps back from the bed. Rain swings his legs to the side of the bed and stands up. Rain smiles because he feels great. He feels refreshed and energetic. He looks in the mirror at his nude body, and he is a mess. He has huge scars up and down his legs, across his arms, his face, and all over his chest, but he does not care; he feels great. Rain turns to the doctors and starts to hug them.

"I don't know how you did it. I don't know how you fixed me, but I feel great. I feel exhilarated. I feel like dancing," says Rain.

Rain grabs the hands of one of the female doctors and swings in circles, dancing with the doctor, who laughs with Rain. Rain can hear loud laughter, which takes his joy away. Rain lets go of the doctor and looks out the windows. He sees Glamfury looking in.

"Feeling better, Rain? I am so glad the good doctors were able to fix you up," says Glamfury.

The huge hand of Glamfury breaks through the window into the room, grabbing hold of Rain. Glamfury pulls Rain from the room and holds him high above the ground. Glamfury looks at Rain held tight in the palm of his right hand.

"So you are feeling better? You are feeling better than ever before? I am glad. Now, Rain, let's have some fun," says Glamfury.

Rain cries, screams, and yells, "No!" as he is raised high in the air, and Glamfury throws him face-first at the road many tens of feet below. Rain is thrown at the road, and he knows the terrible pain of his body being broken is coming his way as he hits the road face-first, and everything goes black.

Chapter 37

Wild Animals

Rain wakes up with a terrible headache. It's the middle of the night, and he can hear the hard-pouring rain landing on the roof of his house. He sits up, rubbing his head. Looking out the window, he sees the water running down the glass. He walks to the bathroom, swinging open the mirror, looking for aspirin. He finds some and swallows four of them. He stands for a moments, hoping the aspirin works like magic, stopping the splitting headache right on the top half of his forehead. He swears someone has been hitting him in the head with a bat while he was sleeping. At least that is what his head feels like.

Rain does not stand there too long before he hears a noise downstairs in the kitchen, which gets his attention. He walks to the top of the stairs and looks down into the darkness. He hears a hissing a mean hissing, which sends chills up his spine. It sounds to him like a cat is squaring off with another cat; only this cat sounds really big. He walks down the stairs, slowly flipping the switch, turning the light on in the stairway. He looks into the kitchen cautiously and sees nothing, but he still hears the hissing. He looks under the kitchen table and sees nothing. He turns on the light and cannot see anything in the kitchen, but something is there. He does not think the hissing is meant for him, but it sure is making him feel uneasy.

Rain moves closer and closer to the sound, figuring it is coming from the cabinet under the sink. He opens the silverware drawer and pulls the biggest steak knife he can find. He reaches down and grabs hold of the handle on the door and pulls it open. A very large black catlike animal springs from the cabinet lightning fast and digs its claws into Rain's right shin. It bites into his leg under his knee. Its claws and teeth dig in deep, drawing a lot of blood, and the animal squeezes its paws. It bites as hard as it can like it is purposefully trying to cause as much damage to Rain as possible. Rain just about jumps out of his skin when the animal first attacked, and he jumped back into the kitchen table, knocking over two chairs and pushing the table back into the wall. Rain sits up, realizing it is much bigger than a cat, more like a large raccoon, and it is clawing and biting his leg. Rain is suddenly thrown from fright to pain. The animal is clawing his leg, and he is bleeding badly.

Rain yells and finally realizes he grabbed a steak knife, which he uses to stab the animal with. Rain stabs the animal over and over until it retreats, using its claws to defend itself, but Rain is in a rage and he stabs it over and over. Blood from the animal is splattered all over the kitchen walls, and the animal manages to stick its claws in Rain's arm. It holds on and bites his hand, drawing more blood from Rain. Rain screams in fear and rage, yelling at the animal. He grabs it by its throat with his left hand and holds the animal to the floor by its neck, applying all the pressure he can. He is suffocating it and breaking its neck. He starts to stab it repeatedly. The animal fights back, clawing and biting his left hand and forearm. Rain's adrenaline races through his veins, supercharging his anger and aggression. Rain finally stabs the animal to death, but the animal takes a serious toll on him before it stops fighting back. It stops breathing, and Rain steps back, breathing heavily and dripping blood from both his arms, hands, and right leg.

"What the fuck? What the fuck are you? How did you get in my house?" yells Rain.

Rain looks to see his arms and leg have been sliced badly. Blood is dripping from him, and he becomes hysterical. Rain backs into the living room and tries to sit on the couch, but he sits before he gets to the couch and falls on the floor. He cannot believe how much damage that animal did to him in such a short amount of time.

Rain hears the call of an eagle and looks up behind him. Over the couch is an eagle with its wings spread the entire width of the ceiling. The huge bird lunges at Rain, talons first, digging them into his chest. Rain can feel the talons dig into his chest. He can feel one of them actually touching his heart as the talons grip his ribs and squeeze them together. Rain cannot believe how strong the bird's talons are, and they have him in an extremely painful grip. The bird starts to peck at Rain's head with its beak, breaking the skin on the top of his head, and Rain is now bleeding profusely down the front of his face. Rain tries to block the bird's beak with his hands, but the eagle is determined and very strong. It pecks hard, nearly breaking his skull as it pecks at him over and over. Rain bobs and sways his head, trying to avoid the sharp beak of the eagle, but it pecks him in the right eye and rips it from his head.

Rain screams in fear and pain and starts to stab the bird in the breast with the steak knife, which is still in his right hand. This is very effective, causing the eagle to release its talons from Rain's chest. The eagle tries to grab his right arm with its left leg and does; however, Rain is now in a rage. He grabs the eagle by its throat with his left arm and thrusts his right arm into its breast, stabbing it over and over. Feathers are flying all over along with blood from the eagle. Rain continues to stab it in the neck and breast until the bird flaps its wings no more. Rain sits on the couch and starts to cry. He has lost a lot of blood. He has lost his right eye, and his arms, chest, head, and right leg are badly sliced. He leans back on his couch, breathing heavily, trying to catch his breath. He hears growling coming from his kitchen and looks to see a strange dog, the likes he has never seen, standing in the doorway from the kitchen leading into the living room.

"Are you fucking kidding me?" says Rain.

This dog is black as midnight. It has tall hind legs, and its back slants downward to its front legs, which stand a few inches lower than its hind legs. Its neck slants lower yet leaving its head only a foot off the floor. Its head is square shaped, and its black stereoscopic eyes are focused right on Rain. It has very sharp canine teeth, and Rain can feel it is going to attack him. It is growling and showing its teeth. Rain stands and readies his knife. This dog is very muscular, and Rain stomps his feet and yells at it, trying to intimidate it. Rain looks to his right and heads for the door leading outside. The strange dog leaps toward the door and in one strong jump lands in front of the door before Rain gets there and turns to face Rain. Rain halts and takes a step back with steak knife ready. The dog growls, looking mean looking, like it is ready to strike, and Rain is ready. Rain is in an offensive stance focused on the dog, which leaves him no time to be concerned about the blood dripping from his body and the throbbing pain in his limbs. The dog walks slowly toward Rain, licking the blood from the carpet. Rain steps back in step with the advancing dog.

As Rain backs up, he hears the claws of paws walking on the linoleum floor in his kitchen. He turns his head to see another doglike creature walking up behind him like the one in front of him. This one has the catlike creature that Rain had killed earlier in its mouth. Rain notices the creature in front of him eyeing the dead creature, and he steps toward the bedroom on the side of the living room. The door to his bedroom is closed, and as soon as Rain gets just to his door, the dog in front of him lunges at the dead animal in the other dog's mouth. Rain is mesmerized as the two animals each have a mouthful of the catlike creature, and they pull, twist, and turn, tearing the animal in half. They bite, chew, and eat the animal, bones and all. Rain watches for a minute and then opens the bedroom door and steps in, closing the door behind him. He stands in the pitch black, feeling his throbbing body from all the wounds he has suffered, and he is still breathing heavily.

"Rain, is that you? What are you doing?" says a voice from his bed.

"What? Marlene? Is that you?" says Rain.

"Well, who else would be sleeping in your bed besides me?" says Marlene.

"Ahh, no one. I just did not think you were here. Turn on the light, I can't even see you," says Rain.

Marlene reaches over and pulls the chain, turning on the lamp. Rain screams in fear as the light goes on. Marlene sits up on the side of the bed. She stands up wearing just her underwear. Rain points his steak knife at her.

"Stay back. Stay back or I'll stab you. Believe me when I tell you I am lethal with this knife," says Rain.

Marlene sniffs the air, deeply closing her eyes and tilting her head upward.

"Mmmmmm. Wow! Rain, you smell so good wearing the scent of plasma," says Marlene.

She opens her eyes and looks him over. Rain has blood all over himself, which is starting to coagulate.

"Stay back, I'm warning you. Stay back," says Rain.

Marlene steps toward Rain, and fluid runs down her body to the floor. She looks at her legs and body holding up her arms as bodily fluid seeps through her skin. She looks at her arms and realizes her whole body is swollen with a venomous liquid puffing her skin out all over her. She has an orangish hue to her entire body, reminding Rain of when she was bitten by all the spiders and her insides were being digested before the little spiders feasted on her. Marlene smells the air, craving Rain's blood.

"I need your blood. I need your blood to replace mine," says Marlene.

Marlene's skin starts to break, and the orange-colored puss starts to run on her neck, arms, chest, and legs.

"Rain, I need your blood," she says.

"Back, stay back," says Rain.

She moves toward Rain, and the puss runs from more and more places on her body. Every time she moves, another place on her skin cracks, releasing the puss. Rain slashes at her face, her arms, and her chest. She screams a screeching cry as she starts to flow a disgusting mixture of blood, puss, venom, and bodily fluids. She is very weak and still tries reaching for Rain, but he slashes at her every time, and she falls weaker with every second. She falls to her knees, screeching and trying to hold her flesh together, which starts to fall off her bones.

"Rain, why did you let them eat me? Why did you let all those spiders eat me? They ate me, Rain. They ate me!" cries Marlene, and then she starts to laugh.

Her body melts and shrinks before Rain. The fluids from her body soak the carpet and spread until they hit Rain's feet, and this is all he can take. Rain is truly grossed out; he catches his throat before he pukes. He freaks out, turning to the bedroom door, opening it, and running out of the room, closing the door behind him. Rain stands at the door, holding the door handle like he is waiting for someone to pull on it from the other side. He hears a growl and the crunching of bones behind him. "Oh, shit," he says, turning his head. One of the dogs is sitting, chewing on what is left of the cat creature. Rain turns his head to the other side, and the other dog creature is standing there, dripping saliva from its mouth. It lunges forward, digging its teeth into Rain's left calf muscle. It bites hard and deep. Rain cries out in pain, stabbing the animal in the small of its back. Rain stabs the steak knife into it all the way down to the hilt. The animal howls in obvious pain and backs away. It backs into the kitchen, screeching, howling, and crying. The other dog creature follows into the kitchen while keeping its eyes on Rain.

The bedroom door behind Rain opens slowly, and Rain is unaware of it because he is watching the animals walk into the kitchen and out of sight. Marlene walks from the bedroom with her skin stretched, torn, and sagging all over her body. The muscles all over her body are a network of pitted, decaying flesh. She is truly a gory sight that would make most people puke just by looking at her. Marlene takes a step and swings her right hand around Rain's head, slapping her puss-coated hand on his face. She pulls his head to her and bites him on the neck below his left ear. She rips a chunk of flesh from his neck, causing blood to squirt out all over.

Rain screams in pain, and the two dog creatures run back into the living room. Each of them bite into one of Rain's legs and start to thrash back and forth as hard as they can. Marlene reaches her left arm around Rain's chest and holds on. She looks up and laughs with flesh in her mouth and blood dripping down her neck, mixing with her bodily fluids. Rain screams and kicks. He elbows Marlene in the stomach, causing her to back away and bend down. Rain makes a fist and punches down as hard as he can on the dog at his left leg. The dog pauses to screech a painful howl and then digs its teeth into Rain's leg before he can get away.

Rain notices the knife still in the back of the other dog and slams his clenched fist on it, driving it into the body of the dog biting into his right leg. The dog howls and backs away, swaying its head back and forth in obvious discomfort. Rain punches and kicks the other dog, which is still thrashing his left leg back and forth violently, causing massive blood loss to Rain. Rain makes fists with both hands and punches simultaneously on either side of the dog's throat. These dogs are tough with sturdy bones and hefty muscles, but this action causes the dog to lose its grip on Rain, allowing him to jump over it, and he runs up on the couch, turning to see the two dogs pause and look at him from the center of the living room floor. Marlene is on her knees by the bedroom door, and she starts to whimper.

"Rain, it is you who started all this. It is you that the servant of hell is after. It is you that can end all this suffering for all of us. Rain, it is you, it was always you. You don't get it, do you? You cannot escape your fate. You cannot get away from the hell that is after you. You can only draw more and more of us into your nightmare. You can only cause more pain and suffering to more and more people. They want you to hold out. They want you to fight on and on because it only makes them stronger. The longer you hold out, the more youth and the more souls they collect. They are hell, and you are no match. How can you be?" says Marlene.

"What do you mean I started this? I did not start this. They came after me, and if not me, it would just be someone else. They probably want everyone, and you are probably in on this with them. There has to be a way to defeat them or at least prevent them from hurting other people, and I am going to figure it out. Help me, help me defeat them or at least contain them. If you know it is hell that is after me, then you must know something that can help me keep them in hell," says Rain.

"They are too smart for you. They have you running in circles. You don't even know where you are. You don't know if you are coming or going. You don't know if you are in a dream or if you are in the real world. You have no chance, but if you think you can fight them, you must remember—remember how you got here and remember all you have seen in your dreamworld. Remember who you are and who your friends really are. Remember what is reality and what is dream. Remember," says Marlene.

The dogs turn to Marlene, who is on her knees, and they charge, biting into her neck and her abdomen. The dogs thrash and rip her softened body, easily ripping flesh and bone. Her head rolls off her back as her neck is bitten in half. Her ribs break as the other dog rips them from the right side of her chest. The dogs bite and chew, eating her ravenously. Rain again has to catch his throat and prevent himself from throwing up in disgust. He is still a bloody mess himself. He can feel his arms sticking to the wall he is leaning against. He is still standing on the couch, and he can feel his legs sticking to the couch from the blood all over him that has been coagulating. He seizes the moment and runs for the door while the dogs eat Marlene. He opens the door and runs outside, closing the door behind him. He steps back from the door slowly with his hands held toward the door like he is waiting for the dogs to burst out and come after him.

Rain hears a hiss behind him and turns his head slowly to see what new horror awaits him. He feels pain in his left ankle and is pulled violently, falling hard on the ground. He has no time to see what has him as he is twisted and turned. He is scooped up by what is obviously a very large constricting snake. The constrictor wraps up Rain's body in seconds. The snake is large enough to wrap him all the way to his neck. Rain was caught so off guard he had no time to react, and the snake wrapped him with his arms to his sides. There is nothing Rain can do as the snake begins squeezing the life out of him. Rain feels the strength of the snake as it covers his whole body like a blanket. Every time he exhales, the snake, which feels like one huge muscle, squeezes tighter, and Rain cannot breathe in. This happens over and over until Rain cannot breathe in any air at all, and without a sound, Rain watches the stars in the sky. They are beautiful, he thinks, as all the stars in the whole sky start to fade to black, and blackness is all he sees.

Chapter 38

Sucked Out

Ajaunta sits up and reaches to the light on the nightstand next to Rain's bed. She pulls the chain, turning the light on. There is a small wooden vial holder holding ten small glass vials. All of them are empty except one. Ajaunta picks the wooden holder and looks at the one vial holding a lavender-colored liquid. She turns to Rain, who is sleeping on his side. She leans over and kisses him on his cheek.

"I am sorry, Rain. Only one more to go and our hell will be coming to an end. I am sorry," says Ajaunta.

Ajaunta gets up and walks to the top of the stairs. She pauses, holding the wooden holder close to her chest.

"Come, my dear. No need to hold back now. We are near the end. Come, my child, I am waiting," says a voice from downstairs.

Ajaunta walks down the stairs into the kitchen and walks into the living room. Glamfury is sitting on the couch.

"Come, my dear, sit by me," says Glamfury.

He is patting the large couch cushion with his hand. Ajaunta walks over and sits beside him. She holds the wooden vial holder up.

"This is it the last vial. I have kept him asleep for over a month now just as you have asked. I have been in his dreams and loved him just like you wanted. This is the last vial. It is all coming to an end now, right?" says Ajaunta.

"Yes, my dear, it is. Just this one last vial to administer, and he will awake. He will awake, and your responsibility will be over," says Glamfury.

"So I don't give him this one like all the other ones. I don't just put this in his food when he wakes up?" she asks.

"No, my dear. This one has to be injected right into his bloodstream. This will wake him. He will already be very weak from sleeping for so long, but this philter here will keep his mind stuck on your love. He will see me, but the thought of your love will keep his muscles weak. The thought of you being hurt in any way will keep him docile until the end," says Glamfury.

Glamfury pulls a syringe from his jacket and fills it with the lavender-colored fluid from the vial. He hands it to Ajaunta.

"Now, my dear, it is time. Time to bring this all to an end. All this suffering, all this pain, all the torture and mayhem come to an end when you administer this final elixir," says Glamfury.

"It all comes to an end, and I am free—free from your grasp forever," says Ajaunta.

"Yes, my dear, you will be free. Now go administer the final dose," says Glamfury.

Ajaunta gets up and walks into the kitchen. She walks up the stairs into Rain's bedroom where the light still shines. She sits next to Rain.

"I am sorry, Rain. I am so sorry," she says.

Ajaunta sticks the needle into Rain's arm and injects the fluid. She steps back, looking at Rain. Glamfury is standing behind Ajaunta, and he grabs her shoulders with his hands. He turns her and kisses her. Ajaunta falls weak from the kiss. Her arms fall to her sides, and the syringe falls to the floor.

Ajaunta opens her eyes to see she is wearing a beautiful silk dress that fits her body perfectly. It has obviously been professionally tailored to fit her. She loves the way it fits, snug to her body, and flexes as moves. She loves the way every man in the ballroom watches her move, sway, and dance alone on the hardwood floor. Her dress shows her every curve and is cut short just above her knees to give the right amount of provocativeness as she bends and sways. The music is her favorite, created just for her, and the music gets more intense as she comes to a halt in the center of the floor. She smiles looking at the crowd and comes to a motionless pose in the center of the room. She turns her head to the side with a seductive smile and reaches her left arm out to her companion.

Glamfury, dressed in a perfectly fitting black tuxedo, moves gracefully across the floor, reaching out, grabbing hold of Ajaunta's hand. The two of them move gracefully like professional dancers, creating moves and physical rhythms to fit and flow with the music created just for the two of them. The crowd applauds as Glamfury pulls Ajaunta to him, and she twirls in his arm until tight with him and then thrust back to arm's length. She falls, nearly hitting the floor with her face, only to be swept up back into the tight hold of her companion in exhilarating moves that hush the crowd. The crowd cheers when the two of them complete and execute moves that have been choreographed to perfection. Glamfury twirls on a dime while holding Ajaunta's hand, and she falls to the ground, sweeping it with her hair and her dress, just barely avoiding the floor with her flesh. Ajaunta smiles, loving the air flowing through her hair. She loves the speed at which she is twirled and hauled with no fear at all her companion will lose his grip or let her hit the floor. Glamfury pulls her to him tight after the last drop to the ground. He holds her with his right arm around her waist, and the two look deep into each other's eyes. The crowd can see the attraction between the well-conditioned dancers and cheer their passion. Glamfury puts his left hand on Ajaunta's face, pushing her back toward the floor. Ajaunta is so flexible she bends at her waist backward as Glamfury runs his left hand down her neck, between her breasts, and down her abdomen until her hair touches the floor and then pulls her back flush to his chest. The two smile, feeding on the applause of the crowd.

The music changes, gaining a more up-tempo beat. The dancers stomp their feet with the beat of the drum and step back from each other. The crowd applauds and cheers as the dancers clap and move with the beat. They approach each other and fight with each other in a perfectly timed routine. They appear to punch, slap, kick, and knee each other so perfectly that the audience thinks they are beating each other up. This is actually a perfectly executed dance routine that lasts for two minutes, and the two dancers end arm in arm with Ajaunta leaning backward while Glamfury holds her around her back. Ajaunta extends her left arm and lowers it until the arch of her back and her arm extend in a straight line until her fingers touch the ground. Ajaunta smiles big, and the crowd cheers and applauds with enthusiasm. The dancers perform their routine to perfection.

The men love the way Ajaunta's dress fits her perfectly, showing off her every muscle, her every nook and curve. The women love the way

Glamfury moves and sways, the way his tuxedo flexes and moves on his muscular body. The women love the way Glamfury controls Ajaunta's every movement while holding her hand and swaying her body with his arms. The crowd loves these two and gives a standing ovation as Ajaunta raises back up to Glamfury's side and the two of them stand side by side and bow. Ajaunta notices the crowd slows down like the applause is happening in slow motion. She hears the sounds of the crowd slow as well.

"What is it? What is happening?" she asks.

"Oh, no, it is as I feared. They know this is our last dance, and they want blood," says Glamfury.

"They? Who are they?" asks Ajaunta.

"Not *who—what*," says Glamfury.

Ajaunta watches as the crowd surrounding them starts to lose their smiles. The clothing starts to rip and fall from their bodies. Their flesh starts to rip, and blood starts to flow from them. They all turn red from blood, and devilish horns grow from their heads. Sharp claws start to grow from their fingertips, and they start to growl.

"I'm scared. What are we going to do?" cries Ajaunta.

"Follow me," says Glamfury.

He runs right at the crowd of hungry demons, holding Ajaunta's hand. She runs behind him, and he clears a path right through the demons, pushing them back as he holds out his hand and creates and invisible barrier, clearing a path to the door. He opens the door, and the two of them run through the door, closing it behind them. He slams the door shut, and Ajaunta laughs like they just came to the end of a fantastic ride.

Glamfury turns to Ajaunta and pulls her flush to his body. He kisses her passionately, and she loves the affectionate kiss. They kiss long and hard. Ajaunta is overtaken with passion. Her body burns with desire as Glamfury pushes her from him. She smiles, pushing the straps of her dress to the sides of her shoulders, and it falls to her swollen breasts. She smiles, raising her arms up as high as she can, and turns with her back to Glamfury. He walks up behind her, reaching his arms around her, rubbing the front of her body. She smiles as he slides the dress down her body until it falls to the ground. She steps over it in her shiny blue high-heeled shoes, and Glamfury unhooks her bra, which falls to the ground, and she steps over it as well. She turns to face Glamfury and hugs him. He kisses her again and moves her backward into the kitchen.

Ajaunta is so caught up in passion she has not realized she and Glamfury have walked through the doors of the ballroom right into the living room of Rain's house. Glamfury now moves her into the kitchen and leans her back on the kitchen table. Ajaunta smiles as he pulls the last of her clothing form her hips and starts to undress himself. Ajaunta watches as he removes his tuxedo. Her smile is automatic as he enters her excited body. Ajaunta smiles, laying her left arm over her breasts and laying her right arm above her head on the table. Glamfury gets a good hold of her legs and thrusts into Ajaunta, making the whole kitchen table sway back and forth on the kitchen floor. The heat of their passion gets hotter. The rhythm of their love speeds up. Ajaunta breathes heavily, ready to climax with her lover, when Glamfury slams his fists on the table on either side of Ajaunta's head. He pounds the table hard, making a very loud thud, holding his fists on the table. He is now face-to-face with Ajaunta, and she opens her eyes.

"What? Where am I? How did I get here? This is real. You are in me for real. This can't be happening. Get off me. Get out of me. Get away from me!" cries Ajaunta.

"Yes, my dear. This is happening. You have been absolutely crucial in my scheme to gain youth. It is true that Rain will most likely be my greatest conquest of youth of all time, and because of you, he is all primed and ready. You, on the other hand, your part is done. You, my sweet Ajaunta, will never cheat on your spouse ever again," says Glamfury.

Glamfury stands with his erection still in Ajaunta. He laughs and starts to pump her. She has not the energy to fight back, and Glamfury laughs louder and louder, getting closer to his climax. He pumps faster and harder on Ajaunta, who is screaming and crying. She can feel he is nearing his climax. She cannot help the way her body responds, climaxing herself. Her mind is crying in anguish while her body bathes in pleasure. She feels Glamfury get larger and explode inside of her. He grinds their loins together harder and harder, causing great friction that starts to become very uncomfortable for Ajaunta.

"OK, you are done. Stop. Stop. That hurts!" cries Ajaunta.

Glamfury laughs, releasing her legs with his hands. Ajaunta tries to pull away from him, but she cannot. It is like they have been glued together. She starts to panic, putting her feet on his chest, trying to break the seal on their loins, but Glamfury laughs. He holds his arms up in the air. Ajaunta starts to feel pain in her abdomen.

"What? What are you doing? Stop. Stop. That hurts!" cries Ajaunta.

"The time has come, my lord. Take this soul as an offering of my continued service to you and your needs. Let the youth of this fine young woman strengthen me, and may her soul help power your everlasting kingdom," says Glamfury.

His words reverberate as if spoken through loud speakers. Ajaunta cries as the pain in her abdomen starts to get very painful. The walls of the kitchen pull away like huge chains have pulled them back. The ceiling pulls up and away out of sight. The floor pulls away, and Ajaunta is suddenly swept with a noxious hot air. She is on a huge boulder, reminding her of the boulder behind the cabin where sacrifices were made. Looking around, she can tell, or at least it seems like, she is in hell. This frightens her terribly, and she panics. She pushes, kicks, screams, cries, and tries as hard as she can to break from Glamfury, but she cannot break the hold on their loins. It is like they are one, like her skin is somehow now joined with Glamfury's skin. She looks down to see the skin around her crotch pull with Glamfury's skin as she tries to break free, like they are one, and the harder she tries to pull away, the more painful it is, like her skin is being torn from her body. She can feel Glamfury moving around inside of her, and he is still getting larger.

"No. No. No. What is this?" she cries.

"Look around you, my child. What do you think this is?" says Glamfury.

She looks around, seeing boiling lava all around. The sky is lined with yellow lightning, and the heat nearly scalds her skin. Glamfury holds his arms up high toward the hellish sky. He laughs and smiles.

"My lord. Come take your soul, my lord," says Glamfury.

Glamfury laughs loudly as the hell wind whips through his hair. Ajaunta feels pain in her abdomen that gets worse and worse until she screams in pain. Ajaunta's abdomen sucks in like Glamfury's penis is a large syringe, and it is sucking her insides into Glamfury. Ajaunta looks down to see her stomach suck down to her spine. Her eyes widen and go white. She screams as Glamfury laughs and moves around inside of her. Ajaunta can see the penis of Glamfury move in her stomach, and it acts like a hose sucking all the insides out of her. Her insides are sucked into Glamfury, and she goes numb. Ajaunta is still conscious, but as her digestive tract and major organs are sucked from her inner cavity and into Glamfury, she goes into a state of severe shock. She can breathe for a few more moments as she watches the life-stealing penis move under her skin. She looks up with her dying eyes to see Glamfury revel in the successful stealing of her youth. Glamfury's penis moves up under her ribs and sucks the lungs from her body. Now the only vital organ in Ajaunta's body is her brain. She looks down to see the horror of her body collapsed and filled with the penis of Glamfury. She cannot breathe; nor can she feel a thing. She will pass within a minute, but before she passes, she looks up to see the ruler of hell rise from the lava.

Lucifer towers above her and Glamfury. She cannot move or say a thing as the ruler of hell puts his massive hands to either side of her head. He points his index fingers toward her and sticks the sharp pointy tips into her ears. The sharp tips of his fingers just pierce her eardrums, and then they start to expand. Ajaunta no longer feels pain; nor does she know her skull is cracking as Lucifer's fingers expand. Her skull cracks from her ears to her jaw, and her face lifts like the lid of a Rolodex. Lucifer runs the tips of his right-hand fingers and thumb over her brain. Lucifer's fingers and thumb grab what seems to be just her brain, but he actually grabs hold of her soul before it makes its ascent into heaven, which has just been stopped.

Lucifer pulls his hand away, pulling Ajaunta's soul from within her body. It is the same shape as her body, but it looks like smoke—smoke that holds its form. Lucifer whips her soul like a wet washcloth, whipping her up and down. Ajaunta's soul screams as Lucifer and Glamfury laugh. Lucifer holds Ajaunta's soul over his mouth and puts her in feetfirst, chewing and devouring her until she is gone. Lucifer laughs and uses his index finger like a scalpel to cut the flesh now joining Ajaunta and Glamfury at their loins. Lucifer grabs hold of Ajaunta's corpse by her head and raises her above his mouth. He puts her in feetfirst, chewing and devouring her. This time, you can hear her bones crunch. Lucifer devours her body in no time and laughs as he descends back into the hell lava.

Glamfury stands on the boulder, nude, with his arms raised in the air. The yellow lightning starts to shoot into him. He grows younger and stronger. His muscles bulge with virility. His eyes whiten, as do his teeth. The yellow lightning in the sky acts like ropes that whip him and grab hold of him. They fling him high into the air toward the outer atmosphere of hell. Glamfury screams in joy as he is flung high and fast. He passes from the hell dimension into Rain's living room. He flips onto the couch, where he sits fully clothed. He is calm, relaxed, and a few years younger.

Chapter 39

Manipulating Dreams

Glamfury gets up from the couch and walks upstairs. He walks into Rain's bedroom and reaches his right hand into the pocket of his unique trench coat. He pulls his hand, and it is full of a very fine purple-colored powder. He grabs hold of Rain's shoulder, pulling him to his back. Rain is starting to wake from his chemically controlled sleep, which has had him asleep for a month now. There was a few breaks where Rain actually woke from his sleep and was not quickly put back into sleep by Ajaunta. Ajaunta has been with Rain for longer than a month now, and both of them have been controlled and tricked by Glamfury the whole time, which is true for Smoke, Bailey, and Marlene as well. Glamfury has used Ajaunta to weaken and break Rain's mind.

It is possible for Glamfury to steal the youth of women who sleep with him even though they are in a dream, but for men, they must beg Glamfury to kill them. They must beg and plead with Glamfury to give their soul to Lucifer, or Glamfury cannot steal their youth. Once Glamfury steals their youth, Lucifer takes their soul, and they become children of hell forever. You would think this an impossible feat, but that is why Glamfury tortures and kills his victims in their dreams. He wears down and breaks the minds of his victims until they beg and plead with him.

Rain is by far the most stubborn, hardheaded individual Glamfury has run into in all seven hundred of his years on earth as Glamfury. Rain will grant Glamfury a glut of youth if Glamfury can get Rain to beg and plead. Glamfury is able to see into the dreams of his victims.

He is able to enter these dreams, and once the victims are in the dream, they act as they would as if they were living the dream in the real world. Glamfury is able to manipulate the dreams, adding and changing images. This is how Glamfury is able to find persons very close to his intended target and use those persons against his intended victims. This is how Glamfury gets new victims to steal youth from as well. Unfortunately, it was Rain whom Glamfury was after the whole time, but Rain is so resistant that Glamfury needed to gain youth. Ajaunta has been taken to hell for real, and now Glamfury is using that vision of what has happened to Ajaunta. He is using that vision and manipulating it against Rain, Smoke, and Bailey in the form of a dream right now. This is how Glamfury manipulates his victims without the victims knowing how or why.

Glamfury waves his right hand over Rain's head and pulls it back quickly. The purple powder floats like a cloud and gently, slowly settles through the air toward Rain's face. When Rain breathes in, the powder is drawn into his nostrils. The last vial of lavender-colored fluid is actually a love potion that Glamfury had Ajaunta administer to Rain, and it is causing him to slowly wake. Glamfury intended for this to happen, and as Rain is now starting to wake, Glamfury starts to work the final stages of his plan to steal youth from his most determined victim yet. Glamfury puts his hands on Rain's shoulders and shakes him a little. Rain opens his eyes, seeing Glamfury above him with his eyes closed. His hands are on Rain's shoulders, and instinctively, Rain breathes deeply, opening his mouth, sucking the rest of the purple powder into his lungs. This acts as a sedative washing Rain back to sleep as Glamfury starts to speak to him.

"Your trusted and best friend of a lifetime Smoke has rushed to get you. He has told you your enemy Glamfury has taken your lifelong love Ajaunta and he plans to sacrifice her to the horrors of hell. Smoke has taken you to the gates of hell where the two of you have been once before, and through these gates is Ajaunta being held by Glamfury. You must get in there and rescue her, or she will be sacrificed to hell, where she will be tortured forever. Ha, ha, ha, ha. Ha, ha, ha, ha. Ha, ha, ha, ha," laughs Glamfury.

Glamfury pulls his hands from Rain's shoulders. He gets up and walks toward the doorway leading out of the bedroom. Glamfury turns to Rain, who sleeps.

"Time to bring youth for my aging body. You are strong, Rain, but your friends are not as resistant, and soon they will add to my longevity. You keep holding out once your loves and best friends are gone. What need will you have to resist me? Ha, ha, ha, ha. Ha, ha, ha, ha. Ha, ha, ha, ha," laughs Glamfury as he walks out of the bedroom.

Rain wakes up. Smoke is shaking him by his shoulders.

"Rain, I know you are going to hate me, but we have to go back. We have to go back into the cave. We have to go back to the gates of hell. It's Glamfury. He has Bailey, and he has Ajaunta. We have to get in there, or he is going to sacrifice them," says Smoke.

Smoke puts Rain's rifle on his chest and heads through the jungle toward the cave.

"Come on, Rain. Come on." Smoke's voice echoes as he disappears in the jungle.

"What the fuck, Smoke? What the fuck are you talking about?" says Rain.

Rain gets up. He is in his military gear, and he recognizes the jungle. He walks in the direction Smoke has gone and finds Smoke bent down next to a tree. Rain bends down, and the two of them look at the entrance to the cave.

"Smoke, this is the cave we went in, and it lead us to the gates of hell," says Rain.

"I know," says Smoke.

"This is where we killed Glamfury. Remember I stabbed him with the soul knife and he was blown into hell? This is where Wicks and Smoulder lost their lives. Why would we go back there?" asks Rain.

"Glamfury did not die. He has Bailey and Ajaunta, and they are in there. They are at the gates of hell," says Smoke.

Rain feels a pounding in his head. He lowers his head, rubbing his forehead, and he has visions. He sees Ajaunta falling toward the lava, and Glamfury is there, laughing. Glamfury is laughing and looking right at Rain, taunting him with words of how he is going to torture and kill Ajaunta.

"Smoke, I don't know how, but you are right. We have no time to waste. Glamfury has Ajaunta, and he is going to kill her. They are at the gates of hell, or maybe they are in hell already. I don't know, but we have no time to waste. We have to get in there. Come on," says Rain.

Rain gets up and runs into the cave. Smoke runs behind Rain, and the two of them run right to the trapdoor leading to the lower part of the cave. They descend and follow the cave to the place where they were blown into the wall, but there is no doorway—no way for them to descend to the gates of hell, at least not that they can see.

"Smoke, this is it. This is where Glamfury had Smoulder, and we were all blown into the wall, landing near the gates of hell," says Rain.

"I know, but where is the hole in the wall?" says Smoke.

The two of them feel the earth wall, looking for a doorway, but they find nothing. That matters not as a massive gust of wind like before blows in, and the two of them are sucked into the wall, which seems to vanish, and they fall landing on metal gates. They can see through the metal gates below them, and they can see Glamfury has Ajaunta on a large boulder. The boulder is on a very large granite slab, and there is Bailey chained to a granite wall, which rises up from the large slab of granite. All around the granite is flowing molten lava and very hot gusts of hell wind blowing and creating very loud noise.

"He has Ajaunta. Come on, we have to get down there. Come on!" yells Rain.

"Bailey is down there too!" yells Smoke.

The two of them run to the gates of hell, which are open, and they look down to see Ajaunta, Bailey, and Glamfury are a long way down.

"How are we going to get down there?" says Smoke.

"I don't know. I guess we are going to jump," says Rain.

"We are going to what?" says Smoke.

"Jump," says Rain.

Rain jumps. Smoke watches as Rain seems to float down toward the granite rock. Smoke takes a deep breath and jumps. They both float like they are birds with their arms and legs held out. They don't know how, but it works, and they both fall down to the granite rock, which is much larger when they get down there. Smoke walks up to Bailey and tries to unshackle her, but she is chained very tight, and he cannot break the chains. Rain walks toward the boulder, and Glamfury halts his advance. Glamfury pulls the soul knife and puts it to Ajaunta's throat. Ajaunta's wrists and ankles are tied with a thin strong rope that reaches over the sides of the granite slab they are all on. Rain cannot see where or what they are attached to, but Ajaunta's limbs are pulled tight, and she is held snug to the boulder on her back with no way to get loose.

"Take another step and I will cut her throat. Drop the gun," says Glamfury.

Rain relaxes his arms, lowering his gun.

"Let her go, Glamfury. I am the one you want. Let her go," says Rain.

"Beg me to kill you. Beg me to send your soul to Lucifer and I will let her go," says Glamfury.

"I will never beg you. I will never succumb to servants of hell. Why don't you take me on man on man?" says Rain.

"I believe you think you will never beg, and I have whipped your ass how many times now? You are no match for me. Now it's time to make you a believer. You will not beg me, so I will take your love, and this time, it is for real," says Glamfury.

Glamfury raises his right arm and swings, stabbing the soul knife right through Ajaunta's sternum.

"No!" yells Rain.

Rain and Smoke run toward Glamfury, raising their guns, but Glamfury waves his hand, and both men are stopped almost dead in their tracks, moving in superslow motion. Glamfury rips the soul knife through the center of Ajaunta's rib cage. She screams in pain. Glamfury puts his fingers in between her ribs and rips the left and right side of her rib cage from her body, flinging each side over the side of the granite slab into the molten lava of hell. Glamfury laughs.

"Come, my lord, show these three this is for real. They do not have to beg me to kill them, and the longer they hold out, the more of their loved ones will be sworn into the torture of hell forever," laughs Glamfury.

Rain and Smoke watch as Lucifer rises from the lava. He is absolutely titanic in size and looks exactly like what they thought he would look like. They watch as Lucifer splits Ajaunta's head and rubs his pointed fingers and thumb over her brain and apparently pulls her soul from within her body. They watch as Lucifer whips her soul like a washcloth and eats it. Then he eats her body and sinks back into the hell lava. They watch as Glamfury grows younger right in front of them. Glamfury laughs and waves his hand. Rain and Smoke fall to the ground, and they are breathing heavily like they have been working very hard. They were trying very hard to break free from the slow motion they were in. They stand and point their weapons at Glamfury.

"Now, boys, put your weapons down, or I will just wave my hand again," says Glamfury.

Rain and Smoke both stand at ease, lowering their weapons. They move back toward Bailey, trying their best to protect her.

"Was that for real? He cannot kill us in the dreamworld, right? We are in the dreamworld, right? This can't be real?" cries Bailey.

"I don't know. I don't know if we are in the dreamworld or the real world. This is the first time I saw Glamfury grow young before us. This has to be a dream, right, Rain?" says Smoke.

"We have to be in the dreamworld and none of this is real. He is playing with us, trying to get us to follow his wishes. Do not do what he asks. Do not give in to his demands," says Rain.

"How do we get out of here? This is not like before where we run to the place where we fell in," says Smoke.

"Maybe it is. Maybe it is just like that. Shoot the chains on Bailey's wrists," says Rain.

"What?" says Smoke.

"Come on, shoot the chains on Bailey's wrists," says Rain.

Rain points his gun at Bailey's right wrist, and Smoke follows suit on her left. They shoot, and Bailey is freed from her shackles.

"Now what? What are we supposed to do now?" says Smoke.

"This has to be just like it was before. It just looks a little different. Come on, grab Bailey by her hand and come with me," says Rain.

The three of them hold hands and walk to the side of the granite where they landed. Sure enough, just like before, they are sucked upward and blown back into the cave from where they fell into hell.

"Come on, time to get the fuck out of here," says Rain.

The three of them run out of the cave. They hear Glamfury's voice echo loud through the cave.

"You cannot escape me. You cannot escape. I will find you. I will hunt you. I will eat you all," says Glamfury.

The three of them are running into the forest, and Bailey is crying. She stops and bends over, breathing heavily. Rain and Smoke walk back to her.

"Come on, Bailey, we have to keep moving," says Smoke.

"Keep moving where? Where are we going? Where are we? Why should we keep moving? He just finds us no matter where we go. There is no getting away from him," says Bailey.

"I think I have to agree with you. You are right. Where are we going? I don't know. What are we doing? We keep running, and he keeps catching us. I just keep waking up from one nightmare to be trapped in another nightmare. I escape one nightmare to be thrown into another nightmare. What the fuck are we going to do? We can't kill him. We can't beat him. What are we going to do?" says Smoke.

"I swear I have seen you all die many times. I swear he has killed me over and over but this last time. Him killing Ajaunta just now seemed to have real closure to it. It seemed much more real than before," says Bailey.

"Yeah, the way the devil came up and stole her soul from her body like that, I think it was real for real. What do you think, Rain? I think we are in the dreamworld right now, but I think we always were. I think he is just toying with us, and now he is coming for us for real. There is nothing we can do. Why even try to fight him? I thought he could not kill us in the dreamworld, but now I think he can. We are doomed," says Smoke.

"We have to keep fighting. We have to keep thinking. I don't know what to do, but I know I will not give up. I will not give in to the will of some servant of hell," says Rain.

"So what are we going to do? Seems like we have tried everything. Seems like we never even finish any of the things we start because we are always thrown in a different direction," says Smoke.

"I don't know, Smoke, but we have to try. We have to try until it's over one way or the other. Yeah, he may kill us. He may very well kill me, but it will not be without a fight. We are here, and whether we are in the dreamworld or the real world, he is there, he is here, he is real. There has to be a way to defeat him, and we have to figure it out. No one is going to do it for us, so we have to figure it out. There is no fighting chance in despair. There is no survival for the disheartened. We need to stick together. We need to face our fear. We need to face the demon that Glamfury is. We need to figure out what his weakness is and exploit it. We have to," says Rain.

"I am all for living. I am all for putting down evil, but we are just going to wake somewhere else. We are just going to start some sort of hell somewhere else. I don't even know how to give in because I am always starting over. What we need to figure out is how to know when and where we are. We need to know the end of one traumatic situation is coming to an end so we can be prepared to face this demon in the beginning of our next traumatic situation. I think he is so far ahead of us that he knows we are starting to catch on. We are starting to figure out how to fight him, and now he is killing us for real," says Bailey.

They look at each other, quietly thinking.

Chapter 40

Pulled Apart

Bailey looks around. She is looking very concerned like she is in deep thought.

"What is it? What has you so concerned?" says Smoke.

"This is already very different from all my other dreams, if in fact they are all dreams," says Bailey.

"What do you mean?" says Smoke.

"Well, in my dreams before, where you and Rain are in my dreams with me, we are usually in your house or your bedroom. This is the first time we are in a jungle. That is very different. We always end up having sex or falling asleep on the couch like when Rain and Ajaunta were with us. I always wake up starting a new cycle of seduction from Glamfury. I am usually at a party dressed to the nines. We are eating great foods, and then Glamfury takes me to the dance floor, and it always happens like that. It is always a different time period, and the dance always fits that time period, but I cannot resist. He is always dressed so handsome, and he sweeps me off my feet during and after the dance when he takes me to some bedroom where he makes love with me. This is very different because I feel like I am awake and I am with you two. This is very nerve racking because I can feel something is different, and it is scaring the hell out of me," says Bailey.

"Yeah, I usually wake to some sort of new hell, and it seems like we are stranded in real time, doesn't it?" says Rain.

"Yeah, it does," says Smoke.

The three of them look around, confused.

"I can't tell if we are in the real world. I have to believe we are in a dreamworld because we were just at the gates of hell, and we actually saw the devil himself. The devil took Ajaunta's soul and then ate her body. We have to be dreaming," says Rain.

"Then we are about to experience some sort of torture," says Smoke.

"Like I said, I don't like this because this is not how my dreams start. I'm scared, guys," says Bailey.

"Don't worry, we are right here," says Smoke.

"I remember this mission. This is where we rendezvous on the Bliaston River. Colonel Sanbers is waiting for us," says Rain.

"Yup, that's right. I remember too. Let's get to the Bliaston River. It is this way. Come on, let's go," says Smoke.

Smoke and Rain head on through the jungle. Bailey walks behind them, but there is a problem. She walks, but the ground moves like a treadmill. She walks faster and starts to run, but it matters not; she does not go anywhere. She starts to panic and screams for Rain and Smoke, but they do not hear her. She screams and yells; she runs as fast as she can. It seems like everything around her is moving in slow motion except the ground she is standing on, which moves like a treadmill, and she cannot get off it. She can see flies flying so slow she can see their wings moving. She sees a snake moving toward her, but she moves much faster than it, and she grabs it by the tail and throws it away from her. She calls to Rain and Smoke, and they finally turn to see Bailey is not following them. They start to walk toward her, and they are moving so slow. Bailey calls to them, and she can hear them talking, but she cannot make out their words. They seem to move faster and faster as they get closer to her, and time seems to catch up as they get closer to her.

"Bailey, what's the matter? Come on, let's get out of here," says Smoke.

"I can't. The ground under my feet moves like a treadmill, and I cannot go anywhere. See, watch," says Bailey.

She starts to walk toward them, and everything seems fine. She walks right to them.

"You guys, I am telling you something is going on. I don't like this. Just a minute ago, I could not go anywhere," says Bailey.

"Well, come on, all is good now. Take my hand. We are getting out of here," says Smoke.

Smoke reaches out to take Bailey's hand, and just as he is about to grab hold of her hand, she is pulled by her ankles. Vines have wrapped around her ankles and pull very fast. Bailey falls flat on her face. She falls with her arms at her sides, and she is startled and stunned. Her lips are bloodied, and before she can get up, the vines pull her across the jungle floor. Smoke and Rain run behind her, trying to catch her. The vines pull her just fast enough to keep her out of the reach of Smoke and Rain. This is quickly becoming a serious problem for Bailey, who is being cut, scraped, and jostled along the jungle floor. She is quickly experiencing a lot of pain. She is constantly having the wind knocked out of her as she is dragged over logs and uneven slopes of the ground. She is starting to be bitten by insects that are suddenly all over her body. The shrubs start to become more like prickers that are cutting into her skin. The blades of grass seem to have razor-sharp edges, and she is suddenly bleeding all over her body. Her clothes are starting to cut and shred, and she is now screaming in pain as the entire front portion of her body is full of very painful cuts.

No matter how fast Smoke and Rain run, they cannot catch her, and finally, the vines let go of her. She comes to a stop, lying on her stomach. Smoke and Rain catch up to her. They sit her up, using their shirts to brush off the insects and bugs that are all over her. They do their best to comfort and calm her. Her clothes are tattered, and she is bleeding all over. She is crying and nearly in a state of shock. She is responsive but in a bad way. She needs to get to the ship quickly where her wounds can be cleaned and she can be bandaged.

"We have to get her to the ship," says Smoke.

"I know, I know. Come on, let's help her to her feet and move her as quickly to the ship as we can," says Rain.

Rain lifts Bailey by her right arm, and Smoke lifts her by her left arm. They stand supporting her and start to move through the jungle.

"Stop. Stop. This is not right. Can't you feel it? Can't you feel this is the end? He is here. He is here somewhere, I can feel it," says Bailey.

Rain and Smoke keep moving through the jungle, supporting Bailey.

"What do you mean this is the end? What do you mean you can feel him? What are you talking about?" says Smoke.

"Him, Glamfury he is here. Can't you sense him? This is different than all my dreams. This is a whole lot different. He is here, and he is here to kill me. In my dreams, he always made love with me after he seduced me. Now I can tell he is here, but this is not a dream—this is real. I don't know how I know, I just do. I guess because of all the pain I am in. I guess because my body is a mess. I am all cut and bleeding. He would not want to make love with me like this." Bailey starts to cry. "I thought he was always going to make love with me. I did not know why I did not know he wanted to kill me like he did Ajaunta. He is here to kill me!" Bailey cries.

"Don't worry, we are not going to let him get anywhere near you. No matter what he says, no matter how bad he tortures you, don't beg him to kill you. He has killed me more times than I can count, but it is only real if you beg him to kill you," says Smoke.

"Beg him to kill me? What are you talking about?" says Bailey.

"Doesn't he always tell or ask you to beg him to kill you? That way, he gets to steal your youth and your soul goes to Satan," says Rain.

"No, he has never said that to me. He has said he would kill you (Smoke) if I resisted having sex with him. I tried to resist him. I tried so hard, but he always got me to make love with him. I thought I was protecting you, Smoke. I am so sorry I was leading him to you. I was helping him find weakness in you that he could use against you. I am sorry. I now know he is here to kill me," says Bailey.

Bailey cries.

"He's here, he's here!" she cries.

Rain and Smoke look around and notice the loose debris on the ground start to rise up into the air.

"Come on, Rain, let's get her out of here," says Smoke.

"Yeah, I second that," says Rain.

Rain and Smoke still have Bailey's arms over their shoulders, and they start to move quickly through the woods. It starts to get harder and harder for them to move like there is a very strong wind blowing in their face, but there is no wind. They are leaning forward and stepping high like there is over a foot of snow on the ground, but there is no snow. They are acting just as they would as if it was very cold with a strong wind and a lot of snow on the ground. They all have their heads facing downward and leaning forward as they try to move.

"What the hell is going on? There is no wind or snow. What the hell?" yells Rain.

"I don't know what the fuck is going on. We have to keep moving forward!" yells Smoke.

"He is here!" yells Bailey.

They all hear the laughter of Glamfury echo through the woods. It gets louder and louder, but there is no sign of him. The feeling of strong wind and deep snow goes away, and the debris that are floating in the air fall to the ground. The grass on the ground starts to grow very fast. It grows upward, wrapping around Bailey's legs.

"What the hell? What is going on? It's growing around me. It's going to kill me!" cries Bailey.

"No, it's not," says Smoke.

Smoke bends down and tries to pull the grass from her legs. He pulls, breaking the grass, but more and more grow up and faster, replacing the grass that Smoke has ripped from her. Rain bends down and starts to help remove the grass from her. The tree branches above them that no one is paying attention to start to grow very fast. They grow thicker and denser. They start to swing back and forth, but Rain and Smoke are concentrating on getting the grass off Bailey. No matter how fast they break the grass, it grows back, keeping her constantly in its grip. Rain and Smoke are getting severe cuts on their hands from the grass, which is dangerously sharp. The tree branches start swinging at Rain and Smoke, trying to get them away from Bailey.

"What the fuck? Are you kidding me? The trees are swinging at us," says Smoke.

The branches are still growing larger, and one behind Rain grows down and wraps around him. It swings, throwing him high and far away. A branch behind Smoke swings down, forming a sort of bat, which hits Smoke and sends him flying through the air. Bailey screams as the grass grows very fast, circling around her body. The grass grows thick about an inch and a half in width, and the sides are razor sharp. Bailey starts to scream and cry in pain as the grass growing up her body cuts her all over like razor blades being drawn over her skin. The grass grows up her body on the inside of her clothing and outside of her clothing. Bailey starts to run, but like before, the ground acts like a treadmill, and she goes nowhere no matter how fast she runs, no matter how hard she jumps. She cries and screams as the grass covers more and more of her body. The tree branches that have grown very thick and long swing at her, hitting her like a piñata. They hit her harder and harder. She is thrown into the air, but the grass around her pulls her back to the ground, where she is struck again and again. The branches are whipping her, causing large welts to grow all over her body. The leaves on the branches are sharp like the grass and cause larger, deeper wounds on her body, and blood is splattered as she is struck over and over.

Rain and Smoke have run back to help her, but they cannot move closer than fifteen feet from her, or the branches swing down at them, sending them flying back. Smoke gets as close to Bailey as he can after being thrown back three times now. He gets as close as he can get without having the branches swing at him. Rain runs up next to him after experiencing the same dilemma. They watch as Bailey is covered in the grass. She is being struck over and over, flying up, only to be pulled back to the ground to be struck again. She is crying and bleeding, and both Rain and Smoke are splattered with her blood.

"Stop this. Stop this, you motherfucker. You sick motherfucker!" yells Smoke.

The laughter of Glamfury echoes through the woods. Glamfury rises from the earth, laughing. He walks up to Bailey, raising his hands toward the branches striking her, and the branches halt. The grass descends down her body, releasing her from its grip. Glamfury puts his hands on Bailey and turns her, facing Rain and Smoke. Rain and Smoke gasp seeing what has happened to her. Her clothing is soaked in her blood. Her arms, face, and neck, and her chest and legs have all been cut. Her flesh is swollen all over, and she is in a state of shock. The skin and flesh all over her body is sliced and gouged, causing even hardened veterans of violence to gasp and cover their mouths.

"You sick motherfucker. I will kill you. I will kill you!" yells Smoke.

Smoke runs toward Glamfury. Glamfury waves his hand, and Smoke is thrown back in the air and lands at Rain's feet. Rain helps him up. Glamfury stands with his right arm over Bailey. She is a disgusting bloody mess. Her face is torn ripped and swollen, and Glamfury licks her cheek, showing off the blood on his tongue to Rain and Smoke.

"You two are very resistant. I told both of you that you would be mine, but you resist. You think you can just keep holding off and I will go away. I will not, and I will have all your loved ones if you keep resisting me. Ajaunta is now mine, and soon Bailey will be mine, and there is nothing you can do about it. So I appreciate all the loved ones you send my way. Just keep resisting me, and I will keep young on the youth of your loved ones. Watch as Bailey becomes mine," says Glamfury.

Glamfury steps back away from Bailey, leaving her standing there. She is in a daze, and blood drips from her fingers. Rain and Smoke see vines growing along the ground toward her. They reach her and wrap up her legs, pulling her to the ground. The vines wrap around her legs and her arms, pulling on her, rising her about four feet in the air. A lot of vines wrap and grow, making a bed below her, which she is rested on. Smoke yells and runs toward her, as does Rain, but the ground moves like a treadmill, and they can get no closer to her. The vines grow up her pant legs, cutting them and removing them. The same happens to her shirt. The vines then pull back all except for a few that wrap around her feet and a few that wrap around her shins. They start to pull, and Bailey starts to scream as her feet are pulled from her legs at the ankles. The vines then move to her thighs and shins, pulling until her knees are pulled apart.

Glamfury laughs, and Smoke falls to his knees, crying for his love. Bailey has passed out from the shock, and Glamfury puts his hand on her forehead, waking her up to the excruciating pain, and she cries more. Glamfury laughs. Rain and Smoke still try to run toward Bailey, but they cannot get any closer. The vines move to Bailey's thighs and around her waists and start to pull. Bailey looks down and can barely see through her swollen bloodied eyes. Rain and Smoke can hear Bailey's hips being pulled apart as her left leg pulls out of her hip. Again Bailey falls unconscious from the pain, and again Glamfury wakes her. Glamfury laughs as he waves his right arm over her dismembered body, and her left leg is ripped from her body. Glamfury laughs as Bailey screams in pain. Smoke cannot take any more. He is crying seeing his love being tortured like this.

"Stop. Stop, you freak from hell. You sick motherfucker!" cries Smoke.

"Stop? You want me to stop this? I could stop this. I could put her back together if someone were to take her place," says Glamfury.

"Take me. I will take her place. Let her go," says Smoke.

"Smoke. Smoke, don't do this. This is what he is trying to make you do. Don't give in to him," says Rain.

"Beg me to kill you. Beg for Lucifer to take your soul, and she will be set free," says Glamfury.

"I beg you to kill me. Glamfury, kill me. Take my youth. Send my soul to Lucifer," says Smoke.

"Smoke, no!" yells Rain.

Glamfury laughs. He stands at the head of Bailey, raising his arms in the air, laughing. The vines grow faster in greater numbers, wrapping around Bailey's body. Her arms are pulled from her shoulders. Her elbows are pulled apart, and her wrists are pulled from her forearms. Glamfury grows taller as the bed of vine slants upward, showing off Bailey's dismembered body. Rain and Smoke watch as Glamfury puts both his hands in Bailey's mouth and pulls it apart, almost ripping her jaw from her skull. Glamfury then puts a lip-lock on her bloody mouth and sucks in very hard. He sucks hard and nonstop. Rain and Smoke both watch as the ripped portions of her body pull back together and seem to fuse back together. Glamfury releases his lip-lock and looks up the air. He looks at Rain and Smoke and puts another lip-lock on her. He inhales deeply. Rain and Smoke watch as Bailey's body is sucked in like all her insides are being sucked into Glamfury's mouth.

"No!" cries Smoke.

Glamfury sucks for what seems an hour and pulls back from Bailey's imploded body. She is clearly dead. All her internal organs have been sucked into Glamfury's mouth and consumed. Rain and Smoke watch as Glamfury seems to get younger right in front of them. Glamfury laughs and sinks into the earth. Rain and Smoke try to approach Bailey, but still they cannot move any closer. The air turns red, and a very hot wind sweeps through the forest. The leaves and debris start to blow along the ground. The ground starts to shake. Rain and Smoke fall to the ground and are jostled around for a minute until the shaking stops. They get up, hearing a great noise coming from the earth. Lucifer rises from the ground at the head of Bailey. He looks just as titanic as he did the last time Rain and Smoke saw him. He puts his index fingers in Bailey's ears, and her skull pops along her jaw bone. Lucifer grabs hold of her upper jaw and pulls her skull, exposing her brain. Lucifer runs the fingers and thumb of his right hand over her brain and pulls what must be her soul from her body. He pulls her soul from her neck and holds it to the right. It looks like smoke in the outline of her body. Lucifer holds it above his mouth and drops it in like a sardine, eating it. He then lifts her body and drops it in his mouth the same way, only this time Rain and Smoke see and hear him chewing the bones and flesh. Lucifer chews and swallows all of Bailey and then sinks back into the earth. Smoke falls to his knees.

"I failed her. I could not save her!" cries Smoke.

Rain helps his friend to his feet.

"Come on, Smoke, let's get out of here. This is not real. None of this is real. We are going to wake up and find none of this is real," says Rain.

"He did it. He tricked me into begging him to kill me. He said he would take me and spare Bailey. He said he would let her go. He killed her. Now he is going to kill me," says Smoke.

"Come on, we need to get out of here," says Rain.

Chapter 41

The Burning

The rain starts to pour from the sky in the steamy jungle. Within seconds, everything is a wash. The warm water feels good on the sweaty bodies of Rain and Smoke, who find shelter under a large tree that has very large leaves. They are skilled in handling jungle life, and the two of them make a shelter under leaves and tree branches that keep them dry while the hot sun is blocked out and a deluge of rain water washes the forest. They are both still in military gear with their rifles leaning against the tree. Rain pulls some jerky from his backpack and chews in deep thought, looking at the ground.

"I know that look. What is it? What are you thinking?" asks Smoke.

"I was just thinking about Marlene. The last time I saw her, she was eaten by some sort of wild dogs. It was horrific, and I almost puked," says Rain.

"I thought nothing would make you puke," says Smoke.

"Yeah, me too. I have seen you, Ajaunta, Marlene, and Bailey die so many times now it almost seems like it is supposed to be. This guy comes to us in our dreams and wears us down. He tells us we have to beg him to kill us and we are sent to hell. We resist, and he tortures us and kills us over and over. I keep trying to relate him to any myth or legend, but nothing ever comes to mind. The only things I have to go on that may hurt, kill, or defeat him are the books we found and the soul knife, which have all been recollected by him. This guy, this Glamfury, I don't know how to fight him, but there has to be a way. Marlene told me to remember. Just before she was killed by those dogs, she told me to remember what I had seen and known in the dreamworld. I don't even know what is dream or real anymore. I don't know that we ever knew what was dream or real," says Rain.

"I remember you, Bailey, and Ajaunta sitting on my couch in my house, and we were planning how to fight this guy. We said we would all stick together. We thought we knew what was dreamworld and what was real world. Personally I think it's all dreamworld. One thing is for sure—the last death of Bailey just now. That seemed like it was real. All the deaths I have seen lately seemed real, but this last one feels like Bailey is not coming back. It feels like I have condemned myself to the will of this apparent servant of hell," says Smoke.

"I agree. The last death of Ajaunta seemed like there was real finality to it. It seemed like that was the last time I will see her. It must be that Lucifer was involved in the last two deaths. That's what really freaks me out. I mean, who actually sees the devil? I never even believed in heaven or hell. I guess this really is like you said. You said this is the dreamworld. It's all just one long dream, but still the last things Marlene said to me must have some bearing. It may be what we need to do to end this nightmare," says Rain.

"What was it?" says Smoke.

"She said to remember—remember what I had seen in my dreams," says Rain.

"Hmmm, remember," says Smoke.

"I just don't know what I am trying to remember. I only remember bits and pieces, you know," says Rain.

Smoke stands up. "Shit," he says.

Rain stands up. "What is it?" he asks.

"Glamfury. He is here. Now I know what Bailey was saying. I can feel him. I can sense him. Rain, he has come to kill me. I can't explain it. It's something inside me, something that is pulsing through my veins. I can hear him laugh like he is toying and playing with me. Rain, he is here," says Smoke.

The ground beneath them gives way and falls toward the depths of hell. It is a black hole. Rain quickly grabs the branches above them and hangs over the hole without falling in. Smoke grabs hold of the tree roots along the outer edge of the hole, which is only about four feet across. The rain is still pouring, and now the water is flowing in the hole.

"Hold on, Smoke. Hold on, I am working my way to you!" yells Rain.

Rain swings arm to arm down the branch until he can drop down to solid ground. He runs over to Smoke, who is holding on to the exposed tree roots, and now it's like floodwater rushing over his body into the hole. Smoke has to keep raising his head to breathe because the water is getting greater and greater, nearly covering his whole body as it runs into the hole. Rain kneels down near the hole and is almost swept in by the rushing water. He has to move back or fall in.

"Rain, Rain. Help. I can't hold on much longer. My hands keep slipping down the roots!" yells Smoke.

"Hold on, Smoke, I am coming!" yells Rain.

Rain crawls on his stomach to the hole and reaches for Smoke's hands. The water is rushing over both of them. Rain grabs Smoke's hands. Smoke grabs Rain's hands, but this proves futile as their hands are slippery, and Smoke falls into the hole with the running water.

"Smoke!" yells Rain.

Smoke falls out of sight, and the hole closes up. Rain rolls to his back, and just like that, the rain stops falling from the sky. Rain stands up and walks out of the canopy that he and Smoke had built. He looks to the sky and hears a sweeping noise in the air. Looking to his left, he sees a branch with a lot of leaves swinging right for him, and it hits him hard. Rain is thrown in the air and flies backward through daylight into moonlight and right into the side of Marlene's house on Bender Turn Road. The night is misty and cool, which is a huge shift in atmosphere compared to the hot humidity of the jungle he was just in. He stands with a shiver as he adjusts to the night. The moon is bright, and the clouds shine silver and blue. Rain steps back from the house, looking at it. "This has to be the doing of Marlene. She has to be trying to tell me something. What is it? She said remember. What is it I am supposed to remember? Marlene, help me," says Rain, talking out loud.

Rain walks up onto the porch, and it is not like when he used to go see Marlene and her parents when the house was well kept and comfortable. It is like when he and Smoke had gone there and it was abandoned for what seemed a century. Rain walks on the porch, and the wood breaks in places, and his feet almost fall through. He cautiously walks to the door and turns the doorknob, and the door opens inward with a very eerie screech as it opens. It is dark inside, and Rain slowly walks into the living room. Surprisingly, the moonlight shines in the windows, giving silvery shadows throughout the rooms of the house. Rain walks in, imagining he sees things that are not there. Ghosts and shadow monsters out of the corners of his eyes keep him on defense, and he keeps creeping himself out, looking from side to side. Rain reaches for his rifle, realizing it is still in the jungle. He walks through the living room to the bottom of the stairs and walks up to Marlene's room. He pushes the door, and again it opens inward with an eerie screech. The room is empty, and immediately, he is really creeped out remembering how Smoke had turned into some sort of devil last time Rain was in this room. He remembers seeing Marlene out the window, and she was eaten by that hell lizard in the front yard. Rain walks to the window and looks out. All seems quiet on this cool, misty moonlit night. Suddenly, the lights go on in the hallway. Rain looks out of the bedroom.

"Rain, Rain, run. It's a trap. Rain, get out. Get out of the house. It's a trap, and he is going to kill you. Rain, get out."

Rain knows Marlene's voice, and she is yelling as loud as she can. Her voice is coming from downstairs, and Rain runs downstairs to amazement. Not only is the downstairs lit up, but also the kitchen to the left and the living room to the right are now fully furnished, and all the lights are on. The house now looks like it did when Rain went to visit Marlene and her parents. Marlene is tied up in front of the fireplace, which has a raging fire burning in it. Her arms are tied to posts rising from the mantelpiece, and her back rests against the mantelpiece with her legs free, but she cannot go anywhere. Rain immediately runs to try and free her, but her legs are raised up, and the fire shoots from the fireplace like a flamethrower, engulfing Rain in flames. He is burning. He is screaming and swiping at his body with his arms. Immediate pain and panic engulf his body and senses. Rain drops and rolls, but the flames and fire cover his whole body. He grabs the long thick window curtains and pulls them from the windows. He rolls in them, which help smother the flames. It takes a few minutes, but Rain is able to extinguish the flames.

Marlene is crying. The tears are rolling down her face to see Rain burned. Rain gets out of the curtains, and all his clothing has been burned from his body. His hair is gone, all of it. His skin has all been burned off, and his flesh has seared his whole body over. Rain has thought he has felt the most excruciating and unimaginable pain a person could experience in this never-ending nightmare, but nothing compares to the kind of pain he is experiencing now. The air makes his body hurt. Where he touches the floor or anything is beyond pain that can be explained. Rain stands, and as he cries, the tears that fall down his face hurt like nothing he has ever felt. He looks at his body to see the most ugly, horrific sight he has ever seen in his life. His flesh looks like pulp held together with superglue. He stinks of burned meat mixed with shit. He cannot believe he is able to remain conscious. He cannot believe he can see, hear, or smell, but he can. He cries with no idea what to do. He is constantly overcome with pain and fear. Rain screams as yet more intense pain shoots from his shoulder and pulses throughout his entire body in streams of pain.

Glamfury laughs as he steps from Rain toward Marlene after slapping Rain on the shoulder a few times. Glamfury looks at his hand covered in Rain's blood and licks it from his palm. He holds his palms, facing Rain, and steam starts to rise from his hands.

"Ah, the warmth of fire. The burning sensation of flame. So wonderful, yes?" says Glamfury.

Glamfury's arms and face turn red like they are becoming very hot.

"How many times do I have to tell you, if you are going to kill me, then kill me. I will not beg you to kill me," says Rain.

"I am starting to believe you. I mean, I have never known anyone who could take the pain you are taking and for so long. You are truly something unique. You saw your love of a lifetime killed and her soul taken by Lucifer, and you did not flinch. I am quite sure you are going to watch the beautiful Marlene be tortured, murdered, and eaten by Lucifer right here, right now because you do not care. You think you are strong. You think you are going to hold out and win something. You will win nothing, and I appreciate it because her youth will be mine. Her youth will continue my longevity. I can't thank you enough, Rain. You never get it, and I appreciate it. You continue my eternal life here on this earth. Thanks to you, I will live forever," says Glamfury.

Glamfury turns toward the fire and stands before Marlene.

"Rain, remember and never give in. Never give in to his demands—never," says Marlene.

Glamfury raises his arms in the air, and the fire shoots from the fireplace, engulfing Marlene in flames. She screams in pain, the same pain Rain has just gone through. "No!" yells Rain. He runs into

Glamfury, tackling him to the ground. Rain is screaming in pain and starts to punch Glamfury. The pain is unconscionable, and the flesh falls off Rain's hand as he punches Glamfury. Glamfury laughs even as he is punched in the face. Marlene screams as flames rise from her burning body. Rain gets up and grabs the curtains, wrapping them around Marlene. It takes a few moments, but he stops the flames and steps back from Marlene. Her body has been scorched just as Rain's body was, and somehow, she too is conscious. They look at each other, crying, as they see what has happened to their bodies. They are burned flesh that easily falls from their bones.

"Look out. Rain, behind you," says Marlene.

Rain is grabbed from behind by Glamfury. Glamfury throws Rain at the wall opposite of the fireplace, and large metal nails extend from the wall. Rain's body slams onto the nails, and he sticks to the wall. The pain has exhausted him to where he cannot move. He is barely awake, and flesh is falling from his bones, making him yet another gruesome sight of gore in this never-ending horror. His head droops as he can barely keep it up, and he barely is conscious.

"Rain, Rain. Never forget, never forget to never give in to him. Never," says Marlene.

"Quiet!" yells Glamfury.

Glamfury slaps Marlene across the face, and the flesh on the right side of her face is ripped from her face. She screams as Glamfury starts to grab the flesh on her bones, and he pulls it from her body. Glamfury grabs hold of her fleshy breasts and rips them from her body, throwing them into the fire. He strips the flesh from her ribs so her internal organs can be seen. Rain can see her heart pumping blood, which squirts and drips from her ripped flesh. Marlene screams and kicks at Glamfury, so he grabs the muscles on her legs and rips them from her bones so she cannot move her legs anymore. Marlene hangs from her wrists tied above her head, and her body is still resting against the mantelpiece. Her head droops as her life is fading away. With what seems to be her dying breath, she looks to Rain.

"No matter what happens. No matter what he says, you can never give in to his demands. Rain, remember, never give in to him," says Marlene.

Glamfury laughs and looks at Rain. He walks up to Rain.

"That's right, Rain. Never give in to me. Never do as I ask, and never think for one second that I am anything less than 100 percent pure evil.

I will kill everything you know. I will eat, suck, and destroy everything that makes you, you. I have stolen the youth of Ajaunta, Bailey, and now Marlene because you are not man enough to save them. You are not man enough to take their place as my life, and I appreciate it. You are a never-ending supply of youth. You are my eternal salvation, my eternal youth, my eternal life," says Glamfury with powerful laughter.

Glamfury turns his back to Rain and lowers his pants. Rain can tell Glamfury puts his excitement into Marlene's burned skinless flesh. Glamfury bites the burned lips on her mouth and rips them from her jaw. He chews and turns his face so Rain can see her blood running down his neck. He chews and swallows. Marlene screams in pain through her lipless mouth, and Glamfury puts his open mouth on hers. Rain can see her internal organs as they are drawn toward Glamfury's mouth and his hips until all her organs have been sucked into Glamfury's body, all except her brain. Glamfury steps back from Marlene, zipping up his pants. He turns toward Rain and steps to the side so Rain can see Marlene has no internal organs except her brain and most the flesh on her body has fallen off.

"You could have saved her. You could have saved them all. I am grateful to you, Rain. It is as I have always said. You will be my greatest conquest of youth probably ever. You are too stupid to get it. You are to pigheaded, and I appreciate it. Oh, you don't think her horror is over, do you?" says Glamfury.

Glamfury walks over to Rain and puts his arm behind Rain. He swings his arm, pulling Rain's body from the nails, and Rain falls to the floor. The pain is so intense Rain cannot move. He cries as Glamfury grabs him by the back of his neck. Glamfury lifts Rain in the air, facing him toward Marlene's body hanging on the fireplace.

"Give in to me. Beg me to kill you. Beg for Lucifer to take your soul, or watch as Marlene is sentenced to an eternity of rape, torture, and pain. Give in to me now," says Glamfury.

"Go to hell," says Rain.

"So be it," says Glamfury.

The walls of the house pull away. The upstairs and roof fly away, exposing the living room to the red haze of hell, which fills the sky. Molten lava in the form of raindrops fall on the living room, and little sounds of searing wood can be heard. The burning starts on the floor, and shallow flames cover the floor. Rain is whipped like a snake.

Glamfury still holds him by his neck and easily whips him up and down. After a few whips, Rain looks down to see he has been healed and restored to his normal healthy body. He makes his left hand a fist and swings at Glamfury's face. Glamfury waves his hand and walks away, falling off the side of the floor into the lava. Rain has been put in slow motion, and he moves but very slowly. He turns to see Marlene and the fireplace tilt and lie horizontally. The titanic Lucifer rises from the lava and puts his pointed index fingers in Marlene's ears.

"No!" yells Rain.

Rain can hear Marlene's skull crack, and Lucifer lifts the top of her skull, exposing her brain. He runs the fingers and thumb on his right hand across her brain and pulls her soul from within her body. Lucifer whips her soul like a washcloth and raises it above his mouth, dropping it in and consumes it. He then grabs her head and raises her body above his mouth, dropping it in his mouth as he chews, crunching her bones and eating her entire body. Lucifer falls back into the lava, and Rain falls to the floor, able to move in real time again. He looks around but cannot leave the floor because he is surrounded by molten lava. The floor is on fire, and he hears a great noise from above. He looks up to see a large burning boulder falling from above, and everything goes black as it falls on Rain.

Chapter 42

Smoke's Descent

Smoke grabs Rain's hands as tight as he can, but he cannot hold on and falls in the black hole with the water. He falls for what seems a mile and splashes in a soupy pool of mud and water. The last of the water falls on him from the hole that he just fell in. He yells Rain's name as loud as he can, but he cannot even see a light from where he fell from. He can see up, and what he sees seems to be the long roots of trees hanging from very far up, much higher than he can reach. He stands up wiping mud and water from himself. He is soaking wet and a muddy mess. There is only one way for him to go, and that is down a tunnel he is in. The walls and floor are all mud, and the ceiling way up seems to be the underside of the forest. The ceiling, as far as Smoke can tell, is tree and plant roots. Smoke follows the tunnel, which is ten to twelve feet wide. As Smoke walks down the tunnel, trying to figure how there is enough light for him to see, he can hear chanting. He walks toward the sound, and he can now see a yellow light, which must be from a fire. He continues down the tunnel, and it veers to the right and then it makes a sharp right turn. Smoke walks around and steps back, hiding behind the wall. He saw Glamfury standing, and he was the one chanting a foreign language. Smoke saw three Egengyns and a large fire behind Glamfury.

"Come on out, Smoke. We know you are there. We have been waiting for you. I think you will find this part very interesting. Did you know that you and your friend Rain are responsible for killing more of my followers than anyone? You call them Egengyns. They are my disciples. Come on out. You can see how my disciples are born. Come on, don't be afraid," says Glamfury.

Smoke walks out from behind the corner. He can see a very large boulder just like the one that was behind the cabin. There are three Egengyns standing around the boulder with coconut shells over their heads and long vines that fall down to their knees. Glamfury continues to chant in a language that Smoke does not understand. The Egengyn standing on one side of the boulder by himself turns and walks to the wall, collecting a coconut shell that hangs on a hook with vines hanging down from it. He walks to the boulder, and Glamfury chants louder. The boulder seems to melt in the middle. The center of the boulder turns red and starts to simmer like bubbling lava. The Egengyn holding the coconut shell holds it above the center of the boulder, and a skull rises from the lava and then neck bones. From the neck down, Smoke can see an actual human body that is intact flesh and all rising from the lava. It is obviously female. The Egengyn slowly places the coconut shell over the skull.

"Wait, hold on one moment. Do not put the coconut shell on just yet," says Glamfury.

The Egengyn lifts up on the coconut shell.

"You see, the great thing about taking one's youth is that I live eternally. More importantly, Lucifer is granted yet another soul that feeds the flames of hell. Lucifer eats the souls of mortal men and women. He eats their flesh and bones and spits them out for me. What do you mean, you say? Let me show you what I mean," says Glamfury.

Glamfury waves his hands, and Smoke can see an outline of the person's face that would normally be on this skull. Smoke can see it is Bailey.

"No!" yells Smoke.

Smoke charges Glamfury. He reaches for his rifle, but he does not have it; nor does he have his secondary firearms. He does have a knife, which he wields like the professional killer that he is. He runs two steps, and Glamfury waves his right hand, stopping Smoke in time. Smoke is actually moving but at an incredibly slow rate. Smoke can see and hear everything going on around him, but he is not able to keep up. Glamfury and the Egengyns continue on with their ceremony. Glamfury waves his hand, and the image of Bailey's head is gone, revealing the skull with no flesh on it or brains in it. Glamfury waves on the Egengyn, and he places the coconut shell over the skull, and the rest of the female body rises up from the center of the boulder. The newest addition to the Egengyns walks to the one position around the boulder not occupied, and now there are four Egengyns standing around the bolder. Glamfury pulls a book from under the cloak he is wearing and starts to read from the book. The Egengyns all turn toward the wall and walk to it each of them, grabbing a piece of rope. They all walk to Smoke, tying his wrists and ankles with the rope. Smoke is now laid on his back on the boulder. Each Egengyn pulls on their rope, pulling Smoke tight. Glamfury waves his hands, releasing Smoke back to real time. Glamfury walks over to the knife Smoke had in his hand, which has fallen on the floor. He picks the knife and looks at it.

"You were going to use this to cause me harm? Here, let me show you a knife that causes harm," says Glamfury.

Smoke pulls with his arms and legs as hard as he can. He struggles, but the Egengyns pull on the ropes with their body weight, and Smoke cannot overpower them. Smoke is held tight to the boulder just as the victims he has saved or tried to save in the past. His arms and legs are held out, and he cannot escape. Glamfury pulls a knife from under his cloak and throws the knife Smoke brought off to the side. Glamfury holds his soul knife up in the air with both hands and chants some words Smoke does not understand.

"You fucking dick-sucking, devil-worshipping piece of shit. Quit fucking around. You have me. So if you are going to kill me, then do it. What are you waiting for?" yells Smoke.

Glamfury lowers the knife and runs it under Smoke's clothing, slicing the arm and pant legs. All his clothing is removed except for his underwear. Glamfury runs the knife blade along Smoke's skin in a way that does not cut him.

"I am waiting for your friend Rain. Where is he? I wonder. He is not going to let his lifelong friend die right here right now, is he? Where could he be?" says Glamfury.

"You tricked me, you devil scum, but you will never trick Rain. Rain will figure out how to defeat you, and when he does, I will be cheering from hell. As a matter of fact, I will be waiting for you in hell. I will be waiting to return the favor, you can count on that," says Smoke.

"In that case, let me get you on your way," says Glamfury.

Glamfury turns the knife so the tip of the blade is on Smoke's neck under his right ear. He slices Smoke's neck in a half circle to the underside of his left ear. He does not cut very deep, just deep enough to cause blood to seep from the wound. Smoke cries in pain. He cannot believe how bad it hurts like a torch burning his flesh. Glamfury continues to cut down his neck along the top of his right shoulder and down his arm all the way to the tip of his middle finger. Smoke screams in unbelievable pain. Glamfury cuts down his left arm the same way. The longer he cuts, the more painful it becomes. Glamfury does not stop. He cuts and cuts, crisscrossing and dotting all of Smoke's skin until he is a patchwork of drying blood drops.

"You are mine, but you are not the main course. The main course is on the way. The louder you scream, the harder you cry, the sooner he will be here. So let us get you on your way—on your way to hell," says Glamfury.

Glamfury raises his soul knife high in his right hand and chants a few words. The knife starts to glow red down the center of the blade like a blood vein runs down it. It glows blood red throughout the hilt and throbs just as if blood were pumping through the veins showing on it. Glamfury stabs Smoke just to the right of his heart on the outer side of his chest. Smoke cries out in pain, looking at the knife stuck in his chest all the way to the hilt.

"Yes, my son. Yes. You are now becoming a part of me. Your youth will give me lasting life. Your soul will strengthen Lucifer's reign," says Glamfury.

Glamfury waves his hands toward the Egengyns. They release the ropes, which fall to the ground. Smoke has barely enough energy to raise his head. His arms and legs fall limp to the side of the boulder and the veins on the soul knife pump blood as if they were being pumped by Smoke's heart with Smoke's blood.

"Time to call Rain. Time to scream and make your final descent to eternal damnation. Are you ready?" says Glamfury.

Glamfury grabs hold of Smoke's right hand and pulls a tool from underneath his cloak. It is a form of pliers, which he uses to grab hold of Smoke's thumbnail. He starts to pull, twist, and turn on the nail. Smoke screams as he watches Glamfury pull, twist, and turn until his thumbnail finally gives way and is pulled off. Smoke screams out as loud as he can.

"Rain! Rain! Ahh! Stop! Rain, where are you? Rain, he is killing me. Rain, it's a trap. Please kill me. Rain!" cries Smoke.

Rain has his rifle pointed ahead as he searches for Smoke. He can hear Smoke calling for him, and obviously, he is being tortured. Rain desperately tries to reach his friend but does not let his heavy heart take away from his caution. He is searching down an unknown tunnel, and he can feel it is a trap. Rain pushes forward slowly, steadily observing all the surroundings. The tunnel veers to the right and then makes a hard turn to the right. He is quite sure his buddy is right around the corner. Rain steadies himself and takes a deep breath. He turns the corner, facing his gun, and horror fills his eyes. Smoke is lying on the boulder with the soul knife sticking out of his chest. Glamfury has Smoke's right hand in his left hand, and he watches what seems to be slow motion as Glamfury takes his pliers and pulls all the fingernails from Smoke's right hand. Smoke cries and screams in pain. He looks to Rain and uses all his energy to raise and extend his left arm toward Rain.

"No!" yells Rain.

Rain can tell he is in slow motion. He yells for Glamfury to stop, but Glamfury grabs Smoke's left hand and pulls all his fingernails and thumbnail. Smoke holds his bleeding hands to his face, looking at them, and becomes an emotional mess, crying at the way his body is being deformed, and he cannot stop it.

"Rain, it's a trap. Leave me. It's too late for me. Rain, remember, always remember to never give in. That is what Marlene meant when she said to remember. Remember to never give in. He is always trying to trick you. Don't let him make you forget. Always remember to never submit to him!" yells Smoke.

"No! Stop!" yells Rain.

His voice and words along with his movements are severely slowed. There is nothing Rain can do. He tries to run toward Smoke, forgetting his rifle until he sees it, and he starts to pull the trigger. He can see from the corner of his eyes the Egengyns that approach him, and before he can pull the trigger, the Egengyns hack at his knees with machetes. Rain falls to the ground, and his gun is pulled from his grasp before he hits the ground. He looks up to see Glamfury pull all the toenails from Smoke's feet. Rain is lifted up by the Egengyns, so he can see clearly what is happening to Smoke. Glamfury takes a heated nail that is very sharp, and he puts the point of it on Smoke's front tooth and pushes until it pushes right through his tooth. Smoke cries in agony as Glamfury slowly pulls the tooth from his upper jaw. Blood runs out of Smoke's mouth as Glamfury continues to pull all the teeth out of Smoke's mouth in this brutal fashion. Rain cries seeing Smoke tortured in this way, and all just to please Glamfury and his quest for youth.

"That is right, Rain. I did not even ask you to beg me to kill you because I know you will not give in. I know you will resist even when the ones you love are being tortured and sacrificed to eternal damnation. I know you will watch as the ones you love are beaten, tortured, and drained of life. That is why I like you so much, Rain. You are my partner. You will be here with me as I continue to kill and steal youth. The best part is that you are the one supplying all my life. Oh, you did not get it, did you? Like I have said to you before, you will be my greatest conquest of youth ever. Oh, you thought I was talking about your person, didn't you? No. That is not what I meant at all. What I meant is that through your dreams, all the ones you love, all those close to you will be introduced to me, and they will not hold out like you. They will give in, and they will feed my need for youth. Your friends will keep me alive forever. Now you see, don't you? Now you understand how you are my greatest conquest of youth ever," says Glamfury.

Glamfury waves his hands toward the Egengyns, and the coconut shells fall off them. They are complete bodies of three women and one man. Glamfury waves his hands toward them, and the image of the faces on the bodies appear. Rain can see Smoulder, Bailey, Marlene, and Ajaunta.

"No!" cries Rain.

The Egengyns let go of him, and he falls to his knees, crying.

Glamfury laughs loudly. He laughs and grabs hold of Smoke's head in his left hand and raises his head up so Rain can see him.

"This one here was very tough, but not as tough and not as smart as you, Rain," says Glamfury.

Rain looks up and watches, and Glamfury pounds on Smoke's face with his bare fist. Glamfury punches him with fury and power, crushing his face, breaking the bones, and pushing his nose, eyes, and mouth back into his brain. This kills Smoke, and Smoke's body falls limp on the boulder. Glamfury grabs the soul knife and pulls it from Smoke's chest. He slams it back into his sternum and slices up the center of Smoke's ribs. Rain cannot move and watches as Glamfury rips Smoke's ribs from his body, exposing his internal organs. Glamfury grabs hold of Smoke's heart and pulls it from his chest cavity. He raises

Smoke's heart in the air and squeezes the blood from it, which runs down his arm. He eats it while Rain watches. Glamfury ages in reverse, getting younger. The walls of the cave pull away, exposing a deep red sky all around for as far as Rain can see. Lucifer rises from the molten lava that surrounds the patch of ground Glamfury, Rain, and the Egengyns are on. He grabs the bones from the front of Smoke's face and pulls them off with surprising precision since his fingers are so large. He then rubs his fingers and thumb across the brain of Smoke and pulls his soul from his body. He then shakes it like a washcloth and drops the soul in his mouth, consuming it. He then grabs hold of Smoke by his head and lifts his body, dropping it feetfirst into his mouth. Rain can hear Smoke being chewed, his bones crunching and his body consumed by Lucifer. Lucifer then falls back into the lava, and the cave walls come flying back from the red sky and close them all in the cave once more.

"Rain, beg me to kill you. Tell me to send your soul to Lucifer. Beg me," says Glamfury.

Rain finally feels the pain in his knees. The Egengyns have hacked his kneecaps, and they are sliced very badly. Both his knee caps are splintered, sliced, and bleeding. Rain rolls on his back, crying.

"This is not happening. This is not real. You are not real. None of this is real. Go away and leave me alone. I can beat you. I will beat you. It's all in your head, Rain. It is all in your head!" cries Rain.

Rain rolls over onto his side and opens his eyes. He stares into the dirt floor with tears falling from the corners of his eyes.

"Wake up, Rain, wake up. This is all a dream. This is all a bad dream. None of this is real!" cries Rain.

Rain closes his eyes, and the throbbing in his knees is unbearable. He lays his head on the dirt and concentrates on sleeping. He concentrates on sleeping so he can wake from this nightmare where pain, torture, and death have ruled.

This has to be a dream, and I have to wake from this already, Rain thinks to himself, and he fades to black.

Chapter 43

Remember

"Hello."

"Terry!"

"Yeah."

"Terry, are you OK?"

"Phil? This sounds like Phil. Phil, is that you?" says Terry.

"Yeah, Terry, this is Phil. I was calling to see if you are OK," says Phil.

"Yeah, Phil, I am fine. Oh my god! Phil, what time is it? Oh my god! Phil, it is almost 9:00 a.m. What day is it?" says Terry.

"It is Friday, and, yeah, it is almost nine. You have not missed a day of work or been late a single day in over twenty years. Kathy and Fred came to my office and asked if you had called in sick today, and I told them no. As a matter of fact, they are standing here right now. They said you were not here yet, so I immediately called. This is very unlike you. Is everything OK?" says Phil.

"Yeah, everything is all right. I just overslept. I guess I forgot to set my alarm last night. I must have been really tired," says Terry.

"Well, good. I am just glad you are OK. Listen, take your time. There is no rush to get here. Take your time. We will be fine a few hours without you," says Phil.

"Wow, I am so sorry, Phil. I will be there in an hour," says Terry.

"No problem. Take your time. We will see you in a little bit. Bye," says Phil.

"OK, bye," says Terry.

Terry hangs up the phone and sits on the edge of his bed, rubbing his head. He gets up and into the shower after shaving. He takes his time getting ready to go to work. He is never late, and since he has already missed a few hours, he is tempted to just take the day off, but he gets ready and into his car. Driving to work, he keeps thinking to himself that there is something he has forgotten about or something he is supposed to remember. This thought of trying to remember something has bothered him since he woke today. It takes him less than thirty minutes to get to work, and as he parks and walks into the metal factory where he cuts sheets of metal, it finally hits him—the horrible dream he had last night. All the way to the time clock, he has little visions and remembers little bits and pieces of his dream last night. He gets to the time clock and punches in right as everyone is going to break and walks into the break room just as his colleagues are coming here for break.

"Well, look who decided to come into work today. We all thought something was wrong with you. I am glad to see you made it in today," says Sonya.

"Yeah, man, is everything all right? None of us could believe you were a no-call, no-show," says Fred.

"You couldn't believe it. I still can't believe it. I must be getting old. I thought I was going to be the only one ever with a perfect attendance record," says Terry.

"Come over here and sit down. You might as well have a break with us," says Karen.

Terry puts his lunch in the refrigerator and walks over to the table his friends are sitting at. Terry sits down, and as he sits down, it is like an explosion of visions breaking into his head. He can see Bailey with her wrists restrained and the tubes in her neck sucking the blood out of her body. He can see Marlene being eaten by those dog creatures. He can see Ajaunta being molested by the devil-worshipping creatures (Egengyns) in the bed in the cabin in the woods. He can see Smoke being dragged into the pond by the croc man. He can see this man holding Ajaunta and putting her over his shoulder and rubbing her ass while Rain cannot move. He can see this man standing by Smoke, Bailey, and Marlene, and Rain cannot move. Terry looks up seeing his friends talking, but he cannot hear a word they are saying. He realizes his four friends right here represent his four friends in his nightmare.

Terry stands up suddenly breathing heavily. He cannot hear a sound and looks to the clock. Everything in his vision with the exception of the clock becomes blurry. His sight is commandeered by the vision of Marlene saying to him, "Remember." Then the vision of Smoke saying the same thing, "Remember."

Terry is shaken from his vision. Kathy is shaking him gently by his left shoulder.

"Rain, Rain. Hey, Rain, wake up," says Ajaunta.

Terry looks at Kathy, realizing she is Ajaunta in his nightmare.

"Yeah, yeah, I am fine. I just . . ." says Terry.

Terry realizes he is not dreaming and sits still, breathing heavily.

"Hey, buddy, what is wrong?" says Fred.

Fred smacks Terry on the shoulder.

"Yeah, yeah, guys, I have to admit I am really weirded out here. I have to tell you something, and it is something really scary," says Terry.

"What? What is it?" says Sonya.

"I had this really horrible dream last night. I keep seeing visions of it—you know, like little bits and pieces. You all were in it. I mean, you went by different names, but you were all in it. Kathy, you were a girl named Ajaunta, a girl I was in love with my whole life," says Terry.

"So it was just like real life, then," says Kathy.

"Well, yeah, but, Fred, you were a guy named Smoke, and we were partners all our lives," says Terry.

"So you mean just like in real life," says Fred.

"Well, yeah, but we were retired Special Forces. In my dream, we were military, and we were bad, but not as bad as the man that was hunting us. Sonya, you were a girl named Marlene, and she was my girlfriend in my dream," says Terry.

"So you mean just like in real life. I mean, for a while, we were boyfriend and girlfriend, and what a nightmare that was. I am glad we are just friends now," says Sonya.

"Well, yeah, and, Karen, you were a girl named Bailey. She was married to Smoke for a little while, I think?" says Terry.

"So you mean just like in real life. Fred and I were married for four years, and somehow, we are best friends now and not married anymore," says Karen.

"Yeah, yeah. Guys, this is not good. I am seriously freaked out—I mean, for real. This was more than a dream. I think this was for real. He is after me. He is going to kill me," says Terry.

"Wait, wait a minute. Terry, did you and I have sex?" says Kathy.

"What?" says Terry.

"In your dream, did you and I have sex in your dream or your nightmare or whichever it was?" asks Kathy.

"Ah, ah, ah. I think we did, but it was all you. It was you who initiated the sex. I did not mind at all, and it was great. I could not say no," says Terry.

"Oh, that's it. That's it. I'm outta here. I don't want to hear anymore," says Kathy.

Kathy throws her arms in the air and stands up.

"Hey, wait a minute, where are you going?" asks Terry.

"I'm outta here. It's always the girl's fault. If they have sex, they have to die. I mean, for real, we girls can't just have some good old-fashioned sex. No, we can't just make love and get our happy faces on. No, we have to be killed if we get naked. I don't want to hear anymore because I already know the ending—I died. I died, didn't I?" says Kathy.

"Well, yeah. You all died," says Terri.

"I knew it. I knew it. I am outta here. You all have fun. See you at lunch," says Kathy.

Kathy walks out of the break room.

"Wait, wait a minute," says Terry.

"Hey, Terry. I will bite into this. So Kathy died. What about me and the rest of us? You said we all died?" says Sonya.

"Yes. This guy was after us, and he killed us, but he could not just kill us. I mean, he could, but there was something we had to do before he killed us. I think it was different for girls and for guys. I think? I can't remember. Wait a minute, yes. I remember. Girls, if girls had sex with him in the dreamworld, he could kill them. So Kathy was right," says Terry.

"You said *us*. So he killed all of us including you?" says Fred.

"Well, no. I am the only one whom he has not killed yet. I went by the name Rain," says Terry.

"So if he had sex with the girls, he could kill them. What about the guys? What did we have to do to be killed by this guy? I hope it was not to have sex with him. I can guarantee he would not have killed me," says Fred.

"No, it was different for guys. We had to . . . we had to . . . Wait, I remember. For guys, we had to beg him to kill us. Then he could kill us. I mean, he could kill us at any time, but there was a reason why girls had to sleep with him and guys had to beg him to kill us," says Terry.

"Well, what was it? What was the reason? What was or is this guy after?" asks Karen.

"Youth. He is after our youth. If he steals our youth, he can live forever. He serves Lucifer. He serves the devil, and I saw him. I saw the devil in my nightmare. The devil took your souls, and Glamfury—that is his name. His name is Glamfury. That is the guy after me. He is coming for me. He is going to get me. Glamfury is going to steal my youth and send my soul to hell," says Terry.

Terry gets noticeably shaken, and his friends notice it.

"Hey, hey, buddy, relax. It was just a dream—a dream that has you all shaken. But we are right here. None of us are dead, and none of us could get that lucky. You know why? Because we have to go back out there on that floor and do the same boring shit we do day after day, all day long. Now come on, Terry, snap out of it. You are freaking me out," says Fred.

"Yeah, Terry, relax. Why would any guys beg someone to kill them unless they wanted to die, right? Why would I or any girls have sex with this guy? I'm too old for that shit," says Karen.

"It's not like you just have sex with him. This guy works for the devil. Deceit is his gift. He seduces you girls so well you never have a chance. He comes to you in your dreams. He dresses you in the finest clothes. He dines on fantastic meals with you and dances with you in different time periods. He sweeps you off your feet and into the nicest bedrooms where you have passionate heated love. Hell, I'd have sex with him—how could anyone resist?" says Terry.

"Yeah, well, why would I ever beg anyone to kill me? I would not," says Fred.

"That's another thing. What he does is genius. It's hell at its best. He comes to us in our dreams and tortures us. He kills our loved ones, and he does it over and over and over until we can't take it anymore, and then we beg him to kill us, but then we are sent to hell," says Terry.

"Wow! You saw all this? You experienced all this in one dream? One dream that you had last night?" says Sonya.

"It sure felt like a whole lot more than one dream. It felt like a month's worth of dreams. It felt like he tortured me for years," says Terry.

"Well, buddy, I have to go take a piss before I head back to the real world—the real world of working for a living. You know what? You could just beg this guy to kill you and be done with it. I mean, you can't kill someone who serves the devil, right? So why torture yourself any longer? Just beg him to kill you. Do it right now and be done with it," says Fred.

"Fred!" says Karen.

Karen slaps Fred on the shoulder as he gets up. Fred laughs.

"I'm just kidding, buddy. No one wants you or any of us to die," says Fred.

Fred leaves the break room. Karen gets up.

"Well, time to get back to the grindstone. Hey, Terry, don't worry about it. It was just a dream," says Karen.

Karen leaves the break room.

"Maybe I should. Maybe I should just beg this guy to kill me right now. I mean, this is the real world, not a dream. I can't be a slave to a dream—slave to some fictional made-up character from one of my dreams. Fuck it, then. Go ahead kill me. What are you waiting for, Glamfury? Go ahead and kill me. I beg you to kill me. There, I did it. Phew, I am still alive. Well, that feels better. Well, not really," says Terry.

"Terry, you jerk, you better not die on me now," says Sonya.

Kathy, Fred, and Karen walk back into the break room.

"Hey, Terry, what do you want for lunch? We are getting lunch from Sandy's. You want anything? I'll put it on the list if you do," says Fred.

"Yeah, I'll take a cheeseburger and fries," says Terry.

"OK, I'll add it to the list. Renee is working today, and she said she would be here a little after twelve," says Fred.

Terry gets shivers up and down his neck. The name Renee snaps him back to the nights he and Smoke would have coffee in the diner in his dreams.

"Oh my god! He got Renee too. Sandy's was in my dream. It is where Smoke and I, or you (Fred) and I would go to have coffee and talk," says Terry.

"Oh, you mean just like now in real life. Listen, get to work. We will all meet for lunch. Bye," says Fred.

Terry's friends leave and go back to work. Terry stands up and shakes his head back and forth, figuring he might as well get to work, and hopefully, he will have forgotten about this whole nightmare by lunch.

Fred has his welding gear on when someone taps him on the shoulder. He turns off the torch and flips up his face shield to see who is trying to get his attention. Sonya is tapping him on his shoulder, and Fred turns to see a lot of people heading toward the other side of the building.

"What? What is going on?" says Fred.

"Come on, there has been an accident," says Sonya.

"What accident? What has happened?" asks Fred.

"It is Terry. Something bad has happened to Terry. Come on," says Sonya.

Fred takes off his protective gear and walks with Sonya toward the east side of the building. They quickly see a crowd of people has formed and move through it. They come up to Kathy and Karen, and Fred has to cover his mouth to the horror lying there on the floor.

"What the fuck? Terry, what the fuck happened?" says Fred.

Karen holds Fred back as he tries to enter the circle of people around Terry.

"No, Fred. No. Stay back. There is nothing we can do. The band saw had a malfunction. The blade broke somehow and sliced Terry up like that," says Karen.

"Sliced him up. It tore his heart out. What the fuck?" says Fred.

"Fred, come on, let's get out of here. We don't need to see this," says Sonya.

Sonya, Kathy, and Karen are all crying, and they grab hold of Fred. They pull him from the crowd. Phil shows up and puts a jacket over Terry's remains. Phil starts to disperse the crowd of people around Terry. The girls start to cry a lot as they escort Fred back to the break room. Workers around the whole facility are quickly hearing about what has happened and coming to the area where Terry has had his fatal accident. People are in disarray and walking and whispering all around. As the girls and Fred get back to the break room, a lot of people are already there and talking about the accident.

"Shut up! All of you, shut up!" yells Fred.

Fred and the girls sit at a table in the break room.

"What the fuck! This is not happening. He was just telling us how this guy from his dream was going to kill him, and now he is dead," says Fred.

"Come on, Fred, no one from his dream killed him. You saw the blade from the band saw. It was a freak accident. Terry weirded himself out and did something stupid, that is all," says Karen.

"Are you fucking serious? You tell me how a blade from a band saw breaks and then rips up the center of a man's chest and cuts his heart out. That was no accident. That was some fucking shit, that's what that was," says Fred.

"Fred, we are all hurting right now. We need to stay calm. No matter what happened, there is nothing we can do about it now. We have to be strong for Terry and his family," says Kathy.

"We are his family, Kathy," says Fred.

"Then we will bury him," says Sonya.

Chapter 44

I'll Take Your Youth Now

Harvey is being escorted to the break room by Phil. Harvey is obviously distraught. Phil is doing everything he can to get Harvey away from all the other employees, and he is doing his best to calm Harvey down.

"Harvey, sit down. Take a deep breath. Calm down, Harvey, calm down. We all are upset, but we have to keep our heads and stay calm," says Phil.

"You weren't there. You didn't see what actually happened. That was some freaky shit. It was not real. It was not of this earth," says Harvey.

Phil coaxes Harvey into a chair and gets him a coffee.

"Harvey, here, drink this and calm down," says Phil.

"Harvey, what are you talking about? What happened?" asks Fred.

"Dude! Terry went to his saw like always, but then something crazy happened. You won't believe me if I tell you, but I saw it. I saw it with my own eyes," says Harvey.

"What, Harvey? What did you see?" asks Sonya.

"He was standing there like he was talking to someone, but no one was there. He started to scream and yell like he was scared, and he was calling for help. I said, 'What, Terry? What do you need?' But he did not even know I was there. It was like he was in a different world. He started to lift up into the air, but how? I don't know how. There was nothing there. Then he started screaming, and his chest split up the middle, and his ribs were pulled from his body. Then his heart was pulled from his chest, and he fell dead. It was the craziest thing I have ever seen in my life. It was not real, but it happened. I saw it," says Harvey.

"Terry was saying there was this guy after him—this guy he saw in his dream last night. That is why he was late today. He said it really freaked him out, and he was definitely scared," says Karen.

Harvey starts to really freak out, and he starts to cry like he is having a nervous breakdown.

"Glamfury. Terry stopped my machine and told me some guy named Glamfury was after him. It pissed me off that he stopped my machine while I was working. I got mad at him. I did not think some guy for real was trying to kill him, but there was no one there. There was no one there. That's not all. That's not even the scariest part. I saw the devil. I saw the lord of hell, and I was in hell. The devil popped Terry's skull. His head broke apart, and the devil pulled Terry's soul out of his body. I saw it. I saw it happen. Then the devil ate Terry's soul and his body. I saw it, I swear I saw it," says Harvey.

Karen, Kathy, Sonya, and Fred all look at each other with wonder in their eyes. They each wonder if the other person is thinking what they are thinking.

Terry gets up from the break room table. He walks to his work area, talking to himself.

"It was just a dream. None of it was real. Just a dream. It was just a dream. Just get to work and take care of business. Everything is going to be fine. Just get to work, Terry," he says to himself out loud as he walks to his machine.

Terry starts to collect sheets of aluminum, steel, and stainless steel like he always does. He collects his work orders and starts the process of setting up his measurements so he can cut the sheets to their correct widths and heights. He starts to cut his first sheet when his heart begins to flutter. He turns his saw off and rubs his chest. His veins feel cold like the blood in his veins is ice water. He hears eerie sounds coming from the back of him and then in front of him and to the sides.

"Oh, shit, he is here!" yells Terry.

"Harvey, he is here. He's here!" yells Terry.

Harvey has his hearing and his eye protection on, and he is concentrating on cutting his sheets of metal, so he does not hear Terry yelling. Terry yells as loud as he can, and still Harvey does not notice him. Terry walks over to Harvey's machine and hits the emergency stop, which shuts down Harvey's machine, and the saw stops. Harvey lifts the visor over his face, getting noticeably irritated with Terry.

"What the fuck, Terry? You know I'm working here. Why did you stop my machine? Now I have to go through all the bullshit of starting it up again and right in the middle of a job. What the fuck, Terry?" says Harvey.

"Harvey, he is here. He's here. He is going to kill me and steal my youth. He is going to send my soul to Satan," says Terry.

"Terry, shut the fuck up! Get to work and don't hit the emergency stop on my machine while I am working. You know better," says Harvey.

Harvey ignores Terry and starts to restart his machine when he notices Terry start to rise up in the air. Harvey backs away and starts to yell for help when he bumps into something. He turns to see nothing. He reaches out with his hands and can feel an invisible barrier.

"What the fuck!" says Harvey.

He turns to watch what is an unexplainable horror. The roof of the factory lifts up and blows away. The walls and all the machinery pull outward and are blown away, all except for the floor, which remains and is surrounded by flowing molten lava. Harvey can see Terry is being lifted toward the sky, and he runs up, grabbing Terry by his legs, and pulls him down to the floor. Terry falls, and Harvey falls on him.

"Terry, what the fuck is going on? What the hell is this?" asks Harvey.

"This is the dreamworld. This is not real, but he is real," says Terry.

Terry points to a man rising from the lava and walking toward the two men. Terry and Harvey get up.

"What the fuck are you talking about? This is no dream. This is the real world, and we are at work—at least I thought we were," says Harvey.

Glamfury waves his hand at Harvey, and Harvey is thrown back, landing on his ass and sliding into an invisible barrier, which stops him before he falls into the lava. Harvey falls unconscious.

"You think I did not know you would come? You think I have not figured you out? You got a big surprise coming, and it is time for you to meet your maker. I realized a long time ago you walk unseen with us in the real world in real time, and then you bring our reality to the dreamworld, where you have the power of Satan. You manipulate our minds to see what you want us to see. You can see our friends and our loved ones, so this is how you bring them into our dreams and manipulate the scenes to happen as you want them to happen. You twist our reality into dreams, and then you use the power of deceit to steal our youth and send our souls to the devil. Your treachery will not work on me. I figured you out long ago," says Rain.

"Ah, so you figured me out. Very nice. Figure this out," says Glamfury.

Glamfury holds his right arm out to his side, and Rain charges Glamfury. Rain does not attack Glamfury. Instead, he dives and grabs the soul knife, which rises from the lava and is flying toward Glamfury's right hand. Rain grabs the knife and falls to the ground, rolling to his feet and facing Glamfury. Rain stands with lightning-fast reflexes, already aware he is going to attack. Rain jumps at Glamfury with the soul knife held tight in both his hands. Rain comes down, stabbing the knife into Glamfury just under his throat.

"What are you doing? I told you before you do not know what you are doing. You do not have the ability to defeat me," says Glamfury.

Rain holds the handle of the knife with both hands. The knife is buried in Glamfury's chest just under his throat, and this seems to immobilize Glamfury. Rain pulls Glamfury inches from his face with the look of stern determination. Glamfury, for the first time, shows a little concern to the fact that he is not in control at this moment.

"That is right, Glamfury. I did not know what I was doing before, but now I do know what I am doing. I realized the last time I held this knife that you could not freeze me in time. I also realized there is no defeating you in the sense that you can be killed and our nightmare will be over. You are a servant of Satan, and although you walk the world of the living, you have been dead all along. That is why the living cannot see you. You are dead, but you walk with us eternally and see what we see. You bring our reality to dreams where you manipulate women and get them to sleep with you. You get women to commit adultery so you can steal their youth and send their souls to the devil. You torture men over and over by using their loved ones and friends for life. You use this to your benefit, torturing us with our most intimate thoughts and feelings. This is how you can kill us and our loved ones over and over, and yet we never die. This is how you get us to beg you to kill us, granting our youth to you so you can walk among the living forever, and this is how you continue to send souls to the devil in hell where he reigns supreme. I figured you out long ago, Glamfury.

I cannot kill you. I may not be able to live among my friends in the real world anymore, but I can send you to hell. I can take your place, because if there is one thing the devil most certainly is, it is selfish. He does not care about you. He does not care about me. He only cares about himself and what benefits him the most. You, Glamfury, are a powder puff. Compared to me, you are a choir boy and I am your master," says Rain.

Rain squeezes the soul knife with both hands and pulls as hard as he can down the chest of Glamfury.

"No!" yells Glamfury.

Rain pulls down, breaking through the sternum of Glamfury. He pulls hard and strong, splattering blood all over the front of his body. Lightning starts to shoot across the hell sky and into the soul knife. The soul knife starts to pulsate. The red vein traveling down the center of the knife and the veins spiderwebbed throughout the handle start to pulsate and throb as Glamfury sinks to his knees.

"No. You don't know what you are doing. You cannot defeat me. You cannot take my place," cries Glamfury.

Glamfury cannot help but lean backward. He is on his knees and at Rain's mercy as Rain has cut all the way down Glamfury's ribs. Rain pulls the knife from Glamfury's abdomen and slams the blade right through the top of his skull, sending Glamfury into the dumfounded look of a man with a knife stuck in the top of his head. Lightning strikes the handle of the knife and cooks Glamfury's brain. Rain reaches his fingers into Glamfury's chest and rips the ribs from his body. Rain throws each side of Glamfury's rib cage into the burning hell lava. Glamfury's heart is exposed and still beating.

"Lucifer, my master, I know what I must do. I must take the place of Glamfury. I am your new servant. I am the new stealer of souls for you. I am earth's lord of hell. Let me welcome the unsuspecting to my phantasmagoria!" yells Rain.

Rain holds his arms up toward the hell heaven. He feels the wind blow harder, and lightning shoots into his fingertips, scorching his body. Rain reaches his right hand into Glamfury's chest cavity and grabs the beating heart, ripping it from its holdings. Rain raises the heart as high as he can in his right hand, squeezing the blood from it, which runs down his arm and down his chest. Lightning strikes the heart, cooking it in an instant, and Rain bites into the piece of meat, eating it like a ravenous dog. Rain consumes the entire heart, and the whole hell world explodes.

Terry starts up his band saw and starts cutting his first sheet of metal for the day. He looks over and sees Harvey is concentrating on his work. Terry starts to push the metal into the band saw when the blade breaks. The blade whips around very fast and amazingly swings below the cutting table and ricochets off the machine and into Terry's chest. Terry takes a few steps back in a daze. He is instantly thrown into shock and falls to his knees. Harvey sees the blade break and whip around until it ends up in Terry's chest. Harvey comes over to help, but it is too late. The saw blade has ripped up through Terry's chest and tore out his heart. It is not even real looking. Soon there is a gathering of people, and the whole plant is abuzz with the accident. People come running from all over. 911 is called, and emergency rescue is on the way. Phil shows up and tries to calm Harvey, who is now crazy in panic, realizing everything he has seen. Kathy, Fred, Sonya, and Karen have gone back to the break room, and everyone is in disbelief that Terry is dead.

Rain is on his knees. He can see himself (Terry) lying on the floor with the band saw in his chest. He sees Phil put a jacket over his lifeless body, and he sees everyone all around him sobbing and crying. Rain walks around the crowd of people, and no one knows he is there. No one can see him. Rain looks at himself, and he is covered in Glamfury's blood. He is a bloody mess, and for the first time in as long as he can remember, he is covered in blood that is not his own. Rain looks at his arms, his chest, his stomach, and his legs.

"No one can see me. No one knows I am here. It worked. I killed Glamfury. I took his place. I am the seducer of women. I am the stealer of youth and the sender of souls to hell. I am eternal!" yells Rain.

Rain realizes he is a bloody mess and walks to the bathroom. No one is in there, and he goes to the sink to wash as much of the blood from him as he can. He takes his shirt off and puts it in the sink to the right of him. He lets the water run, filling the sink, while he washes off in the sink in front of him. He hears noise behind him and looks in the mirror, seeing nothing. He turns the water off in the sink with his bloody shirt in it and turns to look at the four stalls. He gets an eerie feeling like something is not right; something is spooking him, which should not be, he thinks to himself. He turns and continues to wash in the sink when he hears the stall directly behind him swing open and slam shut. He turns and kicks the stall door violently with his right foot, slamming it against the stall wall, and it slams shut. "That's what I thought," says Rain.

Rain turns and lowers his head to the sink, where he washes his arms and chest. The bathroom stall door directly behind him creaks as it slowly opens. There is nothing in the stall except a black hole leading into what looks like space. Rain gets a very bad feeling. The hair on his neck stands. He does not look; he does not turn around at all. He freezes, hoping he is invisible. He hears breathing behind him and slowly turns around to face the stall. He can see the black hole leading into the unknown. There is no toilet, just a black hole. Rain slowly walks toward the stall and reaches in, slowly grabbing the door, pulling it shut. The outside of the door is mirrored, and he sees Glamfury in the mirror behind him.

"You were worth the wait, Rain. I'll take your youth now," says Glamfury.

Glamfury breaks through the mirror above the sink, grabbing Rain from behind him. Glamfury pulls Rain into the mirror. Rain yells and screams, kicking and punching as he is pulled into the mirror, and the glass of the mirror follows him until the mirror has replaced itself and Rain is gone. All the bloody water and Rain's shirt in the sinks are drawn toward and into the black hole in the stall. The black hole shrinks unit it is gone, and the toilet is back, and Glamfury's laugh is heard until the mirror and bathroom stall have replaced themselves. The sinks are clean, and no trace of Rain or clothing or blood is present. Once the toilet is back and the mirror has replaced itself, the sound of Glamfury is gone. So is Rain.